Praise for *Firefly Lane*

"Hannah's latest is a moving and realistic portrait of a complex and enduring friendship." —*Booklist*

"A lovely, touching read that examines one of the most important things in our lives: enduring friendship."
—Elizabeth Buchan, author of *Revenge of the Middle-Aged Woman*

"In *Firefly Lane*, Kristin Hannah has moved to a new level of fiction. Reminiscent of the works of Cassandra King and Lorna Landvik, Kristin Hannah has created a book that women will want to cozy up to a fire with, reading until the last page is finished. Book groups are sure to love it too!" —Karen Ford, McLean & Eakin Books

"Although I look forward to every one of her books, *Firefly Lane* just may be Kristin Hannah's most important work yet. It is a gift you should give to yourself and then share with every other woman in your life." —Rene Kirkpatrick, All for Kids Books & Music

"A tearjerker that is sure to please the author's many fans."
—*Library Journal*

"I can't remember the last time a book haunted me this much. Long after I turned the last page, I shed tears for the love, laughter, heartache, and loyalty tenderly depicted in *Firefly Lane*. A stunner."
—Danielle Marshall, Powell's Books

"You will love *Firefly Lane*, Kristin Hannah's poignant, warmhearted valentine to a thirty-year friendship between two fascinating women. Heartbreaking and funny, clear-eyed and sweet, *Firefly Lane* is honest, deeply felt, and addictive. It reminds us why we love to read."

—Patricia Gaffney, author of *The Saving Graces*

"This exceptional story will move you and reaffirm the needs of life that only women can fill for each other."

—Holly Frakes, Schuler Books & Music

"This terrific buddy saga about two best girlfriends who survive all sorts of escapades and catastrophes will inevitably provoke comparisons with Iris Dart's *Beaches*, but the story is all Hannah's own."

—*The Seattle Times*

"I just finished wiping my tears after reading *Firefly Lane*. Kristin Hannah's story of *TullyandKate* captures the essence of true friendship and love between women as they grow and change through the years. . . . A beautiful story that every woman should read!!"

—Marcia Vanderford, Vanderford's Books

"*Firefly Lane* is a fat, juicy book filled with the stuff of women's lives: mothers, daughters, triumphs, disappointments, illicit cigarettes, and dancing to favorite songs."   —*The Sunday Oregonian*

"No one writes more insightfully about women's friendships with all of their messy wonder, humor, pain, and complexity more than Kristin Hannah. She's a marvel."

—Susan Elizabeth Phillips, author of *The Great Escape*

FIREFLY LANE

LANE

Kristin Hannah

ST. MARTIN'S GRIFFIN

New York

FIREFLY LANE. Copyright © 2008 by Kristin Hannah. All rights reserved. Printed in the United States of America. For information, address St. Martin's Press, 175 Fifth Avenue, New York, N.Y. 10010.

www.stmartins.com

Design by Kathryn Parise

The Library of Congress has cataloged the hardcover as follows:

Hannah, Kristin.
   Firefly Lane / Kristin Hannah.—1st ed.
      p. cm.
   ISBN 978-0-312-36408-3
   1. Best friends—Fiction. 2. Friendship in adolescence—Fiction.
3. Female friendship—Fiction. 4. Nineteen seventies—Fiction. I. Title.
   PS3558.A4763F57 2008
   813'.54—dc22

2007040442

ISBN 978-0-312-53707-4 (trade paperback)

45 47 49 50 48 46

This book is dedicated to "us." The girls.
Friends who see one another through the hard times, big and small,
year in and year out. You know who you are.
Thanks;

To the people who make up so many of my memories:
my father, Laurence; my brother, Kent; my sister, Laura;
my husband, Benjamin; and my son, Tucker.
Wherever we all go in the world,
you are in my heart;

And to my mom, who inspires so many of my novels;
this one most of all.

ACKNOWLEDGMENTS

Thanks go out to:

Marianne McClary, for helping out on the TV and broadcasting stuff. Your expertise was invaluable. Thanks.

Jennifer Enderlin, Jill Marie Landis, Kim Fisk, Andrea Cirillo, and Megan Chance. Each of you helped me find the path of this story. Thanks.

The fabulous team at St. Martin's Press: Thank you for this opportunity.

The best mirror is an old friend.

—GEORGE HERBERT

FIREFLY
LANE

CHAPTER ONE

They used to be called the Firefly Lane girls. That was a long time ago—more than three decades—but just now, as she lay in bed listening to a winter storm raging outside, it seemed like yesterday.

In the past week (unquestionably the worst seven days of her life), she'd lost the ability to distance herself from the memories. Too often lately in her dreams it was 1974; she was a teenager again, coming of age in the shadow of a lost war, riding her bike beside her best friend in a darkness so complete it was like being invisible. The place was relevant only as a reference point, but she remembered it in vivid detail: a meandering ribbon of asphalt bordered on either side by gullies of murky water and hillsides of shaggy grass. Before they met, that road seemed to go nowhere at all; it was just a country lane named after an insect no one had ever seen in this rugged blue and green corner of the world.

Then they saw it through each other's eyes. When they stood together on the rise of the hill, instead of towering trees and muddy potholes and distant snowy mountains, they saw all the places they would someday go. At night, they sneaked out of their neighboring houses and met on that road. On the banks of the Pilchuck River they smoked stolen cigarettes, cried to the lyrics of "Billy, Don't Be a Hero," and told each other everything, stitching their lives together until by summer's end no one knew where one girl ended and the other began. They became to everyone who knew them simply TullyandKate, and for more than thirty years that friendship was the bulkhead of their lives: strong, durable, solid. The music might have changed with the decades, but the promises made on Firefly Lane remained.

Best friends forever.

They'd believed it would last, that vow, that someday they'd be old women, sitting in their rocking chairs on a creaking deck, talking about the times of their lives, and laughing.

Now she knew better, of course. For more than a year she'd been telling herself it was okay, that she could go on without a best friend. Sometimes she even believed it.

Then she would hear the music. Their music. "Goodbye Yellow Brick Road." "Material Girl." "Bohemian Rhapsody." "Purple Rain." Yesterday, while she'd been shopping, a bad Muzak version of "You've Got a Friend" had made her cry, right there next to the radishes.

She eased the covers back and got out of bed, being careful not to waken the man sleeping beside her. For a moment she stood there, staring down at him in the shadowy darkness. Even in sleep, he wore a troubled expression.

She took the phone off its hook and left the bedroom, walking down the quiet hallway toward the deck. There, she stared out at the storm and gathered her courage. As she punched in the familiar numbers, she wondered what she would say to her once-best friend after all these silent months, how she would start. *I've had a bad week . . . my life is falling apart . . .* or simply: *I need you.*

Across the black and turbulent Sound, the phone rang.

Part One

THE SEVENTIES

Dancing Queen

young and sweet,
only seventeen

CHAPTER
TWO

For most of the country, 1970 was a year of upheaval and change, but in the house on Magnolia Drive, everything was orderly and quiet. Inside, ten-year-old Tully Hart sat on a cold wooden floor, building a Lincoln Log cabin for her Liddle Kiddles, who were asleep on tiny pink Kleenexes. If she were in her bedroom, she would have had a Jackson Five forty-five in her Close 'N Play, but in the living room, there wasn't even a radio.

Her grandma didn't like music much, or television or board games. Mostly—like now—Grandma sat in her rocking chair by the fireplace, doing needlepoint. She made hundreds of samplers, most of which quoted the Bible. At Christmastime she donated them to the church, where they were sold at fund-raisers.

And Grandpa . . . well, he couldn't help being quiet. Ever since his stroke, he just stayed in bed. Sometimes he rang his bell, and that was the only time Tully ever saw her grandma hurry. At the first tinkling of the bell, she'd smile and say, "Oh, my," and run for the hallway as fast as her slippered feet would take her.

Tully reached for her yellow-haired Troll. Humming very quietly, she made him dance with Calamity Kiddle to "Daydream Believer." Halfway through the song, there was a knock at the door.

It was such an unexpected sound that Tully paused in her playing and looked up. Except for Sundays, when Mr. and Mrs. Beattle showed up to take them to church, no one ever came to visit.

Gran put her needlework in the pink plastic bag by her chair and got up, crossing the room in that slow, shuffling way that had become normal in the last few years. When she opened the door, there was a long silence, then she said, "Oh, my."

Gran's voice sounded weird. Peering sideways, Tully saw a tall woman with long messy hair and a smile that wouldn't stay in place. She was one of the prettiest women Tully had ever seen: milky skin, a sharp, pointed nose and high cheekbones that slashed above her tiny chin, liquid brown eyes that opened and closed slowly.

"Thass not much of a greeting for your long-lost daughter." The lady pushed past Grandma and walked straight to Tully, then bent down. "Is this my little Tallulah Rose?"

Daughter? That meant—

"Mommy?" she whispered in awe, afraid to believe it. She'd waited so long for this, dreamed of it: her mommy coming back.

"Did you miss me?"

"Oh, *yes*," Tully said, trying not to laugh. But she was so happy.

Gran closed the door. "Why don't you come into the kitchen for a cup of coffee?"

"I didn't come back for coffee. I came for my daughter."

"You're broke," Grandma said tiredly.

Her mother looked irritated. "So what if I am?"

"Tully needs—"

"I think I can figure out what my daughter needs." Her mother seemed to be trying to stand straight, but it wasn't working. She was kind of wobbly and her eyes looked funny. She twirled a strand of long, wavy hair around her finger.

Gran moved toward them. "Raising a child is a big responsibility, Dorothy. Maybe if you moved in here for a while and got to know Tully you'd be ready . . ." She paused, then frowned and said quietly, "You're drunk."

Mommy giggled and winked at Tully.

Tully winked back. Drunk wasn't so bad. Her grandpa used to drink lots before he got sick. Even Gran sometimes had a glass of wine.

"Iss my birthday, Mother, or have you forgotten?"

"Your birthday?" Tully shot to her feet. "Wait here," she said, then ran to her room. Her heart was racing as she dug through her vanity drawer, scattering her stuff everywhere, looking for the macaroni and bead necklace she'd made her mom at Bible school last year. Gran had frowned when she saw it, told her not to get her hopes up, but Tully hadn't been able to do that. Her hopes had been up for years. Shoving it in her pocket, she rushed back out, just in time to hear her mommy say,

"I'm not drunk, Mother, dear. I'm with my kid again for the first time in three years. Love is the ultimate high."

"Six years. She was four the last time you dropped her off here."

"That long ago?" Mommy said, looking confused.

"Move back home, Dorothy. I can help you."

"Like you did last time? No, thanks."

Last time? Mommy had come back before?

Gran sighed, then stiffened. "How long are you going to hold all that against me?"

"It's hardly the kind of thing that has an expiration date, is it? Come on, Tallulah." Her mom lurched toward the door.

Tully frowned. This wasn't how it was supposed to happen. Her mommy hadn't hugged her or kissed her or asked how she was. And everyone knew you were supposed to pack a suitcase to leave. She pointed at her bedroom door. "My stuff—"

"You don't need that materialistic shit, Tallulah."

"Huh?" Tully didn't understand.

Gran pulled her into a hug that smelled sweetly familiar, of talcum powder and hair spray. These were the only arms that had ever hugged Tully, this was the only person who'd ever made her feel safe, and suddenly she was afraid. "Gran?" she said pulling back. "What's happening?"

"You're coming with me," Mommy said, reaching out to the door-frame to steady herself.

Her grandmother clutched her by the shoulders, gave her a little shake. "You know our phone number and address, right? You call us if you get scared or something goes wrong." She was crying; seeing her strong, quiet grandmother cry scared and confused Tully. What was going on? What had she done wrong already?

"I'm sorry, Gran, I—"

Mommy swooped over and grabbed her by the shoulder, shaking her hard. "Don't *ever* say you're sorry. It makes you look pathetic. Come on." She took Tully's hand and pulled her toward the door.

Tully stumbled along behind her mother, out of the house and down the steps and across the street to a rusted VW bus that had plastic flower decals all over it and a giant yellow peace symbol painted on the side.

The door opened; thick gray smoke rolled out. Through the haze she saw three people in the van. A black man with a huge afro and a red headband was in the driver's seat. In the back was a woman in a fringed vest and striped pants, with a brown kerchief over her blond hair; beside her sat a man in bell-bottoms and a ratty T-shirt. Brown shag carpeting covered the van floor; a few pipes lay scattered about, mixed up with empty beer bottles, food wrappers, and eight-track tapes.

"This is my kid, Tallulah," Mom said.

Tully didn't say anything, but she hated to be called Tallulah. She'd tell her mommy that later, when they were alone.

"Far out," someone said.

"She looks just like you, Dot. It blows my mind."

"Get in," the driver said gruffly. "We're gonna be late."

The man in the dirty T-shirt reached for Tully, grabbed her around the waist, and swung her into the van, where she positioned herself carefully on her knees.

Mom climbed inside and slammed the door shut. Strange music pulsed through the van. All she could make out were a few words: *somethin' happenin' here . . .* Smoke made everything look soft and vaguely out of focus.

Tully edged closer to the metal side to make room beside her, but Mom sat next to the lady in the kerchief. They immediately started talking about pigs and marches and a man named Kent. None of it made sense to Tully and the smoke was making her dizzy. When the man beside her lit up his pipe, she couldn't help the little sigh of disappointment that leaked from her mouth.

The man heard it and turned to her. Exhaling a cloud of gray smoke right into her face, he smiled. "Jus' go with the flow, li'l girl."

"Look at the way my mother has her dressed," Mommy said bitterly. "Like she's some little doll. How's she s'posed to be *real* if she can't get dirty?"

"Right on, Dot," the guy said, blowing smoke out of his mouth and leaning back.

Mommy looked at Tully for the first time, really *looked* at her. "You remember that, kiddo. Life isn't about cooking and cleaning and havin' babies. It's about bein' free. Doin' your own thing. You can be the fucking president of the United States if you want."

"We could use a new president, thass for sure," the driver said.

The woman in the headband patted Mom's thigh. "Thass tellin' it like it is. Pass me that bong, Tom." She giggled. "Hey, that's almost a rhyme."

Tully frowned, feeling a new kind of shame in the pit of her stomach. She thought she looked pretty in this dress. And she didn't want to be the president. She wanted to be a ballerina.

Mostly, though, she wanted her mommy to love her. She edged sideways until she was actually close enough to her mother to touch her. "Happy birthday," she said quietly, reaching into her pocket. She pulled out the necklace she'd worked so hard on, agonized over, really, still gluing glitter on long after the other kids had gone out to play. "I made this for you."

Mom snagged the necklace and closed her fingers around it. Tully waited and waited for her mom to say thank you and put the necklace on, but she didn't; she just sat there, swaying to the music, talking to her friends.

Tully finally closed her eyes. The smoke was making her sleepy. For most of her life she'd missed her mommy, and not like you missed a toy you couldn't find or a friend who stopped coming over to play because you wouldn't share. She *missed* her mommy. It was always inside her, an empty space that ached in the daytime and turned into a sharp pain at night. She'd promised herself that if her mommy ever came back, she'd be good. Perfect. Whatever she'd done or said that was so wrong, she'd fix or change. More than anything she wanted to make her mommy proud.

But now she didn't know what to do. In her dreams, they'd always gone off together alone, just the two of them, holding hands.

"Here we are," her dream mommy always said as they walked up the hill to their house. "Home sweet home." Then she'd kiss Tully's cheek and whisper, "I missed you so much. I was gone because—"

"Tallulah. Wake up."

Tully came awake with a jolt. Her head was pounding and her throat hurt. When she tried to say, *Where are we?* all that came out was a croak.

Everyone laughed at that and kept laughing as they bundled out of the van.

On this busy downtown Seattle street, there were people everywhere, chanting and yelling and holding up signs that read MAKE LOVE NOT WAR, and HELL NO, WE WON'T GO. Tully had never seen so many people in one place.

Mommy took hold of her hand, pulled her close.

The rest of the day was a blur of people chanting slogans and singing songs. Tully spent every moment terrified that she'd somehow let go of her mother's hand and be swept away by the crowd. She didn't feel any safer when the policemen showed up because they had guns on their belts and sticks in their hands and plastic shields that protected their faces.

But all the crowd did was march and all the police did was watch.

By the time it got dark, she was tired and hungry and her head ached, but they just kept walking, up one street and down another. The crowd was different now; they'd put away their signs and started drinking. Sometimes she heard whole sentences or pieces of conversation, but none of it made sense.

"Did you see those pigs? They were *dyin'* to knock our teeth out, but we were peaceful, man. Couldn't touch us. Hey, Dot, you're bogarting the joint."

Everyone around them laughed, Mommy most of all. Tully couldn't figure out what was going on and she had a terrible headache. People swelled around them, dancing and laughing. From somewhere, music spilled into the street.

And then, suddenly, she was holding on to nothing.

"Mommy!" she screamed.

No one answered or turned to her, even though there were people everywhere. She pushed through the bodies, screaming for her mommy until her voice failed her. Finally, she went back to where she'd last seen her mommy and waited at the curb.

She'll be back.

Tears stung her eyes and leaked down her face as she sat there waiting, trying to be brave.

But her mommy never came back.

For years afterward, she tried to remember what had happened next, what she did, but all those people were like a cloud that obscured her memories. All she ever remembered was waking up on a dirty cement stoop along a street that was totally empty, seeing a policeman on horseback.

From his perch high above her, he frowned down at her and said, "Hey, little one, are you all alone?"

"I am," was all she could say without crying.

He took her back to the house on Queen Anne Hill, where her grandma held her tightly and kissed her cheek and told her it wasn't her fault.

But Tully knew better. Somehow today she'd done something wrong, been bad. Next time her mommy came back, she'd try harder. She'd promise to be the president and she'd never, ever say she was sorry again.

Tully got a chart of the presidents of the United States and memorized every name in order. For months afterward, she told anyone who asked that she would be the first woman president; she even quit taking ballet classes. On her eleventh birthday, while Grandma lit the candles on her cake and sang a thin, watery version of "Happy Birthday," Tully glanced repeatedly at the door, thinking, *This is it,* but no one ever knocked and the phone didn't ring. Later, with the opened boxes of her gifts around her, she tried to keep smiling. In front of her, on the coffee table, was an empty scrapbook. As a present, it sort of sucked, but her grandma always gave her stuff like this—projects to keep her busy and quiet.

"She didn't even call," Tully said, looking up.

Gran sighed tiredly. "Your mom has . . . problems, Tully. She's weak and confused. You've got to quit pretending things are different. What matters is that you're strong."

She'd heard this advice a bazillion times. "I know."

Gran sat down on the worn floral sofa beside Tully and pulled her onto her lap.

Tully loved it when Gran held her. She snuggled in close, rested her cheek on Gran's soft chest.

"I wish things were different with your mama, Tully, and that's the God's honest truth, but she's a lost soul. Has been for a long time."

"Is that why she doesn't love me?"

Gran looked down at her. The black horn-rimmed glasses magnified her pale gray eyes. "She loves you, in her way. That's why she keeps coming back."

"It doesn't feel like love."

"I know."

"I don't think she even likes me."

"It's me she doesn't like. Something happened a long time ago and I didn't . . . Well, it doesn't matter now." Gran tightened her hold on Tully. "Someday she'll be sorry she missed these years with you. I'm certain of that."

"I could show her my scrapbook."

Gran didn't look at her. "That would be nice." After a long silence, she said, "Happy birthday, Tully," and kissed her forehead. "Now I'd best go sit with your grandfather. He's feeling poorly today."

After her grandmother left the room, Tully sat there, staring down at the blank first page of her new scrapbook. It would be the perfect thing to give her mother one day, to show her what she'd missed. But how would Tully fill it? She had a few photographs of herself, taken mostly by her friends' moms at parties and on field trips, but not many. Her gran's eyes weren't good enough for those tiny viewfinders. And she had only the one picture of her mom.

She picked up a pen and very carefully wrote the date in the upper right-hand corner; then she frowned. What else? *Dear Mommy. Today was my eleventh birthday . . .*

After that day, she collected artifacts from her life. School pictures, sports pictures, movie ticket stubs. For years whenever she had a good day, she hurried home and wrote about it, pasting down whatever receipt or ticket proved where she had been or what she'd done. Somewhere along the way she started adding little embellishments to make herself look better. They weren't lies, really, just exaggerations. Anything that would make her mom someday say she was proud of her. She filled that scrapbook and then another and another. On every birthday, she received a brand-new book, until she moved into the teen years.

Something happened to her then. She wasn't sure what it was, maybe the breasts that grew faster than anyone else's, or maybe it was just that she got tired of putting her life down on pieces of paper no one ever asked to see. By fourteen, she was done. She put all her little-girl books in a big cardboard box and shoved them to the back of her closet, and she asked Gran not to buy her any more.

"Are you sure, honey?"

"Yeah," had been her answer. She didn't care about her mother anymore and tried never to think about her. In fact, at school, she told everyone that her mom had died in a boating accident.

The lie freed her. She quit buying her clothes in the little-girls departments and spent her time in the juniors area. She bought tight, midriff-baring shirts that showed off her new boobs and low-rise bell-bottoms that made her butt look good. She had to hide these clothes from Gran, but it was easy to do; a puffy down vest and a quick wave could get her out of the house in whatever she wanted to wear.

She learned that if she dressed carefully and acted a certain way, the cool kids wanted to hang out with her. On Friday and Saturday nights, she told Gran she was staying at a friend's house and went roller-skating at Lake Hills, where no one ever asked about her family or looked at her as if she were "poor Tully." She learned to smoke cigarettes without coughing and to chew gum to camouflage the smell on her breath.

By eighth grade, she was one of the most popular girl in junior high, and it helped, having all those friends. When she was busy enough, she didn't think about the woman who didn't want her.

On rare days she still felt . . . not quite lonely . . . but something. Adrift, maybe. As if all the people she hung around with were place-holders.

Today was one of those days. She sat in her regular seat on the school bus, hearing the buzz of gossip go on around her. Everyone seemed to be talking about family things; she had nothing to add to the conversations. She knew nothing about fighting with your little brother or being grounded for talking back to your parents or going to the mall with your mom. Thankfully, when the bus pulled up to her stop, she hurried off, making a big show of saying goodbye to her friends, laughing loudly and waving. Pretending; she did a lot of that lately.

After the bus drove away, she repositioned her backpack over her shoulder and started the long walk home. She had just turned the corner when she saw it.

There, parked across the street, in front of Gran's house, was a beat-up red VW bus. The flower decals were still on the side.

CHAPTER THREE

It was still dark when Kate Mularkey's alarm clock rang. She groaned and lay there, staring up at the peaked ceiling. The thought of going to school made her sick.

Eighth grade blew chips as far as she was concerned; 1974 had turned out to be a totally sucky year, a social desert. Thank God there was only a month left of school. Not that the summer promised to be any better.

In sixth grade she'd had two best friends; they'd done everything together—showed their horses in 4-H, gone to youth group, and ridden their bikes from one house to the next. The summer they turned twelve, all that ended. Her friends went wild; there was no other way to put it. They smoked pot before school and skipped classes and never missed a party. When she wouldn't join in, they cut her loose. Period. And the "good" kids wouldn't come near her because she'd been part of the stoners' club. So now books were her only friends. She'd read *Lord of the Rings* so often she could recite whole scenes by memory.

It was not a skill that aided one in becoming popular.

With a sigh, she got out of bed. In the tiny upstairs closet that had recently been turned into a bathroom, she took a quick shower and braided her straight blond hair, then put on her spazo horn-rimmed glasses. They were hopelessly out of date now—round and rimless were what the cool kids wore—but her dad said they couldn't afford new glasses yet.

Downstairs, she went to the back door, folded her belled pant leg around each calf, and stepped into the huge black rubber boots they kept on the concrete steps. Moving like Neil Armstrong, she made her way through the deep mud to the shed out back. Their old quarterhorse mare limped up to the fence, whinnied a greeting. "Heya, Sweetpea," Kate said, throwing a flake of hay onto the ground, and then scratching the horse's velvety ear.

"I miss you, too," she said, and it was true. Two years ago they'd been inseparable; Kate had ridden this mare all that summer, and won plenty of ribbons at the Snohomish County Fair.

But things changed fast. She knew that now. A horse could get old overnight and go lame. A friend could become a stranger just as quickly.

"'Bye." She clomped back up the dark, muddy driveway and left her dirty boots on the porch.

When she opened the back door, she stepped into pandemonium. Mom stood at the stove, dressed in her faded floral housedress and fuzzy pink slippers, smoking an Eve menthol cigarette and pouring batter into an oblong electric frying pan. Her shoulder-length brown hair was divided into two scrawny pigtails; each one was held in place by a strand of hot-pink ribbon. "Set the table, Katie," she said without glancing up. "Sean! Get down here."

Kate did as she was told. Almost before she was finished, her mother was behind her, pouring milk into the glasses.

"Sean—breakfast," Mom yelled up the stairs again. This time she added the magic words: "I've poured the milk."

Within seconds eight-year-old Sean came running down the stairs and rushed toward the beige speckled Formica table, giggling as he tripped over the Labrador puppy who'd recently joined the family.

Kate was just about to sit down at her regular place when she happened to glance across the kitchen and into the living room. Through the large window above the sofa, she saw something that surprised her: A moving van was turning into the driveway across the street.

"Wow." She carried her plate through the two rooms and stood at the window, staring out over their three acres and down on the house across the street. It had been vacant for as long as anyone could remember.

She heard her mother's footsteps coming up behind her; hard on the fake brick linoleum of the kitchen floor, quiet in the moss-green carpeting of the living room.

"Someone's moving in across the street," Kate said.

"Really?"

No. I'm lying.

"Maybe they'll have a girl your age. It would be nice for you to have a friend."

Kate bit back an irritated retort. Only mothers thought it was easy to make friends in junior high. "Whatever." She turned away abruptly, taking her plate into the hallway, where she finished her breakfast in peace beneath the portrait of Jesus.

As expected, Mom followed her. She stood by the tapestry wall hanging of *The Last Supper,* saying nothing.

"What?" Kate snapped when she couldn't take it anymore.

Mom's sigh was so quiet it could hardly be heard. "Why are we always bickering lately?"

"You're the one who starts it."

"By saying hello and asking how you're doing? Yeah, I'm a real witch."

"You said it, not me."

"It's not my fault, you know."

"What isn't?"

"That you don't have any friends. If you'd—"

Kate walked away. Honest to St. Jude, one more if-you'd-only-try-harder speech and she might puke.

Thankfully—for once—Mom didn't follow her. Instead, she went back into the kitchen, calling out, "Hurry up, Sean. The Mularkey school bus leaves in ten minutes."

Her brother giggled. Kate rolled her eyes and went upstairs. It was so lame. How could her brother laugh at the same stupid joke every day?

The answer came as quickly as the question had: because he had friends. Life with friends made everything easier.

She hid in her bedroom until she heard the old Ford station wagon start up. The last thing she wanted was to get driven to school by her mom, who yelled goodbye and waved like a contestant on *The Price Is Right* when Kate got out of the car. Everyone knew it was social suicide to be driven to school by your parents. When she heard tires crunching slowly across gravel, she went back downstairs, washed the dishes, gathered her stuff, and left the house. Outside, the sun was shining, but last night's rain had studded the driveway with inner-tube-sized potholes. No doubt the old-timers down at the hardware store were already starting to talk about the flooding. Mud sucked at the soles of her fake Earth shoes, making her progress slow. So intent was she on saving her only rainbow socks that she was at the bottom of the driveway before she noticed the girl standing across the street.

She was gorgeous. Tall and big-boobed, she had long, curly auburn hair and a face like Caroline of Monaco: pale skin and full lips and long lashes. And her *clothes*: low-rise, three-button jeans with huge, tie-died wedges of fabric in the seams to make elephant bells; cork-bottomed platform shoes with four-inch heels; and an angel-sleeved pink peasant blouse that revealed at least two inches of stomach.

Kate clutched her books against her chest, wishing she hadn't picked her pimples last night. Or that her jeans weren't Sears Rough Riders. "H-hi," she said, stopping on her side of the road. "The bus stops on this side."

Chocolate-brown eyes, rimmed heavily with black mascara and shiny blue eye shadow, stared at her, revealing nothing.

Just then, the school bus arrived. Wheezing and squeaking, it came to a shuddering stop on the road. A boy she used to have a crush on stuck his head out the window and yelled, "Hey, Kootie, the flood's over," and then laughed.

Kate put her head down and boarded the bus. Collapsing into her usual front-row seat—by herself—she kept her head bowed, waiting for the new girl to walk past her, but no one else got on. When the doors thumped shut and the bus lurched forward, she dared to look back at the road.

The coolest-looking girl in the world wasn't there.

Already Tully didn't fit in. It had taken two hours to choose her clothes this morning—an outfit right out of the pages of *Seventeen* magazine—and every bit of it was wrong.

When the school bus drove up, she made a split-second decision. She wasn't going to go to school in this hick backwater. Snohomish might be less than an hour from downtown Seattle, but as far as she was concerned, she might as well be on the moon. That was how alien this place felt.

No.

Hell, no.

She marched down the gravel driveway and shoved the front door open so hard it cracked against the wall.

Drama, she'd learned, was like good punctuation: it underscored your point.

"You must be high," she said loudly, realizing a second too late that the only people in the living room were the moving men.

One of them paused and looked wearily her way. "Huh?"

She pushed past them, grazing the armoire so hard they swore under their breath. Not that she cared. She hated it when she felt like this, all puffed up with anger.

She wouldn't let her so-called mother make her feel twisted up inside, not after all the times that woman had abandoned her.

In the master bedroom, her mom was sitting on the floor, cutting pictures out of *Cosmo*. As usual, her long hair was a wavy, fuzzy nightmare held in check by a grossly out-of-date beaded leather headband. Without looking up, she flipped to the next page, where a naked, grinning Burt Reynolds covered his penis with one hand.

"I'm *not* going to this backwater school. They're a bunch of hicks."

"Oh." Mom flipped to the next page, then reached for her scissors and began cutting out a spray of flowers from a Breck ad. "Okay."

Tully wanted to scream. "Okay? *Okay?* I'm fourteen years old."

"My job is to love and support you, baby, not to get in your face."

Tully closed her eyes, counted to ten, and said again, "I don't have any friends here."

"Make new ones. I heard you were Miss Popular at your old school."

"Come on, Mom, I—"

"Cloud."

"I'm not calling you Cloud."

"Fine, Tallulah." Mom looked up to make sure her point had been made. It had.

"I don't belong here."

"You know better than that, Tully. You're a child of the earth and sky; you belong everywhere. The Bhagavad Gita says . . ."

"That's it." Tully walked away while her mother was still talking. The last thing she wanted to hear was some drug-soaked advice that belonged on a black-light poster. On the way out, she snagged a pack of Virginia Slims from her mom's purse and headed for the road.

For the next week, Kate watched the new girl from a distance.

Tully Hart was boldly, coolly different; brighter, somehow, than everyone else in the faded green hallways. She had no curfew and didn't care if she got caught smoking in the woods behind the school. Everyone talked about it. Kate heard the whispered awe in their voices. For a group of kids who'd grown up in the dairy farms and paper mill workers' homes of the Snohomish Valley, Tully Hart was exotic. Everyone wanted to be friends with her.

Her neighbor's instant popularity made Kate's alienation more unbearable. She wasn't sure why it wounded her so much. All she knew was that every morning, as they stood at the bus stop beside each other and yet worlds apart, separated by yawning silence, Kate felt a desperate desire to be acknowledged by Tully.

Not that it would ever happen.

". . . before *The Carol Burnett show* starts. It's ready now. Kate? Katie?"

Kate lifted her head from the table. She'd fallen asleep on her open social studies textbook at the kitchen table. "Huh? What did you say?" she asked, pushing her heavy glasses back up into place.

"I made Hamburger Helper for our new neighbors. I want you to take it across the street."

"But . . ." Kate tried to think of an excuse, anything that would get her out of this. "They've been here a week."

"So I'm late. Things have been crazy lately."

"I've got too much homework. Send Sean."

"Sean's not likely to make friends over there, now, is he?"

"Neither am I," Kate said miserably.

Mom faced her. The brown hair she'd curled and teased so carefully this morning had fallen during the day and her makeup had faded. Now her round, apple-cheeked face looked pale and washed out. Her purple and yellow crocheted vest—a Christmas present from last year—was buttoned wrong. Staring at Kate, she crossed the room and sat down at the table. "Can I say something without you jumping all over me?"

"Probably not."

"I'm sorry about you and Joannie."

Of all the things Kate might have expected, that was not even on the list. "It doesn't matter."

"It matters. I hear she's running with a pretty fast crowd these days."

Kate wanted to say she couldn't have cared less, but to her horror, tears stung her eyes. Memories rushed at her—Joannie and her on the Octopus ride at the fair, sitting outside their stalls at the barn, talking about how much fun high school would be. She shrugged. "Yeah."

"Life is hard sometimes. Especially at fourteen."

Kate rolled her eyes. If there was one thing she knew, it was that her mother knew nothing about how hard life could be for a teenager. "No shit."

"I'm going to pretend I didn't hear that word from you. It'll be easy because I'll never hear it again. Right?"

Kate couldn't help wishing she was like Tully. *She'd* never back down so easily. She'd probably light up a cigarette right now and dare her mom to say something.

Mom dug through the baggy pocket of her skirt and found her cigarettes. Lighting up, she studied Kate. "You know I love you and I support you and I would never let anyone hurt you. But Katie, I have to ask you: What is it you're waiting for?"

"What do you mean?"

"You spend all your time reading and doing homework. How are people supposed to get to know you when you act like that?"

"They don't want to know me."

Mom touched her hand gently. "It's never good to sit around and wait for someone or something to change your life. That's why women like Gloria Steinem are burning their bras and marching on Washington."

"So that I can make friends?"

"So that you know you can be whatever you want to be. Your generation is so lucky. You can be anything you want. But you have to take a risk sometimes. Reach out. One thing I can tell you for sure is this: we only regret what we don't do in life."

Kate heard an odd sound in her mom's voice, a sadness that tinted the word *regret*. But what could her mother possibly know about the battlefield of junior high popularity? She hadn't been a teenager in decades. "Yeah, right."

"It's true, Kathleen. Someday you'll see how smart I am." Her mom smiled and patted her hand. "If you're like the rest of us, it'll happen at about the same time you want me to babysit for the first time."

"What are you talking about?"

Mom laughed at some joke Kate didn't even get. "I'm glad we had this talk. Now go. Make friends with your new neighbor."

Yeah. That would happen.

"Wear oven mitts. It's still hot," Mom said.

Perfect. The mitts.

Kate went over to the counter and stared down at the red-brown glop of a casserole. Dully, she fitted a sheet of foil across the top, curled the edges down, and then put on the puffy, quilted blue oven mitts her Aunt Georgia had made. At the back door, she slipped her stockinged feet into the fake Earth shoes on the porch and headed down the spongy driveway.

The house across the street was long and low to the ground, a rambler-style in an L shape that faced away from the road. Moss furred the shingled roof. The ivory sides were in need of paint, and the gutters were overflowing with leaves and sticks. Giant rhododendron bushes hid most of the windows, runaway junipers created a green spiky barrier that ran the length of the house. No one had tended to the landscaping in years.

At the front door Kate paused, drawing in a deep breath.

Balancing the casserole in one hand, she pulled off one oven mitt and knocked.

Please let no one be home.

Almost instantly she heard footsteps from inside.

The door swung open to reveal a tall woman dressed in a billowy caftan. An Indian-beaded headband circled her forehead. Two mismatched earrings hung from her ears. There was a strange dullness in her eyes, as if she needed glasses and didn't have them, but even so, she was pretty in a sharp, brittle kind of way. "Yeah?"

Weird, pulsing music seemed to come from several places at once; though the lights were turned off, several lava lamps burped and bubbled in eerie green and red canisters.

"H-hello," Kate stammered. "My mom made you guys this casserole."

"Right on," the lady said, stumbling back, almost falling.

And suddenly Tully was coming through the doorway, sweeping through, actually, moving with a grace and confidence that was more movie star than teenager. In a bright blue minidress and white go-go boots, she looked old enough to be driving a car. Without saying anything, she grabbed Kate's arm, pulled her through the living room, and into a kitchen in which everything was pink: walls, cabinets, curtains, tile counters, table. When Tully looked at her, Kate thought she saw a flash of something that looked like embarrassment in those dark eyes.

"Was that your mom?" Kate asked, uncertain of what to say.

"She has cancer."

"Oh." Kate didn't know what to say except, "I'm sorry." Quiet pressed into the room. Instead of making eye contact with Tully, Kate studied the table. Never in her life had she seen so much junk food in one place. Pop-Tarts, Cap'n Crunch and Quisp boxes, Fritos, Funyuns, Twinkies, Zingers, and Screaming Yellow Zonkers. "Wow. I wish my mom would let me eat all this stuff." Kate immediately wished she'd kept her mouth shut. Now she sounded hopelessly uncool. To give herself something to do—and somewhere to look besides Tully's unreadable face—she put the casserole on the counter. "It's still hot," she said, stupidly, considering that she was wearing oven mitts that looked like killer whales.

Tully lit up a cigarette and leaned against the pink wall, eyeing her.

Kate glanced back at the door to the living room. "She doesn't care if you smoke?"

"She's too sick to care."

"Oh."

"You want a drag?"

"Uh . . . no. Thanks."

"Yeah. That's what I thought."

On the wall, the black Kit-Kat Klock swished its tail.

"Well, you probably have to get home for dinner," Tully said.

"Oh," Kate said again, sounding even more nerdy than she had before. "Right."

Tully led the way back through the living room, where her mother was now sprawled on the sofa. "'Bye, girl from across the street with the cool neighbor attitude."

Tully yanked the door open. Beyond it, the falling night was a blurry purple rectangle that seemed too vivid to be real. "Thanks for the food," she said. "I don't know how to cook, and Cloud is cooked, if you know what I mean."

"Cloud?"

"That's my mom's current name."

"Oh."

"It'd be cool if I *did* know how to cook. Or if we had a chef or something. With my mom having cancer and all." Tully looked at her.

Tell her you'll teach her.

Take a risk.

But she couldn't do it. The potential for humiliation was sky-high. "Well . . .'bye."

"Later."

Kate stepped past her and into the night.

She was halfway to the road when Tully called out to her, "Hey, wait up."

Kate slowly turned around.

"What's your name?"

She felt a flash of hope. "Kate. Kate Mularkey."

Tully laughed. "Mularkey? Like bullshit?"

It was hardly funny anymore, that joke about her last name. She sighed and turned back around.

"I didn't mean to laugh," Tully said, but she didn't stop.

"Yeah. Whatever."

"Fine. Be a bitch, why don't you?"

Kate kept walking.

CHAPTER
FOUR

Tully watched the girl walk away.

"I shouldn't have said that," she said, noticing how small her voice sounded beneath the enormous star-spangled sky.

She wasn't even sure why she'd said it, why she'd suddenly felt the need to make fun of the next-door neighbor. With a sigh, she went back into the house. The moment she stepped into the room, the smell of pot overwhelmed her, stung her eyes. On the sofa, her mom lay spread-eagled, one leg on the coffee table, one on the back cushions. Her mouth hung open; drool sparkled the corners of her lips.

And the girl next door had seen this. Tully felt a hot wave of shame. No doubt rumors would be all over school by Monday. *Tully Hart has a pothead mom.*

This was why she never invited anyone over to her house. When you were keeping secrets, you needed to do it alone, in the dark.

She would have given anything to have the kind of mom who made dinner for strangers. Maybe that was why she'd made fun of the girl's name. The thought pissed her off and she slammed the door shut behind her. "Cloud. Wake up."

Mom drew in a sharp, snorting breath and sat up. "Whass the matter?"

"It's dinnertime."

Mom pushed the gob of hair out of her eyes and worked to focus on the wall clock. "What are we—in a nursing home? Iss five o'clock."

Tully was surprised her mom could still tell time. She went into the kitchen, served the casserole onto two white CorningWare plates, and returned to the living room. "Here." She handed her mother a plate and fork.

"Where'd we get this? Did you cook?"

"Hardly. The neighbor brought it over."

Cloud looked blearily around. "We have neighbors?"

Tully didn't bother answering. Her mother always forgot what they were talking about anyway. It made any real conversation impossible, and usually Tully didn't care—she wanted to talk to Cloud like she wanted to watch black and white movies—but now, since that girl's visit, Tully felt her differentness keenly. If she had a real family—a mom who made casseroles and sent them as gifts to new neighbors—she wouldn't feel so alone. She sat down in one of the mustard-colored beanbag chairs that flanked the sofa and said cautiously, "I wonder what Gran's doing right now."

"Pro'ly making one of those god-awful PRAISE JESUS samplers. As if that'll save her soul. Ha. How's school?"

Tully's head snapped up. She couldn't believe her mom had just asked about her life. "Lots of kids hang around with me, but . . ." She frowned. How could she put her dissatisfaction into words? All she really knew was that she was lonely here, even among her new friends. "I keep waiting for . . ."

"Do we have ketchup?" her mother said, frowning down at her heap of Hamburger Helper, poking at it with her fork. She was swaying to the music.

Tully hated the disappointment she felt. She knew better than to expect anything from her mother. "I'm going to my room," she said, climbing out of the beanbag chair.

The last thing she heard before she slammed her bedroom door was her mother saying, "Maybe it needs cheese."

Late that night, long after everyone else had gone to bed, Kate crept down the stairs, put on her dad's huge rubber boots, and went outside. It was becoming a habit lately, going outside when she couldn't sleep. Overhead, the huge black sky was splattered with stars. It made her feel small and unimportant, that sky. A lonely girl looking down at an empty street that went nowhere.

Sweetpea nickered and trotted toward her.

She climbed up onto the top rail of the fence. "Hey there, girl," she said, pulling a carrot out of her parka's pocket.

She glanced over at the house across the street. The lights were still on at midnight. No doubt Tully was having a party with all the popular kids. They were probably laughing and dancing and talking about how cool they were.

Kate would give everything she owned to be invited to just one party like that.

Sweetpea nudged her knee, snorted.

"I know. I'm dreaming." Sighing, she slid off the fence, petted Sweetpea one last time, and then went back to bed.

A few nights later, after a dinner of Pop-Tarts and Alpha-Bits cereal, Tully took a long, hot shower, shaved her legs and underarms carefully, and dried her hair until it fell straight from her center part without a single crease or curl. Then she went to her closet and stood there, trying to figure out what to wear. This was her first high school party. She needed to look just right. None of the other girls from the junior high had been invited. She was The One. Pat Richmond, the best-looking guy on the football team, had chosen Tully for his date. They'd been at the local hamburger hangout last Wednesday night, his group of friends and hers. All it had taken was one look between them. Pat had broken free of the crowd of huge guys and walked right over to Tully.

She'd seen him heading her way and practically fainted. On the jukebox, "Stairway to Heaven" had been playing. Talk about romantic.

"I could get in trouble just for talking to you," he said.

She tried to look mature and worldly as she said, "I like trouble."

The smile he gave her was like nothing she'd ever seen before. For the first time in her life, she felt as beautiful as people always said she was.

"You wanna come to the party with me on Friday?"

"I could make that work," she said. It was a phrase she'd heard Erica Kane use on *All My Children*.

"I'll pick you up at ten." He leaned closer. "Unless that's past your curfew, little girl?"

"Seventeen Firefly Lane. And I don't have a curfew."

He smiled again. "I'm Pat, by the way."

"I'm Tully."

"Well, Tully, I'll see you at ten."

Tully still couldn't believe it. For the past forty-eight hours she'd obsessed over this first real date. All the other times she'd gone out with boys it was in a group or to a school dance. This was totally different, and Pat was practically a man.

They could fall in love; she knew it. And then, with him holding her hand, she'd stop feeling so alone.

She finally made her clothes choice.

Low-rise, three-button bell-bottom jeans, a pink scoop-necked knit top that showed off her cleavage, and her favorite cork platforms. She spent almost an hour on her makeup, layering more and more on until she looked foxy. She couldn't wait to show Pat how pretty she could be.

She grabbed a pack of her mom's cigarettes and left her bedroom.

In the living room, Mom looked up blearily from her magazine. "Hey, iss almos' ten o'clock. Where are you going?"

"This guy invited me to a party."

"Is he here?"

Right. Like Tully would invite anyone to come in. "I'm meeting him on the road."

"Oh. Cool. Don't wake me up when you get home."

"I won't."

Outside, it was dark and cold. The Milky Way stretched across the sky in a path of starlight.

She waited by her mailbox on the main road, moving from foot to foot to keep warm. Goose bumps pebbled her bare arms. The mood ring on her middle finger changed from green to purple. She tried to remember what that meant.

Across the street and up the hill, the pretty little farmhouse glowed against the darkness. Each window was like a pat of warm, melting butter. They were probably all at home, clustered around a big table, playing Risk. She wondered what they'd do if she just visited one day, showed up on the porch and said hey.

She heard Pat's car before she saw the headlights. At the roar of the engine, she forgot all about the family across the street and stepped into the road, waving.

His green Dodge Charger came to a stop beside her; the car seemed to pulse with sound, vibrate. She slid into the passenger seat. The music was so loud she knew he couldn't hear what she said.

Grinning at her, Pat hit the gas and they were off like a rocket, blasting down the quiet country lane.

As they turned onto a gravel road, she could see the party going on below. Dozens of cars were parked in a huge circle in a pasture, with their headlights on. Bachman-Turner Overdrive's "Taking Care of Business" blared from someone's car radio. Pat parked over in the stand of trees along the fence line.

There were kids everywhere, gathered around the flames of the bonfire, standing beside the kegs of beer set up in the grass. Clear plastic cups littered the ground. Down by the barn, a group of guys were playing touch football. It was late in May, and summer was still a ways away, so most people were wearing coats. She wished she hadn't forgotten hers.

Pat held her hand tightly, leading her through the crowd of couples toward the keg, where he poured two cups full.

Taking hers, she let him lead her down to a quiet spot just beyond the perimeter of cars. There, he spread his letterman's jacket down on the ground and motioned for her to sit down.

"I couldn't believe it when I first saw you," Pat said, sitting close to her, sipping his beer. "You're the prettiest girl ever to live in this town. All the guys want you."

"But you got me," she said, smiling at him. It felt as if she were falling into his dark eyes.

He took a big drink of his beer, practically finishing it, then he set it down and kissed her.

Other guys had kissed her before; mostly they were fumbling, nervous attempts made during a slow dance. This was different. Pat's mouth was like magic. She sighed happily, whispering his name. When he drew back, he was staring at her with pure, sunshiny love in his eyes. "I'm glad you're here."

"Me, too."

He finished off his beer and got up. "I need more brew."

They were in line at the keg when he frowned at her. "Hey, you aren't drinking. I thought you were cool with partying."

"I am." She smiled nervously. She'd never really drank before, but he wouldn't like her if she acted like a nerd, and she was desperate for him to want her. "Bottoms up," she said, tilting the plastic tumbler to her lips and drinking the whole amount without stopping. When she finished, she couldn't help burping and giggling.

"Far out," he said, nodding, pouring two more beers.

The second one wasn't so bad, and by the third beer Tully had completely lost her sense of taste. When Pat brought out a bottle of Annie Green Springs wine, she guzzled some of that, too. For almost an hour, they sat on his jacket, tucked close together, drinking and talking. She didn't know any of the people he talked about, but that didn't matter. What mattered was the way he looked at her, the way he held her hand.

"Come on," he whispered, "let's dance."

She felt woozy when she stood up. Her balance was off and she kept stumbling during their dance. Finally, she fell down altogether. Pat laughed, took her hand to pull her up, and led her to a dark, romantic spot in the trees. Giggling, she hobbled awkwardly behind him, gasping when he took her in his arms and kissed her.

It felt so good; made her blood feel tingly and hot. She pressed up against him like a cat, loving the way he was making her feel. Any minute he was going to draw back and look down at her and say, *I love you,* just like Ryan O'Neal in *Love Story.*

Maybe Tully would even call him preppie when she said it back to him. Their song would be "Stairway to Heaven." They'd tell people they met while—

His tongue slipped into her mouth, pressing hard, sweeping around like some kind of alien probe. Suddenly it didn't feel good anymore, didn't feel right. She tried to say, *Stop,* but her voice had no sound; he was sucking up all her air.

His hands were everywhere: up her back, around her side, plucking at her bra, trying to undo it. She felt it come free with a sickening little pop. And then he was touching her boob.

"No . . ." she whimpered, trying to push his hands away. This wasn't what she wanted. She wanted love, romance, magic. Someone to love her. Not . . . this. "No, Pat, don't—"

"Come on, Tully. You know you want it." He pushed her back and she stumbled, fell to the ground hard, hitting her head. For a second, her vision blurred. When it cleared, he was on his knees, between her legs. He held both her hands in one of his, pinning her to the ground.

"That's what I like," he said, pushing her legs apart.

Shoving her top up, he stared down at her naked chest. "Oh, yeah . . ." He cupped one breast, tweaked her nipple hard. His other hand slipped into her pants, beneath her underwear.

"Stop. Please . . ." Tully tried desperately to get free, but her wriggling only seemed to excite him.

Between her legs, his fingers probed her hard, moving inside her. "Come on, baby, let yourself like it."

She felt herself starting to cry. "Don't—"

"Oh, yeah . . ." He covered her body with his, pressed her into the wet grass.

She was crying so hard now she could taste her own tears, but he didn't seem to care. His kisses were something else now—slobbering, sucking, biting; it hurt, but not as much as his belt, hitting her stomach when he pulled it off, or his penis, ramming—

She squeezed her eyes shut as pain ripped between her legs, scraped her insides.

Then, suddenly, it was over. He rolled off her, lay beside her, holding her close, kissing her cheek as if what he'd just done to her had been love.

"Hey, you're crying." He gently smoothed the hair away from her face. "What's the matter? I thought you wanted it."

She didn't know what to say. Like every girl, she'd imagined losing her virginity, but it had never felt like this in her dreams. She stared at him in disbelief. "Wanted *that*?"

An irritated frown creased his forehead. "Come on, Tully, let's dance."

The way he said it, so quietly, as if he were actually confused by her reaction, only made it worse. She'd done something wrong, obviously, been a prick tease, and this was what happened to girls who played at it.

He stared at her for a minute longer, then stood up and pulled his pants up. "Whatever. I need another drink. Let's go."

She rolled onto her side. "Go away."

She felt him beside her, knew he was staring down at her. "You acted like you wanted it, damn it. You can't lead a guy on and then just go cold. Grow up, little girl. This is your fault."

She closed her eyes and ignored him, thankful when he finally left her. For once she was glad to be alone.

She lay there, feeling broken and hurt and, worst of all, stupid. After an hour or so, she heard the party break up, heard the car engines start, and the tires pealing through loose gravel as they drove away.

And still she lay there, unable to make herself move. This was all her fault; he was right about that. She was stupid and young. All she'd wanted was someone to love her.

"Stupid," she hissed, finally sitting up.

Moving slowly, she got dressed and tried to stand. At the movement, she felt sick to her stomach and immediately puked all over her favorite shoes. When it was over, she bent down for her purse, clutched it to her chest, and made her long, painful way back up to the road.

There were no cars out this late at night, and she was glad for that. She didn't want to have to explain to anyone why her hair was full of pine needles and her shoes were stained with vomit.

All the way home she relived what had happened—the way Pat had smiled at her when he asked her to the party; the gentle first kiss he'd given her; the way he talked to her as if she mattered; then the other Pat, with his harsh hands and his probing tongue and fingers, with his hard cock and how roughly he'd stuck it up inside her.

The more she replayed it in her mind, the lonelier and more desolate she felt.

If only she had someone she trusted to talk to. Maybe that would ease a little of this pain. But, of course, there was no one.

This was another secret she'd have to keep, like her weirdo mother and unknown father. People would say she had it coming, a junior high girl at a high school party.

As she neared her driveway, she walked a little more slowly. The thought of going home, of feeling alone in a place that should be a refuge for her, with a woman who was supposed to love her, was suddenly unbearable.

The neighbors' old gray horse trotted up to the fence line and nickered at her.

Tully crossed the street and walked up the hill. At the fence, she yanked up a handful of grass and held it out to him. "Hey there, boy."

The horse sniffed the handful of grass, snorted wetly, and trotted away.

"She likes carrots."

Tully looked up sharply and saw her neighbor sitting on the top rail of the fence.

Long minutes passed in silence between them; the only noise was the horse's quiet nickering.

"It's late," the neighbor girl said.

"Yeah."

"I love it out here at night. The stars are so bright. Sometimes, if you stare up at the sky long enough, you'll swear tiny white dots are falling all around you, like fireflies. Maybe that's how this street got its name. You probably think I'm a nerd for even saying that."

Tully wanted to answer but couldn't. Deep, deep inside she'd started to shake and it took all her concentration just to stand still.

The girl—Kate, Tully remembered—slipped down from her perch. She was wearing an oversized T-shirt with a Partridge Family decal on the front that was peeling off. As she moved forward, her boots made a sucking noise in the mud. "Hey, you don't look so good." A retainer drew the s into a long lisp. "And you reek like puke."

"I'm fine," she said, stiffening as Kate drew close.

"Are you okay? Really?"

To Tully's complete horror, she started to cry.

Kate stood there a moment, staring at her from behind those dork-o-rama glasses. Then, without saying anything, she hugged Tully.

Tully flinched at the contact; it was foreign and unexpected. She started to pull away, but found that she couldn't move. She couldn't remember the last time someone had held her like this, and suddenly she was clinging to this weirdo girl, afraid to let go, afraid that without Kate, she'd float away like the S.S. *Minnow* and be lost at sea.

"I'm sure she'll get better," Kate said when Tully's tears subsided.

Tully drew back, frowning. It took her a second to understand.

The cancer. Kate thought she was worried about her mom.

"Do you want to talk about it?" Kate said, taking out her retainer, putting it on the mossy top of a fence post.

Tully stared at her. In the silvery light from a full moon, she saw nothing but compassion in Kate's magnified green eyes, and she wanted to talk, wanted it with a fierceness that made her feel sick. But she didn't know how to start.

Kate said, "Come on," and led her up the hill to the slanted front porch of the farmhouse. There, she sat down, pulling her threadbare T-shirt over her bent knees. "My Aunt Georgia had cancer," she said. "It was grody. Lost all her hair. But she's fine now."

Tully sat down beside her, put her purse on the ground. The smell of vomit was strong. She pulled out a cigarette and lit up to cover the stench. Before she knew it, she'd said, "I went to a party down by the river tonight."

"A high school party?" Kate sounded impressed.

"Pat Richmond asked me out."

"The quarterback? Wow. My mom wouldn't let me stand in the same checkout line as a high school senior. She's so lame."

"She's not lame."

"She thinks eighteen-year-old boys are dangerous. She calls them penises with hands and feet. Tell me that isn't lame."

Tully glanced out over the field and took a deep, steadying breath. She couldn't believe she was going to tell this girl what happened to-night, but the truth was a fire inside her. If she didn't get rid of it, she'd burn up. "He raped me."

Kate turned to her. Tully felt those green eyes boring into her pro-file, but she didn't move, didn't turn. Her shame was so overwhelming that she couldn't stand to see it reflected in Kate's eyes. She waited for Kate to say something, to call her an idiot, but the silence just went on and on. Finally, she couldn't take it anymore. She looked sideways.

"Are you okay?" Kate asked quietly.

Tully relived it all in those few words. Tears stung her eyes, blurred her vision.

Once again, Kate hugged her. Tully let herself be comforted for the first time since she was little. When she finally drew back, she tried to smile. "I'm drowning you."

"We should tell someone."

"No way. They'd say it was my fault. This is our secret, okay?"

"Okay." Kate frowned as she said it.

Tully wiped her eyes and took another drag on her cigarette. "Why are you being so nice to me?"

"You looked lonely. Believe me, I know how that feels."

"You do? But you have a family."

"They *have* to like me." Kate sighed. "The kids at school treat me like I've got an infectious disease. I used to have friends, but . . . you probably don't know what in the heck I'm talking about. You're so popular."

"Popular just means lots of people think they know you."

"I'd take that."

Silence fell between them. Tully finished her cigarette and put it out. They were so different, she and Kate, as full of contrasts as this dark field bathed in moonlight, but it felt so completely easy to talk to her. Tully found herself almost smiling, and on this, the worst night of her life. That was something.

For the next hour, they sat there, talking now and then and sometimes just sitting in silence. They didn't say anything really important or share any more secrets, they just talked.

Finally, Kate yawned and Tully stood up. "I better book."

They got up and walked down to the road. At the mailboxes, Kate stopped. "Well. 'Bye."

"'Bye." Tully stood there a moment, feeling awkward. She wanted to hug Kate, maybe even cling to her and tell her how much this night had been helped by her, but she didn't dare. She'd learned a thing or two about vulnerability from her mother, and she felt too fragile now to risk humiliation. Turning, she headed down to her house. Once inside, she went straight to the shower. There, with the hot water beating down on her, she thought about what had happened to her tonight—what she'd let happen because she wanted to be cool—and she cried. When she was done and the tears had turned into a hard little knot in her throat, she took the memory of this night and boxed it up. She shelved it in the back alongside memories of the times Cloud had abandoned her and immediately began working on forgetting it was there.

CHAPTER
FIVE

Kate lay awake long after Tully had left. Finally, she threw back the covers and got out of bed.

Downstairs, she found what she needed: a small statue of the Virgin Mary, a votive candle in a red glass holder, a book of matches, and her grandmother's old rosary beads. Taking everything back up to her room, she created an altar on top of her dresser, and lit the candle.

"Heavenly Father," she prayed, head bowed and hands clasped, "please watch out for Tully Hart and help her through this hard time. Also, please heal her mother's cancer. I know You can help them. Amen." She said a few Hail Marys, and then went back to bed.

But all night she tossed and turned, dreaming about the encounter with Tully, wondering what would happen in the morning. Should she talk to Tully today at school, smile at her? Or was she expected to pretend it had never happened? There were rules to popularity, secret codes written in invisible ink that only girls like Tully could read. All Kate knew was that she didn't want to make a mistake and embarrass herself. She knew that sometimes the popular girls were "secret friends" with nerds; like, they smiled and said hi when they weren't in school or when their parents were friends. Maybe that was how it would be with her and Tully.

Finally, she quit trying to sleep and got up. Putting on her robe, she went downstairs. In the living room, her dad looked up from the newspaper and smiled. "Top of the mornin' to you, Katie Scarlett. Come give your old man a hug."

She plopped into his lap, rested her cheek against the rough wool of his shirt.

He tucked a strand of hair around her ear. She could see how tired he looked; he was working so hard, doing double shifts at Boeing so they could afford their yearly family camping trip. "How's school going?"

It was the same question he always asked. Once, a long time ago, she'd actually answered, said, "Not so good, Dad," and then waited for his advice or comfort or something, but no such words had come. He'd heard what he wanted to hear, not what she'd said. Her mom had said it was because he worked so many hours at the plant.

Kate could have been upset by his distraction, but somehow it had made her love him even more. He never yelled at her or told her to pay attention or reminded her that she was responsible for her own happiness. Those were her mother's words; her dad just quietly went on loving her no matter what.

"Great," she answered, smiling to reinforce the lie.

"How could it not be?" he said, kissing her temple. "You're the prettiest girl in town, eh? And your mum named you after one of the great literary heroines of all time."

"Yeah, Scarlett O'Hara and I have a ton in common."

"You'll see," he said, chuckling. "There's a fair bit of life still ahead of you, missy."

She looked at him. "Do you think I'll be pretty when I grow up?"

"Ah, Katie," he said. "You're a rare beauty already."

She took those words and tucked them in her pocket like worry stones; every now and again as she got ready for school she felt them, turned them around in her fingers.

By the time she was dressed and ready to go, the house was empty. The Mularkey family bus had left the station.

She was so nervous she arrived at the bus stop early. Every minute that passed seemed to last an eternity, but there was still no sign of Tully when the school bus drove up and came to a shuddering stop.

Kate dropped her chin and took a seat in the first row.

All through morning classes, she looked for Tully, but didn't see her. At lunch she hurried past the crowd of popular kids, who were busy cutting to the front of the food line whenever they felt like it, and sat down at one of the long tables at the very end of the cafeteria. On the other side of the room, kids were laughing and talking and shoving each other; these tables in social Siberia were sadly quiet, though. Kate, like the others seated around her, rarely looked up.

It was a survival skill the unpopular kids learned early: junior high was like the jungles of Vietnam; it was best to crouch low and keep quiet. So intent was she on her lunch that when someone came up to her and said, "Hey," she practically jumped out of her seat.

Tully.

Even on this cool May day, she wore a cut-to-there miniskirt, white go-go boots, shiny black panty hose, and a tube top. Several peace-symbol necklaces bounced against her cleavage. Her hair glinted with copper streaks in the light. A huge macramé-knot purse hung against her thigh. "Have you told anyone about last night?"

"No. Of course not."

"So, we're friends, right?"

Kate didn't know which surprised her more: the question or the vulnerability in Tully's eyes. "We're friends."

"Excellent." Tully pulled a package of Twinkies out of her purse, then sat down beside Kate. "Now let's talk about makeup. You need help, and I'm not being a bitch. Really. I just know about fashion. It's a gift. Can I drink your milk? Good. Thanks. Are you gonna eat that banana? I could come to your house after school . . ."

Kate stood outside the drugstore looking up and down the street for someone who might know her mom. "Are you sure about this?"

"Absolutely."

The answer was slim comfort, actually. In the day they'd officially been friends, Kate had learned one thing about Tully: she was a girl who made Plans.

And today's plan was to make Kate beautiful.

"Don't you trust me?"

There it was, the big question. It was like rolling a Yahtzee: once Tully said it, Kate lost the game. She had to trust her new friend. "Of course I do. It's just that I'm not allowed to wear makeup."

"Believe me, I'm such an expert your mom will never know. Come on."

Tully walked boldly through the drugstore, choosing eye shadow and blush colors that were "right" for Kate, and then—amazingly—she paid for everything. When Kate said something, Tully said airily, "We're friends, aren't we?"

On the way out of the store, Tully bumped her, shoulder to shoulder.

Kate giggled and bumped her back. They made their way through town and followed the river toward home. All the while, they talked about clothes and music and school. Finally, they turned off the old road and went down Tully's driveway.

"My gran would freak if she saw this place," Tully said, looking embarrassed. Rhodies the size of hot-air balloons covered the side of the house. "She owns this house, you know."

"Does she visit you?"

"Nah. It's easier to wait."

"For what?"

"My mom to forget about me again." Tully stepped over a mound of newspapers and around a trio of garbage cans, then opened the door. Inside, the smoke in the room was thick.

Tully's mom was in the living room, lying on the sofa, with her eyes half opened.

"H-hello, Mrs. Hart," Kate said. "I'm Kate from next door."

Mrs. Hart tried to sit up, but obviously she was too weak to manage it. "Hello, girl from nex' door."

Tully grabbed Kate's hand and pulled her through the living room and into her bedroom, then slammed the door shut. She immediately went to her stack of records, pulled out *Goodbye Yellow Brick Road*, and put it on the turntable. When the music started up, she tossed Kate a *Tiger Beat* and dragged a chair over to the vanity. "You ready?"

Kate's nervousness came swooping back. She knew she'd get in trouble for this, but how would she ever make friends or become popular if she didn't take a few risks? "I'm ready."

"Good. Sit down. We'll do your hair first. It needs some highlights. This is exactly what Maureen McCormick uses."

Kate looked at Tully in the mirror. "How do you know that?"

"I read it in last month's *Teen* magazine."

"I'm guessing she goes to professionals." Kate opened the *Tiger Beat* and tried to concentrate on the article ("Jack Wild's Dream Date—It Could Be You!").

"Take that back. I read the instructions twice."

"Is there any chance I'm going to end up bald?"

"Hardly any. Now be quiet. I'm reading the instructions again."

Tully separated Kate's hair into strips and began spraying Sun-In onto the pieces. It took almost an hour to get it done to her satisfaction. "You are going to look like Marcia Brady when I'm done."

"What's it like, being popular?" Kate hadn't meant to ask the question; it just slipped out.

"You'll see. But you'll stay my friend, won't you?"

Kate laughed at that. "Very funny. Hey, that sort of burns."

"Really? That can't be good. And some of your hair is falling out."

Kate managed not to make a face. If going bald was the price of being Tully's friend, she'd pay it.

Tully reached for the blow dryer and turned it on, blasting Kate's hair with heat.

"I got my period," Tully yelled. "So at least assface didn't knock me up."

Kate heard the bravado in her friend's voice and saw it in her eyes. "I prayed for you."

"You did?" Tully asked. "Wow. Thanks."

Kate didn't know what to say to that. To her, praying was like brushing your teeth before bed, just something you did.

Tully clicked off the dryer and smiled, but she looked worried again. Maybe it was the smell of burning hair. "Okay. Take a shower and rinse it out."

Kate did as she was told. A few minutes later, she got out of the shower, dried off, and got dressed again.

Tully immediately grabbed her hand and led her back to the chair. "Is your hair falling out?"

"Some is," she admitted.

"If you're bald, I'll shave my head. Promise." Tully combed and dried Kate's hair.

Kate couldn't look. She closed her eyes and let Tully's voice meld into the whine of the dryer.

"Open your eyes."

Kate looked up slowly. At this distance, she didn't need her glasses, but force of habit made her lean forward. The girl in the mirror had straight streaked blond hair, parted with precision and dried perfectly. For once it looked soft and pretty instead of thin and lank. The white highlights showed off her leaf-green eyes and the hint of pink on her lips. She looked almost pretty. "Wow," she said, too choked up with gratitude to say more.

"Wait till you see what mascara and blush can do," Tully said, "and concealer for those zits on your forehead."

"I'll always be your friend," Kate said, thinking she'd whispered the promise, but when Tully grinned, she knew she'd been heard.

"Good. Now let's go on the makeup. Have you seen my razor?"

"What do you need a razor for?"

"Your eyebrows, silly. Oh, there it is. Close your eyes."

Kate didn't think twice. "Okay."

Kate didn't even bother to hide her face when she came into the house. That was how confident she felt. For the first time ever, she knew she was beautiful.

Her dad was in the living room, sitting in his La-Z-Boy. At Kate's entrance, he looked up. "Good Lord," he said, clanking his drink down on the French provincial end table. "Margie!"

Mom came out of the kitchen, wiping her hands on her apron. She wore her school-day uniform: striped rust and olive polyester blouse, brown corduroy bell-bottoms, and a wrinkled apron that read: A WOMAN'S PLACE IS IN THE HOUSE . . . AND THE SENATE. When she saw Kate, she stopped. Slowly, she untied her apron and tossed it on the table.

The sudden quiet brought Sean and the dog running into the room, tripping over each other. "Katie looks like a skunk," Sean said. "Pee-ew."

"Go wash your hands for dinner," Mom said sharply. "Now," she added when he didn't leave.

Sean grumbled and went upstairs.

"Did you give her permission to do that to her hair, Margie?" Dad said from the living room.

"I'll handle this, Bud," Mom said, frowning at Kate as she crossed the room. "The girl across the street do this to you?"

Kate nodded, trying to hold on to the memory of feeling pretty.

"Do you like it?"

"Yes."

"Well. Me, too, then. I remember when your Aunt Georgia dyed my hair red. Grandma Peet was livid." She smiled. "But you should have asked. You're still young, Kathleen, no matter what you girls want to be true. Now, what have you done to your eyebrows?"

"Tully shaved them. Just to give them shape."

Mom tried not to smile. "I see. Well, plucking is really the way to go. I should have taught you how already, but I thought you were too young." She looked around for her cigarettes. Finding them on the table, she flipped one out and lit up. "After dinner, I'll show you how. And I suppose a little lip gloss and mascara would be all right for school. I'll show you how to make it look more natural."

Kate hugged her mom. "I love you."

"I love you, too. Now get started on the cornbread. And Katie, I'm glad you made a friend, but no more breaking the rules, okay? That's how young girls get into trouble."

Kate couldn't help thinking of the high school party Tully had gone to. "Okay, Mom."

Within a week, Kate became cool by association. Kids raved over her new look and didn't turn away from her in the halls. Being a friend of Tully Hart's meant she was okay.

Even her parents noticed the difference. At dinner, Kate wasn't her usual quiet self. Instead, she couldn't shut up. Story after story spilled out of her. Who was dating whom, who won at tetherball, who got detention for wearing a MAKE LOVE, NOT WAR T-shirt to school, where Tully got her hair cut (in Seattle by a guy named Gene Juarez—how cool was that?), and what movie was playing at the drive-in this weekend. She was still talking about Tully after dinner, while she and Mom did the dishes.

"I can't wait for you to meet her. She's super cool. Everyone likes her, even the heads."

"Heads?"

"Druggies? Stoners?"

"Oh." Mom took the glass meatloaf pan from her and dried it. "I've . . . asked around about this girl, Katie. She tries to buy cigarettes from Alma at the drugstore."

"She's probably buying them for her mom."

Mom set the dry pan down on the speckled Formica counter. "Just do me a favor, Katie. You think for yourself around Tully Hart. I wouldn't want you to follow her into trouble."

Kate threw the crocheted dishrag in the soapy water. "I can't *believe* you. What about all your take-a-risk speeches? For years you tell me to make friends, and the second I find someone, you call her a slut."

"I hardly called her a—"

Kate stormed out of the kitchen. With each step she expected her mother to call her back and ground her, but silence followed her dramatic exit.

Upstairs, she went into her room and slammed the door for effect. Then she sat down on her bed and waited. When Mom came in she'd be sorry; for once Kate had been the strong one.

But Mom didn't show, and by ten o'clock, Kate was starting to feel sort of bad. Had she hurt her mom's feelings? She got up, paced the small room.

There was a knock at the door.

She raced over to the bed and climbed in, trying to look bored. "Yeah?"

The door opened slowly. Mom stood there, wearing the floor-length red velour robe they'd gotten her for Christmas last year. "May I come in?"

"Like I could stop you."

"You could," Mom said quietly. "May I come in?"

Kate shrugged, but scooted to the left to make room for her mom.

"You know, Katie, life is—"

Kate couldn't help groaning. Not another life-is speech.

Mom surprised her by laughing. "Okay, no more speeches. Maybe you're too old for that." She paused at the altar on the dresser. "You haven't made one of these since Georgia was in chemo. Who needs our prayers?"

"Tully's mom has cancer and she was ra—" She snapped her mouth shut, horrified by what she'd nearly revealed. For most of her life she'd told her mother everything; now she had a best friend, though, so she'd need to be careful.

Mom sat down on the bed beside Kate, just as they did after every fight. "Cancer? That's quite a load for a girl your age to carry."

"Tully seems cool with it."

"Does she?"

"She seems cool with everything," Kate said, unable to keep the pride out of her voice.

"How so?"

"You wouldn't understand."

"I'm too old, huh?"

"I didn't say that."

Mom smoothed the hair off Kate's forehead in a touch that was as familiar as breathing. Kate always felt five years old when her mom did that. "I'm sorry you thought I was judging your friend."

"You should be."

"And you're sorry for being so mean to me, right?"

Kate couldn't help smiling. "Yeah."

"I'll tell you what: Why don't you invite Tully over for dinner Friday night?"

"You'll love her. I know you will."

"I'm sure I will," Mom said, kissing her forehead. "'Night."

"'Night, Mom."

Long after her mother had left and the house had gone quiet for the night, Kate lay there, too wound up to sleep. She couldn't wait to invite Tully for dinner. Afterward, they could watch *I Dream of Jeannie*, or play Operation, or practice putting on makeup. Maybe Tully would even want to spend the night. They could—

Tap.

—talk about boys and kissing and—

Tap.

Kate sat up. That wasn't a bird on the roof or a mouse in the walls.

Tap.

It was a small rock, hitting the glass!

She threw the covers back and hurried to the window, shoving it open.

Tully was in her backyard, holding a bike beside her. "Come on down," she said, much too loudly, making a hurry gesture with her hand.

"You want me to sneak out?"

"Uh. Duh."

Kate had never done anything like this, but she couldn't act like a nerd now. Cool kids broke the rules and sneaked out of the house. Everyone knew that. Everyone knew, too, that trouble could follow. And this was exactly what her mom had been talking about.

You think for yourself around Tully Hart.

Kate didn't care about that. What mattered was Tully.

"I'm on my way." Closing the window, she looked around for clothes. Fortunately, her overalls were in the corner, folded neatly beneath a black sweatshirt. She slipped out of her old Scooby-Doo jammies and dressed quickly, then crept down the hall. As she passed her parents' bedroom, her heart was pounding so fast she felt light-headed. The stairs creaked ominously with every footfall, but finally she made it.

At the back door she paused just long enough to think, *I could get in trouble for this,* and then she opened the door.

Tully was there, waiting. Beside her was the most amazing bike Kate had ever seen. It had curly handlebars, a tiny kidney-shaped seat on a platform, and a bunch of cables and wires. "Wow," she said. It would take a lot of berry-picking money to get a bike like that.

"It's a ten-speed," Tully said. "My grandma gave it to me last Christmas. You want to ride it?"

"No way." Kate closed the door quietly behind her. In the carport she found her old pink bicycle with the U-shaped handlebars, flower-decaled banana seat, and white wicker basket. It was hopelessly uncool; a little girl's bike.

Tully didn't even seem to notice. They mounted up and rode down the wet, bumpy driveway to the paved road. There, they veered left and kept going. At Summer Hill, Tully said, "Watch this. Do what I do."

They crested the hill as if they were flying. Kate's hair whipped back from her head; tears stung her eyes. All around them black trees whispered in the breeze. Stars glittered in the velvet black sky.

Tully leaned back and put her arms out. Laughing, she glanced at Kate. "Try it."

"I can't. We're going too fast."

"That's the point."

"It's dangerous."

"Come on. Let go, Katie. God hates a coward." Then, quietly, she added, "Trust me."

Now Kate had no choice. Trust was part of being friends, and Tully

wouldn't hang out with a chicken. "Come on," she said to herself, trying
to sound stern.

Taking a deep breath, she said a prayer and eased her arms out.

She was flying, sailing through the night sky, down the hill. The air
smelled of the riding stable nearby, of horses and sweet hay. She heard
Tully laughing beside her, but before she could even smile, something
went wrong. Her front tire hit a rock; the bike bucked like a Brahman
bull and twisted sideways, catching Tully's tire in its arc.

She screamed, reached for the handlebars, but it was too late. She
was in the air, really flying this time. The pavement rushed up, smacked
her hard, and she skidded across it, landing in a heap in a muddy
ditch.

Tully rolled across the asphalt and slammed into her. The bikes clattered to the ground.

Dazed, Kate stared up at the night sky. Every part of her hurt. Her
left ankle might be broken. It felt swollen, tender. She could feel where
the road had ripped off her skin in patches.

"That was *incredible*," Tully said, laughing.

"Are you kidding? We could have been killed."

"Exactly."

Kate winced in pain as she tried to get up. "We should get out of this
ditch. A car could come along—"

"But wasn't that cool? Wait till we tell the kids about this."

The kids at school. This would be a *story*, and Kate would be one of
the stars in it. People would listen raptly, ooh and aah, say things like,
You sneaked out? Summer Hill without hands? It's gotta be a lie . . .

And suddenly Kate was laughing, too.

They helped each other to their feet and retrieved their bikes. By the
time they were across the road, Kate barely noticed where she was hurt.
She felt like a different girl suddenly—bolder, braver, willing to try
anything. So what if trouble followed a night like this? What was a
sprained ankle or a bloody knee next to an adventure? For the past two
years she'd followed all the rules and stayed home on weekend nights.
No more.

They left their bikes by the side of the road and limped toward the river. In the moonlight, everything looked milky and beautiful—the silvery waves, the jagged rocks along the shore.

Tully sat down by a decaying, moss-covered nurse log in a place where the grass was as thick as shag carpeting.

Kate sat down beside her, so close their knees were almost touching. Together they stared up at the star-spangled sky. The song of the river floated toward them, sounded like a young girl's laugh. Just now, with the world so still and silent, it was as if the breeze had drawn in its cool breath and left them all alone in this place that until right now had been just another bend in a river that flooded every autumn.

"I wonder who named our street," Tully said. "I haven't seen any fireflies."

Kate shrugged. "Over by the old bridge is Missouri Street. Maybe some pioneer was homesick. Or lost."

"Or maybe it's *magic*. This could be a magical street." Tully turned toward her. "That could mean we were meant to be friends."

Kate shivered at the power of that. "Before you moved here, I thought it was just a road that went nowhere."

"Now it's our road."

"We can go all kinds of places when we grow up."

"Places don't matter," Tully said.

Kate heard something in her friend's voice, a sadness she didn't understand. She turned sideways. Tully was staring up at the sky.

"Are you thinking about your mom?" Kate asked tentatively.

"I try not to think about her." There was a long pause, then she dug into her pocket for a Virginia Slims cigarette and lit up.

Kate was careful not to make a face about the smoking.

"You want a drag?"

Kate knew she had no choice. "Uh. Sure."

"If my mom were normal—not sick, I mean—I could have told her about what happened to me at the party."

Kate took a tiny drag, coughed hard, and said, "Do you think about it a lot?"

Tully leaned back against the log, taking the cigarette again. After a long pause, she said, "I have nightmares about it."

Kate wished she knew what to say. "What about your dad? Can you talk to him?"

Tully wouldn't look at her. "I don't think she even knows who he is." Her voice fell. "Or he heard about me and ran."

"That's harsh."

"Life is harsh. Besides, I don't need them. I've got you, Katie. You're the one that helped me through it."

Kate smiled. The sharp tang of smoke filled the air between them, stung her eyes, but she didn't care. What mattered was being here, with her new best friend. "That's what friends are for."

That next night Tully was on the last chapter of *The Outsiders* when she heard her mother yelling through the house. "Tully! Answer the damn door."

She slammed the book down and went out into the living room, where her mother sat sprawled on the sofa, taking a bong hit as she watched *Happy Days.*

"You're right by the door."

Her mother shrugged. "So?"

"Hide your bong."

Sighing dramatically, Cloud leaned over and put her bong beneath the end table beside the couch. Only a blind person would miss it, but that was as good as Cloud was likely to do.

Tully smoothed the hair away from her face and opened the door.

A small, dark-haired woman stood there, holding a foil-covered casserole dish. Electric-blue eye shadow accentuated her brown eyes, and rose-hued blush—applied with too heavy a hand—created the illusion of sharp cheekbones in her round face. "You must be Tully," the woman said in a voice that was higher somehow than expected. It was a girl's voice, full of enthusiasm, and it matched the sparkle in her eyes. "I'm Kate's mom. Sorry to come without calling, but your line has been busy."

Tully pictured the phone by her mother's bed off the hook. "Oh."

"I brought you and your mom a tuna casserole for dinner. I imagine she doesn't feel much like cooking. My sister had cancer a few years ago, so I know the drill." She smiled and stood there. Finally, her smile faded. "Are you going to invite me in?"

Tully froze. *This is going to be bad,* she thought. "Um . . . sure."

"Thank you." Mrs. Mularkey moved past her and went into the house.

Cloud lay on the sofa, sort of spread-eagled; she had a pile of marijuana on her stomach. Smiling blearily, she tried to sit up and failed. The failure made her shoot out a few swear words and then laugh. The whole house reeked of pot.

Mrs. Mularkey came to a stop. Confusion pleated her forehead. "I'm Margie from next door," she said.

"I'm Cloud," Tully's mother said, trying again to sit up. "It's cool to meet you."

"And you."

For a terrible, awkward moment, they just stared at each other. Tully had no doubt at all that Mrs. Mularkey's sharp eyes saw everything— the bong under the end table, the bag of Maui-wowie on the floor, the overturned, empty wineglass, and the pizza boxes on the table. "Also, I wanted to let you know that I'm home most days, and I'd be happy to drive you to the doctor's office or run errands. I know how chemo can make you feel."

Cloud frowned blearily. "Who's got cancer?"

Mrs. Mularkey turned to look at Tully, who wanted to curl up and die.

"Tully, show our cool neighbor with the food where the kitchen is."

Tully practically ran for the kitchen. In that pink hell, junk food wrappers covered the table, dirty dishes clogged the sink, and overflowing ashtrays were everywhere; more evidence of her pathetic life for her best friend's mother to see.

Mrs. Mularkey walked past her, bent over the oven, put the casserole onto the rack, then shut the door with her hip and then turned to study Tully. "My Katie is a good girl," she said at last.

Here it comes. "Yes, ma'am."

"She's been praying for your mother to recover from her cancer. She even has a little altar set up in her room."

Tully looked at the floor, too ashamed to answer. How could she explain why she'd lied? No answer would be good enough, not for a mother like Mrs. Mularkey, who loved her kids. At that, a wave of jealousy joined the shame running through her. Maybe if Tully had had a mother who loved her she wouldn't find it so easy—so necessary—to lie in the first place. And now she'd lose the one thing that mattered to her: Katie.

"Do you think lying to your friends is okay?"

"No, ma'am." So intently was she staring at the floor that she was startled by a gentle touch on her chin that forced her to look up.

"Are you going to be a good friend to Kate? Or the kind that leads her to trouble?"

"I'd never hurt Katie." Tully wanted to say more, maybe fall to her knees and swear to be a good person, but she was so close to tears she didn't dare move. She stared into Mrs. Mularkey's dark eyes and saw something she never expected: understanding.

In the living room, Cloud stumbled over to the television and changed the channel. Tully could see the screen through the rubble of the messy room: Jean Enersen was reporting on the day's top story.

"You do it, don't you?" Mrs. Mularkey said quietly, as if she worried that Cloud might be eavesdropping. "Pay the bills, grocery-shop, clean the house. Who pays for everything?"

Tully swallowed hard. No one had ever seen through her life so clearly before. "My grandmother sends a check every week."

"My dad was a fall-down drunk and the whole town knew it," Mrs. Mularkey said in a soft voice that matched the look in her eyes. "He was mean, too. Friday and Saturday nights, my sister, Georgia, would have to go to the tavern and drag him home. All the way out of the bar he'd be smacking her and calling her names. She was like one of those rodeo clowns, always stepping between the bull and the cowboy. By the end of my junior year I figured out why she ran with the fast crowd and drank too much."

"She didn't want people to look at her like she was pitiful."

Mrs. Mularkey nodded. "She hated that look. What matters, though, isn't other people. That's what I learned. Who your mom is and how she lives her life isn't a reflection of *you*. You can make your own choices. And there's nothing for you to be ashamed of. But you'll have to dream big, Tully." She glanced through the open door to the living room. "Like that Jean Enersen on the TV there. A woman who gets to a place like that in her life knows how to go after what she wants."

"How do I know what I want?"

"You keep your eyes open and do the right thing. Go to college. And trust your friends."

"I do trust Kate."

"So you'll tell her the truth?"

"What if I just promise—"

"One of us is going to tell her, Tully. It should be you."

Tully took a deep breath and released it. Though telling the truth went against every instinct she had, she had no choice, really. She wanted Mrs. Mularkey to be proud of her. "Okay."

"Good. So I'll see you for dinner tomorrow night. Five o'clock. It'll be your chance to start over."

The next night, Tully changed her clothes at least four times, trying to find exactly the right outfit. By the time she was actually ready, she was so late that she had to run all the way across the street and up the hill.

Kate's mom opened the door. She wore a pair of purple gabardine bell-bottoms and a striped V-neck sweater with angel sleeves. Smiling, she said, "I warn you, it's loud and crazy in here."

"I love loud and crazy," Tully said.

"Then you'll fit right in." Mrs. Mularkey put an arm around Tully's shoulder and led her toward the beige-walled living room with its moss-green shag carpeting, bright red sofa, and black recliner. A small gold-framed photo of Jesus and another of Elvis were the only decorations on the walls, but dozens of family pictures cluttered the top of the console TV. Tully couldn't help thinking of the TV in her house; its top was covered with overflowing ashtrays and empty cigarette packs, but no family photos.

"Bud?" Mrs. Mularkey said to the beefy, dark-haired man sitting in the recliner. "This is Tully Hart from next door."

Mr. Mularkey smiled at her and put down his drink. "Well, well. So you're the one we've been hearin' about. It's nice to have you here, Tully."

"It's nice to be here."

Mrs. Mularkey patted her shoulder. "Dinner's not till six. Katie's upstairs in her room. It's the one at the very top of the stairs. I'm sure you girls have plenty to talk about."

Tully got the message and nodded, unable to rouse her voice. Now that she was here, in this warm house that smelled of home-cooked meals, standing shoulder to shoulder with the world's most perfect mom, she couldn't imagine losing it all, becoming unwelcome. "I'll never lie to her again," she promised.

"Good. Now go." With a last smile, Mrs. Mularkey walked into the living room.

Mr. Mularkey put an arm around his wife and drew her into the La-Z-Boy with him. Immediately they bent their heads together.

Tully felt a longing so sharp and unexpected, she couldn't move. Everything would have been different for her if she'd had a family like this. She didn't want to turn away from it just yet. "Are you watching the news?"

Mr. Mularkey looked up. "We never miss it."

Mrs. Mularkey smiled. "Jean Enersen is changing the world. She's one of the first women to anchor a nightly news program."

"I'm going to be a reporter," Tully said suddenly.

"That's wonderful," Mr. Mularkey said.

"There you are," Kate said suddenly, coming up beside her. "Nice of everyone to tell me you were here," she said loudly.

"I was just telling your mom and dad that I'm going to be a news reporter," Tully said.

Mrs. Mularkey beamed at that. In her smile, Tully saw everything that had been missing in her life. "Isn't that a grand dream, Katie?"

Kate looked confused for a moment. Then she hooked her arm through Tully's and pulled her away from the living room and up the stairs. In her small attic bedroom, Kate went to the record player and flipped through a small stack of records. By the time she'd chosen one—Carole King's *Tapestry*—and put it on, Tully was at the window, staring out at the lavender evening.

The surge of adrenaline she'd gotten from her announcement faded, leaving a quiet kind of sadness behind. She knew what she had to do now, but the thought of it made her sick.

Tell her the truth.

If you don't, Mrs. Mularkey will.

"I got the new *Seventeen* and *Tiger Beat*," Kate said, stretching out on the blue shag carpeting. "You want to read 'em? We can take the 'Can You Be Tony DeFranco's Girlfriend?' quiz."

Tully lay down beside her. "Sure."

"Jan-Michael Vincent is so foxy," Kate said, flipping to a picture of the actor.

"I heard he lied to his girlfriend," Tully said, daring a sideways glance.

"I hate liars." Kate turned the page. "Are you really going to be a news reporter? You never told me that."

"Yeah," Tully said, really imagining it for the first time. Maybe she could be famous. Then everyone would admire her. "You'll have to be one, too, though. 'Cause we do everything together."

"Me?"

"We'll be a team like Woodward and Bernstein, only with better clothes. And prettier."

"I don't know—"

Tully bumped her. "Yes, you do. Mrs. Ramsdale told the whole class that you're an excellent writer."

Kate laughed. "That's true. Okay. I'll be a reporter, too."

"When we get famous, we'll tell Mike Wallace we couldn't have done it without each other."

After that, they fell silent, flipping through the magazines. Tully tried twice to bring up the subject of her mother, but both times Kate interrupted her, and then someone was yelling, "Dinner," and her chance for coming clean had slipped away.

All through the best meal of her life, she felt the weight of her lie. By the time they'd cleared the table and washed and dried the dishes, she was stretched to the breaking point. Even dreaming about fame on television couldn't ease her nerves.

"Hey, Mom," Kate said, putting away the last white CorningWare plate, "Tully and me are going to ride our bikes down to the park, okay?"

"Tully and I," her mother answered, reaching down into the magazine pouch of the La-Z-Boy's arm for the TV guide. "And be back by eight."

"Aww, Mom—"

"Eight," her father said from the living room.

Kate looked at Tully. "They treat me like I'm a baby."

"You don't know how lucky you are. Come on, let's get our bikes."

They rode at a breakneck speed down the bumpy county road, laughing all the way. At Summer Hill, Tully flung her arms out and Kate followed.

When they got to the river park, they ditched their bikes in the trees and lay on the grass, side by side, staring up at the sky, listening to the river gurgling against the rocks.

"I have something to tell you," Tully said in a rush.

"What?"

"My mom doesn't have cancer. She's a pothead."

"Your mom smokes dope. Yeah, right."

"It's true. She's always high."

Kate turned to her. "Really?"

"Really."

"You *lied* to me?"

Tully could barely maintain eye contact, she was so ashamed. "I didn't mean to."

"People don't lie accidentally. It's not like tripping over a crack in the sidewalk."

"You don't know how it feels to be embarrassed by your mom."

"Are you kidding? You should have seen what my mom wore out to dinner last—"

"No," Tully said. "You don't know."

"Tell me."

Tully knew what Kate was asking of her; she wanted the truth that had spawned the lie, but Tully didn't know if she could do it, turn all her pain into words and pass them out like cards. All her life she'd kept these secrets close. If she told Kate the reality and then lost her as a friend, it would be unbearable.

Then again, if she didn't tell the truth, she'd lose the friendship for sure.

"I was two years old," she finally said, "when my mom first dumped me at my grandparents' house. She went to town for milk and came back when I was four. When I was ten, she showed up again and I thought it meant she loved me. That time she let go of me in a crowd. The next time I saw her I was fourteen. My gran's letting us live in this house and sending us money every week. That'll last until my mom bails again—which she will do."

"I don't understand."

"Of course you don't. My mom isn't like yours. This is the longest amount of time I've ever spent with her. Sooner or later she'll get bored and move on without me."

"How can a mother do that?"

Tully shrugged. "I think there's something wrong with me."

"There's nothing wrong with you. She's the loser. But I still don't get why you lied to me."

Tully finally looked at her. "I wanted you to like me."

"*You* were worried about *me*?" Kate burst out laughing. Tully was just about to ask her what was so funny when she sobered and said, "No more lies, right?"

"Absolutely."

"We'll be best friends forever," Kate said earnestly. "Okay?"

"You mean you'll always be there for me?"

"Always," Kate answered. "No matter what."

Tully felt an emotion open up inside her like some exotic flower. She could practically smell its honeyed scent in the air. For the first time in her life, she felt totally safe with someone. "Forever," she promised. "No matter what."

Kate would always remember the summer after eighth grade as one of the best times of her life. Every weekday, she rushed through her morning chores without complaint and babysat her brother until three o'clock, when her mom came home from running errands and volunteering on the 4-H council. After that, Kate was free. Weekends were, for the most part, her own.

She and Tully rode their bikes all over the valley and spent hours inner-tubing down the Pilchuck River. In the late afternoons, they stretched out on tiny towels, wearing neon-colored crocheted bikinis, their skin slick with a mixture of baby oil and iodine, listening to Top 40 music on the transistor radio they never left behind. They talked about everything: fashion, music, boys, the war and what was still going on over there, what it would be like to be a reporting duo, movies. Nothing was off-limits; no question couldn't be volleyed over the net. Now it was late August and they were in Kate's bedroom, packing makeup for their trip to the fair. As usual, Kate had to change clothes and put on makeup after she left the house. If she wanted to look cool, anyway. Her mom still thought she was too young for everything. "You got your tube top?" Tully asked.

"Got it."

Grinning at their own brilliant plan, they headed downstairs, where Dad was sitting on the sofa, watching television.

"We're going to the fair now," Kate said, thankful that her mother wasn't here. Mom would notice the bag that was too big for the county fair. Her X-ray vision would probably see through the macramé exterior to the clothes, shoes, and makeup within.

"Be careful, you two," he said without looking up.

It was what he always said now, ever since girls had started disappearing in Seattle. The news was calling the killer "Ted" these days because some girl at Lake Sammamish State Park had actually gotten away and given a description and his first name to the police. Girls all across the state were terrified. You couldn't see a yellow VW bug without worrying that it was Ted's car.

"We'll be super careful," Tully said, smiling. She loved it when Kate's parents worried about them.

Kate crossed the room to kiss her dad goodbye. He curled an arm around her and handed her a ten-dollar bill. "Have fun."

"Thanks, Daddy."

She and Tully headed down the driveway, swinging their bags beside them.

"Do you think Kenny Markson will be at the fair?" Kate asked.

"You worry too much about boys."

Kate bumped her friend, hip to hip. "He has a crush on you."

"Big whoop. I'm taller."

Suddenly Tully stopped.

"Jeez, Tully, be a spaz, why don'tcha? I almost fell over—"

"Oh, no," Tully whispered.

"What's the matter?"

Then she noticed the police car parked in Tully's driveway.

Tully grabbed Kate's hand and practically dragged her down the driveway, across the street, and to the front door, which stood open.

A policeman was waiting for them in the living room.

When he saw them, his fleshy face pleated into clownlike folds. "Hello, girls. I'm Officer Dan Myers."

"What did she do this time?" Tully asked.

"There was a spotted owl protest up by Lake Quinault that got out of hand yesterday. Your mother and several others staged a sit-in that cost Weyerhaeuser a full day's work. Worse, someone dropped a cigarette in the woods." He paused. "They just got the fire under control."

"Let me guess: she's going to jail."

"Her lawyer is seeking voluntary treatment for drug addiction. If she's lucky, she'll be in the hospital for a while. If not . . ." He let the sentence trail off.

"Has someone called my grandmother?"

The officer nodded. "She's expecting you. Do you need help packing?"

Kate didn't understand what was happening. She turned to her friend. "Tully?"

There was a terrible blankness in Tully's brown eyes, and Kate knew that this was big, whatever it was. "I have to go back to my grandma's," Tully said, then she walked past Kate and went into her bedroom.

Kate ran after her. "You *can't* go!"

Tully pulled a suitcase out of the closet and flipped it open. "I don't have any choice."

"I'll *make* your mother come back. I'll tell her—"

Tully paused in her packing and looked at Kate. "You can't fix this," she said softly, sounding like a grown-up, tired and broken. For the first time, Kate understood the stories about Tully's loser mom. They'd laughed about Cloud, made jokes about her drug use and her fashion sense and her various stories, but it wasn't funny. And Tully had known this would happen.

"Promise me," Tully said, her voice cracking, "that we'll always be best friends."

"Always," was all Kate could say.

Tully finished packing and locked up her suitcase. Saying nothing, she headed back to the living room. On the radio "American Pie" was playing, and Kate wondered if she'd ever be able to listen to that song again without remembering this moment. *The day the music died.* She followed Tully out to the driveway. There, they clung to each other until Officer Dan gently pulled Tully away.

Kate couldn't even wave goodbye. She just stood there in the driveway, numb, with tears streaming down her cheeks, watching her best friend leave.

CHAPTER SIX

For the next three years, they wrote letters faithfully back and forth. It became more than a tradition and something of a lifeline. Every Sunday evening, Tully sat down at the white desk in her lavender and pink little-girl's room and spilled her thoughts and dreams and worries and frustrations onto a sheet of notebook paper. Sometimes she wrote about things that didn't matter—the Farrah Fawcett haircut she'd gotten that made her look foxy or the Gunny Sax dress she wore to the junior prom—but every now and then she went deeper and told Katie about the times she couldn't sleep or the way she dreamed of her mother coming back and saying she was proud of her. When her grandfather died, it was Kate to whom Tully turned. She hadn't cried for him until she got the phone call from her best friend that began with, "Oh, Tul, I'm so sorry." For the first time in her life, Tully didn't lie or embellish (well, not too much); she was mostly just herself, and that was good enough for Kate.

Now it was the summer of 1977. In a few short months they'd be seniors, ruling their separate schools.

And today was the day Tully had been working toward for months. Finally, she was going to actually step onto the road Mrs. Mularkey had shown her all those years ago.

The next Jean Enersen.

The words had become her mantra, a secret code that housed the enormity of her dream and made it sound possible. The seeds of it, planted so long ago in the kitchen of the Snohomish house, had sprouted wildly and sent roots deep into her heart. She hadn't realized how much she'd needed a dream, but it had transformed her, changed her from poor motherless and abandoned Tully to a girl poised to take on the world. The goal made her life story unimportant, gave her something to reach for, to hang on to. And it made Mrs. Mularkey proud; she knew that from their letters. She knew, too, that Kate shared this dream. They would be reporters together, tracking down stories and writing them up. A team.

She stood on the sidewalk, staring at the building in front of her, feeling like a bank robber staring at Fort Knox.

Surprisingly, the ABC affiliate, despite its clout and glory, was in a small building in the Denny Regrade section of town. There was no view to speak of, no impressive wall of windows or expensive art-filled lobby. Rather, there was an L-shaped desk, a pretty-enough reception-ist, and a trio of mustard-yellow molded plastic lobby chairs.

Tully took a deep breath, squared her shoulders, and went inside. At the receptionist's desk, she gave her name, and then took a seat along the wall. She made sure not to fidget or tap her feet during the long wait for her interview.

You never knew who was watching.

"Ms. Hart?" the receptionist finally said, looking up. "He'll see you now."

Tully gave her a poised, camera-ready smile and stood up. "Thank you." She followed the receptionist through the doors to another wait-ing area.

There, she came face to face with the man to whom she'd been writ-ing weekly for almost a year.

"Hello, Mr. Rorbach." She shook his hand. "It's excellent to finally meet you."

He looked tired; older than she'd expected, too. There were only a handful of reddish gray hairs growing on his shiny head, and none of them were where they should be. The pale blue leisure suit he wore was decorated with white topstitching. "Come into my office, Miss Hart."

"Ms. Hart," she said. It was always better to start off on the right foot. Gloria Steinem said you'd never get respect if you didn't demand it.

Mr. Rorbach blinked at her. "Excuse me?"

"I'll answer to Ms. Hart, if you don't mind, which I'm sure you don't. How could anyone with a degree in English literature from Georgetown be resistant to change? I'm certain you're on the cutting edge of social consciousness. I can see it in your eyes. I like your glasses, by the way."

He stared at her, his mouth hanging open the slightest bit before he seemed to remember where he was. "Follow me, Ms. Hart." He led her down the bland white hallway to the last fake wood door on the left, which he opened.

His office was a small corner space, with a window that looked directly at the monorail's elevated cement track. The walls were completely bare.

Tully sat on the black fold-up chair positioned in front of his desk.

Mr. Rorbach took his seat and stared at her. "One hundred and twelve letters, Ms. Hart." He patted the thick manila file folder on his desk.

He'd saved all the letters she'd sent. That must mean something. She pulled her newest résumé out of the briefcase and set it on his desk. "As I'm sure you'll notice, the high school paper has repeatedly put my work on its front page. Additionally I've included an in-depth piece on the Guatemalan earthquake, an update on Karen Ann Quinlan, and a heart-wrenching look at Freddie Prinze's last days. They'll surely showcase my ability."

"You're seventeen years old."

"Yes."

"Next month you'll start your senior year of high school."

All those letters had worked. He knew everything about her. "Exactly.

I think that's an interesting story angle, by the way. Going in to senior year; watching the class of '78. Maybe we could do monthly features about what really goes on behind the doors of a local high school. I'm sure your viewers—"

"Ms. Hart." He steepled his fingers and rested his chin on the tips, looking at her. She got the impression he was trying not to smile.

"Yes, Mr. Rorbach?"

"This is the ABC affiliate, for gosh sakes. We don't hire high school kids."

"But you have interns."

"From UW and other colleges. Our interns know their way around a TV station. Most of them have already worked on their campus broadcasts. I'm sorry, but you're just not ready."

"Oh."

They stared at each other.

"I've been at this job a long time, Ms. Hart, and I've rarely seen anyone as full of ambition as you." He patted the folder of her letters again. "I'll tell you what, you keep sending me your writing. I'll keep an eye out for you."

"So when I'm ready to be a reporter, you'll hire me?"

He laughed. "You just send me the articles. And get good grades and go to college, okay? Then we'll see."

Tully felt energized again. "I'll send you an update once a month. You'll hire me someday, Mr. Rorbach. You'll see."

"I wouldn't bet against you, Ms. Hart."

They talked for a few more moments, and then Mr. Rorbach showed her out of his office. On the way to the stairs, he stopped at the trophy case, where dozens of Emmys and other news awards glinted golden in the light.

"I'll win an Emmy someday," she said, touching the glass with her fingertips. She refused to let herself be wounded by this setback, and that was all it was: a setback.

"You know what, Tallulah Hart, I believe you. Now go off to high school and enjoy your senior year. Real life comes fast enough."

Outside, it looked like a postcard of Seattle; the kind of blue-skied, cloudless, picture-perfect day that lured out-of-towners into selling their homes in duller, less spectacular places and moving here. If only they knew how rare these days were. Like a rocket blaster, summer burned fast and bright in this part of the world and went out with equal speed.

Holding her grandfather's thick black briefcase against her chest, she walked up the street toward the bus stop. On an elevated track above her head, the monorail thundered past, making the ground quake.

All the way home, she told herself it was really an opportunity; now she'd be able to prove her worth in college and get an even better job.

But no matter how she tried to recast it, the sense of having failed wouldn't release its hold. When she got home she felt smaller somehow, her shoulders weighted down.

She unlocked the front door and went inside, tossing the briefcase on the kitchen table.

Gran was in the living room, sitting on the tattered old sofa, with her stockinged feet on the crushed velvet ottoman and an unfinished sampler in her lap. Asleep, she snored lightly.

At the sight of her grandmother, Tully had to force a smile. "Hey, Gran," she said softly, moving into the living room, bending down to touch her grandmother's knobby hand. She sat down beside her.

Gran came awake slowly. Behind the thick old-fashioned glasses, her confused gaze cleared. "How did it go?"

"The assistant news director thought I was too qualified, can you believe it? He said the position was a dead end for someone with my skills."

Gran squeezed her hand. "You're too young, huh?"

The tears she'd been holding back stung her eyes. Embarrassed, she brushed them away. "I know they'll offer me a job as soon as I get into college. You'll see. I'll make you proud."

Gran gave her the poor-Tully look. "I'm already proud. It's Dorothy's attention you want."

Tully leaned against her gran's slim shoulder and let herself be held. In a few moments, she knew this pain would fade again; like a sunburn, it would heal itself and leave her slightly more protected from the glare. "I've got you, Gran, so she doesn't matter."

Gran sighed tiredly. "Why don't you call your friend Katie now? But don't stay on too long. It's expensive."

Just the thought of that, talking to Kate, lifted Tully's spirits. With the long-distance charges what they were, they rarely got to call each other. "Thanks, Gran. I will."

The next week Tully got a job at the *Queen Anne Bee*, her neighborhood weekly newspaper. Her duties pretty much matched the measly per-hour wage they paid her, but she didn't care. She was in the business. She spent almost every waking hour of the summer of '77 in the small, cramped offices, soaking up every bit of knowledge she could. When she wasn't bird-dogging the reporters or making copies or delivering coffee, she was at home, playing gin rummy with Gran for matchsticks. Every Sunday night, like clockwork, she wrote to Kate and shared the minute details of her week.

Now she sat at her little-girl's desk in her bedroom and reread this week's eight-page letter, then signed it *Best Friends Forever, Tully* ♥, and carefully folded it into thirds.

On her desk was the most recent postcard from Kate, who was away on the Mularkey family's yearly camping trip. Kate called it Hell Week with Bugs, but Tully was jealous of each perfect-sounding moment. She wished that she'd been able to go on the vacation with them; turning down the invitation had been one of the most difficult things she'd done. But between her all-important summer job and Gran's declining health, she'd had no real choice.

She glanced down at her friend's note, rereading the words she'd already memorized. *Playing hearts at night and roasting marshmallows, swimming in the freezing lake . . .*

She forced herself to look away. It didn't do any good in life to pine for what you couldn't have. Cloud had certainly taught her that lesson.

She put her own letter in an envelope, addressed it, then went downstairs to check on Gran, who was already asleep.

Alone, Tully watched her favorite Sunday night television programs—*All in the Family, Alice,* and *Kojak*—and then closed up the house and went to bed. Her last thought as she drifted lazily toward sleep was to wonder what the Mularkeys were doing.

The next morning she woke at her usual time, six o'clock, and dressed for work. Sometimes, if she arrived early enough at the office, one of the reporters would let her help with the day's stories.

She hurried down the hall and tapped on the last door. Though she hated to wake her grandmother, it was the house rule. No leaving without a goodbye. "Gran?"

She tapped again and pushed the door open slowly, calling out, "Gran . . . I'm leaving for work."

Cool lavender shadows lay along the windowsills. The samplers that decorated the walls were boxes without form or substance in the gloom.

Gran lay in bed. Even from here, Tully could see the shape of her, the coil of her white hair, the ruffle of her nightdress . . . and the stillness of her chest.

"Gran?"

She moved forward, touched her grandmother's velvet, wrinkled cheek. The skin was cold as ice. No breath came from her slack lips.

Tully's whole world seemed to tilt, slide off its foundation. It took all her strength to stand there, staring down at her grandmother's lifeless face.

Her tears were slow in forming; it was as if each one were made of blood and too thick to pass through her tear ducts. Memories came at her like a kaleidoscope: Gran braiding her hair for her seventh birthday party, telling her that her mommy might show up if she prayed hard enough, and then years later admitting that sometimes God didn't answer a little girl's prayers, or a grown woman's, either; or playing cards last week, laughing as Tully swept up the discard pile—again—saying, "Tully, you don't have to have every card, all the time . . ."; or kissing her goodnight so gently.

She had no idea how long she stood there, but by the time she leaned over and kissed Gran's papery cheek, sunlight had eased through the sheer curtains, lighting the room. It surprised Tully, that brightness. Without Gran, it seemed this room should be dark.

"Come on, Tully," she said.

There were things she was supposed to do now; she knew that. She and Gran had talked about this, done things to prepare. Tully knew, though, that no words could have really prepared her for this.

She went over to Gran's nightstand, where a pretty rosewood box sat beneath the photo of Grandpa and alongside the battalion of medications.

She lifted the lid, feeling vaguely like a thief, but Gran expected this of her. *When I go Home,* Gran always said, *I'll leave you something in the box Grandpa bought me.*

Inside, laying atop the cluster of inexpensive jewelry that Tully could rarely remember her Grandmother wearing, was a folded piece of pink paper with Tully's name written on it.

Slowly, she reached out, took the letter, and opened it.

My dearest Tully—

I am so sorry. I know how afraid you are of being alone, of being left behind, but God has His plan for all of us. I would have stayed with you longer if I could have. Your grandfather and I will always be watching out for you from Heaven. You will never be alone if you believe in that.

You were the greatest joy of my life.

Love, Gran

Were.

Gran was gone.

—————

Tully stood outside the church, watching the crowd of elderly people stream past her. A few of Gran's friends recognized her and came over to offer their condolences.

I'm so sorry dear . . .

. . . but she's in a better place . . .

. . . with her beloved Winston.

. . . wouldn't want you to cry.

She took as much of it as she could because she knew Gran would have wanted that, but by eleven o'clock, she was ready to scream. Didn't any of the well-wishers *see*, didn't they realize that Tully was a seventeen-year-old girl, dressed in black and all alone in the world?

If only Katie and the Mularkeys were here, but she had no idea how to reach them in Canada, and since they wouldn't be home for two days, she had to endure this alone. With them beside her, a pretend family, maybe she would have made it through the service.

Without them, she simply couldn't do it. Instead of sitting through the terrible, heart-wrenching memories of Gran, she got up in the middle of the funeral and walked out.

Outside, in the hot August sunlight, she could breathe again, even though the tears were always near to the surface, as was the pointless query, *How could you leave me like this?*

Surrounded by dusty old-model land yachts, she tried not to cry. Mostly, she tried not to remember, or to worry about what would happen to her.

Nearby, a twig snapped and Tully looked up. At first all she saw were the haphazardly parked cars.

Then she saw her.

Over by the property's edge, where a row of towering maple trees delineated the start of the city park, Cloud stood in the shade, smoking a long slim cigarette. Dressed in tattered corduroy bell-bottoms and a dirty peasant blouse, parenthesized by a wall of frizzy brown hair, she looked rail-thin.

Tully couldn't help the tiny leap of joy her heart took. Finally, she wasn't alone. Cloud might be a little nuts, but when the chips were down, she came back. Tully ran toward her, smiling. She would forgive her mother for all the missing years, all the abandonments. What mattered was that she was here now, when Tully needed her most. "Thank God you're here," she said, coming to a breathless stop. "You knew I'd need you."

Her mother lurched toward her, laughing when she almost fell. "You're a beautiful spirit, Tully. All you need is air and to be free."

Tully's stomach seemed to drop. "Not again," she said, pleading for help with her eyes. "Please . . ."

"Always." There was an edge to Cloud's voice now, a sharpness that belied the glassy look in her eyes.

"I'm your flesh and blood and I need you now. Otherwise I'll be alone." Tully knew she was whispering, but she couldn't seem to find any volume for her voice.

Cloud took a stumbling step forward. The sadness in her eyes was unmistakable, but Tully didn't care. Her mother's pseudo-emotions came and went like the sun in Seattle. "Look at me, Tully."

"I'm looking."

"No. *Look*. I can't help you."

"But I need you."

"That's the fucking tragedy of it," her mother said, taking a long drag on the cigarette and blowing smoke out a few seconds later.

"Why?" Tully asked. She was going to add, *Don't you love me?* but before she could form the pain into words, the funeral let out and black-clad people swarmed into the parking lot. Tully glanced sideways, just long enough to dry her tears. When she turned back, her mother was gone.

The woman from social services was as dry as a twig. She tried to say the right things, but Tully noticed that she kept glancing at her watch as she stood in the hallway outside Tully's bedroom.

"I still don't see why I need to pack my stuff. I'm almost eighteen. Gran has no mortgage on this house—I know 'cause I paid the bills this year. I'm old enough to live alone."

"The lawyer is expecting us," was the woman's only answer. "Are you nearly ready?"

She placed the stack of Kate's letters in her suitcase, closed the lid, and snapped it shut. Since she couldn't actually form the words *I'm ready*, she simply grabbed the suitcase, then slung her macramé purse over her shoulder. "I guess so."

"Good," the woman said, spinning briskly around and heading for the stairs.

Tully took one last, lingering look around her bedroom, noticing as if for the first time things she'd overlooked for years: the lavender ruffled bed linens and white twin bed, the row of plastic horses—dusty now—that lined the windowsill, the Mrs. Beasley doll on the top of the dresser, and the Miss America jewelry box with the pink ballerina on top.

Gran had decorated this room for the little girl who'd been dumped here all those years ago. Every item had been chosen with care, but now they'd all be boxed up and stored in the dark, along with the memories they elicited. Tully wondered how long it would be before she could think of Gran without crying.

She closed the door behind her and followed the woman through the now-quiet house, down the steps outside, to the street in front of house, where a battered yellow Ford Pinto was parked.

"Put your suitcase in the back."

Tully did as she was told and got into the passenger seat.

When the lady started up the car, the stereo came on at an ear-shattering level. It was David Soul's "Don't Give Up on Us." She immediately turned it down, mumbling, "Sorry about that."

Tully figured it was as good a song to apologize for as any, so she just shrugged and looked out the window.

"I'm sorry about your grandmother, if I haven't said that already."

Tully stared at her weird reflection in the window. It was like looking at a negative version of her face, colorless and insubstantial. The way she felt inside, actually.

"By all accounts she was an exceptional woman."

Tully didn't answer that. She couldn't have found much of a voice anyway. Ever since the encounter with her mother, she'd been dry inside. Empty.

"Well. Here we are."

They parked in front of a well-kept Victorian home in downtown Ballard. A hand-painted sign out front read: BAKER AND MONTGOMERY, ATTORNEYS AT LAW.

It took Tully a moment to get out of the car. By the time she did, the woman was giving her a soft, understanding smile.

"You don't need to bring your suitcase."

"I'd like to, thanks." If there was one thing Tully understood, it was the importance of a packed bag.

The woman nodded and led the way up the grass-veined concrete walkway to the white front door. Inside the overly quaint space, Tully took a seat in the lobby, close to the empty receptionist's desk. Cutesy drawings of big-eyed kids lined the ornately papered walls. At precisely four o'clock, a pudgy man with a balding head and horn-rimmed glasses came to get them.

"Hello, Tallulah. I'm Elmer Baker, your Grandmother Hart's attorney."

Tully followed him to a small upstairs room with two overstuffed chairs and an antique mahogany desk littered with yellow legal pads. In the corner, a standing fan buzzed and thumped and sent warm air spinning toward the door. The social worker took a seat by the window.

"Here. Here. Sit down, please," he said, moving to his own chair behind the elegant desk.

"Now, Tallulah—"

"Tully," she said quietly.

"Quite right. I recall Ima saying you preferred Tully." He put his elbows on the desk and leaned forward. His buglike eyes blinked behind the thick magnifying lenses of his glasses. "As you know, your mother has refused to take custody of you."

It took all her strength to nod, even though last night she'd practiced a whole monologue about how she should be allowed to live alone. Now, here, she felt small and much too young.

"I'm sorry," he said in a gentle voice, and Tully actually flinched at the words. She'd come to truly loathe the stupid, useless sentiment.

"Yeah," she said, fisting her hands at her sides.

"Ms. Gulligan here has found a lovely family for you. You'll be one of several displaced teens in their care. The excellent news is that you'll be able to continue in your current school placement. I'm sure that makes you happy."

"Ecstatic."

Mr. Baker looked momentarily nonplussed by her response. "Of course. Now. As to your inheritance. Ima left all her assets—both homes, the car, the bank accounts, and stocks—to you. She has left instructions for you to continue with the monthly payments to her daughter, Dorothy. Your grandmother believed it was the best and only way to keep track of her. Dorothy has proven to be very reliable at keeping in touch when there's money coming." He cleared his throat. "Now . . . if we sell both homes, you won't have to worry about finances for quite some time. We can take care—"

"But then I won't have a home at all."

"I'm sorry about that, but Ima was very specific in her request. She wanted you to be able to go to any college." He looked up. "You're going to win the Pulitzer someday. Or that's what she told me."

Tully couldn't believe she was going to cry again, and in front of these people. She popped to her feet. "I need to go to the restroom."

A frown pleated Mr. Baker's pale forehead. "Oh. Certainly. Downstairs. First door to the left of the front door."

Tully got up from her chair, grabbed her suitcase, and made her halting way to the door. Once in the hallway, she shut the door behind her and leaned against the wall, trying not to cry.

Foster care could *not* be her future.

She glanced down at the date on her Bicentennial wristwatch.

The Mularkeys would be home tomorrow.

CHAPTER
SEVEN

The drive home from British Columbia seemed to take forever. The air conditioner in the station wagon was broken, so warm air tumbled from the useless vents. Everyone was hot and tired and dirty. And still Mom and Dad wanted to sing songs. They kept bugging the kids to sing along.

Kate couldn't stand how lame it was. "Mom, will you *please* tell Sean to quit touching my shoulder?"

Her brother burped and started laughing. The dog barked wildly.

In the front seat, Dad leaned forward and turned on the radio. John Denver's voice floated through the speakers with "Thank God I'm a Country Boy." "That's all I'm singing, Margie. If they don't want to join in . . . fine."

Kate returned to her book. The car bounced so much the words danced on the page, but that didn't matter; not with as many times as she'd read *The Lord of the Rings*.

I am glad you are here with me. Here at the end of all things.

"Katie. Kathleen."

She looked up. "Yeah?"

"We're home," her dad said. "Put that dang book down and help us unload the car."

"Can I call Tully first?"

"No. You'll unpack first."

Kate slapped her book shut. For seven days she'd been waiting to make that call. But unloading the car was more important. "Fine. But Sean better help."

Her mother sighed. "You just worry about yourself, Kathleen."

They piled out of the smelly station wagon and began the end-of-vacation ritual. By the time they finished, it was dark. Kate put the last of her clothes into the pile on the laundry room floor, started the first load, then went to find her mom, who was sitting on the sofa with Dad. They were leaning against each other, looking dazed.

"Can I call Tully now?"

Dad consulted his watch. "At nine-thirty? I'm sure her grandmother would really appreciate that."

"But—"

"Goodnight, Katie," her dad said firmly, looping his arm around Mom and pulling her close.

"This is so not fair."

Mom laughed. "Whoever told you life would be fair? Now go to bed."

For almost four hours Tully stood at the corner of her house, watching the Mularkeys unload their car. She'd thought about running up the hill a dozen times, just showing up, but she wasn't ready for the boisterousness of the whole family just yet. She wanted to be alone with Kate, someplace quiet where they could talk.

So she waited until the lights went out and then crossed the street. In the grass beneath Kate's window, she waited another thirty minutes, just to be sure.

Off to her left somewhere, she could hear Sweetpea nickering at her and pawing at the ground. No doubt the old mare was looking for company, too. During the camping trip a neighbor had fed the horse, but that wasn't the same as being loved.

"I know, girl," Tully said, sitting down. She wrapped her arms around her bent legs, hugging herself. Maybe she should have called instead of stalking them like this. But Mrs. Mularkey might have told her to come by tomorrow, that they were tired from their long drive, and Tully couldn't wait anymore. This loneliness was more than she could handle by herself.

Finally, at eleven o'clock, she stood up, brushed the grass off her jeans, and threw a piece of gravel at Kate's window.

It took four tosses before her friend stuck her head out the window. "Tully!" Kate ducked back into her room and slammed the window shut. It took less than a minute for her to appear at the side of the house. Wearing a Bionic Woman nightshirt, her old black-rimmed glasses, and her retainer, Kate ran for Tully, arms outstretched.

Tully felt Kate's arms wrap around her and for the first time in days, she felt safe.

"I missed you so much," Kate said, tightening her hold.

Tully couldn't answer. It was all she could do not to cry. She wondered if Kate knew, really knew, how important their friendship was to her. "I got our bikes," she said, stepping back, looking away so Kate wouldn't see her moist eyes.

"Cool."

Within minutes they were on their way, flying down Summer Hill, their hands outstretched to catch the wind. At the bottom of the hill, they ditched their bikes in the trees and walked down the long and winding road to the river. All around them trees chattered among themselves; the wind sighed, and leaves fluttered down from branches in an early sign of the coming autumn.

Kate flopped down in their old spot, her back rested against the mossy log, her feet stretched out in the grass that had grown tall in their absence.

Tully felt an unexpected pinch of nostalgia for their youth. They'd spent most of one summer here, taking their separate, lonely lives and braiding them into a rope of friendship. She lay down beside Kate, scooting close enough that their shoulders were touching. After the last few days, she needed to know that her best friend was finally beside her. She positioned her transistor radio nearby and turned up the volume.

"Hell Week with Bugs was even worse than usual," Kate said. "I did talk Sean into eating a slug, though. It was worth the week's allowance I lost." She giggled. "You should have seen his face when I started laughing. Aunt Georgia tried to talk to me about birth control. Can you believe it? She said I should—"

"Do you even know how lucky you are?" The words were out before Tully could stop them, spilling like jelly beans from a machine.

Kate shifted her weight and turned, until she was lying sideways in the grass, looking at Tully. "You usually want to hear everything about the camping trip."

"Yeah, well. I've had a bad week."

"Did you get fired?"

"That's your idea of a bad week? I want your perfect life, just for a day."

Kate drew back, frowning. "You sound pissed at me."

"Not at you." Tully sighed. "You're my best friend."

"So, who are you mad at?"

"Cloud. Gran. God. Take your pick." She took a deep breath and said, "Gran died while you were gone."

"Oh, Tully."

And there it was, what Tully had been waiting for all week. Someone who loved her and was truly sorry for her. Tears stung her eyes; before she knew it, she was crying. Big, gulping sobs that wracked her body and made it impossible to breathe, and all the while, Kate held her, letting her cry, saying nothing.

When there were no tears left inside, Tully smiled shakily. "Thanks for not saying you felt sorry for me."

"I am, though."

"I know." Tully lay back against the log and stared up at the night sky. She wanted to admit that she was scared and that as alone as she'd sometimes felt in life, she knew now what real loneliness was, but she couldn't say the words, not even to Kate. Thoughts—even fears—were airy things, formless until you made them solid with your voice, and once given that weight, they could crush you.

Kate waited a moment, then said, "So what will happen?"

Tully wiped her eyes and reached into her pocket, pulling out a pack of cigarettes. Lighting one up, she took a drag and coughed. It had been years since she'd smoked. "I have to go into foster care. It's only for a while, though. When I'm eighteen I can live alone."

"You're not going to live with strangers," Kate said fiercely. "I'll find Cloud and make her do the right thing."

Tully didn't bother answering. She loved her friend for saying it, but they lived in two different worlds, she and Kate. In Tully's world, moms weren't there to help you out. What mattered was making your own way.

What mattered was not caring.

And the best way not to care was to surround yourself with noise and people. She'd learned that lesson a long time ago. She didn't have long here in Snohomish. In no time at all, the authorities would find her and drag her back to her lovely new family, full of displaced teens and the people paid to house them. "We should go to that party tomorrow night. The one you wrote about in your last letter."

"At Karen's house? The summer's-end bash-o-rama?"

"Exactly."

Kate frowned. "My folks would have a cow if they found out I went to a kegger."

"We'll tell them you're staying at my house across the street. Your mom will believe Cloud is back for a day."

"If I get caught—"

"You won't." Tully saw how worried her friend was, and she knew she should stop this plan right now. It was reckless, maybe even dangerous. But she couldn't stop the train. If she didn't do something drastic, she'd sink into the gooey darkness of her own fears. She'd think about the mother who'd so often and so repeatedly abandoned her, and the strangers with whom she'd soon live, and the grandmother who was gone. "We won't get caught. I promise." She turned to Kate. "You trust me, don't you?"

"Sure," Kate said slowly.

"Great. Then we're going to the party."

"Kids! Breakfast is ready."

Kate was the first one to sit down.

Mom had just put a plate of pancakes down on the table when there was a knock at the door.

Kate jumped up. "I'll get it." She ran for the door and yanked it open, feigning surprise. "Mom, look. It's Tully. Gosh, I haven't seen you in *forever*."

Mom stood near the table, wearing her zip-up, floor-length red velour robe and pink fuzzy slippers. "Hey, Tully, it's good to see you again. We missed you on the camping trip this year, but I know how important your job is."

Tully lurched forward. Looking up, she started to say something, but no sound came out of her mouth. She just stood there, staring at Kate's mom.

"What is it?" her mother said, moving toward Tully. "What's going on?"

"My gran died," Tully said softly.

"Oh, honey . . ." Mom pulled Tully into a fierce hug, holding her for a long time. Finally, Mom drew back, put an arm around Tully, and led her to the sofa in the living room.

"Turn off the griddle, Katie," Mom said without even looking back.

Kate turned off the griddle and then followed them to the living room. She hung back, standing in the curl of the archway that separated the two rooms. Neither of them seemed to care that she was there.

"Did we miss the funeral?" Mom asked gently, holding Tully's hand.

Tully nodded. "Everyone said they were sorry. I officially hate those words now."

"People don't know what to say, that's all."

"My favorite part was the ever popular 'she's in a better place.' As if dead is better than being with me."

"And your mom?"

"Let's just say she doesn't call herself Cloud for nothing. She came and went." Tully glanced at Kate and added quickly, "But she's here for now. We're staying across the street."

"Of course she is," Mom said. "She knows you need her."

"Can I spend the night there tonight, Mom?" Kate asked; her heart was beating so hard and fast, she was sure her mom could hear it. She tried to look completely trustworthy, but since she was lying, she expected her mother to see through it.

Mom didn't even look at Kate. "Of course. You girls need to be together. And you remember this, Tully Hart: You're the next Jessica Savitch. You will survive this. I promise."

"You really think so?" Tully asked.

"I know so. You have a rare gift, Tully. And you can be certain that your gran is in Heaven watching out for you."

Kate felt a sudden urge to butt in, to step forward and ask her mother if she believed *she* could change the world. She even went so far as to move forward and open her mouth, but before she could form the question, she heard Tully say,

"I'll make you proud, Mrs. M. I promise I will."

Kate paused. She had no idea how she could make her mother proud; she wasn't like Tully. Kate had no rare gift.

The thing was, though, her own mother should think she did and should point it out. Instead, her mother—like everyone else—was caught in the gravitational pull of Tully's sun.

"We're both going to be reporters," Kate said, more harshly than she intended. At their startled looks, she felt like an idiot. "Come on," she said, forcing a smile this time. "We should eat before everything is ruined."

The party was a bad idea. Taunting-Carrie-at-the-prom bad.

Tully knew it but couldn't turn back. In the days since Gran's funeral and Cloud's encore abandonment, her grief had been slowly replaced by anger. It darted through her blood like a predator, puffing her up with emotions that couldn't be tamped down or contained. She knew she was being reckless, but she couldn't change her course. If she slowed down, even for a moment, her fear would catch up with her and the plan was in motion now. They were in her mother's old bedroom, sup- posedly getting ready.

"Ohmigod," Kate said in an awed voice. "You gotta read this."

Tully marched over to the poorly decoupaged water bed, grabbed the paperback novel out of Kate's hands, and threw it across the room. "I can't believe you brought a book."

"Hey!" Kate tried to sit up; waves rolled around her. "Wulfgar was ty- ing her to the end of the bed. I have to find out—"

"We're going to a party, Kate. Enough with the romance novels. And just for the record, tying a woman to a bed is S-I-C-K."

"Yeah," Kate said slowly, frowning. "I know, but—"

"No buts. Get dressed."

"Okay, okay." She shuffled over to the pile of clothes Tully had laid out for her earlier—a pair of Jordache jeans and a clingy bronze halter top. "My mom would die if she knew I was going out in this."

Tully didn't respond. Truthfully she wished she hadn't heard. Mrs. M. was the last person she wanted to think about right now. She fo- cused instead on getting dressed: jeans, pink tube top, and navy plat- form lace-up sandals. Bending over, she brushed her hair for maximum Farrah volume, then sprayed it with enough Aqua Net to stop a bug in flight. When she was sure she looked perfect, she turned to Kate. "Are you—"

Kate was dressed for the party and back on the bed reading again.

"You are so pathetic."

Kate rolled onto her back and smiled. "It's romantic, Tully. I'm not kidding."

Tully grabbed the book again. She wasn't sure why, but this really pissed her off. Maybe it was Kate's glossy idealism; how could she see Tully's life and still believe in fairy-tale endings? "Let's go."

Without waiting to see if Kate was following, Tully went out to the garage and opened the doors and then slid into the cracked black driver's seat of her grandmother's Queen Victoria, ignoring the way the stuffing poked into her back. She slammed the door shut.

"You have her car?" Kate said, opening the passenger door and poking her head in.

"Technically it's my car now."

Kate slid onto the seat and closed the door.

Tully popped a Kiss tape into the eight-track player and cranked up the volume. Then she put the car in reverse and eased her foot onto the gas.

They sang at the top of their lungs all the way to Karen Abner's house, where at least five cars were already parked. Several of them were tucked into the trees and out of sight. When someone's parents left town, word spread fast; parties sprouted like mushrooms.

Inside, it was a smoke-fest. The sweet smell of pot and incense was almost overpowering. The music was so loud it hurt Tully's ears. She grabbed Kate's hand and led her down the stairs to the rec room in the basement.

The huge room had fake-wood-paneled walls and lime-green indoor-outdoor carpeting. In the center was a cone fireplace surrounded by an orange half-moon-shaped sofa and several brown beanbag chairs. Over to the left, some boys were playing foosball and screaming at every turn of the handle. Kids were dancing wildly, singing to the music. A couple of boys were on the sofa, getting high, and a girl was over by the door, shotgunning a beer beneath a huge painting of a Spanish matador.

"Tully!"

Before she could respond, her old friends surrounded her, pulled her away from Kate. She went to the keg first and let one of the boys give her a plastic cup full of foamy gold Rainier beer. She stared down at it, jolted by the memory that came with it: *Pat, pushing her to the ground . . .*

She looked around for Kate, but couldn't see her friend in the crowd.

Then everyone began chanting her name. "Tu-lly. Tu-lly."

No one was going to hurt her. Not here; tomorrow, maybe, when the authorities caught up with her, but not now. She chugged the beer and held the cup out for another, yelling out Kate's name as she did.

Kate appeared instantly, as if she'd been just out of view, waiting to be called for.

Tully shoved the beer toward her. "Here."

Kate shook her head. It was a slight there-and-gone motion, but Tully saw it and felt ashamed that she'd offered the beer, and then angry that her friend was so innocent. Tully had never been innocent; not that she could remember anyway.

"Ka-tie, Ka-tie," Tully yelled, getting the crowd to chant with her. "Come on, Katie," she said quietly. "We're best friends, aren't we?"

Kate glanced nervously at the crowd around her.

Tully felt that shame again and the jealousy. She could stop this right now, protect Katie—

Kate took the beer and chugged it.

More than half of it spilled down her chin and onto her halter top, making the shimmery fabric cling to her breasts, but she didn't seem to notice.

Then the music changed. ABBA's "Dancing Queen" blared through the speakers. *You can dance, you can j-ive . . .*

"I love this song," Kate said.

Tully grabbed Kate's hand and dragged her over to where the kids were dancing. There, Tully let loose and fell into the music and the movement.

By the time the music changed and slowed down, she was breathing hard and laughing easily.

But it was Kate who was the more changed. Maybe it was the one beer, or the pulsing beat of the music; Tully wasn't sure. All she knew was that Kate looked gorgeous, with her blond hair shining in the light from an overhead fixture and her pale, delicate face flushed with exertion.

When Neal Stewart came up to them and asked Kate to dance, Kate was the only one surprised. She turned to Tully. "Neal wants to dance with me," she yelled during a lull in the song. "He must be drunk." Putting her hands in the air, she danced away with Neal, leaving Tully standing alone in the crowd.

Kate pressed her cheek against Neal's soft T-shirt.

It felt so good, the way he had his arms around her, his hands just above her butt. She felt his hips moving against hers. It made her heartbeat speed up, made her breathing quicken. A new feeling overtook her; it was a kind of breathless anticipation. She wanted . . . what?

"Kate?"

She heard the hesitant way he said her name and it struck her suddenly: Did he feel all these things, too?

Slowly, she looked up.

Neal smiled down at her; he was only a little unsteady on his feet. "You're beautiful," he said, and then he kissed her, right there in the middle of the dance floor. Kate drew in a sharp breath and stiffened in his arms. It was so unexpected that she didn't know what she was supposed to do.

His tongue slid into her mouth, forcing her lips to open a little.

"Wow," he said softly when he finally drew back.

Wow what? *Wow, you're a spaz?* or *Wow, what a kiss!*

Behind her, someone yelled, "Cops!"

In an instant, Neal was gone and Tully was beside her again, taking her hand. They made their lurching, desperate way out of the house, up the hill and through the scrub brush, and back down to the trees. By the time they got to the car, Kate was terrified and her stomach was in open revolt. "I'm gonna puke."

"No, you aren't." Tully yanked open the passenger door and shoved Kate inside. "We are *not* gonna get busted."

Tully ran around the front of the car and opened her door. Sliding into the driver's seat, she stabbed the key into the ignition, yanked the gearshift into reverse, and stomped on the gas. They rocketed back-ward and slammed into something hard. Kate flew forward like a rag doll, cracking her forehead on the dashboard and then slumping back into her seat. Dazed, she opened her eyes, tried to focus.

Tully was beside her, rolling down the driver's-side window.

There, in the darkness, was good old Officer Dan, the man who'd driven Tully away from Snohomish three years ago. "I knew you Firefly Lane girls would be a pain in my ass."

"Fuck," Tully said.

"Nice language, Tallulah. Now, will you please step out of the car?" He bent down, looked at Kate. "You, too, Kate Mularkey. The party's over."

The first thing that happened at the police station was the girls were separated.

"Someone will come talk to you," Officer Dan said, guiding Tully into a room at the end of the hall.

A gunmetal-gray desk and two chairs sat forlornly beneath a bright hanging lightbulb. The walls were a gross green color and the floor was plain bumpy cement. There was a sad, faded stink to the place, a com-bination of sweat and piss, and old spilled coffee.

The entire left wall was a mirror.

All it took was one episode of *Starsky and Hutch* to know that it was really a window.

She wondered if the social worker was on the other side of it yet, shaking her head in disappointment, saying, *That fine family won't want her now,* or the lawyer, who wouldn't know what to say.

Or the Mularkeys.

At that, she made a little sound of horror. How could she have been so stupid? The Mularkeys had liked her until tonight, and now she'd gone and thrown that all away, and for what? Because she'd been de-pressed by her mom's rejection? By now she ought to be used to that. When had it ever been any other way?

"I won't be stupid again," she said, looking right at the mirror. "If someone would give me another chance, I'd be good."

After that, she waited for someone to burst in for her, maybe holding handcuffs, but the minutes just ticked by in smelly silence. She moved the black plastic chair to one corner and sat down.

I knew better.

She closed her eyes, thinking the same thing over and over again. Along with that thought, running alongside it like some shadow forming in the twilight was its twin: *Will you be a good friend to Katie?*

"How could I be so stupid?" This time Tully didn't even glance at the mirror. There was no one behind there. Who would be looking at her anyway, the kid no one wanted?

Across the room, the doorknob twisted, turned.

Tully tensed. Her fingers bit into her thighs.

Be good, Tully. Agree with everything they say. Foster care is better than juvenile hall.

The door opened and Mrs. Mularkey walked into the room. In a washed-out floral dress and worn white Keds, she looked tired and poorly put together, as if she'd been wakened in the middle of the night and dressed in whatever she could find in the dark.

Which, of course, was exactly what had happened.

Mrs. Mularkey reached into her dress pocket for her cigarettes. Finding one, she lit up. Through the swirling smoke, she studied Tully. Sadness and disappointment emanated from her, as visible as the smoke.

Shame overwhelmed Tully. Here was one of the very few people who had ever believed in her, and she'd let Mrs. M. down. "How's Kate?"

Mrs. Mularkey exhaled smoke. "Bud took her home. I don't expect she'll leave the house again for a good long while."

"Oh." Tully squirmed uncomfortably. Her every blemish was on view, she was sure of it, from the lies she'd told to the secrets she'd kept to the tears she'd cried. Mrs. M. saw it all.

And she didn't like what she saw.

Tully could hardly blame her. "I know I let you down."

"Yes, you did." Mrs. Mularkey pulled a chair away from the table and sat down in front of Tully. "They want to send you to juvenile hall."

Tully looked down at her own hands, unable to stand the disappointment she saw on Mrs. M.'s face. "The foster family won't want me now."

"I understand your mother refused to take custody of you."

"Big surprise there." Tully heard the way her voice cracked on that. She knew it revealed how hurt she'd been, but there was no way to hide it. Not from Mrs. M.

"Katie thinks they can find another family for you to live with."

"Yeah, well, Katie lives in a different world than I do."

Mrs. Mularkey leaned back in her chair. Taking a drag on her cigarette, she exhaled smoke and said quietly, "She wants you to live with us."

Just hearing it was like a blow to the heart. She knew she'd spend a long time trying to forget it. "Yeah, right."

It was a moment before Mrs. Mularkey said, "A girl who lived in our house would have to do chores and follow the rules. Mr. Mularkey and I wouldn't stand for any funny business."

Tully looked up sharply. "What are you saying?" She couldn't even put this sudden hope into words.

"And there would definitely be no smoking."

Tully stared at her, feeling tears sting her eyes, but that pain was nothing compared to what was going on deep inside her. It felt suddenly as if she were about to fall. "Are you saying I can live with you?"

Mrs. M. leaned forward and touched Tully's jawline. "I know how hard your life has been up to now, Tully, and I can't stand for you to go back to that."

The falling turned into flying, and suddenly Tully was crying for all of it—Gran, the foster family, Cloud. Her relief was the biggest emotion she'd ever felt. With shaking hands, she pulled the crumpled, half-empty pack of cigarettes out of her purse and handed them over.

"Welcome to our family, Tully," Mrs. M. finally said into the silence, pulling Tully into her arms and letting her cry.

Through all the decades of Tully's life, she would remember that moment as the beginning of something new for her; the becoming of someone new. While she lived with the loud, crazy, loving Mularkey family, she found a whole new person inside her. She didn't keep secrets or tell lies or pretend that she was someone else, and never once did they act as if she were unwanted or not good enough. No matter where she went in her later years, or what she did or whom she was with, she would always remember this moment and those words: *Welcome to our family, Tully.* Always and forever, she would think of that senior year of high school, when she was inseparable from Kate and a part of the family, as the single best year of her life.

CHAPTER EIGHT

G irls! Quit lollygagging. We're going to hit traffic if we don't leave now."

In the creaky attic bedroom, Kate stood at the edge of her twin bed, staring down at the open suitcase that contained all of her prized belongings. A framed picture of her grandparents lay on top, wedged between her ribbon-wrapped packet of long-ago letters from Tully and a photo of her and Tully taken at graduation.

Although she'd been looking forward to this moment for months (she and Tully had spun endless late-night dreams, all of which began with the words *when we're in college*), now that it was here, she felt reluctant to leave home.

Over the course of their senior year in high school, they'd become a pair. TullyandKate. Everyone at school said their two names as one. When Tully became editor of the school paper, Kate was right beside her, helping her to edit the stories. She lived vicariously through her friend's achievements, rode the wave of her popularity, but all of that had taken place in a world she knew, in a place where she felt safe.

"What if I forgot something?"

Tully crossed the room and came up beside Kate. She closed the suitcase and clamped it shut. "You're ready."

"No. *You're* ready. You're always ready," Kate said, trying not to sound as afraid as she was. It occurred to her suddenly, sharply, how much she'd miss her parents and even her little brother.

Tully stared at her. "We're a team, aren't we? The Firefly Lane girls."

"We have been, but—"

"No buts. We're going to college together, we're pledging the same sorority, and we'll be hired by the same TV station. Period. That's it. We can do it."

Kate knew what was expected of her, by Tully and everyone else: she was supposed to be strong and courageous. If only she felt it more deeply. But since she didn't feel it, she did what she often did lately around Tully. She smiled and faked it. "You're right. Let's go."

The drive from Snohomish to downtown Seattle, which usually took about thirty-five minutes, seemed to pass in a blink. Kate barely spoke, couldn't seem to find her voice, even as Tully and her mom chattered on about the upcoming Rush Week at the sororities. Her mother, it seemed, was more excited about their college adventure than Kate was.

In the towering high-rise of Haggett Hall, they made their way through the loud, crowded corridors to a small, dingy dorm room on the tenth floor. Here was where they'd stay during Rush. When it was over, they'd move into their sorority.

"Well. This is it," Mr. Mularkey said.

Kate went to her parents and threw her arms around them, forming the famous Mularkey family hug.

Tully stood back, looking oddly left out.

"Geez, Tully, get over here," Mom called out.

Tully rushed forward and let them all embrace her.

For the next hour they unpacked and talked and took pictures. Then, finally, Dad said, "Well, Margie, it's time. We don't want to get caught in traffic." There was one last round of hugs.

Kate clung to her mom, battling tears.

"It's going to be okay," Mom said. "Trust in all the dreams you've made. You and Tully are going to become the best reporters this state has ever seen. Your dad and I are so proud of you."

Kate nodded and looked up at her mom through hot tears. "I love you, Mom."

Much too soon, it was over.

"We'll call every Sunday," Tully said behind them. "Right after you get home from church."

And then, suddenly, they were gone.

Tully flopped on the bed. "I wonder what Rush will be like. I bet every house will want us. How could they not?"

"They'll want you," Kate said softly, and for the first time in months she felt like the girl they'd called Kootie all those years ago, the girl in the Coke-bottle glasses and high-water Sears jeans. It didn't matter that she'd gotten contacts and lost her braces and learned how to put on makeup to enhance her features. The sorority girls would see through all that.

Tully sat up. "You know I won't join a sorority unless we're in it together, right?"

"That's not fair to you, though." Kate went to the bed and sat down beside her.

"Remember Firefly Lane?" Tully said, lowering her voice. Over the years those words had become a catchall phrase, a kind of shorthand for their memories. It was their way of saying that a friendship begun at fourteen, back when David Cassidy was groovy and a song could make you cry, would last forever.

"I haven't forgotten."

"But you don't get it," Tully said.

"Get what?"

"When my mom dumped me, who was there for me? When my gran died, who held my hand and took me in?" She turned to Kate. "You. That's the answer. We're a team, Kate. Forever friends, no matter what. Okay?" She bumped Kate, made her smile.

"You always get your way."

Tully laughed. "Of course I do. It's one of my more endearing traits. Now let's figure out what we're going to wear for the first day . . ."

The University of Washington was everything Tully had hoped it would be and more. Spread out over several miles and comprised of hundreds of gothic buildings, it was a world unto itself. The size daunted Kate, but not Tully; she figured if she could triumph here, she could triumph anywhere. From the moment they moved into their sorority, she began preparing for a reporting job at the networks. In addition to taking the core classes in communications, she made time to read at least four newspapers a day and watch as many newscasts as possible. When her big break came, she was going to be ready.

It had taken her most of the first few weeks of school to get her bearings and figure out what Phase One of the academic plan should be. She'd met with her School of Communications advisor so often that he sometimes avoided her in the hall when he saw her coming, but she didn't care. When she had questions, she wanted answers.

The problem, once again, was her youth. She couldn't get into the upper-level broadcasting or journalism classes; no amount of cajoling or prodding could move the behemoth bureaucracy of this huge state school. She simply had to wait her turn.

Not something she was good at.

She leaned sideways and whispered to Kate, "Why is there a science requirement? I won't need geology to be a reporter."

"Shhh."

Tully frowned and sat back in her chair. They were in Kane Hall, one of the biggest auditoriums on campus. From her chair in the nosebleed section, crammed in among almost five hundred other students, she could barely see the professor, who'd turned out not to be a professor at all, but rather his teaching assistant.

"We can buy lecture notes. Let's go. The newspaper office opens at ten."

Kate didn't even glance at her, just kept scribbling notes on her paper.

Tully groaned and sat back, crossing her arms in disgust, waiting minute by minute for class to end. The second the bell rang, she shot to her feet. "Thank God. Let's go."

Kate finished with her notes and collected her pages, methodically organizing everything in her notebook.

"Are you *making* paper? Come on. I want to meet the editor."

Kate stood up and slung her backpack over one shoulder. "We are not going to get a job at the newspaper, Tully."

"Your mom told you not to be so negative, remember?"

They went downstairs, merging into the loud crowd of students.

Outside, the sun shone brightly on the brick-covered courtyard known as Red Square. Over by Suzzallo Library, a group of long-haired students were gathered beneath a CLEAN UP HANFORD sign.

"Quit complaining to my mom when you don't get your way," Kate said as they headed for the Quad. "We can't even get into journalism classes until we're juniors."

Tully stopped. "Are you really not going to come with me?"

Kate smiled and kept walking. "We aren't going to get the job."

"But you'll come with me, right? We're a team."

"Of course I'm coming."

"I knew it. You were just messing with me."

They kept talking as they walked through the Quad, where the cherry trees were lush and green, as was the grass. Dozens of students in brightly colored shorts and T-shirts played Frisbee and hacky sack.

At the newspaper office, Tully stopped. "I'll do the talking."

"I'm shocked, really."

Laughing, they went into the building, announced themselves to a shaggy-looking kid at the front desk, and were directed to the editor's office.

The entire meeting lasted less than ten minutes.

"Told you we were too young," Kate said as they walked back to the sorority.

"Bite me. Sometimes I think you don't even want to be a reporter with me."

"That's a complete lie: you hardly ever think."

"Bitch."

"Hag."

Kate put an arm around her. "Come on, Barbara Walters, I'll walk you home."

Tully was so depressed over the meeting at the newspaper that Kate spent the rest of the day cajoling her into a good mood.

"Come on," she finally said, hours later, when they were back in their minuscule room in the sorority house. "Let's get ready. You want to look your best for the exchange."

"What do I care about a stupid exchange? Frat boys are hardly my ideal."

Kate struggled not to smile. Everything about Tully was big—she had such high highs and low lows. Their time at UW had only increased her tendencies. The funny thing was that while this huge crowded campus had somehow released Tully's extravagances, it had had an opposite and calming effect on Kate. She felt stronger every day here, more and more ready to become an adult. "You're such a drama queen. I'll let you do my makeup."

Tully looked up. "Really?"

"It's a time-limited offer. You better move your ass."

Tully jumped up, grabbed her hand, and dragged her down the hall to the bathroom, where dozens of girls were already showering and drying off and blowing their hair out.

They waited their turns, took their showers, and went back to the room. Thankfully, their other two roommates weren't there. The tiny space, filled mostly with dressers and desks and a set of bunk beds for the upperclassmen, barely gave the two of them room enough to turn around. Their own twin beds were in the large sleeping porch down the hall.

Tully spent almost an hour on their hair and makeup, then pulled out the fabric they'd bought for their togas—gold for Tully, silver for Kate—and created a pair of magical garments held in place by tight belts and rhinestone pins.

Kate studied her reflection when they were done. The sparkling silver fabric complemented her pale skin and golden hair and brought out the green in her eyes. After all the nerd years, she was still sometimes surprised that she could look good. "You're a genius," she said.

Tully twirled for inspection. "How do I look?"

The gold toga showed off her big boobs and tiny waist, and a riot of curled, teased, sprayed mahogany hair spilled down over her shoulder, à la Jane Fonda in *Barbarella*. Blue eye shadow and heavy liner made her look exotic.

"You look gorgeous," Kate said. "The guys'll be falling all over themselves."

"You care too much about love; must be all those romance novels you read. This is *our* night. Screw the boys."

"I don't want to screw them, but a date would be nice."

Tully grabbed Kate's arm and led her out into the hallway, which was crowded with laughing, talking girls in various stages of dress, running down the busy corridors with curling irons, hair dryers, and bedsheets.

Downstairs in the formal living room, one of the girls was teaching the others to Hustle.

Outside, Kate and Tully merged into the crowd walking down the street. There were people everywhere on this balmy late September night. Most of the fraternities were having an exchange. There were girls in costume, in ordinary clothes, in almost nothing at all, walking in sorority groups toward their various destinations.

The Phi Delt house was big and square, a fairly modern mixture of glass and metal and brick, that was set on a corner. Inside, the walls were worn, the furniture was broken and ripped and ugly, and the décor was prison-era 1950. Not that most of this could be seen through the crowd.

People were packed in like sardines, chugging beer from plastic cups and swaying to the music. "Shout!" blared through the speakers and everyone was singing along, jumping up in time to the music.

A little bit softer now . . .

The crowd crouched, stilled, then raised their hands and rose up again, chanting along.

As always, the minute Tully stepped into a party, she was "on." Gone
was the edge of depression, the hesitant smile, the irritation at losing
the job. Kate watched in awe; her friend instantly grabbed everyone's
attention.

"Shout!" Tully yelled out, laughing. Boys moved in close, drawn to
her like moths to a flame, but Tully barely seemed to notice. She surged
onto the dance floor, dragging Kate along with her.

It was the most fun Kate had had in years.

By the time she'd group danced to "Brick House," "Twistin' the Night
Away," and "Louie Louie," she was hot and sweaty.

"I'll be right back," she yelled to Tully, who nodded, and then she
went outside, where she sat on the low brick wall that marked the property's edge. Cool night air breezed across her sweaty face. She closed
her eyes and swayed to the music.

"The party's inside, you know."

She looked up.

The guy who'd spoken was tall and broad-shouldered, with wheat-
colored hair that fell across the bluest eyes. "Can I sit with you?"

"Sure."

"I'm Brandt Hanover."

"Kate Mularkey."

"Is this your first frat party?"

"Does it show?"

He smiled and went from good looking to gorgeous. "Just a little. I
remember my first year here. It was like being on Mars. I'm from Moses
Lake," he said, as if that should explain everything.

"Small town?"

"Speck on the map."

"It *is* kind of overwhelming."

The conversation moved easily on from there. He talked about
things she could relate to. He'd grown up on a farm, feeding cows before dawn and driving his dad's hay truck when he was thirteen. He
knew about feeling both lost and found in a place as big and sprawling
as UW.

Inside, the music changed. Someone turned the volume way up. It was ABBA's, "Dancing Queen."

Tully came running out of the house. "Kate!" she yelled, laughing. "There you are."

Brandt immediately stood.

Tully frowned at him. "Who's this?"

"Brandt Hanover."

Kate knew exactly what was going to happen next. Because of what had happened to Tully in the dark woods by the river all those years ago, she didn't trust boys, didn't want anything to do with them, and she was committed to protecting Kate from any kind of harm or heartbreak. Unfortunately, though, Kate wasn't afraid. She *wanted* to date and have fun and even maybe fall in love.

But how could she say that, when Tully was only trying to protect her?

Tully grabbed Kate's arm, pulled her to her feet. "Too bad, Brandt," she said, laughing a little too loudly as she dragged Kate away. "This is our song."

"I saw Brandt at the HUB today. He smiled at me."

Tully fought the urge to roll her eyes. In the six months since that first toga party at the Phi Delts, Kate had found a way to mention Brandt Hanover at least once a day. You'd think they were dating, as often as his name came up. "Let me guess: you pretended not to notice."

"I smiled back."

"Wow. A red-letter day."

"I thought I'd invite him to the spring dance. We could double date."

"I have to write an article on the Ayatollah Khomeini. I figured if I keep sending stuff to the paper, sooner or later they'll publish something. It wouldn't hurt you to try a little harder to—"

Kate turned to her friend. "That's *it*. I renounce our friendship. I know you have no interest in our social life, but I do. If you don't go—"

Tully laughed. "Gotcha."

Kate couldn't help laughing. "Bitch." She slung an arm around Tully. Together they walked along the grass-dotted sidewalk of Twenty-first Street and onto campus.

At the campus security post, Kate said, "I'm headed to Meany. How about you?"

"Drama/TV."

"That's right! Your first broadcast journalism class—and with that famous guy you've been stalking since we got here."

"Chad Wiley."

"How many letters did you have to write to get in?"

"About a thousand. And you should be coming with me. We both need this class."

"I'll get in as a junior. You need me to walk you over?"

Tully loved her friend for that. Somehow Kate knew that despite her show of courage, Tully was nervous about this. Everything she wanted could start today. "No, thanks. How can I make my big entrance with someone else?"

She watched Kate walk away from her. Standing there, alone among the crowd of students moving between the buildings, Tully took a deep, relaxing breath, trying to still herself. She needed to appear calm.

She strolled confidently past the fountain of Frosh Pond and went into the Drama/TV Building, where her first stop was the restroom.

There, she paused in front of the mirrors. Her curled, sprayed hair was perfect, as was her makeup. The skintight, flare-legged jeans and shiny white tunic blouse with gold belt and Nehru collar managed to be both sexy and businesslike at the same time.

When the bell rang, she hurried down the hallway, with her backpack bouncing against her ass as she moved. In the auditorium, she walked boldly down to the first row and took a seat.

In the front of the room, the professor sat slumped in a metal chair. "I'm Chad Wiley," he said in a sexy, whiskey-rough voice. "Those of you who recognize my name get an A in the class."

There was a smattering of laughter around the room. Tully's was the loudest. She knew more than his name. She knew his whole life story.

He'd come out of college as a kind of wunderkind in broadcasting. He'd moved up the ranks fast, becoming a network anchor before he was thirty. Then, quite simply, he'd lost it. A pair of DWIs, a car crash that broke both of his legs and injured a child, and his star had fallen. There'd been a couple of years with no mention of him at all, and then, finally, he'd surfaced at UW, teaching.

Wiley stood. He was unkempt, with long dark hair and at least three days' growth of gray-black beard, but the intelligence in his dark eyes was undiminished. The stamp of greatness was still on him. No wonder he'd made it.

He handed her a syllabus and started to move on.

"Your coverage of the Karen Silkwood case was inspired," she said, smiling brightly.

He paused, looked down at her. There was something unsettling about the way he stared—intensely, but only for a second, like a laser beam switched on and off—and then he kept walking past her and on to the next student.

He thought she was just another front-row suck-up who wanted to curry favor.

She'd need to be more careful in the future. Nothing mattered more to her right now than impressing Chad Wiley. She intended to learn everything she could from him.

Part Two

THE EIGHTIES

Love Is a Battlefield

heartache to heartache,
we stand

CHAPTER NINE

By the end of her sophomore year, there was no doubt in Tully's mind that Chad Wiley knew who she was. She'd taken two of his classes: Broadcast Journalism I and II. Whatever he taught, she took; whatever he asked of her, she did. Full-bore. Balls to the wall.

The problem was this: he didn't seem to recognize her talent. They'd spent all of last week reading the news from a teleprompter. Each time she finished, she immediately looked at him, but he barely glanced up from his notes. Rather, he spooled off a criticism as if he were relaying a recipe to a troublesome neighbor, then called out, "Next."

Day after day, week after week, class after class, Tully waited for him to respond to her obvious talent, to say, *You're ready for KVTS*. Now it was the first week of May. With about six weeks left in her sophomore year, she was still waiting.

Plenty of things had changed in her life the past two years. She'd cut her hair shoulder-length and gone with bangs. Her style icon had gone from Farrah Fawcett-Majors to Jessica Savitch. Nineteen eighty was made for Tully: big hair, bright makeup, glittery fabric, and shoulder pads. No pale colors/sorority-girl styles for her. When she walked into a room these days, people noticed.

Except, of course, for Chad Wiley.

But that was about to change; Tully was sure this time. Last week she'd finally racked enough credits to apply for a summer internship position at KVTS, the local public programming station that was housed on campus. She'd gotten up at six A.M. so that her name appeared first on the sign-up sheet. When she'd been given the audition piece, she'd gone home and practiced it endlessly, trying it at least a dozen different ways until she found the tone of voice that perfectly matched the tone of the story. Yesterday she'd nailed the audition. She was certain of it. Now, finally, it was time to found out what position she'd earned.

"How do I look?"

Kate didn't look up from *The Thorn Birds*. "Awesome."

Tully felt a flash of irritation that was more and more familiar these days. Sometimes she just looked at Kate and felt her blood pressure skyrocket. It was all she could do not to yell.

The problem was love. Kate had spent all of their freshman year mooning over bad-haircut Brandt. By the time they finally dated, it was a letdown that ended fast. Still, Kate didn't seem to care. Through most of sophomore year, she'd dated Ted, who supposedly loved her, and then Eric, who most certainly did not. Kate went to one fraternity dance after another, and though she never fell in love with any of the doofuses she dated—and definitely didn't have sex with them—she talked about them constantly. Every sentence lately seemed to start with some guy's name. Even worse, she hardly ever mentioned the broadcasting plan. She seemed perfectly happy to take classes in other departments. Whenever one of their sorority sisters got engaged, Kate rushed to be a part of the crowd that swooned over the ring.

In truth, Tully was sick of it. She kept writing news stories that the school paper wouldn't publish and hanging around the campus TV station, where no one would give her the time of day, and throughout all of this failure, when she could really use her best friend, Kate just kept yammering on about her latest date. "You totally aren't looking."

"I don't have to."

"You don't know how important this is to me."

Kate finally looked up. "You've been practicing one news story for two weeks. Even when I got up to pee in the middle of the night, I heard you rehearsing. Believe me, I know how psyched you are."

"So how come you're so Joanie about this?"

"I'm no Joanie. I just know you'll get the anchor job."

Tully grinned. "I will, won't I?"

"Of course. You're wicked good. You'll be the first junior to actually be on air."

"Professor Wiley will have to admit it this time." Tully grabbed her backpack and slung it over her shoulder. "Want to come with me?"

"Can't. I'm meeting Josh for a study group in Suzzallo."

"That pretty much falls in the blows-chips category of dating, but to each his own." Tully snagged her sunglasses off the dresser and headed out.

The campus was bathed in cool sunlight on this mid-May day. Every plant was in bloom and the grass was so thick and lush it looked like patches of green velvet tucked neatly between strips of cement. She strode confidently through campus to the building that housed KVTS. There, she paused just long enough to smooth her sprayed hair, then went into the quiet, utilitarian-looking hallway. To her left was a bulletin board thick with notices. *Roommate wanted: pot smoker only* was the first one that caught her eye. She noticed that all the phone-number tabs had been ripped off of it, while the ad next to it (*Roommate wanted: Born-again Christian preferred*) looked sadly intact.

Room 214 was shut. No slice of light ran along the floor beneath the door. Beside it, a piece of paper was tacked to the bulletin board.

SUMMER INTERNSHIP POSITIONS/DEPARTMENT

News/Anchor	Steve Landis
Weather	Jane Turner
Marketing & Community Relations	Gretchen Lauber
Sports	Dan Bluto
Afternoon Planning	Eileen Hutton
Research Desk/Fact Checking	Tully Hart

Tully felt a surge of disappointment, then anger. She yanked open the door and slipped into the dark auditorium where no one could see her, muttering, "Chad Wiley, you sorry-assed loser. You wouldn't know talent if it grabbed your tiny pecker and squeezed—"

"I imagine you're talking about me."

She jumped at the sound of his voice.

He was not twenty feet away from her, standing in the shadows. His dark hair was even messier than usual; it hung in curly disarray to his shoulders.

He moved closer, his fingers trailing on the back of the chair to his right. "Ask me why you aren't an evening news intern and I'll tell you."

"I couldn't care less why."

"Really?" He looked at her for another long minute, unsmiling, then walked away from her, down the aisle and up onto the stage.

She could either keep her pride or risk her future. By the time she made her decision and hurried after him, he was backstage.

"Okay . . ." The word seemed to catch on something in her throat. "Why?"

He stepped toward her. For the first time she noticed the lines on his face, the creases in his cheeks. The dim overhead lighting accentuated every flaw, every hollow and mark on his skin. "Whenever you come to class, I can tell you've chosen your clothes carefully and spent a lot of time on your hair and makeup."

He was looking at her now, *seeing* her. And she could see him, too. Past the shaggy unkemptness to the sharp bone structure that had once made him so handsome. But it was his eyes that grabbed her; liquid brown and sad, they spoke to the empty places inside of her. "Yeah. So?"

"You know you're beautiful," he said.

No stammering, no desperation. He was cool and steady. Unlike the boys she met at frat parties or on campus or in the taverns playing pool, he wasn't half drunk and desperate for a feel.

"I'm talented, too."

"Maybe someday."

The way he said it pissed her off. She was gathering her wits for a scathing comeback when he closed the distance between them. All she had time for was a bewildered, "What are—" before he kissed her.

At the touch of his lips, gentle yet firm, she felt something exquisite and tender blossom inside her; for no reason at all, she started to cry. He must have tasted her tears, because he drew back, frowned at her. "Are you a woman, Tully Hart, or a girl?"

She knew what he was asking. As hard as she'd tried to conceal her innocence, he'd sensed it, tasted it. "Woman," she lied, with only the barest wobble on the *w*. She knew now, after just one kiss, that whatever there was to know about sex, her pathetic rape in the woods had taught her none of it. Although she wasn't a virgin, she was something worse somehow, a reservoir of bad and painful memories, and yet, now, with him, for the first time she wanted more.

That was how she'd felt with Pat that night, too.

No. This was different. She was a long way from that desperate, lonely girl who would have gone into any dark woods to be loved.

He kissed her again, murmuring, "Good." This time the kiss went on and on, deepening into something that pulled at her insides and made her ache with need. By the time he began pressing his hips against hers, igniting a fire between her legs, she'd forgotten all about being scared.

"You want more?" he whispered.

"Yes."

He swept her into his arms and carried her to a broken-down sofa tucked against the shadowy back wall. There, he laid her down onto the bumpy, scratchy cushions and slowly, gently began to undress her. As if from far away, she felt her bra unsnap, her underpants peel off. And still his kiss went on and on, stoking this fire inside her.

When they were both naked, he lowered himself to the sofa and took her in his arms. The springs sagged beneath their weight, pinged in protest. "No one has taken time with you, have they, Tully?"

She saw her own desire reflected in his eyes, and for the first time she wasn't afraid in a man's arms. "Is that what you're going to do—take your time?"

He brushed the damp hair away from her face. "I'm going to teach you things, Tully. Isn't that what you wanted from me?"

It took Tully almost two hours to find Kate. She began her search at the study tables in the basement of the sorority. Next, she spun through the TV room and their bedroom; she even checked on the sleeping porch, although at four o'clock on a sunny May day, it was understandably empty. She tried the undergraduate library and Kate's favorite carrel, then the graduate reading room, where several hippie-looking older students shushed her just for walking through the stacks. She was about ready to give up when she remembered the Annex.

Of course.

She ran through the sprawling campus to the small, two-story, peaked-roof house that they called the Annex. Sixteen lucky upper-class girls got to move out of the main house and into this place every quarter. It was party central. No house mothers, no one to monitor the doors; it was as close to the real world as any of them were likely to get until they left the sorority altogether.

She opened the front door and called out Kate's name. Someone in another room answered.

"I think she's on the roof."

Tully grabbed a pair of TaBs from the fridge and went upstairs. In a back bedroom, the window was open. She leaned through the opening and looked out on the roof of the carport.

There was Kate, all by herself, in a skimpy white crocheted bikini, lying on a beach towel, reading a paperback novel.

Tully climbed out onto the ledge and crossed the carport roof, which they all called Black Beach. "Hey," she said, offering Kate a TaB. "Let me guess: you're reading a romance novel."

Kate cocked her head and squinted into the sun, smiling. "*The Promise* by Danielle Steel. It's really sad."

"You want to hear about real romance?"

"Like you would know anything about it. You haven't gone on a date since we got here."

"You don't have to go on a date to have sex."

"Most people do."

"I'm not most people. You know that."

"Yeah, right," Kate said. "Like I'm supposed to believe you got laid."

Tully grabbed one of the towels that had been left there and stretched out on it. Trying not to smile, she stared up at the blue sky and said, "Three times, to be exact."

"But you were just going to check on the summer internship . . ." Kate gasped and sat up. "You *didn't*."

"You're going to say we're not supposed to have sex with our professors. I think it's really more of a recommendation. A guideline. Still, you can't tell anyone."

"You had sex with Chad Wiley."

Tully sighed dreamily at the way that sounded. "It was totally cool, Katie. I mean it."

"Wow. What did you do? What did he do? Did it hurt? Were you scared?"

"I was scared," Tully said quietly. "At first all I could think about was . . . you know . . . the night with Pat. I thought I was going to get sick, or maybe run, but then he kissed me."

"And?"

"And . . . I just sort of melted. He had my clothes off before I was even paying attention."

"Did it hurt?"

"Yeah, but not like before." It surprised Tully how easy it was suddenly to mention the night she was raped. For the first time it was a more distant memory, something bad that had happened to her as a kid. Chad's gentleness had shown her that sex didn't have to hurt, that it could be beautiful. "After a while it felt amazingly good. Now I know what all those *Cosmo* articles are about."

"Did he say he loved you?"

Tully laughed, but deep inside, it wasn't as funny as she wished it were. "No."

"Well, that's good."

"Why? I'm not good enough to fall in love with? That's for nice Catholic girls like you?"

"He's your *prof*, Tully."

"Oh, that. I don't care about stuff like that." She looked at her friend. "I thought you'd go all romance-novel on me and say it was some kind of fairly tale."

"I need to meet him," Kate said firmly.

"It's not like we can double-date."

"Then I guess I'll be the third wheel. Hey, he can probably get the senior rate if we go out to dinner."

Tully laughed. "Bitch."

"Maybe, but I'm a bitch who wants more details. I want to know *everything*. Can I take notes?"

Kate got off the bus and stood on the sidewalk, looking down at the directions in her hand.

This was the address.

All around her, people milled about the sidewalk. Several jostled her as they passed. She squared her shoulders and headed for the door. There was no point in worrying about this meeting—she'd been worrying for more than a month, and for most of that time she'd also been nagging. It had not been easy to get Tully to agree to tonight.

But in the end, Kate had said the magic words—thrown the Yahtzee: *Don't you trust me?* After that, it had only been a matter of scheduling.

So now, on this warm evening, she was moving toward a building that looked like a tavern, on a mission to save her best friend from making the biggest mistake of her life.

Sleeping with a professor.

Really, what good could come of that?

Inside the Last Exit on Brooklyn, Kate found herself in a world unlike

anything she'd ever seen before. First off, the place was huge. There had
to be seventy-five tables—marble ones along the walls and big, rough
wooden ones in the center of the room. An upright piano and stage area
seemed to be the centerpiece. On the wall beside the piano, a graying,
curling poster of the "Desiderata" poem grabbed her attention. *Go placidly
amid the noise and haste, and remember what peace there may be in silence.*

Not that there was peace or silence in here. Or breathable air.

A thick blue-gray haze hung suspended, collecting in the high ceil-
ings. Almost everyone was smoking. Cigarettes zipped up and down
throughout the room, caught between fingers that gestured with each
word. At first she didn't see any empty tables; every one was full of
people playing chess, or reading tarot cards, or arguing politics. Several
people sat in chairs around a mic, strumming their guitars.

She made her way through the tables toward the back corner.
Through an open door, she could see another area out back filled with
picnic tables, where more people sat around talking and smoking.

Tully sat at a table way in the back, tucked in the shadowy corner.
When she saw Kate, she stood up and waved.

Kate eased past a woman smoking a clove cigarette and sidled around
a post.

That was when she saw him.

Chad Wiley.

He wasn't at all what she'd expected. He sat lazily in the chair, with
one leg stretched out. Even in the smoke and shadows, she could see
how handsome he was. He didn't *look* old. Tired, maybe, but in a world-
weary kind of way. Like an aging gunslinger or a rock star. The smile he
gave her started slowly, crinkling up his eyes, and in those eyes, she saw
a knowledge that surprised her, made her miss a step.

He knew why she was here: a best friend coming to save a girl making a mistake by dating the wrong man.

"You must be Chad," she said.

"And you must be Katie."

She flinched at the unexpected use of her nickname. It was a forcible
reminder that Chad knew Tully, too.

"Sit down," Tully said. "I'll go get a waitress." She was on her feet and gone before Kate could stop her.

Kate looked at Chad; he eyed her back, smiling as if at some secret. "This is an interesting place," she said to make conversation.

"It's like a tavern without beer," he said. "The kind of place where you can change who you are."

"I thought change started from within."

"Sometimes. Sometimes it's forced upon you."

His words caused something to darken his eyes, an emotion of some kind. She was reminded of his backstory suddenly, the bright career he'd lost. "They'd fire you—the university—if they found out about you and Tully, wouldn't they?"

He drew his leg back, sat up straighter. "So that's how you want to play it. Good. I like direct. Yes. I'd lose this career, too."

"Are you some kind of risk junkie?"

"No."

"Have you slept with your students before?"

He laughed. "Hardly."

"So, why?"

He glanced sideways, at Tully, who was at the crowded coffee bar, trying to order. "You, of all people, shouldn't have to ask that. Why is she your best friend?"

"She's special."

"Indeed."

"But what about her career? She'd be ruined if word got out that she was with you. They'd say she slept her way to a degree."

"Good for you, Katie. You should be looking out for her. She needs that. She's . . . fragile, our Tully."

Kate didn't know which upset her more—his description of Tully as fragile or the way he said *our Tully*. "She's a steamroller. I don't call her Tropical Storm Tully for nothing."

"That's on the outside. For show."

Kate sat back, surprised. "You actually care about her."

"More's the pity, I imagine. What will you tell her?"

"About what?"

"You came here to find a way to convince her not to see me anymore, didn't you? You can certainly say I'm too old. Or the prof angle is always a winner. Just so you know, I drink too much, too."

"You want me to tell her those things?"

He looked at her. "No. I don't want you to tell her those things."

Behind them, a young man with wild hair and ratty-looking pants stepped up to the microphone. He introduced himself as Kenny Gorelick, then began playing a saxophone. His music was wildly romantic and jazzy; for a few moments the talk in the place died down. Kate felt swept up in the music, transported by it. Gradually, though, it became background music and she looked at Chad. He was studying her intently. She knew how much it meant to him, this conversation, and how much Tully meant to him. That turned the tables neatly; she was surprised by the suddenness of the switch. Now, sitting here, she was worried that Tully would ruin this man, who frankly looked as if he didn't have the stamina to take another hit like that. Before she could answer the question he'd posed, Tully was back, dragging a purple-haired waitress with her.

"So," she said, frowning and a little breathless, "are you friends yet?"

Chad was the first to look up. "We're friends."

"Excellent," Tully said, sitting on his lap. "Now who wants apple pie?"

Chad dropped them off two blocks from the sorority house, on a dark street lined with aging boardinghouses that were filled with the kind of students who paid no attention to what sorority girls did.

"It was nice to meet you," Kate said as she got out of the car. She stood on the sidewalk, waiting for Tully to quit making out with him.

Finally, Tully got out of the car and waved goodbye as Chad's black Ford Mustang drove away.

"Well?" she demanded suddenly, turning to Kate. "He's handsome, isn't he?"

Kate nodded. "He sure is."

"And cool, right?"

"Definitely cool." She started to walk away, but Tully grabbed her sleeve, stopped her, and spun her around.

"Did you like him?"

"Of course I liked him. He's got a great sense of humor."

"But?"

Kate bit her lip, stalling for time. She didn't want to hurt Tully's feeling or piss her off, but what kind of friend would she be if she lied? The truth was, she *had* liked Chad and she believed he truly cared about Tully; it was also true that she had a bad feeling about their relationship and meeting him had only made it worse.

"Come on, Katie, you're scaring me."

"I wasn't going to say anything, Tully, but since you're forcing me . . . I don't think you should be going out with him." Once her opinion broke through the dam, she couldn't stop. "I mean, he's thirty-one years old. He has an ex-wife and a four-year-old daughter he never sees. You can't be seen publicly with him or he'll get fired. What kind of relationship is that? You're missing your college years."

Tully took a step back. "Missing my college years? You mean going to dances in Tahitian costumes and shotgunning beer? Or dating guys like the nerds you seem to choose—most of them are only slightly smarter than a pet rock."

"Maybe we should just agree to disagree . . ."

"You think I'm with him for my career, don't you? To what—get better grades or a spot at the station?"

"Aren't you? Just a little bit?" Kate knew instantly she shouldn't have said it. "I'm sorry," she said, reaching for her friend. "I didn't mean it."

Tully wrenched free. "Of course you meant it. Miss Perfect with the best family and the flawless grades. I don't even know why you hang around with me: I'm such a slut career hound."

"Wait!" Kate called out, but Tully was already gone, running down the dark street.

CHAPTER
TEN

Tully ran all the way to the bus stop on Forty-fifth.

"Bitch," she muttered, wiping her eyes.

When the bus came, she paid her fare and climbed aboard, muttering, "Bitch," twice more as she found a seat and sat down.

How could Kate have said those things to her?

"Bitch," she said again, but this time the word leaked out, sounding forlorn.

The bus stopped less than a block from Chad's house. She rushed up the sidewalk toward the small Craftsman-style home and knocked on the door.

He answered almost instantly, dressed in a pair of old gray sweats and a Rolling Stones T-shirt. She could tell by the way he smiled at her that he had expected her. "Hey, Tully."

"Take me to bed," she whispered throatily, pushing her hands up underneath his shirt.

They made their fumbling, kissing way through the house and to the small bedroom in the back. She stayed close to him, locked in his arms, kissing him deeply. She didn't look at him, couldn't, but it didn't matter. By the time they fell onto the bed, they were both naked and greedy.

Tully lost herself and her pain in the pleasure of his hands and mouth, and when it was over and they lay there, entwined, she tried not to think of anything except how good he made her feel.

"Do you want to talk about it?"

She stared up at the plain, high-pitched ceiling that had become as familiar to her as her own dreams. "What do you mean?"

"Come on, Tully."

She rolled on to her side and stared at him, propping her head into her hand.

He touched her face in a gentle caress. "You and Kate fought about me, and I know how much her opinion means to you."

The words surprised her, though they shouldn't have. In the time they'd been sleeping together, she'd somehow begun to reveal pieces of herself to him. It had begun accidentally, a comment here or there after sex or while they were drinking, and somehow grown from there. She felt safe in his bed, free from judgment or censure. They were lovers who didn't love each other, and that made talking easier. Still, she saw now that he'd listened to all of her babble and let the words form a picture. The knowledge of that made her feel less lonely all of a sudden, and even though it scared her, she couldn't help being comforted by it.

"She thinks it's wrong."

"It is wrong, Tully. We both know that."

"I don't care," she said fiercely, wiping her eyes. "She's my best friend. She's supposed to support me no matter what." Her voice broke on the last words, the promise they'd made to each other all those years ago.

"She's right, Tully. You should listen to her."

She heard something in his voice, a barely-there quaver that made her look deeply into his eyes. In them, she saw a sadness that confused her. "How can you say that?"

"I'm falling in love with you, Tully, and I wish I weren't." He smiled sadly. "Don't look so scared. I know you don't believe in it."

The truth of that settled heavily on her, made her feel old suddenly. "Maybe someday I will." She wanted to believe that, at least.

"I hope so." He kissed her gently on the lips. "And now, what are you going to do about Kate?"

"She won't talk to me, Mom." Kate leaned back against the cushioned wall of the tiny cubby known as the phone room. She'd had to wait almost an hour for her turn on this Sunday afternoon.

"I know. I just hung up with her."

Of course Tully would call first. Kate didn't know why that irritated her. She heard the telltale lighting of a cigarette through the phone lines. "What did she tell you?"

"That you don't like her boyfriend."

"That's all?" Kate had to be careful. If Mom found out Chad's age, she'd blow a gasket and Tully would *really* be pissed if she thought Kate had turned Mom against her.

"Is there more?"

"No," she said quickly. "He's all wrong for her, Mom."

"Your vast experience with men tells you this?"

"She didn't go to the last dance because he didn't want to. She's missing out on college life."

"Did you really think Tully would be your average sorority girl? Come on, Katie. She's . . . dramatic. Full of dreams. It wouldn't hurt you to have a little of that fire, by the way."

Kate rolled her eyes. Always there was the subtle—and not so subtle— pressure to be like Tully. "We're not talking about my future. Focus, Mom."

"I'm just saying—"

"I heard you. So what do I do? She is avoiding me completely. I was trying to be a good friend."

"Sometimes being a good friend means saying nothing."

"I'm just supposed to watch her make a mistake?"

"Sometimes, yes. And then you stand by to pick up the pieces. Tully's such a big personality; it's easy to forget her background and how easily she can be hurt."

"So what do I do?"

"Only you can answer that. My days of being your Jiminy Cricket are long past."

"No more life-is speeches, huh? Great. Just when I could have used one."

Through the phone line came the hiss of exhaled smoke. "I do know that she's going to be in the editing room at KVTS at one o'clock."

"You're sure?"

"That's what she said."

"Thanks, Mom. I love you."

"Love you, too."

Kate hung up and hurried back to her room, where she dressed quickly and put on a little makeup: concealer, mostly, to cover the zits that had broken out across her forehead since their fight.

She made her way across campus in record time. It was easy. This late in the quarter people were busy studying for finals. At the door to KVTS, she paused, steeling herself as if for battle, and then went inside.

She found Tully exactly where Mom had predicted: hunched in front of a monitor, logging the raw footage and interviews. At Kate's entrance, she looked up.

"Well, well," Tully said, standing up. "If it isn't the head of the Moral Majority."

"I'm sorry," Kate said.

Tully's face crumpled at that, as if she'd been holding her breath in and suddenly let it go. "You were a real bitch."

"I shouldn't have said all that. It's just . . . we've never held back from each other."

"So that was our mistake." Tully swallowed, tried to smile. Failed.

"I wouldn't hurt you for the world. You're my best friend. I'm sorry."

"Swear it won't happen again. No guy will ever come between us."

"I swear." Kate meant it with every fiber of her being. If she had to staple her tongue down, she'd do it. Their friendship was more important than any relationship. Guys would come and go; girlfriends were forever. They knew that. "Now it's your turn."

"What do you mean?"

"Swear you won't bail on me again without talking. These last three days really sucked."

"I swear it."

Tully wasn't quite sure how it had happened, but somehow this sleeping with her professor had graduated into a full-blown affair. No pun intended. Perhaps Kate had been right and it *had* begun as a kind of career move for her; she no longer remembered. All she knew was that in his arms she felt content, and that was a new emotion for her.

And, of course, he *was* her mentor. In their time together he'd taught her things it would have taken her years to discover by herself.

More importantly, he'd shown her what making love was. His bed had become her port; his arms her life ring. When she kissed him and let him touch her with an unimaginable intimacy, she forgot that she didn't believe in love. Her first time, back in those dark Snohomish woods, faded from her memory a little more each day, until one day she discovered that she no longer carried it around inside of her. It would always be a part of her, a scar on her soul, but like all scars, it faded in time from a bright and burning red to a slim, silvery line that could only sometimes be seen.

But even with all that, with all that he'd shown and given her, it was beginning not to be enough. By fall semester of her senior year, she was growing impatient with the rarefied world of college. CNN had changed the face of broadcasting. Out in the real world, things were happening, things that mattered. John Lennon had been shot and killed outside his New York apartment; a guy named Hinckley had shot President Reagan in a pathetic attempt to impress Jodie Foster; Sandra Day O'Conner had become the first female Supreme Court justice; and Diana Spencer had married Prince Charles in a ceremony so fairy-tale perfect that every girl in America believed in love and happy endings for the entire summer. Kate talked about the wedding so often and in such detail you'd think she'd been invited.

All of it was headline news, made during Tully's life, and yet because she was in school, it was before her time. Oh, sure, she wrote the articles for the school paper and sometimes even got to read a few sentences here and there on air, but it was all make-believe, warm-up exercises for a game she wasn't yet allowed to play.

She yearned to swim in the real waters of local or national news. She'd grown even more tired of sorority dances and frat parties and that most archaic of all rituals—the candle passings. Why all those sorority girls wanted to get engaged was beyond her. Didn't they know what was going on in the world, didn't they see the possibilities?

She'd done everything UW had to offer, taken every broadcast and print journalism class that mattered, and learned what she could from a year's worth of interning at the public affairs station. It was time now to jump into the dog-eat-dog world of TV news. She wanted to surge into the crowd of reporters and elbow her way to the front.

"You're not ready," Chad said, sighing. It was the third time he'd said it in as many minutes.

"You're wrong," she said, leaning toward the mirror above his dresser, applying one more coat of mascara. In the glam early eighties, you couldn't wear too much makeup or have too big a hairdo. "You've made me ready and we both know it. You got me to change my hair to this boring Jane Pauley bob. Every suit I own is black and my shoes look like a suburban housewife's." She put the mascara brush back in the holder and slowly turned around, studying the Lee press-on nails she'd applied this morning. "What more do I need?"

He sat up in bed. From this distance he looked either saddened by their discussion or tired; she wasn't sure which. "You know the answer to that question," he said softly.

She dug through her purse for another color of lipstick. "I'm sick of college. I need to get into the real world."

"You're not ready, Tully. A reporter needs to exhibit a perfect mix of objectivity and compassion. You're too objective, too cold."

This was the one criticism that bugged her. She'd spent years *not* feeling things. Now she was suddenly supposed to be both compassionate and objective at the same time. Empathetic but professional. She couldn't quite pull it off and she and Chad both knew it. "I'm not talking about the networks yet. It's just one interview for a part-time job until graduation." She walked over to the bed. In her black suit and white blouse, she was the picture of conservative chic. She'd even tamed the sexiness of her shoulder-length hair by pulling it back into a banana clip. Sitting on the edge of the mattress, she pushed a long lock of hair away from his eyes. "You're just not ready for me to go out into the world."

He sighed, touched her jawline with his knuckle. "It's true I prefer you in my bed to out of it."

"Admit it: I'm ready." She'd intended to sound sexy and grown-up, but the vulnerable tremble in her voice betrayed her. She needed his approval like she needed air or sunlight. She'd go without it, of course, but less confidently, and today she needed every scrap of confidence she could find.

"Ah, Tully," he said finally. "You were born ready."

Smiling triumphantly, she kissed him—hard—then got up and grabbed her vinyl briefcase. Inside it was a handful of résumés printed on heavy ivory stock; several business cards that read, *Tallulah Hart, TV news reporter;* and a videotape of a story she'd done on-air for KVTS.

"Break a leg," Chad said.

"I will." She caught the bus in front of the Kidd Valley hamburger stand. Even though she was a senior, she hadn't bothered with bringing her car to school. Parking was expensive and hard to find. Besides, the Mularkeys loved having her gran's old land yacht.

All the way through the U District and into the city, she thought about what she knew about the man she was going to meet. At twenty-six, he was already a well-respected former on-air reporter who'd won some big reporting award during a Central American conflict. Something—none of the articles said what—had brought him home, where he'd suddenly changed career tracks. Now he was a producer for the smaller office of one of the local stations. She had practiced endlessly what she would say.

It's nice to meet you, too, Mr. Ryan.

Yes, I have had an impressive amount of experience for a woman of my age.

I'm committed to being a first-rate journalist and hope, no, expect to—

The bus came to a smoking, wheezing stop on the corner of First and Broad.

She hurried off the bus and down the steps. As she stood beneath the bus stop sign, consulting her notes, it started to rain, not hard enough to require an umbrella or a hood, but just enough to ruin her hair and poke her in the eyes. She ducked her head to protect her makeup and ran up the block to her destination.

The small concrete building with curtainless windows sat in the middle of the block with a parking lot beside it. Inside, she consulted the tenant board and found what she was looking for: KCPO—SUITE 201.

She perfected her posture, smiled professionally, and went up to Suite 201.

There, she opened the door and almost walked right into someone.

For a moment Tully was actually taken aback. The man standing in front of her was gorgeous—unruly black hair, electric-blue eyes, shadowy stubble of a beard. Not what she'd expected at all.

"Are you Tallulah Hart?"

She extended her hand. "I am. Are you Mr. Ryan?"

"I am." He shook her hand. "Come in." He led her through a small front room cluttered with papers and cameras and stacks of newspapers everywhere. A couple of open doors revealed other empty offices. Another guy stood in the corner, smoking a cigarette. He was huge, at least six-foot-five, with shaggy blond hair and clothes that looked as if he'd slept in them. A giant marijuana leaf decorated his T-shirt. At their entrance, he looked up.

"This is Tallulah Hart," Mr. Ryan said by way of introduction.

The big guy grunted. "She the one with the letters?"

"That's her." Mr. Ryan smiled at Tully. "He's Mutt. Our cameraman."

"Nice to meet you, Mr. Mutt."

That made them both laugh and the sound of their laughter only cemented her anxiety that she was too young for this.

He led her into a corner office and pointed to a metal chair in front of a wooden desk. "Have a seat," he said, closing the door behind him.

He took a seat behind the desk and looked at her.

She sat up straight, trying to look older.

"So, you're the one who has been clogging my mail with tapes and résumés. I'm sure, with all your ambition, you've researched us. We're the Seattle team for KCPO in Tacoma. We don't have an internship program here."

"That what your letters said."

"I know. I wrote them." Leaning back in his chair, he wishboned his arms behind his head.

"Did you read my articles and watch my tapes?"

"Actually, that's why you're here. When I realized you weren't going to stop sending me audition tapes, I figured I might as well watch one."

"And?"

"And you'll be good one day. You've got that thing."

One day? Will be?

"But you're a long way from ready."

"That's why I want this internship."

"The nonexistent one, you mean."

"I'll work twenty to thirty hours a week for free, and I don't care if I get college credit or not. I'll write copy, fact-check, do research. Anything. How can you go wrong?"

"Anything?" He was looking at her intently now. "Will you make coffee and vacuum and clean the bathroom?"

"Who does all that now?"

"Mutt and me. And Carol, when she's not following a story."

"Then absolutely I will."

"So you'll do whatever it takes."

"I will."

He sat back, studying her closely. "You understand you'd be a grunt, and an unpaid one at that."

"I understand. I could work Mondays, Wednesdays, and Fridays."

Finally he said, "Okay, Tallulah Hart." He stood up. "Show me what you can do."

"I will." She smiled. "And it's Tully."

He walked her back through the office. "Hey, Mutt, this is our new intern, Tully Hart."

"Cool," Mutt said, not looking up from the camera equipment in his lap.

At the door, Mr. Ryan paused and looked at her. "I hope you intend to take this job seriously, Ms. Hart. Or this is an experiment that will have a shorter shelf life than milk."

"You can count on me, Mr. Ryan."

"Call me Johnny. I'll see you Friday. Say eight A.M.?"

"I'll be here."

She played and replayed the encounter over and over in her head as she walked briskly down the street to the bus stop and caught a ride.

She'd actually made her own internship. Someday, when Phil Donahue interviewed her, she'll tell this story to show her gutsy determination.

Yes, Phil. It was a bold move, but you know broadcasting. It's a dog-eat-dog world, and I was a girl with ambition.

But she'd tell Katie first. Nothing was quite perfect until she shared it with Kate.

This was the start of their dream.

The cherry trees in the Quad marked the passing of time better than any calendar. Pink and full of blossoms in the spring; lush and green in the warm, quiet days of summer; gloriously hued for the start of school; and now, bare on this November day in 1981.

For Kate, life was moving much too quickly. She was light-years away from the shy, quiet girl she'd been on arrival. In her years at UW, she'd learned to direct Rush Week skits, to organize and plan a dance for three hundred people, to chug a glass of beer and shoot a raw oyster, to work the room at a frat party and be comfortable around people she didn't know, to write edgy news stories with a hook and a splash, and to film that same story even if she was moving while it happened. Her journalism professors had graded her highly and told her repeatedly that she had a gift.

The problem, it seemed, was her heart. Unlike Tully, who could barrel forward and ask any question, Kate found it hard to intrude on people's grief. More and more often lately, she held back on her own stories and edited Tully's instead.

She didn't have what it took to be a network news producer or a first-rate reporter. Every day, as she sat in her broadcast and communications classes, she was lying to herself.

She dreamed lately of other things, of going on to law school so that she could fight the injustices she reported on, or writing novels that made people see the world in a better, more positive light . . . or—and this was the most hidden dream of all—falling in love. But how could she tell Tully these things?

Tully, who had taken her hand all those years ago when no one else would, who'd spun the gossamer dream of their lives as partners in TV news. How could she tell her best friend that she no longer shared their dream?

It should be easy to say. They'd been girls all those years ago when they'd chosen to embark on their tandem life. In the years between then and now, the world had changed so much. The war in Vietnam had been lost, Nixon had resigned, Mount St. Helens had blown up, and cocaine had become the Chex mix for a new generation of partygoers. The U.S. hockey team had pulled off a miracle win at the Olympics and a B-rate actor was president. Dreams could hardly remain static in such uncertain times.

She simply had to stand up to Tully, for once, and tell her the truth, say, *Those are your dreams, Tully, and I'm proud of you, but I'm not fourteen anymore and I can't follow you forever.*

"Maybe today," she said aloud, dragging her backpack along beside her as she walked through the gray, foggy campus.

If only she really had a dream of her own, something to replace the twin-TV news stars. Tully might accept that; Kate's vague, *I don't know*, wouldn't hold much water with Tropical Storm Tully.

On the edge of campus, she merged into the stream of kids and crossed the street, smiling and waving at friends as she passed them. At the sorority house, she went right to the living room, where girls sat packed like hot dogs on the sofas and chairs and on every patch of the celery-green carpet.

She tossed her backpack to the floor and found a spot on the floor between Charlotte and Mary Kay. "Has it started?"

About thirty people shushed her as the *General Hospital* theme music started. Laura's face filled the screen. She looked beautiful and dewy-eyed in a gorgeous white headdress. A collective sigh went around the room.

Then Luke appeared in his gray morning suit, smiling at his bride-to-be.

Just then, the sorority door banged open. "Kate!" Tully yelled, walking into the room.

"Ssshhh," everyone said at once.

Tully squatted behind Kate. "We need to talk."

"Shh. Luke and Laura are getting married. You can tell me about your interview—you got it: congratulations—when it's over. Now be quiet."

"But—"

"Shhh."

Tully sank to her knees, mumbling, "How can you all be so gaga over some skinny white guy with a bad perm? And he's a rapist. I think—"

"SHHH."

Tully sighed dramatically and crossed her arms.

As soon as it was over and the music started up again, she popped to her feet. "Come on, Katie. We need to talk." She grabbed Kate's hand and led her away from the publicness of the TV room, through the halls, and down a flight of stairs to the sorority's dirty little secret: the smoking lounge. It was a tiny room, tucked behind the kitchen, with two love seats, a coffee table littered with full ashtrays, and air so thick and blue it hurt your eyes, even when no one was in the room. It was *the* place for after-party gossip and late-night laughter.

Kate hated it down here. The habit that had seemed so cool and defiant at thirteen was gross and stupid now. "So, tell me everything. You got the internship, right?"

Tully grinned. "I did. Mondays, Wednesdays, and Fridays. Some weekends. We're on our way, Katie. I'll nail this job and by the time we graduate, I'll talk them into hiring you. We'll be a team, just like we always said."

Kate took a deep breath. *Do it. Tell her.* "You shouldn't be worrying about me, Tully. This is your day, your start."

"Don't be ridiculous. You still want to be a team, don't you?" Tully paused, stared at Kate, who screwed up her courage and opened her mouth. Then Tully laughed. "Of course you do. I knew it. You were just messing with me. Very funny. I'll talk to Mr. Ryan—he's my new boss—just as soon as he can't live without me. Now I gotta run. Chad will want to hear about the interview, but I had to tell you first." Tully hugged her fiercely and left.

Kate stood there, in the small, ugly room that smelled of stale cigarettes, staring at the open door. "No," she said softly. "I don't want to do that."

There was no one listening.

CHAPTER ELEVEN

Thanksgiving in the Mularkey household was always a spectacle. Aunt Georgia and Uncle Ralph drove over from eastern Washington, bringing enough food with them to feed an entire community. In years past, they'd had their four children with them, but now those kids were adults themselves and sometimes had other families to visit on the holiday. This year, Georgia and Ralph were alone, and looking a little dazed by their situation. Georgia had poured herself a drink before she even bothered saying hello to anyone in the house.

Kate sat on the threadbare arm of the cherry-red sofa that had been the centerpiece of this living room for as long as she could remember. Tully sat cross-legged on the floor at Mom's feet. It was her usual spot on holidays. Tully rarely liked to be too far from the woman she considered the perfect mother. Mom, in Dad's La-Z-Boy, was across from Georgia, who sat on the sofa.

It was the girlfriend hour—a family tradition. Georgia had devised it years ago—before there were any kids to care about, or so family legend had it. Every holiday, for one hour, while the men were watching football, the women gathered in the living room to have cocktails and catch up on the news. They all knew that soon enough there would be a Herculean amount of work to do in the kitchen, but for sixty minutes, no one cared.

This year, for the first time ever, Mom had poured glasses of white wine for Kate and Tully. It made Kate feel very grown up to sit here on the arm of the sofa, sipping her wine. Already the first Christmas album of the year was on the turntable. Elvis, naturally, singing about the little boy in the ghetto.

It was funny how an album, or even just a song, could remind you of so many moments in your life. Kate didn't think there had ever been any family event—Christmas, Thanksgiving, Easter, the yearly camping trip—that had been Elvis-free. It just wasn't a Mularkey family moment without him. Mom and Georgia made sure of that. His death hadn't changed the tradition at all, but sometimes, if they drank enough, they'd hug each other and cry for the loss of him.

"You should see what I got to do this week," Tully said, rising to her knees in her excitement. Kate couldn't help noticing that she looked like a supplicant, waiting for Mom's blessing. "You know the Spokane rapist case? Well," she said dramatically, luring them in, "the guy they arrested? His mother hired someone to kill the judge and prosecutor. Can you believe it? And Johnny—that's my boss—he let me do a first draft of the copy. They even used a sentence I wrote. It was so cool. Next week he's letting me tag along to an interview with a guy who invented some new kind of computer."

"You're really on your way now, Tully," Mom said, smiling down at her.

"Not just me, Mrs. M.," Tully said. "It's going to work out with Kate, too. I'll get her an internship at the station; you'll see. I'm already starting to drop hints. Someday you'll see us both on TV. The first pair of female anchors on a network news show."

"Think of it, Margie," Georgia said dreamily.

"Anchors?" Kate said, straightening. "I thought we were going to be reporters."

Tully grinned. "With our ambition? Are you kidding? We're going straight to the top, Katie."

Kate had to say something now. This was spinning out of control, and honestly, today was a good time to come clean. A round of drinks had softened everyone. "I should tell you—"

"We'll be more famous than Jean Enersen, Mrs. M.," Tully said, laughing. "And definitely richer."

"Imagine being rich," Mom said.

Aunt Georgia patted Kate's thigh. "Everyone in the family is so proud of you, Katie. You'll make a name for all of us."

Kate sighed. Once again she'd lost her chance. Getting up, she walked across the room, past the corner where soon the Christmas tree would be placed, and stood at the window, looking out over the pasture. A blanket of glittery white coated the field, created sparkly mounds on the fence posts. Moonlight turned everything a beautiful frosty blue and white; with the black velvet sky, it looked like a greeting card. As a girl, she'd waited impatiently for this unexpected weather, prayed for it for months, and no wonder. Covered in snow, Firefly Lane looked like something out of a fairy tale. The kind of place where nothing could ever go wrong, where a girl should be able to simply tell her family that she'd changed her mind.

The last few months of their senior year were perfection. Although Tully spent more than twenty-five hours a week at the station where she was interning, and Kate spent an equal number of hours working at Starbucks, the new designer coffee shop in the Pike Place Market, they made sure to spend a lot of their weekend time together, playing pool and drinking beer at Goldies or listening to music at the Blue Moon Tavern. Tully spent a lot of her nights at Chad's, but Kate didn't say much about that. Truthfully, she was having too much fun dating to hassle Tully about her choices.

The only problem in Kate's life—and it was a biggie—was her upcoming graduation. She was going to graduate next month with honors, with a degree in communications/broadcast journalism, and she still hadn't told anyone that it wasn't her dream job.

Now, though, she was going to come clean. She was in one of the third-floor phone rooms, folded up to fit, and she'd just dialed home.

Mom answered on the second ring. "Hello?"

"Hey, Mom."

"Katie! What a great surprise. I can't remember the last time you called in the middle of the week. You must be psychic: Dad and I just got home from the mall. You should see the dress I got for graduation. It's beautiful. Don't let anyone tell you JC Penney doesn't have great clothes."

"What does it look like?" Kate was stalling; with half an ear, she listened to her mom's description. Mom had just said something about shoulder pads and glitter when Kate jumped in. "I just applied for a job at Nordstrom, Mom. In the advertising department."

There was a noticeable pause on the other end, then the telltale sound of a cigarette being lit. "I thought you and Tully were going to be—"

"I know." Kate leaned back against the wall. "A reporting team. World-famous and rich."

"What's really going on, Kathleen?"

Kate tried to put her indecision into words. She just didn't know what she wanted to do with the rest of her life. She believed there had to be something special out there for her, a path that was hers alone and held happiness at its end, but where was the start of it? "I'm not like Tully," she finally said, admitting the truth she'd known for a long time. "I don't eat, sleep, and breathe the news. Sure, I'm good enough to get all A's and my profs love me because I'm never late with an assignment, but journalism—TV or print—is a jungle. I'll be eaten alive by people like Tully who'll do anything for a scoop. It's just not realistic to think I can make it."

"Realistic? Realistic is your dad and me trying to manage our expenses when they keep cutting his hours at the plant. Realistic is me being a smart woman who can't get a job at anything better than minimum wage because I have no education and all I've done is raise kids. Believe me, Katie, you don't want to be realistic at your age. There's plenty of time for that. Now you should dream big and reach high."

"I just want something different."

"What?"

"I wish I knew."

"Oh, Katie . . . I think you're afraid to reach for the brass ring. Don't be."

Before Katie could answer, there was a knock at the door. "I'm in here," she called out.

The door swung open to reveal Tully. "There you are. I've been looking everywhere. Who are you talking to?"

"Mom."

Tully yanked the phone from Kate and said, "Hey, Mrs. M. I'm kidnapping your daughter. We'll call back later. 'Bye." She hung up, then turned to Kate. "You're coming with me."

"Where are we going?"

"You'll see." Tully led her out of the house and down to the parking lot, where her new blue VW bug waited.

All the way into downtown Seattle, Kate asked where they were going and what was up until they pulled up in front of a small office building.

"This is where I work," Tully said when she turned off the engine. "I can't believe you've never been here before. Oh, well, you're here now."

Kate rolled her eyes. Now she knew what was happening: Tully wanted to show off some new triumph—a reel, a tape, a story she'd done that had actually been aired. As usual, Kate followed. "Look, Tully," she said as they made their way down the colorless hallway and into the small, cluttered space that was the Seattle office of KCPO-TV, "I need to tell you something."

Tully opened the door. "Sure. Later. That's Mutt, by the way." She pointed to a huge, long-haired, hunched-over guy standing by the open window, who was blowing his cigarette smoke outside.

"Hey," he said, barely lifting a single finger in greeting.

"Carol Mansour—she's the reporter—is at a city council meeting," Tully said, leading Kate toward a closed door.

As if Kate hadn't been hearing Carol Mansour stories forever.

Tully stopped at the door and knocked. When a male voice answered, Tully opened the door and pulled Kate inside. "Johnny? This is my friend Katie."

A man looked up from behind his desk. "You're Kate Mularkey, huh?"

He was, hands down, the best-looking man Kate had ever seen. He was older than they were, but not by much; maybe five or six years. His long black hair was thick and feathered back, with the barest hint of curl at the ends. Prominent cheekbones and a smallish chin could have made him look pretty, but there was nothing feminine about him. When he smiled at her, she drew in a sharp breath, feeling a jolt of pure physical attraction that was unlike anything she'd ever experience before.

And here she stood, dressed for work in her preppy Gloria Vanderbilt jeans, penny loafers, and red V-neck sweater. All of last night's curl had fallen out of her hair and she hadn't redone it this morning. She hadn't bothered with makeup, either.

She was going to kill Tully.

"I'll leave you two alone," Tully said, skipping out of the office, closing the door behind her.

"Please. Have a seat," he said indicating the empty chair across from his desk.

She sat down, perching nervously on the edge of the chair.

"Tully tells me you're a genius."

"Well, she is my best friend."

"You're lucky. She's a special girl."

"Yes, sir, she is."

He laughed at that; it was a rich, contagious sound that made her smile, too. "Please, don't call me sir. It makes me think some old guy is behind me." He leaned forward. "So, Kate, what do you think?"

"About what?"

"The job."

"What job?"

He glanced at the door, said, "Hmmm, that's interesting," then looked at her again. "We have an opening for an office person. Carol used to do all of the phones and filing, but she's going to have a baby, so the cheap-ass station manager has finally kicked in for a little help."

"But Tully—"

"She wants to stay an intern. Says that thanks to her grandmother she doesn't need the money. Between you and me, she's not great at answering the phones anyway."

This was all coming at Kate too fast. Only an hour ago, she'd finally admitted that she didn't want to go into broadcasting, and now here she was being offered a job every kid in her department at UW would kill for.

"What's the pay?" she asked, stalling.

"Minimum wage, of course."

She did the math in her head. With tips, she made close to double that much at Starbucks.

"Come on," he said, smiling. "How can you turn me down? You can be a receptionist in an ugly office for next to no money. Isn't it every college grad's dream?"

She couldn't help laughing. "When you put it that way, how could I refuse?"

"It's a start in the glamorous world of TV news, right?"

His smile was like some kind of superpower that scrambled her thoughts. "Is it? Glamorous, I mean?"

He looked surprised by the question, and for the first time he really looked at her. His fake smile faded, and the look in his blue eyes turned hard, cynical. "Not in this office."

He got to her. She didn't know why, but it was powerful, this attraction she felt. Nothing like how she'd responded to college boys. It was another reason not to take the job.

Behind her, the door opened. Tully came through, practically bouncing. "Well, did you say yes?"

It was crazy to take a job because you were hot for the boss.

Then again, she was twenty-one years old and he was offering her a start in television.

She didn't look at Tully. If she did, Kate knew she'd feel as if she were selling out, following again, and for all the wrong reasons.

But how could she say no? Maybe in a real job she'd find that passion and brilliance she needed. The more she thought about it, the more possible it seemed. School wasn't the real world. Perhaps that was why the news business hadn't seized hold of her. Here, the stories would matter.

"Sure," she said at last. "I'll try it, Mr. Ryan."

"Call me Johnny." The smile he gave her was so unsettling she actually had to look away. She was sure somehow that he could see inside her or hear how fast he made her heart beat. "Okay, Johnny."

"All *right*," Tully said, clapping her hands together.

Kate couldn't help noticing how her friend instantly seized Johnny's full attention. He was sitting at his desk now, staring at Tully.

That was when Kate knew she'd made a mistake.

Kate stared at herself in the small oval mirror above the dresser. Her long, straight, highlighted hair was drawn back from her face and held in place by a black velvet headband. Pale blue eye shadow and two coats of green mascara accentuated the color of her eyes, and pink lip gloss and blush gave her skin some color.

"You'll learn to love the news," she said to her reflection. "And you're not just following Tully."

"Hurry up, Kate," Tully called out, knocking hard on the bedroom door. "You don't want to be late on your first day of work. I'll be down in the parking lot."

"Okay, so maybe you *are* following her." Grabbing her briefcase off the twin bed that was hers, she left her bedroom and headed downstairs.

In this last week of school, the hallways were crazy-busy with girls studying for finals, saying goodbye, and packing up their things. Kate wound through the melee and went out to the small parking lot behind the house, where Tully sat in her brand-new VW Bug, with the engine running.

The second Kate sat down and slammed the door shut, they were off. Prince's *Purple Rain* soundtrack blared from the tiny speakers. Tully had to yell over the music.

"This is so great, isn't it? Us finally going to work together."

Kate nodded. "It sure is." She had to admit she was excited. After all, she was a college graduate—or would be soon—and she'd found an excellent starter position in her major field. It didn't matter that Tully had gotten the job for her, or that she was essentially following her best friend. What mattered was doing this job to the best of her abilities and finding out if broadcast journalism was for her. "Tell me about our boss," she said, turning down the stereo.

"Johnny? He's totally good at what he does. Used to be a war correspondent. In El Salvador or Libya; who the hell knows? I hear he misses combat, but he's a great producer. You can learn a lot from him."

"Have you ever wanted to go out with him?"

Tully laughed. "Just because I slept with my prof doesn't mean every boss is fair game."

Kate was relieved by that; more so than she should be. She wanted to ask if Johnny was married—she'd wanted to ask the question for almost a week—but she couldn't quite form the words. They'd be too revealing.

"Here we are." Tully pulled up to the curb outside the building and parked. All the way up the stairs and down the hall, she talked about how great it was going to be to work together, but once they were in the small, cramped set of offices, she made a beeline for Mutt and huddled with him.

Kate stood there, clutching her fake leather briefcase to her chest, wondering what she should do.

She had just decided to take off her jacket when Johnny appeared, looking both incredibly handsome and profoundly pissed off.

"Mutt! Carol!" he yelled, even though they were all standing right there. "That new company, Microsoft, is announcing something. I don't know what the hell it is. Mike is faxing the info. They want you to go to the company headquarters and see if you can talk to the boss. Bill Gates."

Tully surged forward. "Can I tag along?"

"Who cares? It's a bullshit story," Johnny said, then went back into his office and slammed the door.

The next few moments were a blur of chaotic movement. Carol, Tully, and Mutt gathered up their supplies and rushed out of the office.

Kate stood there after they left, in the now-quiet, vacant office, wondering what in the hell she was supposed to do.

Beside her, the phone rang.

She peeled out of her jacket, hung it over her chair back and sat down, then answered. "KCPO news. This is Kathleen. How may I help you?"

"Hey, honey, it's Mom and Dad. We just wanted to call and say have a great first day at work. We're so proud of you."

Kate was hardly surprised. Some things in life never changed; her family was one of them. She loved them for it. "Thanks, guys."

For the next few hours, she found it remarkably easy to fill her time. The phone rang almost constantly, and the in-box on her desk looked as if it hadn't been touched in years. The files were an absolute mess.

She became so engrossed in her work that the next time she looked at the clock it was one o'clock and she was starving.

Certainly she was allowed a lunch break? She got up from her desk and crossed the now-clean office. At Johnny's door, she paused, gathered her courage to knock, but before she could do it, she heard yelling from his side of the door. He was on the phone, arguing with someone.

It was better not to interrupt. She set the phone's answering machine on automatic pickup and ran downstairs to the deli. There, she bought herself half a ham and cheese sandwich. On impulse, she bought a cup of clam chowder and a BLT as well. A pair of Cokes finished her order. Bag in hand, she ran upstairs and switched the phones back on.

Then she went to Johnny's door again; silence came from the other side.

She knocked timidly.

"Come in."

She opened the door.

He sat at his desk, looking tired. His long hair was a mess, as if he'd been running his fingers through it constantly, shoving it back from his face. Dozens of newspapers covered his desk, so many that even the phone was hidden. "Mularkey," he said, sighing. "Shit. I forgot you started today."

Kate wanted to make a joke about it, but her voice wouldn't cooperate. She was so keenly aware of him, it was vaguely disturbing that he hadn't even known she was here.

"Come on in. What do you have there?"

"Lunch. I thought you might be hungry."

"You bought me lunch?"

"Was that wrong? I'm sorry, I—"

"Sit down." He pointed at the chair opposite his desk. "I appreciate it, really. I can't remember the last time I ate."

She moved to the desk, began unpacking their lunch. All the while she felt him watching her, those flame-blue eyes of his intently staring. It made her so nervous she almost spilled the chowder.

"Hot soup," he said, his voice low now, intimate. "So you're one of those."

She sat down, looking at him, unable not to. "One of those?"

"A caretaker." He picked up the spoon. "Let me guess: You grew up in a happy family. Two kids and a dog. No divorce."

She laughed. "Guilty. How about you?"

"No dog. Not so happy."

"Oh." She tried to think of something else to say. "Are you married?" popped out before she could stop it.

"Nope. Never. You?"

She smiled. "No."

"Good for you. This is a job that takes focus."

Kate felt like an imposter. Here she was, sitting across from her boss, trying to focus on saying something that would make him admire her, and she couldn't even make eye contact. It was crazy. He wasn't *that* good-looking. Something about him just hit her so damn hard she couldn't think straight. Finally she said, "You think they'll come up with a good story at Microsoft?"

"Israel invaded Lebanon yesterday. Did you know that? They've driven the Palestinians back to Beirut. That's the real story. And we're in the shit-ass office, dicking around with soft news." He sighed. "I'm sorry. I'm just having a bad day. And it's your first." He smiled, but it didn't reach his eyes. "And you bought me soup. Tomorrow I'll play nice, I promise."

"Tully told me you used to be a war correspondent."

"Yeah."

"I guess you loved that, huh?"

She saw something flash through his eyes then; her first instinct would have been to label it sadness, but how could she know? "It was insane."

"How come you quit?"

"You're too young to understand."

"I'm not that much younger than you. Try me."

He sighed. "Sometimes life kicks the shit out of you; that's all. It's like the Stones said: You can't always get what you want."

"The song says something about getting what you need instead."

He looked at her then, and for a split second, she knew she'd gotten his attention. "Did you find enough to keep yourself busy this morning?"

"The files were a mess. So was the in-box. And I organized and shelved all those tapes that were in the corner."

He laughed. It transformed his face, made him so handsome she drew in a sharp breath. "We've been trying to get Tully to do all that for months."

"I didn't mean—"

"Don't worry. You didn't get your friend in trouble. Believe me, I know what to expect from Tully."

"What's that?"

"Passion," he said simply, packing the empty sandwich wrapper into the Styrofoam soup cup.

Kate almost flinched at the way he said it, and she knew suddenly that she was in trouble. No matter how often she reminded herself that he was her boss, it didn't matter. In the end, what mattered was how she felt when she was near him.

Falling. There was no other word to describe it.

And yet, for the rest of the day, as she answered the phones and filed papers, she replayed in her head that last moment with him and the easy, straightforward way he'd answered her question about Tully: *passion.*

Mostly she remembered the way he'd smiled in admiration when he'd said it.

CHAPTER
TWELVE

The summer after graduation came as close to Heaven as Tully could imagine. She and Kate found a cheap 1960s-style apartment in a great location—above the Pike Place Market. They brought in furniture from Gran's house and filled the kitchen with forty-year-old Revereware pots and Spode china. On the walls, they tacked up favorite posters and put pictures of themselves on all the end tables. Mrs. Mularkey had surprised them one day with bags of groceries and several silk plants, to give the place a homey feel, she said.

The neighborhood created their lifestyle. They were within walking distance of several bars—their favorites were the Athenian inside the Market, and the smoky old Virginia Inn on the corner. At six o'clock in the morning, amid the beeping of delivery trucks and the honking of horns, they walked across the street for lattes from Starbucks and bought croissants from La Panier, a French bakery.

As working single girls, they fell into an easy routine. Each morning they went out for breakfast, sat at ironwork tables on the sidewalk, and read the various papers that they collected. *The New York Times*, *The Wall Street Journal*, and the *Seattle Times* and *Post-Intelligencer* became their bibles. When they were done, they drove to the office, where every day they learned something new about the business of TV news, and after work, they changed into glittery big shoulder-padded tunics and peg-legged pants and went to one of the many downtown clubs. On any given night they could listen to punk rock, new wave, rock 'n' roll, or pop— whatever they felt like.

And since Tully didn't have to hide Chad's existence anymore, he often took both Katie and her out, and they had a blast.

It was everything she and Kate had dreamed of, all those years ago on the dark banks of the Pilchuck River, and Tully loved every minute of it.

Now they were pulling up to the office. All the way out of the car and into the building, they talked.

But the minute Tully opened the door, she knew something was up. Mutt was near the window, hurriedly packing up his camera gear. Johnny was in his office, yelling at someone on the phone.

"What's going on?" Tully asked, tossing her purse on Kate's neat-as-a-pin desk.

Mutt looked up. "There's a protest going on. It's our story."

"Where's Carol?"

"In the hospital. Labor."

This was Tully's chance. She went straight into Johnny's office, without even bothering to knock. "Let me go on air. I know you think I'm not ready, but I am. And who else is there?"

He hung up the phone and looked at her. "I already told the station you'd do the report. That's what all the yelling was about." He came around the desk and moved toward her. "Don't let me down, Tully."

Tully knew it was unprofessional, but she couldn't help herself: she hugged him. "You're the best. I'll make you proud. You'll see."

She was halfway to the door when he cleared his throat and said her name. She stopped, turned.

"Don't you want to read the background stuff? Or do you want to go in blind?"

Tully felt her cheeks heat up. "Whoops. I'll read it."

He handed her a sheath of slippery fax paper. "It's about some housewife in Yelm who channels ghosts. J. Z. Knight."

Tully frowned.

"Is that a problem?"

"No. I just . . . know someone who lives out there. That's all."

"Well, there won't be time for visiting friends. Now go. I want you back by two to edit."

Without Mutt and Tully, the office was quiet. It was only the second time all summer that Kate had been alone in the office with Johnny. A little unnerved by the silence—as well as by the sight of his open door and the knowledge that he was just on the other side of it—she tended to answer the phone too quickly and even sound a little breathless when she did it.

When Tully was here, there was the noise and commotion. She lived for TV news and no moment of it was beneath her contemplation. All day, every day, she badgered Johnny and Carol and Mutt with questions; she continually sought their collective advice on every topic.

Kate had lost track of the times she'd seen Mutt roll his eyes as Tully walked away from a conversation. Carol was even less accommodating; the lead reporter barely talked to Tully lately. Not that Tully seemed to care. What mattered to Tully was the news: first, last, and always.

Kate, on the other hand, cared about the people in the office more than she cared about the stories they followed. She had been befriended almost instantly by Carol, who often took her out to lunch to talk about her impending birth, and just as often called upon Kate to edit her copy or research stories. Mutt, too, had chosen Kate as his confidante. He spent long hours talking to her about his family problems and the woman who refused to marry him.

The only person Kate hadn't connected with was Johnny.

She was a nervous wreck around him. All he had to do was look her way and smile, and she'd drop whatever was in her hand. She consistently stuttered when giving him his messages and tripped over the ripped carpet edge in his office.

It was pathetic.

At first, Kate figured it was his looks. He was Irish-Catholic-boy per-fect, with his black hair and blue eyes, and when he smiled his whole face crinkled in a way that made her breath catch in her throat.

She'd assumed her infatuation wouldn't last, that in time, as she got to know him, his looks would be less arresting for her. At the very least, she thought she'd develop an immunity to his smile.

No such luck. Everything he said and did tightened the noose around her heart. Beneath his cynical veneer, she'd glimpsed an idealist, and even more: a wounded one. Something had broken Johnny, left him here, on the fringes of the big story, and the mystery of it tanta-lized her.

She went over to the corner, where a stack of tapes lay in a heap, waiting to be put away. She'd just picked up an armful when Johnny ap-peared in the doorway of his office. "Hey," he said. "Are you busy?"

She dropped the stack of tapes. *Idiot.* "No," she said. "Not really."

"Let's grab a real lunch. It's a slow news day and I'm sick of deli sand-wiches."

"Uh . . . sure." She concentrated on the tasks in front of her: switch-ing on the answering machine, putting on her sweater, picking up her purse.

He came up beside her. "Ready?"

"Let's go."

She walked alongside him down the block and across the street. Now and then his body brushed against hers, and she was acutely aware of every contact.

When they finally got to the restaurant, he led her over to a table in the corner that overlooked Elliott Bay and the shops at Pier 70. A wait-ress showed up almost instantly to take their orders.

"Are you old enough to drink, Mularkey?" he asked with a smile.

"Very funny. But I don't drink on the job." At the words, which couldn't have sounded more prim, she winced and thought, *Idiot,* again.

"You're a very responsible girl," he said when the waitress left; he was obviously trying not to smile.

"Woman," she said firmly, hoping she didn't blush.

He smiled at that. "I was trying to compliment you."

"And you chose *responsible?*"

"What would you prefer?"

"Sexy. Brilliant. Beautiful." She laughed nervously, sounding more like a girl than she would have wished. "You know: the words every woman wants to hear." She smiled. This was her chance to make an impression on him, get his attention as he'd gotten hers. She didn't want to blow it.

He leaned back in his chair, hopefully not because he suddenly wanted distance between them. She wished now, fervently, in fact, that she'd slept with one of her college boyfriends. She was certain he could see the stamp of virginity on her. "You've been at the station, what—two months now?"

"Almost three."

"How do you like it?"

"Fine."

"Fine? That's an odd answer. This is a love-it-or-hate-it business." He leaned forward, put his elbows on the table. "Do you have a passion for it?"

That word again: the one that separated her and Tully as cleanly as wheat from chaff.

"Y-yes."

He studied her, then smiled knowingly. She wondered how deeply into her soul that blue gaze had seen. "Tully certainly does."

"Yes."

He tried to sound casual as he asked, "Is she seeing anyone?"

Kate considered it a personal triumph that she didn't flinch or frown. Now, at least, she knew why he'd asked her out for lunch. She should have known. She wanted to say, *Yes; she's been with the same man for years,* but she didn't dare. Tully might not hide Chad anymore, but she didn't flaunt him, either. "What do you think?"

"I think she sees a lot of men."

Thankfully, the waitress returned with their orders and she pretended to be fascinated by her plate. "What about you? I get the feeling you're not exactly passionate about your job."

He looked up sharply. "What makes you say that?"

She shrugged and kept eating, but she was watching him now.

"Maybe not," he said quietly.

She felt herself go still; her fork stayed in midair. For the first time they weren't making idle chitchat. He'd just revealed something important; she was somehow certain of that. "Tell me about El Salvador."

"You know what went on down there? The massacre? It was a blood-bath. Things have been getting worse lately, too. The death squads are killing civilians, priests, nuns."

Kate hadn't known all of that, or any of it, really, but she nodded anyway, watching the play of emotions cross his face. She'd never seen him so animated, so passionate. Again there was an unreadable emotion in his eyes, too. "You sound as if you loved it. Why did you leave?"

"I don't talk about this." He finished his beer and stood up. "We better get back to work."

She looked down at their barely eaten lunches. Obviously she'd gone too far, probed too much. "I got too personal, I'm sorry—"

"Don't be. It's ancient history. Let's go."

All the way back to the office, he said nothing. They walked briskly upstairs and into the quiet office.

There, she couldn't help herself, she touched his arm. "I really am sorry. I didn't mean to upset you."

"Like I said, it's old news."

"It isn't, though, is it?" she said quietly, knowing instantly that she'd overstepped again.

"Get back to work," he said brusquely, and went into his office, slamming the door shut behind him.

Yelm slept in the verdant green valley between Olympia and Tacoma. It had always been the kind of town where people dressed in flannel shirts and faded jeans and waved to one another as they passed.

All that had changed a few years ago, on the day a thirty-five-thousand-year-old warrior from Atlantis supposedly appeared in the kitchen of an otherwise ordinary housewife.

The locals, who believed in the Northwest creed of "live and let live," looked the other way for a long time. They ignored the "weirdos" who came to Yelm (many of them in expensive cars, wearing designer clothes—"Hollywood types") and paid no attention as SOLD signs started appearing on prime pieces of land.

When the whispers began that J. Z. Knight was gearing up to build some kind of compound to house a school for her followers, though, the townsfolk had had enough. According to the South Sound bureau chief at KCPO, people were picketing the Knight property.

The "crowd" protesting the proposed development turned out to be about ten people holding up signs and chatting with one another. It looked more like a coffee klatch than a political gathering—until the news van showed up. Then the crowd started marching and chanting.

"Ah," Mutt said, "the power of the media." He pulled over to the side of the road and turned to Tully.

"Here's what they didn't teach you in college: Get into the middle of it. Wade in. If it looks like there's going to be a fight, I want you there, got it? Just keep asking questions, keep talking. And if I give you the sign, get the hell out of the shot."

Tully's heart was going a mile a minute as she followed his lead.

The protesters surged toward them. Everyone was talking at once, trying to make their point, elbowing each other out of their way.

Mutt shoved Tully, hard. She stumbled forward and came face to chest with a huge, burly guy with a Santa-like beard and a sign that read: JUST SAY NO TO RAMTHA.

"I'm Tallulah Hart from KCPO. What are you out here for today?"

"Get his name," Mutt yelled.

Tully winced. *Shit.*

The man said, "I'm Ben Nettleman. Me and my family's lived in Yelm for nearly eighty years. We don't want to see it turn into some super-market for new age weirdos."

"They got California for that!" someone yelled.

"Tell me about the Yelm you know," Tully said.

"It's a quiet place, where people look out for each other. We start our day with prayer and mostly we don't care what our neighbors do . . . until they start building shit that don't belong and bringing crazies by the busloads."

"And you say crazies because—"

"They are! That lady channels some dead guy who says he lived in Atlantis."

"I can do an Indian accent, too. It don't make me Ramtha," someone yelled.

For the next twenty minutes, Tully did what she did best: she talked to people. Six or seven minutes in, she found her groove and remembered what she'd been taught. She listened and asked the follow-up questions she would have asked anyone on an ordinary day. She had no idea if they were the right questions or if she was always standing in the best place, but she did know that by her third interview, Mutt had stopped directing her and started letting her lead. And she knew that she *felt* good. People really opened up to her, sharing their feelings and concerns and fears.

"Okay, Tully," Mutt said behind her. "That's it. We're done."

The minute the camera was off, the crowd broke up.

"I did it," she whispered. It was all she could do not to actually jump up and down. "What a rush."

"You did good," Mutt said, giving her a smile that she'd never forget.

Mutt packed up his camera gear in record time and climbed into the van.

Tully was on an adrenaline high.

Then she saw the campground sign.

"Turn off here," she said, surprising herself.

"Why?" Mutt asked.

"My mom is . . . on vacation. She's staying at this campground. Give me five minutes to say hi."

"I'll take a smoke break. That'll give you fifteen. But then we gotta boogie."

The van pulled up in front of the campground's reservation desk.

Tully went to the desk and asked about her mother. The man on duty nodded. "Site thirty-six. Tell her she needs to pay when you see her."

Following the path through the trees, Tully almost turned around a dozen times. Honestly, she had no idea why she was here. She hadn't seen or spoken to her mother since Gran's funeral, and although Tully had become the executor of Gran's estate at eighteen, and responsible for the monthly disbursement to Cloud, she'd never once received a thank-you for the money. Just a series of I've-moved-please-send-money-to-this-address postcards. This campground in Yelm was the most recent.

She saw her mother standing by a row of Sani-cans, smoking a ciga-rette. Wearing a coarse gray Cowichan sweater and pajamalike pants, she looked like an escapee from a women's prison. The years had sanded down some of her beauty and left a network of fine lines across her hollowed cheeks.

"Hey, Cloud," she said when she got close.

Her mother took a drag of her cigarette and exhaled slowly, watch-ing her through heavily lidded eyes.

She could see how bad her mother looked, how the drugs were ag-ing her. Not even forty yet, Cloud looked fifty, easy. As usual her eyes had the glassy, unfocused gaze of an addict.

"I'm here on assignment for KCPO news." Tully tried to keep the pride out of her voice, knowing it was stupid to expect anything from her mother, but it was there anyway, in her eyes and her voice, the shadowy remnant of that pathetic little girl who'd filled twelve memory books so that someday her mother would know her and be proud. "It was my first on-air report. I told you I'd be on TV someday."

Cloud's body swayed ever so slightly, as if there were music in the air that only she could hear. "TV is the opiate of the masses."

"Well, if there's anyone who'd know about drugs, it's you."

"Speaking of that, I'm kinda short this month. You got any cash?"

Tully dug in her purse, found the fifty-dollar bill she kept in her wallet for emergencies, and handed it to her mother. "Don't give it all to one dealer."

Cloud took a clumsy step forward and palmed the money.

Tully wished she'd never come here. She knew what to expect from her mother: nothing. Why couldn't she seem to remember that? "I'll send money for your next rehab, Cloud. Every family has its traditions, right?" On that, she turned and walked back to the van.

Mutt was waiting for her. Dropping his cigarette, he ground it out with his heel and grinned at her. "Mommy proud of her college girl?"

"Are you kidding?" Tully said, grinning brightly and wiping her eyes. "She cried like a baby."

When Tully and Mutt came back, the team clicked into high gear. The four of them crammed into the editing room and turned twenty-six minutes of tape into a sharp, impartial thirty-second story. Kate tried to keep her thoughts focused on the story, just the story, but lunch with Johnny had dulled her senses; or heightened them. She wasn't entirely sure which. All she really knew was that whatever schoolgirl crush she'd had on him before he asked her out to lunch had deepened into something else.

When they finished working, Johnny picked up the phone and called the Tacoma station manager. He talked for a few moments, then hung up and looked at Tully. "They'll air it tonight at ten unless something comes up."

Tully jumped up and clapped her hands. "We did it!"

Kate couldn't help feeling a stab of envy. Just once, she wanted Johnny to look at her the way he looked at Tully.

If only she were like her friend—confident and sexy and willing to make a grab at whatever—and whomever—she wanted. Then she might have a chance, but the thought of Johnny's rejection, of a blank-eyed, *Huh?* kept her standing in the shadows.

Tully's shadow, to be precise. As always, Kate was the backup singer who never stepped into the spotlight.

"Let's go celebrate," Tully said. "Dinner's on me."

"Count me out," Mutt said. "Darla's waiting for me."

"I can't do dinner, but how about drinks at nine?" Johnny said.

"We can do that," Tully said.

Kate knew she should say no. The last thing she wanted to do was sit at the table and watch Johnny watch Tully—but what choice did she have? She was the sidekick. Rhoda Morgenstern. And wherever Mary went, Rhoda had to follow, even if it hurt like hell.

Kate chose her clothes with care: a cap-sleeved white T-shirt, black vintage jacquard vest, and tight jeans tucked into scrunchy ankle boots. After curling her hair, she combed it carefully to one side and anchored it into a ponytail. She thought she looked pretty good until she went out into the living room and saw Tully standing there, dressed in a green jersey dress with a plunging neckline, padded shoulders, and a wide metallic belt, swaying to the music.

"Tully? You ready?"

Tully stopped dancing, flicked off the stereo, and linked arms with Kate. "Come on. We're so outta here."

Down on the street in front of their apartment, they found Johnny leaning against his black El Camino. In faded jeans and an old Aerosmith T-shirt, he looked totally sexy in a casual, rumpled kind of way.

"Where are we going?" Tully asked. She immediately linked her other arm with his.

"I've got a plan," Johnny said.

"I love a man with a plan," Tully said. "Don't you, Kate?"

The word *love* paired with his name hit a little close to home, so she didn't look at him when she said, "I do."

Three abreast, they walked down the cobblestone street of the empty market.

At the neon-lit sex shop on the corner, Johnny guided them to turn right.

Kate frowned. There was an invisible line, like the equator, that ran down Pike Street. To the south, it got ugly fast. This was where the tourists didn't go unless they were looking for drugs or hookers. The shops and businesses on both sides of the street were seedy-looking.

They walked past two adult bookstores and an X-rated theater where the *Debbie Does Dallas* sequel was playing on a double feature with *Saturday Night Beaver*.

"This is great," Tully said. "Kate and I never go down here."

Johnny came to a stop beside a ratty-looking wooden door that had obviously once been painted red. "Ready?" he said with a smile.

Tully nodded.

He opened the door. The music was earsplittingly loud.

A huge black man sat on a stool at the entrance. "ID, please," he said, turning on a flashlight to study their driver's licenses. "Go on."

Tully and Kate showed their IDs, then moved on ahead, down the dark narrow hallway that was covered with flyers and posters and bumper stickers.

The hallway opened into a long, rectangular room that was packed with people dressed in metal-enhanced black leather. Kate had never seen so many bizarre hairdos in one room. There were dozens of people with six-inch-long Mohawks gelled to sawblade perfection and dyed in rainbow colors.

Johnny led them through the dance floor, past a few wooden tables, to the bar, where a girl with magenta hair cut into spidery spikes and a safety pin in her cheek took their orders. At the end of the bar, suspended up in the corner, was a good-sized TV that was currently tuned to MTV. No one was paying the slightest attention to it.

When the bartender returned, Johnny gave her a healthy tip and a bright smile, then led Kate and Tully to a table back in the corner, beneath the TV.

Tully immediately lifted her margarita for a toast. "To us. We totally rocked today."

They clinked glasses and drank.

And drank.

By their third round, Tully was drunk. When the right song started—"Call Me," or "Sweet Dreams (Are Made of This)," or "Do You Really Wanna Hurt Me?"—she was on her feet, dancing all by herself right next to the table.

Kate wished she could find that kind of ease in herself, but two drinks weren't enough to undo who she was. Instead, she sat there, watching Johnny watch Tully.

He didn't really look at Kate until Tully went to the bathroom. "She never slows down, does she?"

Kate tried then to think of a response that would steer the conversation away from her best friend, maybe even reveal her own passionate side, but who was she kidding? She had no passionate side. Tully was candy-apple-red silk; Kate was beige cotton. "Yeah."

Tully rushed back from the bathroom, skidded drunkenly into the bar. "Hey, it's ten o'clock. Can we change the channel on the TV? No one is watching it anyway."

"Whatever." The bartender, who looked like an extra from some apocalyptic war movie, climbed up on to a stepladder and changed the channel.

Tully moved toward the TV, looking like a penitent approaching the Pope.

Then her face filled the screen. *"I'm Tallulah Hart in Yelm, Washington. This sleepy town was the site of protest today when followers of J. Z. Knight and the thirty-five-thousand-year-old spirit she calls Ramtha clashed with locals over the proposed building of a compound . . ."*

When it was over, Tully turned to Kate, said, "Well?" in a quiet, nervous voice.

"You were totally bitchin'," Kate said, meaning it. "Excellent."

Tully threw her arms around Kate and held her tightly, then grabbed her hand. "Come on. I want to dance. You, too, Johnny. We can all dance together."

There were men dancing together, and women making out to the beat of the Sex Pistols. The girl beside Kate, wearing a black plastic miniskirt and combat boots with fishnet stockings, was dancing alone.

Tully was the first to start dancing, then Johnny, and finally Kate. At first she felt awkward—literally a third wheel—but by the end of the song, she'd softened. The alcohol was a lubricant, making her body more fluid somehow, and when the music changed and slowed down, she barely hesitated to step into Tully and Johnny's arms. The three of them moved together with a natural ease that was surprisingly sexy. Kate stared up at Johnny, who was gazing at Tully, and she couldn't help wishing just once he'd look at her that way.

"I'll never forget this night," Tully said to both of them.

He leaned down and kissed Tully. Kate was drunk enough that it took her a second to register what she was seeing. Then came the pain.

Tully pulled out of the kiss. "Bad Johnny." She laughed, pushing him away.

He moved his hand down Tully's back, tried to pull her close. "What's wrong with bad?"

Before Tully could answer, someone called out her name and she spun around.

Chad was pushing through the gyrating, slam-dancing crowd. With his long hair and ragged Springsteen T-shirt, he looked like a hard rock guy in a new wave world.

Tully ran for him. They kissed as if they were alone in the room, then Kate heard her friend say, "Take me to bed, old man."

Without a wave or a goodbye or a hello, they were gone. Kate stood there, still in Johnny's arms. He was staring at the door as if he expected Tully to return, to shout out April Fools and start dancing with them again.

"She won't be coming back," Kate said.

Johnny snapped out of it. Letting go of her, he went back to the table and ordered two drinks. In the silence that followed, she stared at him, thinking: *Look at me*.

"That was Chad Wiley," he said.

Kate nodded.

"No wonder . . ." He stared at the blank hallway on the other side of the dance floor.

"They've been together a long time." She studied his profile. For a crazy second, she thought about making a move, reaching for him. Maybe she could get him to forget about Tully or change his mind; maybe tonight she didn't care if she would be his second choice, or if it would be because of the booze. Love could grow from drunken passion, couldn't it? "You thought you and Tully might—"

He nodded before she could finish and said, "Come on, Mularkey. I'll walk you home."

All the way back to her apartment, she told herself it was for the best.

"Well, goodnight, Johnny," she said at her front door.

"Goodnight." He started for the elevator. Halfway there, he stopped and turned to her. "Mularkey?"

She paused, glanced back. "Yeah?"

"You were really good today. Did I tell you that? You're one of the most talented writers I've ever seen."

"Thanks."

Later, lying in her bed, staring into the darkness, she remembered his words, and how he'd looked when he'd said them.

In some small way, he'd noticed her today.

Maybe it wasn't as hopeless as she'd thought.

CHAPTER
THIRTEEN

From the moment Tully did her first on-air broadcast, everything changed. They became the fearsome foursome; Kate and Tully and Mutt and Johnny. For two years they were together constantly, huddled together in the office, working on stories, going from place to place like gypsies. The second story that Tully covered was about a snowy owl who'd taken up residence on a streetlamp in Capitol Hill. Next, she followed the gubernatorial campaign of Booth Gardner, and though she was one of dozens of reporters on the case, it seemed that Gardner often answered her questions first. By the time the first Microsoft millionaires began driving through downtown in their mint-new Ferraris, listening to geek music on supersized headphones, everyone at KCPO knew that Tully wouldn't last on the smallest local channel for long.

They all knew it, but perhaps Johnny most of all. So, although the three of them didn't talk about the future, they felt its shadowy presence constantly, and somehow that made their time together sweeter and more intense. On the rare night when they weren't working on a story, Johnny, Tully, and Kate met at Goldies to play pool and drink beer. By the end of their second year together, they knew all there was to know about each other; at least, all that each was willing to share.

Except the stuff that truly mattered. Kate often thought it ironic that three people who searched through the rubble of life to find pebbles of truth could be so stubbornly blind about their own lives.

Tully had no idea that Johnny wanted her, and he was completely unaware that Kate wanted him.

So their weird, silent triangle went on, day after day, night after night. Tully always asked Kate why she didn't date. She longed to come clean, tell Tully the truth, but every time she started to confess, she backed out. How could she tell the truth about Johnny, after the crap she'd given Tully about Chad? Your boss, after all, was worse than your professor.

And besides, what did Tully know about unrequited love? Her friend would just start pushing Kate to ask Johnny out. What would Kate say then? *I can't. He's in love with you.* Deeper down, in a dark place she rarely acknowledged, there was another fear, one she only recognized in her dreams and nightmares. In the cold light of day, she didn't believe it, but at night, alone, she worried that if Tully found out about Kate's love, it might actually make Johnny more attractive to Tully. That was the thing about her best friend; it wasn't that she wanted what she couldn't have. It was that she wanted everything, and sooner or later, Tully got what she wanted. Kate couldn't risk it. Not having Johnny she could live with. Losing him to Tully would be unbearable.

So Kate kept her head down, her hands busy, and her dreams of love hidden away. She smiled easily when Mom or Dad or Tully teased her about her social life, joked that her standards were higher than some people she could name, an answer which was always good for a laugh.

She tried not to be alone with Johnny too much, either, just to stay on the safe side. Although she no longer fumbled things or got tongue-tied around him, she always sensed that he was quite perceptive, and that, given too many opportunities, he might sense that which she worked so hard to hide.

Her plan went pretty well, all things considered, until a cold November day in 1984 when Johnny called her into his office.

They were alone again, that day. Tully and Mutt were tracking down a Sasquatch sighting in the Olympic rain forest.

Kate smoothed her angora sweater and schooled her face into an impersonal smile as she went into his office and found him standing at the dirty window. "What is it, Johnny?"

He looked terrible. Haggard. "Remember when I told you about El Salvador?"

"Sure."

"Well, I still have friends down there. One of them, Father Ramón, is missing. His sister thinks they've taken him somewhere for torture, or that they've killed him. She wants me to come down and see if I can help."

"But it's dangerous—"

"Danger is my middle name." He smiled, but it was like a reflection on water, distorted and unreal.

"This isn't something to joke about. You could be killed. Or disappear like that journalist in Chile during the coup. He was never seen again."

"Believe me," he said, "I'm not joking. I've been there, remember? I know what it's like to be blindfolded and shot at." He turned his head. His eyes took on a vague, unfocused look, and she wondered what he was remembering. "I can't turn my back on the people who protected me down there. Could you turn away from Tully if she begged you for help?"

"I would help her, as you well know. Although I don't expect to see her in a war zone, unless you count the anniversary sale at Nordstrom."

"I knew you were my girl. So you'll keep this place running while I'm gone?"

"Me?"

"Like I said once, you're a responsible girl."

She couldn't help herself; she moved toward him, looked up. He was leaving, could be hurt down there, or worse. "Woman," she said.

He stared down at her, unsmiling. She felt the mere inches between them. It would take nothing, barely a movement to touch.

"Woman," he said.

Then he left her there, standing alone, surrounded by word ghosts; things she could have said.

When Johnny was gone, Kate learned how elastic time was, how it could stretch out until minutes felt like hours. All it would take was a phone call, though, an official saying he was sorry, to make it snap like a rubber band. Every time the phone rang, she tensed. By the end of the first day, she had a pounding headache.

She learned another lesson that first week, too. Life went on. The head honchos in Tacoma still called, and a producer was assigned to oversee the assignments the team was given, but in truth, the way it worked out, Kate began to take over some of the producing responsibilities. Mutt and Tully trusted her, and she knew how to make things work on the shoestring budget they'd been given. All that longing of hers had paid off; it seemed she'd watched Johnny closely enough that she knew how to do his job. She was a seamstress to his couturier, of course, but still, she was competent. By Thursday of the first week, the out-of-town producer had thrown up his hands, said he had better things to do than follow crazy people around all day, and returned to Tacoma.

On Friday, Kate produced her first segment. It was soft and unimportant—an update on former children's TV star Brakeman Bill— but still it was hers, and it hit the air.

What an adrenaline rush it had been to see her work on-screen, even if it was Tully's face and voice that everyone remembered. She'd called her parents and they drove down to watch the broadcast with Kate and Tully. Afterward, they'd toasted to "the dream" and agreed that it was that much closer to coming true.

"I always thought Katie and I would be on air together, an anchoring team, but I guess I was wrong," Tully had said. "She'll be the producer of my show someday instead. And when Barbara Walters interviews me, I'll say I couldn't have done it without her."

Kate had toasted when it was expected of her, smiling purposely and reliving every moment through Tully's chatter. She'd been proud of herself, truly she had, and she'd loved doing the piece and celebrating with her parents. It had been especially poignant when Mom took her aside and said, "I'm proud of you, Katie. You're on your way now. Aren't you glad you didn't give up?"

But all the while, a part of her was watching the clock, thinking how slowly time was moving.

"You look terrible," Tully said the next day, dropping a stack of tapes on Kate's desk.

The clattering sound startled Kate. She realized she'd been staring at the clock again. "Yeah, well, your singing sucks."

Tully laughed at that. "Everyone has something they can't do." She put her palms on Kate's desk and leaned forward. "Chad and I are going to the Backstage tonight. Junior Cadillac is playing. You want to come?"

"Not tonight."

Tully eyed her. "What in the hell is wrong with you? You've been moping around for more than a week. I know you're not sleeping—I hear you up walking around in the middle of the night—and you won't go anywhere. It's like living with the Elephant Man."

Kate couldn't help glancing at Johnny's door and then up at her friend. Longing welled up inside her, sharp and strong; if only she could tell Tully the truth: that she'd accidentally fallen in love with Johnny and now she was worried about him. It would take such a load off of her. In ten years, this was the first thing she'd ever hidden from Tully and it physically hurt to conceal it.

But her feelings for Johnny were so fragile; she knew that Tropical Storm Tully would rain all over them, ruin them.

"I'm just tired," she said. "This producing is hard work. That's all."

"But you love it, don't you?"

"Sure. It's great. Now go on, meet Chad. I'll close up." After Tully left, Kate lingered in the dark, quiet office. The strange thing was, she liked being here; she felt close to him.

"You're an idiot," she said aloud. Truthfully, she said it to herself at least twice a day lately. She was acting like—felt like—a left-behind lover, but it was all in her imagination. At least she wasn't so far gone that she'd forgotten that.

She went home by herself. The bus dropped her off at the corner of First and Pine. Amid the colorful crowd of tourists and weirdos and hippies, she picked up some food for dinner. Back in her apartment, she curled up on the couch, ate her dinner out of white cardboard containers, and watched the nightly news. Afterward, she made some notes on story ideas, called her mom, then turned the channel to NBC for *Dynasty* and *St. Elsewhere*.

Halfway through the medical drama, the doorbell rang.

Frowning, she went to the door. "Who is it?"

"Johnny Ryan."

The jolt Kate felt almost knocked her off her feet. Relief. Joy. Fear. She experienced all three emotions in a heartbeat of time.

She glanced in the mirror hanging on the wall beside her and gasped. She looked like a fashion magazine "before" photo—limp hair, no makeup, eyebrows untrimmed.

He pounded on the door again.

She opened it.

He stood there, leaning heavily against the doorframe, wearing dirty Levi's and a torn BORN IN THE USA tour T-shirt. His hair was long and uncombed, and though he was tanned, his face looked worn, older. She could smell alcohol, too.

"Hey," he said, opening his fingers from along the doorframe in greeting. At the movement he lost his balance and almost fell.

Kate moved toward him. Holding him up, she guided him into the apartment, kicked the door shut, and led him to the sofa, where he half stumbled to a sit.

"I've been sitting over in the Athenian," he said, "trying to get up the nerve t' come over here." He glanced blearily around the place. "Where's Tully?"

"She's not here," Kate said, feeling a clutch in her heart.

"Oh."

She sat down beside him. "How did it go in El Salvador?"

When he turned to her, the look in his eyes was so devastating that she reached out, put her arm around him, and drew him close.

"He was dead," he said after a long silence. "Before I even got there, he was dead. But I had to find him . . ." He pulled a flask out of his back pocket and took a long drink. "Y' want some?"

She took a sip, felt it burn all the way down her throat and settle like a hot coal in the pit of her stomach.

"It's damned heartbreaking wha's going on. And not enough is getting on air. No one cares."

"You could go on assignment," she said, even though she hated the idea.

"I wish I could . . ." His voice faded away, then turned sharp. "Old news." He took another drink.

"Maybe you should slow down a little." She tried to take the flask from him. Instead, he grabbed her wrist and pulled her onto his lap. He touched her face with his other hand, caressing her cheek as if he were blind and trying to come up with an image of what she looked like.

"You're beautiful," he whispered.

"You're drunk."

"You're still beautiful." He slid one hand up her arm and the other down her throat until he was holding her in his arms. She knew he was going to kiss her, felt the knowledge in every nerve ending in her body, just as she knew she should stop him.

He pulled her closer and all her good intentions disappeared. She gave herself over to the pressure of his hands, let herself be guided down, down toward his mouth.

The kiss was like nothing she'd ever experienced before: tender and sweet at first, then searching, demanding.

She surrendered to him as completely as she'd dreamed of doing. His tongue electrified her, sparked a new and painful desire. She became greedy for him, desperate. Without thinking, she shoved her hands up under his T-shirt, feeling his warm skin, needing to be closer . . .

Her hands were at his collarbone, pushing the soft warm cotton upward, when she realized he'd gone still.

Her senses were so scrambled it took her a moment to clear her head. Breathing hard, aching with this new need, she drew back enough to look at him.

He lay back against the sofa, his eyes at half mast. He lifted his hand slowly, jerkily, almost as if he weren't quite controlling his own movements, and touched her lips, tracing their contour with his fingertip. "Tully," he whispered. "I knew you'd taste good."

And with that blow to the heart, he fell asleep.

Kate wasn't sure how long she sat on his lap, staring down at his sleeping face. Once again, time seemed elastic between them. It felt as if she were bleeding—but it wasn't blood that leaked out of her, not something that could be so easily transfused. Instead, she was losing her dreams. The fantasy flower of love she'd planted all by herself and tended so carefully.

She climbed off him and settled him onto the sofa, taking off his shoes and covering him with a blanket.

In her own bed, with a door closed between them, she lay awake for a long time, trying not to replay it over and over in her mind, but it was impossible. She kept tasting his lips, feeling his tongue against hers, and hearing him whisper, *Tully*.

When she finally fell asleep, it was already well past midnight and morning came much too quickly. At six o'clock, she slammed the silencer on her alarm, brushed her teeth and hair, put on a robe, and hurried into the living room.

Johnny was up, sitting at the kitchen table, drinking coffee. At her entrance, he put the cup down and got up. "Hey," he said, shoving his fingers through his hair.

"Hey."

They stared at each other. She tightened the belt on her terrycloth robe.

He glanced at Tully's door.

"She's not here," Kate said. "She spent last night at Chad's."

"So you put me to bed on the couch and covered me."

"Yep."

He moved toward her. "I was pretty baked last night. I'm sorry. I shouldn't have come by."

She wasn't sure what to say.

"Mularkey," he finally said, "I know I was out of it . . ."

"Yes, you were."

"Did . . . anything happen? I mean, I'd hate to think—"

"Between us? How could it?" she said before he could finish saying how much he would regret a liaison between them. "Don't worry. Nothing happened."

The smile he gave her was so relieved she wanted to cry. "Then I guess I'll see you at work today, huh? And thanks for taking care of me."

"Sure." She crossed her arms. "What are friends for?"

CHAPTER
FOURTEEN

Late in 1985, Tully got her big break. Assigned to do a live broadcast from Beacon Hill, she was surprised by the flurry of nerves that made her fingers tremble and her voice break, but when it was over, she felt invincible.

She'd been good. Maybe even amazing.

Now she sat upright in the passenger seat of the live truck, a van specifically designed for the technical requirements of a live broadcast, bouncing slightly with enthusiasm. When she closed her eyes, she relived every second of it: the way she'd pushed into the front of the crowd and asked her questions, her flawless wrap-up at the end, shot in front of the well-lit bank, with the red and yellow police lights cutting through the darkening night. Afterward, it had taken forever to load up all the gear and get back on the road, but she didn't care. The longer this night lasted, the better. She hadn't even taken off her earpiece, battery pack, wireless microphone, or walkie-talkie. They were badges of honor.

"Pull over at that 7-Eleven," Johnny said from the back of the van. "I'm thirsty. Mutt, jump out and get a few establishing shots while we're here. It's your turn to make the drink dash, Tully."

Mutt drove into the parking lot. "Cool."

When they parked, Tully collected their money, then got out of the van and headed for the brightly lit mini-mart.

"None of that New Coke for me," Johnny said into her earpiece.

She pulled the walkie-talkie off her belt, switched it on, and said, "You say that to me every time. I'm not an idiot."

Inside the brightly lit store, she looked around for the cooler case, found it, and walked down the medicine aisle.

"Hey, look," she said, talking into the walkie-talkie, "they have Geritol. You need some, Johnny?"

"Smartass," he answered in her earpiece.

Laughing, she reached for the cooler case's handle when she noticed a shadow move across the glass. Turning, she saw a man in a gray ski mask point a gun at the cashier.

"Oh, my God."

"Are you talking about me?" Johnny said. "Because it's about time—"

She fumbled for the volume on the walkie-talkie and switched it off before the robber heard something. She clipped it to her belt and pulled her jacket over it, hiding her battery pack at the same time.

At the register, the robber swung to face her.

"You! Get on the floor." The masked man pointed his gun at the ceiling and pulled the trigger to make his point.

"Tully? What the *hell* is going on?" came Johnny's voice through the earpiece.

Tully fumbled with the earpiece cord, trying to conceal it under her jacket. Then she turned up the volume on the walkie-talkie's outgoing message, hoping like hell Johnny would be able to pick up some sound. "Someone's robbing the store," she whispered as loudly as she dared, depressing the outgoing button.

In her earpiece, she heard Johnny say, "Holy shit. Mutt, call 911 and then start shooting. Tully, keep calm and get the hell to the floor. We can go live with this. Turn on your mic. I'm getting hold of the station. They're on air now. Stan, can you hear me?"

A few seconds later, Johnny said, "Okay, Tully. We're putting this through to Mike. He's on air now with the ten o'clock news. Your audio is going on live. You won't be able to hear him, but he'll hear you."

Tully turned on her mic, whispered into it, "I don't know, Johnny. How do—"

"Your mic is hot, Tully," he said urgently. "You're on live. Go."

The masked man must have heard something; he suddenly swung toward her again, pointing his gun at her. "I told you to get down, damn it."

She just had time to process "I've had enough o' this shit" when he pulled the trigger.

There was a loud crack of sound. Tully barely had time to scream before the bullet hit her in the shoulder and knocked her off her feet. She crashed into the shelves beside her, was vaguely aware of colored boxes crumbling and falling around her. Her head hit the linoleum floor hard.

For a moment, she lay there, gasping, staring up at a wiggling snake of fluorescent lighting.

"Tully?"

It was Johnny's voice, in her ear. She eased slowly—slowly—onto her side. Her shoulder throbbed with pain, but she gritted her teeth and kept moving. Keeping low, she crawled to the end of the aisle, ripped open a box of Kotex, and shoved a pad over her wound, holding it in place. The pressure hurt like hell and made her dizzy.

"Tully? What happened? Talk to me. Are you okay?"

"I'm here," she said. "I just put . . . a dressing on my wound. I think I'm fine."

"Thank God," Johnny said. "You want to turn off your mic?"

"No way."

"Okay. You're live, remember? Keep talking. They can't hear me, but they can hear you. This is your big break, kiddo, and I'm right here to help you. Can you describe the scene?"

She got to a crouch, wincing at the pain, and moved forward slowly, trying to gauge when she could actually look up. "Moments ago, a masked man came into this mini-mart on Beacon Hill, wielding a handgun and demanding money from the clerk. He fired once into the air to make his point and once into me." Her voice was as loud a whisper as she dared.

She heard a noise; it sounded like crying. Keeping low, she came around the corner and found a little boy, huddled against the neon candy aisle.

"Hey," she said, holding out her hand. He took it greedily, squeezing so tightly she couldn't pull away. "Who are you?"

"Gabe. I'm here with my grandpa. Did you see that guy shoot his gun?"

"I did. I'm going to go find your grandpa to make sure he's okay. You stay here. What's your last name, Gabe, and how old are you?"

"Linklater. I'm gonna be seven in July."

"Okay, Gabe Linklater. You stay low and keep quiet. No more crying, okay? Be a big boy."

"I'll try."

She tucked her chin toward her chest and talked quietly into the mic. She wasn't sure what the station could hear, but she just kept talking. "I found seven-year-old Gabe Linklater in the candy aisle. He came in with his grandfather, who I'm looking for now. I can hear the gunman over at the register, threatening the cashier. Tell the police there's only one robber." She turned the corner.

There she found an old man, sitting cross-legged on the floor, holding a box of Purina Dog Chow. "Are you Gabe's grandfather?" she whispered.

"Is he okay?"

"A little scared, but fine. He's in the candy aisle. What did you see?"

"The robber drove up in a blue car. I saw him through the window." He looked at her shoulder. "Maybe you should—"

"I'm going to move in closer." She compressed the pad against her wound again, winced at the pain, and waited for the nausea to pass. This time, her hand came away bloody. Ignoring it, she reported in again to the anchor she couldn't hear. "Apparently, Mike, the lone gunman arrived in a blue car, which should be parked outside in front of one of the windows. I'm happy to say that Gabe's grandfather is also alive and unharmed. Now I'm working my way toward the register. I can hear the gunman yelling that there has to be more money and the cashier saying that he can't open the safe. I can see the flash of lights outside. So the police have arrived. They're shining the lights into the store, telling him to come out with his hands up." She scuttled out in the open for just a second and then crouched behind a life-sized standee of Mary Lou Retton eating Wheaties. "Tell the police he's taken off his mask, Mike. He's blond-haired, with a snake tattoo that wraps around his neck. The gunman is extremely agitated. He's screaming obscenities and waving his gun around. I think—"

Another gunshot rang out. Glass shattered. Seconds later a SWAT team stormed through the glass doors.

"Tully!" It was Johnny, calling out for her.

"I'm okay." She stood up slowly, feeling a wave of pain and nausea at the movement. She saw the live truck through the broken window. Mutt was there with the camera, shooting all of it, but she couldn't see Johnny. "Seattle SWAT has just shot the glass out of the window and come in. They have the robber on the ground. I'll see if I can get close enough to ask them some questions."

She eased around the standee and moved slowly forward. She was near the cereal aisle now, and for a split second she thought about Saturday morning breakfasts at the Mularkeys'. Mrs. M. used to let her have Quisp. Only on the weekends, though.

That was her last conscious thought before she passed out.

The drive to the hospital seemed to last forever. All the way there, through the stop-and-go city traffic, Kate sat in the backseat of the smelly cab and prayed that Tully would be okay. Finally, at just past eleven o'clock, they pulled up out front. She paid the driver and ran into the brightly lit lobby.

Johnny and Mutt were already there, slumped in uncomfortable plastic chairs, looking haggard. At her entrance, Johnny stood.

She ran to him. "I saw the news. What happened?"

"A man shot her in the shoulder and she kept on broadcasting. You should have seen her, Mularkey, she was brilliant. Fearless."

Kate heard the admiration in his voice, saw it in his eyes. Any other time it might have wounded her, that obvious pride; now it pissed her off. "That's why you're in love with her, isn't it? Because she has the guts you don't. So you put her in harm's way and get her shot and you're proud of her *passion*." Her shaking voice drew the last word out like a piece of poisoned taffy. "Screw the heroics. I wasn't talking about the news. I was asking about her life. Have you even asked how she is?"

He looked startled by her outburst. "She's in surgery. She—"

"Katie!"

She heard Chad call out her name and she turned, seeing him run into the lobby. They came together as naturally as wind and rain, clinging to each other.

"How is she?" he whispered against her ear, his voice as fragile as she felt.

She drew back. "In surgery. That's all I know. But she'll be fine. Bullets can't stop a storm."

"She's not as tough as she pretends to be. We both know that, don't we, Kate?"

She swallowed, nodded. In an awkward silence they stood together, bound by the invisible threads of their mutual concern. She saw it in his eyes, as clear as day; he *did* love Tully, and he was scared. "I better go call my mom and dad. They'll want to be here."

She waited for him to respond, but he just remained there, glassy-eyed, his hands flexing into fists at his sides like a gunslinger who might soon have to draw his weapon. With a tired smile, she walked away. As she passed Johnny, she couldn't help but say, "That's how real people help each other through hard times."

At the bank of pay phones, she put in four quarters and dialed home. When her dad answered—thank God it wasn't her mother; Kate would have lost it then—she gave him the news and hung up.

She turned around and Johnny was there, waiting for her. "I'm sorry."

"You should be."

"One of the things about this business, Katie, is that you learn to compartmentalize, to put the story first. It's a hazard of the trade."

"It's always about the story with people like you and Tully." She left him standing there and went to the sofa, where she sat down. Bowing her head, she prayed again.

After a moment she felt him come up beside her. When he didn't say anything, she looked up.

He didn't move, didn't even blink, but she could see how tense he was. He seemed to be holding on to his composure by a rapidly fraying thread. "You're tougher than you look, Mularkey."

"Sometimes." She wanted to say that love gave her strength, especially during a time like this, but she was afraid to even say the word while she was looking at him.

He sat down slowly beside her. "When did you get to know me so well?"

"It's a small office."

"That's not it. No one else knows me like you do." He sighed and leaned back. "I did put her in danger."

"She wouldn't have it any other way," she conceded. "We both know that."

"I know, but . . ."

When he let his sentence trail off, she looked at him. "Do you love her?"

He didn't respond at all, just sat there, leaning back, with his eyes closed.

She couldn't stand it. Now that she'd finally dared to ask the question, she wanted it answered. "Johnny?"

He reached over for her, put an arm around her shoulder, and drew her to him. She sank into the comfort he offered. It felt as natural as breathing being beside him like this, though she knew how dangerous that feeling was.

There, saying nothing more, they sat together through the long, empty hours of the night. Waiting.

———

Tully came awake slowly, taking stock of her surroundings: white acoustic-tile ceiling, bars of fluorescent lighting, silver rails on her bed, and a tray beside her.

Memories trickled into her consciousness: Beacon Hill. The mini-mart. She remembered the gun being pointed at her. And the pain.

"You'll do anything to get attention, won't you?" Kate stood by the door, wearing a pair of baggy UW sweatpants and an old Greek Week T-shirt. As she approached the bed, tears filled her eyes. She wiped them away impatiently. "Damn. I swore I wouldn't cry."

"Thank God you're here." Tully hit the button on her bed control until she was sitting up

"Of course I'm here, you idiot. Everyone is here. Chad, Mutt, Mom, Dad. Johnny. He and my dad have been playing cards for hours and talking about the news. Mom has made at least two new afghans. We've been so worried."

"Was I good?"

Kate laughed at that even as tears spilled down her cheeks. "That would be your first question. Johnny said you kicked Jessica Savitch's ass."

"I wonder if *60 Minutes* will want to interview me."

Kate closed the distance between them. "Don't scare me like that again, okay?"

"I'll try not to."

Before Kate could say anything, the door opened and Chad stood in the doorway, holding a pair of Styrofoam coffee cups. "She's awake," he said quietly, putting the cups down on the table beside him.

"She just opened her eyes. Of course, she's more interested in her chances of winning an Emmy than in her recovery." Kate looked down at her friend. "I'll leave you two alone for a minute."

"You won't leave, though?" Tully said.

"I'll come back later, when everyone else has gone home."

"Good," Tully said. "'Cause I need you."

As soon as Kate was gone, Chad moved closer. "I thought I'd lost you."

"I'm fine," she said impatiently. "Did you see the broadcast? What do you think?"

"I think you're not fine, Tully," he said softly. "You're farther from fine than anyone I know, but I love you. And all night I've been thinking about what my life would be without you and I don't like what I see."

"Why would you lose me? I'm right here."

"Marry me, Tully."

She almost laughed, thinking it was a joke; then she saw the fear in his eyes. He really was afraid of losing her. "You mean it," she said, frowning.

"I got offered a job at Vanderbilt in Tennessee. I want you to come with me. You love me, Tully, even if you don't know it. And you need me."

"Of course I need you. Is Tennessee a top forty market?"

His rough face crumpled at that; his smile faded. "I love you," he said again, softly this time and without the kiss to seal the words and give them weight.

The door behind him opened. Mrs. Mularkey stood there, arms akimbo, wearing a cheap jean skirt and a plaid blouse with a Peter Pan collar. She looked like an extra from *Footloose*. "The nurse said five more minutes with visitors and then they're throwing us all out."

Chad bent down and kissed her. It was a beautiful, haunting kiss that somehow managed both to bring them together and highlight how far apart they could be. "I loved you, Tully," he whispered.

Loved? Had he said *loved?* As in past tense? "Chad—"

He turned away from the bed. "She's all yours, Margie."

"Sorry to kick you out," Mrs. Mularkey said.

"Don't worry about it. I think my time was up. Goodbye, Tully." He walked past her and left the room, letting the door bang shut behind him.

"Hey, little girl," Mrs. Mularkey said.

Tully surprised herself by bursting into tears.

Mrs. Mularkey just stroked her hair and let her cry.

"I guess I was really scared."

"Shhh," Mrs. Mularkey said soothingly, drying her tears with a Kleenex. "Of course you were, but we're here now. You're not alone."

Tully cried until the pressure in her chest eased and the tears dried up. Finally, feeling better, she wiped her eyes and tried to smile. "Okay. I'm ready for my lecture now."

Mrs. Mularkey gave her The Look. "Your professor, Tallulah?"

"Ex-professor. That's why I never told you. And you'd say he was too old for me."

"Do you love him?"

"How would I know?"

"You'd know."

Tully stared up at Mrs. M. For once, she felt like the older of them, the one with more experience. The Mularkeys all saw love as a durable, reliable thing, easy to recognize. Tully might be young, but she knew they were wrong. Love could be more fragile than a sparrow's bone. But she wouldn't say it out loud. Instead, all she said was, "Maybe."

Overnight, Tully became a media sensation in Seattle. Newspaperman Emmett Watson took a break from ranting about the Californication of Washington State to write a column about courage under fire and how proud we should be of Tallulah Hart's commitment to the news. Radio station KJR dedicated a whole day of rock 'n' roll songs to the "news chick who used a microphone to stop a robbery," and even *Almost Live,* the local comedy show, aired a segment that made fun of the bumbling robber and showed Tully in a Wonder Woman outfit.

Flowers and balloons poured into her hospital room, many of them signed by people who normally made the news themselves. By Wednesday, she'd had to start donating the beautiful bouquets and arrangements to other patients. The nurses in charge of her learned how to be bodyguards and bouncers in addition to their normal jobs.

"So, you're the genius here. What do I do?" She sat up in bed, going through the pile of pink While You Were Out messages that Kate had brought with her from the office. It was an impressive list of names, but she was having trouble concentrating. Her arm hurt and the sling made even little tasks difficult. Worst of all, she couldn't stop thinking about Chad's out-of-left-field proposal. "I mean: Tennessee. I might as well be in Nebraska."

"For sure."

"How can I get to the top in a place like that? Or maybe that's exactly where I could get to the top fast and get noticed by the networks."

Kate sat at the other end of the bed, her legs stretched out alongside Tully's. "Look. We've been talking about this for, like, an hour. Maybe I'm not the best person to ask, but it seems to me that at some point you've got to at least mention love."

"Your mom said I'd know if I loved him." She looked down at her bare left hand, trying to imagine a diamond ring.

"You said I was supposed to shoot you if you even thought about marriage before thirty." Kate grinned. "You want to amend that?"

"Very funny."

The bedside phone rang. Still staring at her hand, she picked it up quickly, hoping it was Chad. "Hello?"

"Tallulah Hart?"

She sighed, disappointed. "This is she."

"I'm Fred Rorbach. You may remember me . . ."

"Of course I remember you. KILO-TV. I sent you a résumé every week for my entire senior year of high school, and then I sent you tapes in college. How are you?"

"I'm fine, thanks, but I'm at KLUE-TV now, not KILO. I'm running the evening news."

"Congratulations."

"Actually, that's why I'm calling. We're probably not the first station to call you, but we feel certain we'll make the best offer."

He had her full attention now. "Oh, really?"

Kate slid off the bed and stood next to Tully, mouthing: *What's the buzz?*

Tully waved her off. "Tell me about it."

"We want to do whatever it takes to make you part of the KLUE news family. When can you come in to talk to me about this?"

"I'm being discharged right now. How about tomorrow? Ten A.M."

"We'll see you then."

Tully hung up the phone and shrieked. "That was KLUE-TV. They want to hire me!"

"Oh, my gosh," Kate said, jumping up and down. "You're going to be a star. I knew it. I can't wait to—" She stopped in the middle of her sentence; her smile fell.

"What?"

"Chad."

Tully felt something twist deep inside her. She wanted to pretend there was something to think about, a decision to be made, but she knew the truth, and so did Kate.

"You're going to be a huge star," Kate said firmly. "He'll understand."

CHAPTER
FIFTEEN

K ate pretended to focus all of her attention on driving Tully's car, but it wasn't easy. Ever since she'd picked her up from the interview, Tully hadn't stopped talking, spinning out the old little-girl dreams. *We're on our way, Kate. As soon as I get an anchor spot, I'll make sure they hire you as a reporter.*

Kate knew she should put the brakes—finally—on this dual future of theirs. She was tired of following Tully, and besides, she didn't want to quit her job. She had a reason, finally, to stay where she was.

Johnny.

How pathetic was that? He didn't love her, but she couldn't help thinking that maybe with Tully gone, she'd have a chance.

It was ridiculous, and embarrassing, but her dreams centered more on him and less on broadcasting. Not that she could admit that to anyone. Twenty-five-year-old college-educated women were expected to dream of more money and higher positions on the corporate ladder and running the very companies that had refused to hire their mothers. Husbands were to be avoided in the pre-thirty years. There was always time for marriage and children, was the common refrain. You couldn't give up *you* for *them.*

But what if you wanted *them* more than you wanted a singular, powerful you? No one ever talked about that. Kate knew that Tully would laugh at such thoughts, say Kate was stuck in the fifties. Even her mother would say she was wrong and bring up that weighted word: *regret*. She'd parrot the words that filled the pages of *Ms.* magazine—that being *just* a mother was a waste of talent. Her mother wouldn't even notice how sad she looked as she spoke, as if the life she'd chosen had been for nothing.

"Hey, you missed the turn."

"Oh. Sorry." Kate turned at the next block and circled back, pulling up in front of Chad's house. "I'll wait here. I've got *The Talisman* to finish."

Tully didn't open her door. "He'll understand why I can't marry him yet. He knows how much this means to me."

"He certainly knows," Kate agreed.

"Wish me luck."

"Don't I always?"

Tully got out and walked up to the front door.

Kate opened her paperback and dove into the story. It wasn't until much later that she looked up, noticing it had begun to rain.

Tully should have come back by now, told her to drive on home, that she'd be spending the night with Chad. Kate closed the book and got out of the car. As she walked up the cement path, she had a bad feeling that something was wrong.

She knocked twice, then opened the door.

Tully was in an empty living room, kneeling in front of the fireplace, crying.

Tully handed her a piece of paper that was splotched with tears. "Read it."

Kate sat back on her heels and looked down at the bold black handwriting.

Dear Tully,

   I was the one who recommended you to KLUE, so I know all about the job you've come to tell me about, and I'm proud of you, baby. I knew you could do it.

When I took the job at Vanderbilt I knew what it meant for us.
I hoped . . . but I knew.

You want a lot from this world, Tully. Me, I just want you.

It ain't exactly lock-and-key perfect, is it?

Here's what matters: I'll always love you.

Light the world on fire.

It was signed simply, C.

"I thought he loved me," Tully said when Kate handed her back the letter.

"It sounds like he does."

"Then why would he leave me?"

Kate looked at her friend, hearing the distant echo of all the times Tully had been abandoned by her mother. "Did you ever tell him you loved him?"

"I couldn't."

"Maybe you don't love him, then."

"Or maybe I do," Tully said, sighing. "It's just so damned hard to believe in."

That was the fundamental difference between them. Kate believed in love with all her heart; unfortunately, she'd fallen in love with a man who didn't know she existed. "What matters now is your career, anyway. There's always time for love and marriage."

"Yeah. When I've made it."

"Yeah."

"Someone will definitely love me then."

"The whole world will love you."

But later, long after Tully had said, "Screw him anyway," and laughed a little desperately, Kate couldn't expel those last words from her mind. Suddenly she was worried.

What if someday the whole world loved Tully and it still wasn't enough?

Tully had forgotten how long and lonely a night could be. For so many years, Chad had been her protection, her port. With him, she'd learned to sleep through the night, breathing peacefully, dreaming only of her bright future, and because he'd loved her, she'd slept well in her own bed, too, on their nights apart, comforted by the knowledge that she could go to him anytime.

She threw the covers back and got out of bed. A quick glance at the alarm clock on her nightstand revealed that it was just past two o'clock in the morning.

As she'd thought: long and lonely.

In the kitchen, she put a pot of water on the stove and stood there, waiting for it to boil.

Maybe she'd made a mistake. Maybe this emptiness she felt right now was love. With the life she'd led it made sense that she would notice the negative of an emotion rather than the positive. But if she did love him, what difference did it make? What would she do? Follow him to Tennessee and settle in university housing and become Mrs. Wiley? How would she be the next Jean Enersen or Jessica Savitch then?

She got a big KVTS cup out of the cupboard and poured her tea, then went to the living room, where she sat on the couch, tucking her feet beneath her, warming her cold hands on the porcelain. Fragrant steam floated upward. She closed her eyes and tried to let her mind clear.

"Can't sleep?"

She glanced up and saw Kate, who stood in front of her bedroom door, wearing the same flannel nightgown she'd worn for years. Tully usually teased her that she looked like one of the Waltons, but tonight she appreciated the familiarity. It was funny how a single garment could remind you of years together—slumber parties and makeovers and breakfasts spent watching Saturday morning cartoons. "I'm sorry if I woke you."

"You walk like an elephant. Is there more tea water?"

"The pot is on the stove."

Kate went into the kitchen and came back with a cup of tea and a box of Screaming Yellow Zonkers. Tossing the box between them, she sat down facing Tully, leaning against the arm of the sofa. "You okay?"

"My shoulder hurts like hell."

"When did you take your last pain pill?"

"I'm overdue."

Kate put down her cup, went into the bathroom, and came out with a Percodan and a glass of water.

Tully took the pill and washed it down.

"Now," Kate said, retaking her seat. "You want to talk about what's really wrong?"

"No."

"Come on, Tully. I know you're thinking about Chad, wondering if you did the right thing."

"This is the problem with forever friends. They know too much."

"Maybe."

"And what do you and I know about love anyway?"

Kate's face took on that sad, semi-judgmental look that Tully hated. It was almost a poor-Tully look. "I know about love," she said quietly. "Maybe not being in love or being loved, but I know about loving someone and how much it can hurt. I think if you really loved Chad, you'd know it, and you'd be in Tennessee right now. At least, if I loved someone, I'd know it."

"Everything is always black and white with you. How do you always know what you want?"

"You know what you want, Tully. You always have."

"So I don't get to fall in love? That's my price for fame and success? Always being alone?"

"Of course you can fall in love. You just have to let yourself. They don't call it falling for nothing."

The words should have comforted Tully; they were intended to be hopeful, she knew that, but just then, she couldn't feel that optimism. Rather, she felt colder and emptier having heard them from Kate. "There's something missing in me," she said quietly. "First my dad saw it. Whoever the hell he is; he must have taken one look at me and run. And let's not even discuss my loving mother. I'm . . . easy to leave. Why is that?"

Kate scooted down the couch, leaned against Tully just the way they used to, all those years ago on the banks of the Pilchuck. The snack box poked into her back and she pulled it out from behind her and tossed it onto the messy, newspaper-strewn coffee table. "There's nothing missing in you, Tully. It's the opposite, in fact. You're *more* than most people. You are really, really special, and if Chad didn't see that—or couldn't wait for you to be ready for him—then he wasn't the guy for you. Maybe that's a normal problem when you're with an older guy. He's ready to land when you're just taking off."

"That's true. I am young. I forgot about that. He should have understood that and waited for me. I mean, if he really loved me, how could he have left me? Could you leave someone you loved?"

"It depends."

"On what?"

"If I thought he was ever going to love me back."

"How long would you wait?"

"A long time."

That made Tully feel better for the first time since she'd read the note from Chad. "You're right. I loved him, but I guess he didn't love me. Not enough anyway."

Kate frowned. "That's not exactly what I said."

"Close enough. We're way too young to get tied down by love. How could I have forgotten that?" She gave Kate a hug. "What would I do without you?"

It wasn't until much later, after a long and sleepless night, as Tully lay in bed watching another day dawn through the window, that her own words came back to her, haunting in their intensity. *Easy to leave.*

CHAPTER SIXTEEN

From the moment Tully took the new job, Kate found herself watching her friend's life from a distance. Month after month passed with them living separate lives, connected only by place. By the following summer's end, their tiny apartment, once the container of their lives, had become something of a way station. Tully spent twelve hours a day, seven days a week, working. When she wasn't technically at work, she was chasing down leads and following stories, trying like hell to do something—anything—that would put her in front of the camera.

Without Tully, Kate's life lost its shape, and like some overwashed sweater, no amount of positioning or folding could make it right again. Her mother told her repeatedly to snap out of her funk and start dating, have some fun, but how could she date when she had no interest in the guys who had interest in her?

Tully did not suffer from the same malaise. While she still cried about Chad when they were drinking late at night, she had no problem meeting guys and bringing them home. Kate had yet to see the same guy come out of Tully's bedroom twice. According to Tully, that was the plan. She had, or so she said, no intention of falling in love. In retrospect, of course, Tully came to believe that she'd loved Chad desperately, so much so that no other man could measure up. But not enough, as Kate repeatedly pointed out, to call him or move to Tennessee.

To be honest, Kate was growing tired of her friend's drunken reminiscences about the epic love she'd had for Chad.

Kate knew what love was, how it could turn you inside out and dry up your heart. An unreturned love was a bleak and terrible thing. All day long, every day, she moved like a lesser planet in Johnny's orbit, watching him, wanting him, aching for him in lonely silence.

After that long night spent together in the hospital waiting room, Kate had thought there might actually be some hope. She'd felt that a door had opened between them; they'd talked easily, and about important things. But whatever inroads had been made in the bright light of the waiting room had faded with the dawn. She'd never forget the look on his face when he learned that Tully would be fine. It was more than relief.

That was when he'd pulled away from her.

Now finally it was time for her to pull away from him. Time to leave her little girl fantasies in the sandbox along with other forgotten toys and move on. He didn't love her. Any dreams to the contrary were simply that.

It couldn't go on anymore. That was the decision she'd made at work today, while she stood in the doorway to his office, waiting for him to notice she was there.

As soon as her workday had ended, she'd gone to the newsstand in the Public Market and purchased all the local papers. While Tully was out bar-hopping with her guy du jour, or working late, Kate intended to rechart the course of her life.

Sitting at the kitchen table, with her half-eaten dinner still in cartons around her, she opened the *Seattle Times* and turned to the classified section. There, she saw several interesting choices. Reaching for a pen, she was about to circle one when the door behind her opened.

She turned around and saw Tully in the doorway; her friend wore her dating clothes—an artfully torn sweatshirt that exposed one bare shoulder, jeans tucked into slouchy ankle boots, and a big low-slung belt. Her hair had been puffed up around her face and pulled into a bright banana clip over her left ear. An ornate set of crucifixes hung from around her neck.

Of course she had a guy with her; she was draped all over him.

"Hey, Katie," she said in a slurred I've-already-had-three-margaritas voice. "Look who I ran into."

The guy stepped out from behind the door.

Johnny.

"Hey, Mularkey," he said, smiling. "Tully wants you to come dancing with us."

She closed the newspaper with exaggerated care. "No, thanks."

"Come on, Katie. It'll be like old times," Tully said. "The Three Musketeers."

"I don't think so."

Tully let go of Johnny's hand and half stumbled, half lunged toward her. "Please," she said. "I had a bad day today. I need you."

"Don't," Kate started, but Tully wasn't listening.

"We'll go to Kells."

"Come on, Mularkey," Johnny said, moving toward her. "It'll be fun."

The way he smiled made it impossible to say no, even though she knew it was a bad idea to join them.

"Okay," she said. "I'll get dressed."

She went into her bedroom and put on a sparkly blue dress with shoulder pads and a cinch belt. By the time she came back out of her room, Johnny had Tully pressed up against the wall, with her hands over her head and his hands covering hers, and was kissing her.

"I'm ready," Kate said dully.

Tully wiggled out from underneath Johnny and grinned at her. "Excellent. Let's rock 'n' roll."

Three abreast, their arms linked, they walked out of the apartment and down the empty cobblestone street. At Kells Irish Pub, they found a small empty table close to the dance floor.

The minute Johnny left to get them drinks, Kate looked across the table. "What are you doing with him?"

Tully laughed. "What can I say? We ran into each other after work and had a few drinks. One thing led to another, and . . ." She looked sharply at Kate. "Do you *care* if I sleep with him?"

There it was. The question that mattered. Kate had no doubt that if she bared her soul and told the truth, this horrible night would be over. Tully would shut Johnny down faster than a storm door in a tornado, and she wouldn't tell Johnny why.

But what good would come of that? Kate knew how Johnny felt about Tully, how he'd always felt. He wanted a woman with passion and fire; losing Tully wouldn't make him turn to Kate. And maybe it was time for drastic measures, finally. Kate's hope had endured so much, but this—him sleeping with Tully—would be the end of it.

She lifted her gaze, praying her eyes were dry. "Come on, Tully, you know better than that."

"Are you sure? Do you want—"

"No. But . . . he cares about you, you do know that, right? You could break his heart."

Tully laughed at that. "You Catholic girls worry about everyone, don't you?"

Before Kate could answer, Johnny returned to the table with two margaritas and a bottle of beer. Setting them down, he took Tully's hand and dragged her onto the floor. There, they melted into the crowd, where he took her into his arms and kissed her.

Kate reached for her drink. She had no idea what that kiss meant to Tully, but she knew what it meant to Johnny, and the knowledge seeped through her like some kind of poison.

For the next two hours, she sat with them, drinking heavily, pretending she was having fun. All the while something inside of her was slowly dying.

At some point during the endless, excruciating evening, Tully went to the bathroom and left Johnny and Kate alone. She tried to think of something to say to him, but frankly, she didn't dare make eye contact. With his damp, curling hair and flushed cheeks, he looked so damned sexy it made her chest ache.

"She's really something," he said. Behind him, the band finished their song and turned to their sheet music for inspiration. "I was starting to think it would never happen . . . her and me," he said, sipping his beer, gazing back toward the bathroom, as if he could draw her back by will alone.

"You should be careful," Kate said almost too quietly to be heard. She knew the words, and the warning, would reveal something of her heart, but she couldn't help herself. Johnny might wear the suit of a cynic at work, but at the hospital she'd learned the truth. Inside, where it mattered, he was an idealist. No one bruised as easily as a believer. She should know.

Johnny leaned toward her. "What was that, Mularkey?"

She shook her head. There was no way she could say it again, and besides, Tully was back.

Much later, when she lay in her lonely bedroom, listening to the sound of lovemaking coming from another room, she finally cried.

In the months since their party night at Kells Pub, Kate was not the only one to notice the change in Johnny. As autumn settled into the city and stripped it of color, the mood in the office became sullen and quiet. Mutt kept completely to himself, cleaning and rearranging his equipment, filing negatives in notebooks. Carol, who had been cajoled back to work after Tully's departure, stayed in her own office, with the door shut, barely saying a word to everyone, even when she got her coffee.

No one said a word about Johnny's appearance, but everyone saw that he seemed lately to be simply rolling out of bed and coming to work. His hair was too long and beginning to curl in all kinds of weird ways. He hadn't shaved in days; his beard grew in dark, shadowed patches on his hollowed cheeks, and his clothes often didn't match.

The first few times he'd come to work this way, they'd rallied around him like geese, clucking their worry. Quietly but firmly he'd shut the door to his office, saying he was fine. Mutt had mounted an offensive that began with an offer of pot and ended with, "Whatever, man. I'm here if you wanna talk."

Carol had tried in her own way to swim the invisible moat Johnny had ringed around himself; her attempts failed as utterly as Mutt's.

The only one who didn't try to reach Johnny was Kate, and she was the only one who knew what the problem was.

Tully.

Just that morning, as they'd been having breakfast, Tully had said, "Johnny keeps calling me. Should I go out with him again?"

Fortunately for Kate, it had turned out to be a rhetorical question.

Tully answered it herself. "No way. I want a relationship like I want a lethal injection. I thought he knew that."

Now Kate sat at her desk, supposedly filing their new insurance information.

She and Johnny were alone in the office for the first time in days. Carol and Mutt were out on assignment.

She got up slowly, walked to his closed office door. It made no sense for her to go to him; certainly if the tables were turned he wouldn't have gone to her, but he was hurting right now, and she couldn't stand that. After a long minute, she knocked.

"Come in."

She opened the door.

He was at his desk, hunched over, writing furiously on a yellow legal pad. Hair fell across his profile; he impatiently tucked it behind his ear and looked up at her. "Yeah, Mularkey?"

She went to the fridge in the corner of his office and got two Henry Weinhard's beers. Opening them, she handed one to him, then sat down on the edge of his cluttered desk. "You look like a man who is drowning," she said simply.

He took the beer. "It shows, huh?"

"It shows."

He glanced at the door. "Are we alone?"

"Mutt and Carol left about ten minutes ago."

Johnny took a long drink of his beer and leaned back in his chair. "She won't return my phone calls."

"I know."

"I don't get it. That night—our night together, I mean—I thought . . ."

"Do you want the truth?"

"I know the truth."

They sat there in silence for a long time, each sipping beer.

"It's fucking awful to want someone you can't have."

And with those few words, Kate knew: she had never had a chance with him. "Yeah, it is." She paused, looking down at him. It was time—past time, really—for her to let go of this dream and move on. "I'm sorry, Johnny," she finally said, getting up from the edge of his desk.

"What are you sorry about?"

She wished she had the nerve to answer him, to tell him how she felt, but some things were better left unspoken.

Seated in an uncomfortable chair in an unfamiliar office, Kate stared out the window at a bare, leafless tree and the gray sky behind it. She wondered idly when the last tangerine-colored leaves had fallen away.

"Well, Ms. Mularkey, you have a very impressive résumé for someone your age. May I ask why you're considering a career change to advertising?"

Kate tried to look relaxed. She'd dressed carefully for today in a plain black wool gabardine suit, with a white blouse and a silk paisley tie tamed into a floppy bow at her throat. She hoped it was a look that said professional through and through. "In my years in TV news I've learned a few things about myself and a few things about the world. The news, as you know, is go-go-go. We're always moving at top speed, just getting the facts and then moving on. I often find myself more interested in what comes after the story than the story itself. I'm better, I believe, at long-range thinking and planning. Details, rather than broad strokes. And I'm a good writer. I'd like to learn more about that, but I won't do it in ten-second sound bites."

"You've given this a lot of thought."

"I have."

The woman across the desk leaned back, studying Kate through a pair of trendy, bead-encrusted glasses. She seemed to like what she saw. "Okay, Ms. Mularkey. I'll discuss this with my partners and we'll get back to you. Just so I know, when could you start work?"

"I'd need to give two-weeks notice and then I'd be ready to go."

"Excellent." The woman stood. "Do you need a parking voucher?"

"No, thank you." Kate shook the woman's hand firmly and left the office.

Outside, Pioneer Square huddled beneath a stern charcoal-hued sky. Cars clogged the narrow, old-fashioned streets, but very few pedestrians walked past the brick-faced buildings. Even the homeless people who usually slept on these park benches and bummed smokes and money from passersby were somewhere else on this cold afternoon.

Kate walked briskly along First Avenue, buttoning up her old college coat as she went. She caught the uptown bus and got off at the stop in front of the office at exactly 3:57.

Surprisingly, the main office room was empty. Kate hung up her coat and tossed her purse and briefcase under her desk, then went around the corner to Johnny's office. "I'm back."

He was on the phone, but he motioned for her to come in. "Come on," he was saying in an exasperated voice, "how am I supposed to help you with that?" He was silent for a moment, frowning. Then, "Fine. But you owe me one." He hung up the phone and smiled at Kate, but it wasn't the old smile, the one that had taken her breath away. She hadn't seen that one since the night with Tully.

"You're wearing a suit," he said. "Don't think I haven't noticed. Around here, that means only two things, and since I know you aren't anchoring the news . . ."

"Mogelgaard and Associates."

"The ad agency? What position did you apply for?"

"Account executive."

"You'd be good at that."

"Thanks, but I don't have the job yet."

"You will."

She waited for him to say more, but he just stared at her, as if something troubled him. No doubt she reminded him of the night with Tully. "Well, I better get back to work."

"Wait. I'm working on this story for Mike Hurtt. I could use some help."

"Sure."

For the next few hours, they sat huddled together at his desk, working and reworking the problematic script. Kate tried to keep her distance from him and told herself never to make eye contact. Both resolutions failed. By the time they finished work, night had fallen outside; the quiet outer offices were banked in shadows.

"I owe you dinner," Johnny said, putting his papers away. "It's almost eight."

"You don't owe me anything," she answered. "I was just doing my job."

He looked at her. "How will I get along without you?"

Months ago, when there was still hope, she would have blushed at a moment like this. Maybe even a week ago she would have. "I'll help you hire someone."

"You think replacing you will be easy?"

She had no answer for that. "I'm going now—"

"I owe you dinner. That's all there is to it. Now get your coat. Please."

"Okay."

They went downstairs and got into his car. In minutes, they were pulling up to a beautiful cedar-shaked houseboat on Lake Union.

"Where are we?" Kate asked.

"My house. Don't worry, I'm not going to make you dinner. I just want to change my clothes. You're all dressed up."

Kate steeled herself against the emotion knocking on her heart. She would not let it in. For too long she'd let herself be pulverized by dreams of a happy ending that wasn't to be. She followed him down the dock and into a house that was surprisingly spacious.

Johnny immediately went to the fireplace, where a fire was already set. He bent down, lighting the newspapers and kindling fire roared to life. Then he turned to her. "Would you like a drink?"

"Rum and Coke?"

"Perfect." He went to the kitchen, poured two drinks, and returned. "Here you go. I'll be right back."

She stood there a moment, uncertain of what to do. She glanced around the living room, noticing how few photographs he had. On the television cabinet there was a single picture of a middle-aged couple, dressed in brightly colored clothing, squatting together in a jungle-looking setting with children clustered around them.

"My parents," Johnny said, coming up behind her. "Myrna and William."

She spun around, feeling as if she'd been caught snooping. "Where do they live?" she said, going to the couch, sitting down. She needed distance between them.

"They were missionaries. They were killed in Uganda by Amin's death squads."

"Where were you?"

"When I was sixteen, they sent me to school in New York. That was the last time I saw them."

"So they were idealists, too."

"What do you mean, 'too'?"

She saw no reason to put it into words, this knowledge she'd gleaned over the years, cobbled together into an image of his life. "It doesn't matter. You were lucky to be raised by people who believed in something."

He stared at her, frowning.

"Is that why you became a war correspondent? To fight in your own way?"

He sighed and shook his head, then walked over to the sofa and sat down beside her. The way he looked at her, as if she were somehow watery or out of focus, made her heartbeat speed up. "How do you do that?"

"What?"

"Know me?"

She smiled, hoping it didn't look as brittle as it felt. "We've worked together a long time."

It was a long moment before he said, "Why are you really quitting, Mularkey?"

She leaned back a little. "Remember when you said it was awful to want something you can't have? I'm never going to be a kick-ass reporter or a first-rate producer. I don't live and breathe the news. I'm tired of not being good enough."

"I said, it was awful to want some*one* you couldn't have."

"Well . . . it's all the same."

"Is it?" He put his drink on the coffee table.

She shifted her weight to face him, pulled her legs up underneath her. "I know about wanting someone."

He looked skeptical. No doubt he was thinking about the times Tully teased her about never dating. "Who?"

She knew she should lie, gloss over the question, but just now, with him so close, she felt a wave of longing that nearly overwhelmed her. God help her, but that door seemed opened again. Though she knew it wasn't, knew it was an illusion, she walked through it anyway. "You."

He drew back; it was obvious that he'd never imagined this. "You never . . ."

"How could I? I know how you feel about Tully."

She waited for him to say something, but he just looked at her. In the silence, she could make up anything. He hadn't said no, hadn't laughed. Maybe that meant something.

For years, she'd expended effort to keep the faucet of her longing for him turned off, but now that he so close, there was no holding back. This was her last chance. "Kiss me, Johnny. Show me I'm wrong to want you."

"I wouldn't want to hurt you. You're a nice girl, and I'm not looking for—"

"What if not kissing you hurts me?"

"Katie . . ."

For once, she wasn't Mularkey. She leaned closer. "Now who's afraid? Kiss me, Johnny."

Just before her lips touched his, she thought she heard him say, "This is a bad idea," but before she could reassure him, he was kissing her back.

It wasn't the first time Kate had been kissed; it wasn't even the first time she'd been kissed by a man she cared about, and yet, absurdly, she started to cry.

He tried to pull away when he noticed her tears, but she wouldn't let him. One moment they were on the sofa, making out like teenagers; the next thing she knew, she was on the floor in front of the fire, naked.

He knelt beside her, still clothed. Shadows concealed half his body and highlighted the sharp angles and hollows of his face. "Are you sure?"

"That would have been a good question *before* my clothes came off." Smiling, she angled up and began unbuttoning his shirt.

He made a sound that was part desperation, part surrender, and let her undress him. Then he took her in his arms again.

His kisses were different now, harsher, deeper, more erotic. She felt her body responding in a way it never had before; it was as if she became nothing and everything, just a ragged collection of nerve endings. His touch was her torture, her salvation.

Sensations became everything, all that she was, all that she cared about; pain, pleasure, frustration. Even her breathing wasn't her own. She was gasping, choking, crying out for him to stop, and not to stop, and to make it go on and make it go away.

She felt her body arching up, as if the whole of her were reaching for something, needing it with a desperation that made her ache, but she didn't even know what it was.

And then he was inside her, hurting her. She gasped at the suddenness of the pain but made no sound. Instead, she clung to him, kissing him and moving with him until the pain dissolved and there was none of her left; there was only this, the feelings of them where they came together, the sharp, aching need for something more . . .

I love you, she thought, holding him, rising to meet him. The withheld words filled her head, became a soundtrack to the rhythm of their bodies.

"Katie," he cried out, thrusting deep inside her.

Her body exploded, like some star in space, breaking apart, floating away. Time stopped for a moment, then settled slowly back in place.

"Wow," she said, flopping back onto the warm carpet. For the first time in her life, she got what all the hype was about.

He stretched out beside her, his sweat-dampened body tucked in close to hers. Keeping one arm around her, he stared up at the ceiling. Like hers, his breathing was ragged.

"You were a virgin," he said, sounding frighteningly far away.

"Yes," was all she could say.

She rolled onto her side, slid her naked leg over him. "Is it always like that?"

When he turned to her, she saw something in his blue eyes that confused her: fear.

"No, Katie," he said after a long time. "It's not."

Kate woke in Johnny's arms. They both lay on their backs, with the sheets puddled around their hips. She stared up at the planked ceiling, feeling the heavy, unfamiliar weight of his hand between her naked breasts.

Dawn's pale glow slanted through the open window, collecting in a buttery smear on the hardwood floor. The endless slapping of waves against the pilings echoed the slow and steady beat of her heart.

She didn't know what she was supposed to do now, how she was supposed to act. From their first kiss, this had been a magical and unexpected gift. They'd made love three times during the night, the last time only a few hours ago. They'd kissed, they'd made omelettes and eaten in front of the fire, they'd talked about their families and their job and their dreams. Johnny had even told a series of extremely stupid jokes.

What they hadn't talked about was tomorrow, and it was here now, as much a presence between them as the soft sheets and the sound of their breathing.

She was glad she'd waited to make love, even though waiting for the right guy was unfashionable these days. Everything about last night had rocked her world, just as the poets predicted.

But what if Johnny didn't think she was the right girl? He hadn't said he loved her—of course he hadn't—and without those words, how was a woman to put passion in context?

Was she supposed to get dressed and sneak out and pretend it never happened? Or should she go downstairs and make breakfast and pray to God that last night was a beginning and not an ending?

When she felt him stir beside her, she tensed up.

"Morning," he said in a gravelly voice.

She didn't know how to play coy or act indifferent. She'd loved him too long to pretend otherwise. What mattered now was that they didn't just get up and go their separate ways. "Tell me something I don't know about you."

He stroked her upper arm. "Hmmm. I used to be an altar boy."

It was surprisingly easy to picture him like that, a young, skinny boy, with his hair slicked back from his face with water, walking carefully up the aisle. The image made her giggle. "My mother would love you."

"Now tell me something about you."

"I'm a science fiction geekess. *Star Wars, Star Trek, Dune.* I love them all."

"I would have pegged you for a romance reader."

"That, too. Now tell me something that matters. Why did you quit reporting?"

"You always go right for deep water, don't you?" He sighed. "I think you've figured it out anyway. El Salvador. I went down there like some kind of white knight, ready to shine my light on the truth. And then I saw what was happening . . ."

She said nothing, just kissed the curl of his shoulder.

"My folks had hidden so much from me. I thought I was prepared, but you can't be. It's blood and death and body parts being blown off. It's dead kids in the street and boys with machine guns. I got captured . . ." His voice faded away; he cleared his throat and reinforced it. "I don't know why they let me live, but they did. Lucky me. I tucked my tail between my legs and ran home."

"You didn't do anything to be ashamed of."

"I ran like a coward. And I failed. So now you know it all, why I'm in Seattle."

"Do you think it changes how I feel about you?"

It was a moment before he said, "We need to take this slow, Katie."

"I know." She rolled over, so that she was pressed against him. She tried to memorize everything about his face and how he looked first thing in the morning. She saw the shadow of a beard that had grown in their sleeping hours and thought: *Already, changes.*

He tucked the hair behind her ear. "I don't want to hurt you."

She wanted to say simply, *Then don't,* but this wasn't a time for simple answers or pretense. Honesty mattered now. "I'll take the risk of getting hurt if you will," she said evenly.

A hint of a smile played at the edges of his mouth, but she didn't see it in his eyes. In fact, he looked more than a little worried. "I knew you'd be dangerous."

She didn't understand. "Me? You must be joking. No one has ever thought I was dangerous."

"I do."

"Why?"

He didn't answer; instead, he leaned forward just enough to kiss her. She closed her eyes, waiting for it. She wasn't sure, but maybe, just before his lips touched hers, he said, "Because you're the kind of girl a guy could fall in love with."

He didn't sound particularly happy as he said it.

Outside her front door, Kate paused. Only moments before she'd been flying high, reveling in the night spent in Johnny's arms, but now she was back in the real world, where she'd just slept with a man her best friend had slept with first.

What would Tully say?

She opened the door and went inside. On this gray, rainy morning, the apartment was surprisingly quiet. She tossed her purse on the kitchen table and made herself a cup of tea.

"Where the hell have you been?"

She turned, flinched.

Tully stood there, her hair dripping wet, wearing nothing but a towel. "I almost called the cops last night. Where— You're wearing the suit from yesterday." A slow, knowing smile crept across her face. "Did you spend the night with someone? Oh, my *God*, you did. You're blushing." Tully laughed. "And I thought you were going to die a virgin." She grabbed Kate's arm and dragged her over to the sofa. "Talk."

Kate stared at her best friend, wishing she'd come home after Tully had left for work. This needed thought, planning. Tully could ruin it all with a word, a look. *He's mine*, her friend could say, and what would Kate do?

"Talk," Tully said again, bumping her.

Kate took a deep breath. "I'm in love."

"Whoa there, Penelope Pitstop. Love? After one night?"

It was now or never, and though never sounded good, there was no point in putting off the inevitable. "No," she said. "I've loved him for years."

"Who?"

"Johnny."

"*Our* Johnny?"

Kate refused to let the pronoun wound her. "Yes. Last night—"

"He slept with me, what? A few months ago, then wouldn't stop calling. He's on the rebound, Katie. He can't be in love with you."

Kate tried not to let the word *rebound* find purchase, but it did. "I knew you'd make it about you."

"But . . . he's your boss, for God's sake."

"I quit. I'm starting a job in advertising in two weeks."

"Oh, great. Now you're giving up your career for a guy."

"We both know I'm not good enough to make it at the networks. That's your dream, Tully. It always was." She could see that her friend wanted to argue the point; she saw, too, that any argument would be a lie. "I'm in love with him, Tully," she said finally. "I have been for years."

"Why didn't you tell me?"

"I was scared."

"Of what?"

Katie couldn't answer.

Tully stared at her. In those dark, expressive eyes, she saw everything: fear, worry, and jealousy. "This has disaster written all over it."

"I didn't trust Chad all those years ago, remember? But I put it aside because you needed me to."

"Speaking of love disasters."

"Can you be happy for me?"

Tully stared at her, and though she finally smiled, it wasn't the real thing and both of them knew it. "I'll try."

Rebound. The word, like the image it represented, kept springing into Kate's mind.

He slept with me, what? A few months ago . . .

. . . can't be in love with you . . .

As soon as Tully left the apartment, Kate called in sick to work and crawled into bed. She hadn't been there more than twenty minutes when a knock at the front door startled her out of her thoughts. "Damn it, Tully," she muttered, pulling on her pink velour robe and slipping into her bunny slippers. "Can't you ever remember your key?" She opened the door.

Johnny stood there. "You don't look sick."

"Liar. I look terrible."

He reached forward, untied the belt, and pushed the robe off her shoulders. It fell around her feet in a poufy pink puddle. "A flannel nightgown. How sexy." He closed the door behind them.

She tried not to think about her conversation with Tully—

rebound

can't love you

—but the words chased one another across her mind, tripping every now and then over his: . . . *don't want to hurt you.*

She saw now, suddenly, the danger she'd accepted so naïvely. He could shatter her heart and there was no way to protect herself.

"I thought you'd be happy to see me," he said.

"I told Tully about us."

"Oh. And was there a problem?"

"She thinks I'm a rebound girl."

"She does, does she?"

Kate swallowed hard. "Do you love her?"

"That's what this is about?" He swept her up into his arms, carrying her toward her bedroom as if she weighed nothing at all. Once they were in bed, he began unbuttoning her nightgown, planting kisses along the way. "It doesn't matter," he whispered against her bare skin. "She didn't love me."

She closed her eyes and let him rock her world again, but when it was over and she was curled against him again, the uncertainty returned. She might not be the most experienced girl in the world, but neither was she the most naïve, and there was one thing of which she was sure: it mattered whether Johnny had loved Tully.

It mattered very much.

CHAPTER
SEVENTEEN

Falling in love was everything Kate had dreamed it would be. By the time spring came again, painting the landscape with vibrant color, she and Johnny were an honest-to-God couple; they spent most of their weekends together and as many weeknights as possible. In March she'd brought him home to meet the parents and they'd been ecstatic. A nice Irish Catholic boy with a great career and a good sense of humor who liked to play board games and cards. Dad called him a "good egg" and Mom declared him to be perfect. "Definitely worth waiting for," she'd whispered at the end of the first meeting.

For his part, Johnny had fit into the Mularkey clan as if he'd been born into it. He'd never admitted it, but Kate was certain that he liked being part of a family again after so many solitary years. Although they didn't talk about the future, they enjoyed every minute of the present.

But that was all about to change.

Now she was in bed, staring up at the ceiling. Beside her, Johnny lay sleeping. It was just past four o'clock in the morning and already she'd thrown up twice. There was no point in putting off the inevitable any longer.

She peeled the covers back gently, careful not to wake him, and got out of bed. Barefoot, she crossed the thick pad of carpet and went into his bathroom, closing the door behind her.

Opening her purse, she dug through the clutter and withdrew the package she'd purchased yesterday. Then she opened the package and followed the directions.

Slightly less than two hours later, she had an answer: pink for pregnant.

She stared down at it. Her first ridiculous thought was that for a girl who'd dreamed of becoming a mother, she was damned close to crying.

Johnny wouldn't be happy about this. He was nowhere near ready for fatherhood. He hadn't even said he loved her yet.

She loved him so much, and everything had been so great for the past few months. Still, she couldn't shake the feeling that it was fragile, this relationship of theirs, that the balance was tenuous. A baby could ruin them.

She hid the package and indicator back in her purse—the extraordinary thing mixed in the ordinary debris of her life—and took a long hot shower. By the time she was dressed and ready for work, the alarm was going off. She went to the bed and sat beside him, stroking his hair as he woke up.

He smiled up at her, said, "Hey," sleepily.

She wanted to say simply, *I'm pregnant,* but the admission wouldn't come. Instead, she said, "I've got to go in early today. The Red Robin account."

He looped a hand around the back of her neck and pulled her down for a kiss. When it was over, she meant to ease away. "I love you," she whispered.

He kissed her again. "And that makes me the luckiest guy in the world."

She said goodbye as if this were just another in the string of mornings they'd woken up together, and went to work. In her office, she slammed her door shut and stood there, trying not to cry.

"I'm pregnant," she said to the ad-covered walls.

Now, if only she could say it to Johnny. She ought to be able to say anything to him, wasn't that how love was supposed to work? God knew she loved him enough, maybe even more than enough. She could no longer imagine a life without him. She loved the routine of their lives, the way they often had breakfast together in the kitchen of his houseboat, standing side by side in front of the sink, or the way they sat in bed at night, snuggled together, watching Arsenio Hall. When he kissed her, whether it was a quiet goodnight kiss or a passionate let's-start-something one, her heart always kicked into high gear. They talked all the time, about anything and everything; until today, she would have said there were no words she couldn't say to him.

For most of the day, she moved forward on autopilot, but somewhere around four o'clock, her will failed her. Picking up the phone, she dialed the familiar number and waited impatiently.

"Hello?" Tully said.

"It's me. I'm having a crisis."

"I'll be there in twenty," Tully said without hesitation.

For the first time all day, Kate smiled. Just being with Tully would help; it always had. Fifteen minutes later, she tidied up her already neat desk, grabbed her purse, and left her office.

Outside, the sun was a pale white ball in a washed-out blue sky. A few hardy tourists walked up and down Pioneer Square. Across the street, the homeless people who lived in Occidental Park lay sprawled out on the cobblestoned ground and the ironwork benches, huddled beneath filthy blankets and old sleeping bags. The trees around them were in full bloom.

Kate buttoned up her coat just as Tully pulled up in her brand-new metallic-blue Corvette convertible.

As always, the car made Kate both shake her head and smile. It was so damned . . . phallic, and yet somehow Tully fit it perfectly. Her wool pants and silk blouse were even the same color blue as the car.

Kate hurried around to the passenger side and got in.

"Where do you want to go?"

"Surprise me," Kate answered.

"You got it."

In no time at all, they'd snaked through the downtown traffic, rocketed over the West Seattle Bridge, and arrived at a restaurant on Alki Beach. On this faded spring day the place was empty, and they were seated instantly at a table overlooking the steely Sound.

"Thank God you called," Tully said. "This was the week from hell. They've had me traveling to every armpit town in the state. Last week I interviewed a guy in Cheney who's built a truck that runs on wood. I kid you not. He has a stove in the bed that's the size of an aircraft carrier and it takes a half a cord a week. I could barely see the damn truck through the black smoke it belched out, and he wanted me to report that he'd discovered the future. Tomorrow I'm supposed to go to Lynden to interview some Hutterite chick who won thirty-two blue ribbons at the fair. Yippee. Oh, and last week—"

"I'm pregnant."

Tully's mouth dropped open. "Are you kidding me?"

"Do I look like I'm kidding?"

"Holy shit . . ." Tully leaned back in her seat, looking stunned. "I thought you were on the pill."

"I am. And I've never missed one."

"Pregnant. Wow. What did Johnny say?"

"I haven't told him yet."

"What are you going to do?" The question was heavy, weighed down as it was by the unspoken option.

"I don't know." Kate looked up, met Tully's gaze. "But I know what I'm not going to do."

Tully stared at her for a long time, saying nothing. In those amazingly expressive dark eyes, Kate saw a parade of emotions—disbelief, fear, sadness, worry, and finally, love. "You'll be a great mother, Katie."

She felt the start of tears. It was what she wanted; now, here, for the first time she dared to admit it to herself. That was what a best friend did: hold up a mirror and show you your heart. "He's never said he loved me, Tully."

"Oh. Well . . . You know Johnny."

With that, Kate felt the past rear up between them. She knew Tully was feeling it, too, this thing they tried so hard to forget: their shared knowledge of John Ryan. "You're like him," she finally said. "How will he feel when he finds out?"

"Trapped."

It was exactly what Kate had told herself. "So what do I do?"

"You're asking me? The woman who can't keep a goldfish alive for more than a week?" Tully laughed; it sounded only the tiniest bit bitter. "You go home and tell the man you love that he's going to be a dad."

"You make it sound so easy."

Tully reached across the table, taking her hand. "Trust him, Katie."

She knew it was the best advice she could get. "Thanks."

"Now let's talk about the important shit, like names. You don't have to name her after me. Tallulah sort of sucks. No wonder dopehead picked it, but my middle name is Rose. That's not so bad . . ."

The rest of the afternoon passed in quiet conversation. They avoided talk of the baby and focused on inconsequential things. By the time they'd left the restaurant and driven back to town, Kate's desperation had eased. It wasn't gone, but having a plan of action helped.

When Tully parked behind the houseboat, Kate gave her friend a fierce hug and said goodbye.

Alone in Johnny's house, she changed into a pair of sweats and an old T-shirt, then went into the living room to wait for him.

As she sat there, knees pressed together (too late for that), her hands clasped, she listened to the ordinary sounds of this life she'd grown accustomed to—the slap of the waves on the pilings around her, the squawking of seagulls, the ever-present chug of a motorboat going past. It had never felt quite so fragile before, or so bittersweet. All her life she'd imagined love as a durable thing, a polyester emotion that could handle the wear and tear of everyday action, but now she saw how dangerous that perception was. It lulled you, put you at risk.

Across the room, the lock clicked and the door opened. Johnny smiled when he saw her. "Hey, there. I called you before I left the office. Where were you?"

"I played hooky with Tully."

"Happy hour, huh?" He pulled her up into his arms and kissed her.

She let herself melt against him. When she put her arms around him, she found that she couldn't let go.

She held on so tightly he had to actually pull her away. "Katie?" he said, stepping back enough to look down at her. "What's wrong?"

In the last hour she'd imagined a dozen different ways to tell him, to ease him into the news, but now, standing here in front of him, she saw what a waste all those plans were. This wasn't a gift that could be wrapped in pretty paper and she wasn't the kind of woman who could stay silent.

"I'm pregnant," she said in as firm a voice as she could manage.

He stared at her for an eternity, uncomprehending. "You're what? How did that happen?"

"The normal way, I'm pretty sure."

He let out a long, slow breath and sank to the sofa. "A baby."

"I didn't mean for it to happen." She sat down beside him. "I don't want you to feel trapped."

The smile he gave her was a stranger's, not the one she loved, that crinkled up his eyes and made her smile back. "You know how much I want to just pick up and leave when I'm finally ready. Follow a big story and redeem myself. It's been in my head for so long . . . ever since I screwed up in El Salvador."

She swallowed hard, nodded. Her eyes stung, but she refused to draw attention to her tears by wiping them away. "I know."

He reached out, touched her flat stomach. "But I couldn't just leave anymore, could I?"

"Because of the baby?"

"Because I love you," he said simply.

"I love you, too, but I don't want to—"

He slid off the couch, positioned himself on one knee, and she drew in a sharp breath. "Kathleen Scarlett Mularkey, will you marry me?"

She wanted to say yes, scream it, but she didn't dare. Fear was still too much a part of how she felt. So she had to say instead, "Are you sure, Johnny?"

And then, finally, she saw his smile. "I'm sure."

Kate had taken Tully's advice—of course—and gone for timeless elegance. Her wedding dress was an ivory silk gown with a heavily beaded bodice and an off-the-shoulder neckline. Her hair, carefully lightened in a trio of blonds, had been drawn back from her face and coiled into a Grace Kelly twist. The veil, when she put it on, would float over her face and fall down to her shoulders like a sparkling cloud. For the first time in her life she felt movie-star beautiful. Mom thought so, too; she took one look and started to cry. A few moments ago she had hugged Kate fiercely, kissed her cheek, and gone into the church, leaving Kate and Tully alone for the first time all day.

Now, standing in front of a full-length mirror that captured her fairy-tale reflection, Kate glanced over at Tully, who'd been uncharacteristically quiet on this grand poobah of hair and makeup days. Dressed in the pale pink strapless taffeta bridesmaid's gown, she looked vaguely out of place and fidgety.

"You look like you're gearing up for a funeral instead of a wedding."

Tully looked at her, trying to make a smile look real, but they'd been friends too long to pass each other such counterfeit emotions. "Are you sure about getting married? I mean really sure? There's no—"

"I'm sure."

Tully appeared unconvinced; more than that, she looked afraid. "Good," she said, biting her lower lip, nodding stiffly. "'Cause it's forever."

"You know what else is forever?"

"Dirty diapers."

Kate reached out for Tully's hand, noticing how cold her friend's skin was. How could she convince Tully that this was the Y in their lives, the inevitable separation, but not an abandonment? "Us," she said pointedly. "We'll be friends through jobs and kids and marriages." She grinned. "I'm sure I'll outlast several of your husbands."

"Oh, that's nice." Tully laughed, bumping her shoulder into Kate's. "You think I won't be able to stay married."

Kate leaned against her friend. "I think you'll do whatever you want, Tully. You're such a bright light. Me, I just want Johnny. I love him so much it hurts sometimes."

"How can you say you only want Johnny? You have a great career. Someday you're going to be running that agency. This pregnancy won't throw you off course. These days women can have it all."

Kate smiled. "That's you, Tully. And I'm so proud of you that I can't stand it. Sometimes at Safeway I tell complete strangers that I'm your friend. But I need you to be proud of me, too. No matter what I do. Or don't do."

"I'm always there for you. You know that."

"I know."

They stared at each other, and in that moment, with both of them dressed up like princesses and standing in front of a mirror, they were fourteen years old again, planning the whole of their lives.

Tully finally smiled. This time it was the real thing. "When are you going to tell your mom about the baby?"

"After I'm married." Kate laughed. "I'll confess to God, but I'm not telling my mom till I'm Mrs. Ryan."

For a single, glorious moment, time simply stopped. They were TullyandKate again; girls sharing secrets.

Then the door opened.

"It's time," Dad said. "The church is full. Tully: you're up."

Tully gave Kate a big hug, then hurried out of the dressing room.

Kate stared at her dad in his rented tux, with his newly cut hair, and felt a rolling wave of love for him. Through the doors, they heard the music start up.

"You look beautiful," he said after a moment. His voice was uneven, not his usual sound at all.

She went to him, looked up, remembering a hundred moments in the space of a heartbeat. The way he read her bedtime stories when she was little and tucked spare money in her back pocket when she was older, the way he sang off-key at church.

He touched her chin, tilted her face up. That was when she saw the tears in his eyes. "You'll always be my little girl, Katie Scarlett. Don't you forget that."

"I could never forget it."

Inside, the music changed to "Here Comes the Bride." They linked arms and walked toward the church's double doors. One halting step after another, they made their way down the aisle.

Johnny stood at the altar, waiting for her. When he took her hand in his and smiled down at her, she felt that swelling in her chest again, the sweet knowing that this was the man for her. No matter what else would happen to her in this life, she knew that she was marrying her true love, and that made her one of the lucky ones.

From then on, the night took on the hazy, insubstantial edges of a dream. They stood at the end of the receiving line, kissing friends and relatives and collecting their well-wishes.

The world felt wide open. Anything was possible. Kate found that she couldn't stop smiling or crying.

When the music started—Madonna's "Crazy for You"—Johnny found her in the crowd and reached for her hand.

"Hey, Mrs. Ryan."

Touch me once and you'll know it's true . . .

She moved into the circle of his arms, loving the feel of him against her.

All around them, people stepped back, making room for the newly-weds to dance. She could feel them watching, smiling, saying how romantic the song was and how beautiful the bride looked.

It was the Cinderella-at-the-ball moment that Kate had dreamed of all her life. "I love you," she said.

"You'd better," he whispered, kissing her gently.

When the song ended, the audience burst into applause. Champagne glasses were raised alongside bottles of beer and cocktail glasses; guests shouted, "To the Ryans!"

It wasn't until the tail end of the most magical of nights that Kate's smile first left her. She was at the bar, getting another glass of sparkling cider and talking to her Aunt Georgia, when it happened.

Later, over the years that followed, especially in troubled times, she'd wonder why she looked up at precisely that instant, or why, with all the people in the room, dancing and talking and laughing, she'd had to look up at just that moment to see Johnny, standing all by himself, sipping a beer.

And looking at Tully.

CHAPTER EIGHTEEN

I don't know who writes these directions, but I don't think the assholes speak English."

Kate smiled and stepped cautiously down the ladder. They were in the downstairs bedroom of the houseboat, readying the nursery. She could tell that Tully was about thirty seconds away from throwing the screwdriver at the freshly painted wall. "Let me look at the sheet."

From her place in the middle of the floor, surrounded by piles of white sticks and boards and groupings of screws and washers, Tully held up the long, wrinkled piece of paper. "Be my guest."

Kate studied the ridiculously complicated directions. "We start with that long flat piece. It dovetails into that piece, see? Then you screw that part on there . . ."

For the next two hours, they sat or stood, hunkered together and hunched over, putting together the most complicated crib of all time.

When it was done, and tucked in place against the sunshine-yellow wall with the Winnie-the-Pooh border, they stood back and admired it. "What would I do without you, Tully?"

Tully put an arm around her. "Thankfully you'll never have to know. Come on, I'm making margaritas."

"I can't drink. You know that."

Tully grinned at her. "My deepest apologies for that, but you'll notice that I have no bun in the oven. I don't believe I'm within eight hundred miles of a bun, in fact. So, not only can I have a margarita, but after putting together that crib—a job which, I might add, is totally Johnny's and in fact required a scrotum to complete in less than a full day—I deserve a margarita. And you, O fattening one, can have a virgin drink. Ironic, don't you think?"

Arm in arm, they went to the kitchen and made the drinks. All the way there, and back to the living room, where they sat in front of the fire, they talked. About little things, mostly—the speeding ticket Tully got last week, Sean's new girlfriend, the class Mom was taking at the local community college.

"What's it like," Tully asked when Kate got up to put a log on the fire, "being married?"

"Well, it's only been three months, so I'm hardly an expert, but so far it's great." She sat back down and put her feet on the coffee table, resting her hand on the barely noticeable bump of her stomach. "You'll think I'm crazy, but I love the routine, the way we have breakfast together, each reading our own stuff; I love that he's the first person I see every morning and that he kisses me goodnight before I fall asleep." She smiled at Tully. "But I miss sharing a bathroom with you. He's constantly moving my stuff and putting it away—and then he forgets where he put it. How about you, Tully? How's life in our old apartment?"

"Lonely," Tully said, shrugging and smiling as if she didn't care. "I'm getting used to it again."

"You can call anytime, you know."

"And I do." Tully laughed and poured herself a second margarita. "Have you guys figured out the plan for life after my godchild's birth? Will they let you have a few weeks off?"

This was the subject Kate had tried to avoid. She'd known what she wanted to do from the moment Johnny had married her, but she hadn't had the courage to tell Tully. She took a deep breath. "I'm quitting."

"What? Why? They've got you on the best accounts, and you and

Johnny are making good money. It's 1987 for crying out loud. You don't have to quit your job to be a mother. You can hire a nanny."

"I don't want someone else raising this baby. At least not until kindergarten."

That got Tully on her feet. "Kindergarten? What is that, eight years?"

Kate smiled at that. "Five."

"But—"

"No buts. It's important to me to be a good mother. You, of all people, should understand how much it matters to a kid."

Tully sat back down. They both knew there was nothing she could really say to that. Tully still bore the scars of a bad mother. "Women can do both, you know. This isn't the fifties."

"My mom went on every field trip I ever took. She was a helper in the classroom every year until I begged her to please stop coming. I didn't take the bus until I was in junior high and still remember talking to my mom on the ride home after school. I want my child to have all that. I can always go back to work later."

"And you think that will be enough for you—carpools and field trips and classroom-volunteering?"

"If it's not, I'll find something else. Come on, it's not like I'm an astronaut." She smiled. "So, tell me about your job. I'll live vicariously through you, so make the stories good."

Tully immediately launched into a hilarious story about her most recent assignment.

Kate leaned back and closed her eyes, listening.

"Kate? Kate?"

She was so lost in her thoughts it took her a moment to realize that Tully was talking to her. She laughed. "Sorry about that. What were you saying?"

"You fell asleep on me. I was telling you about this guy who asked me out and when I looked over, you were out like a light."

"I was not," Kate said quickly, but the truth was that she did feel drowsy, kind of light-headed, too. "I think I need a cup of tea." She stood up and swayed precariously, reaching out for the back of the couch. "Wow, that was—" In the middle of her sentence, she looked at Tully and frowned. "Tully?"

Tully got to her feet so quickly, she knocked over her margarita. She put an arm around Kate, steadying her. "I'm right here."

Something was wrong; a wave of dizziness struck her so hard and suddenly that she stumbled.

"Hold on, honey," Tully said, moving her gently toward the door. "We need to get to a phone."

A phone? Kate shook her head in confusion; her vision blurred. "I don't know what's happening," she mumbled. "Is this a surprise party for me? Is it my birthday?"

Then she looked down at the sofa where she'd been sitting.

A dark pool of blood stained the cushion and splattered the decking at her feet. "Oh, no," she whispered, touching her stomach. She wanted to say more, pray to God to for help, but while she was grasping for words, the world tilted sickeningly and she passed out.

Tully forced them to let her stay in the ambulance. She sat by Kate, saying, "I'm right here," over and over.

Kate was conscious, but barely so. Her skin was as pale as an old overwashed sheet; even her green eyes, usually so bright, were dull and glassy. Tears leaked down her temples.

The ambulance pulled up to the hospital. Tully was pushed aside in their haste to get Kate out of the van and into the bright lights of the hospital. She stood there in the open doorway, watching them take her best friend away. Suddenly she felt the full impact of what was happening.

Women having miscarriages could bleed to death.

"Please, God," she said, wishing for the first time in her life that she really knew how to pray, "don't let me lose her."

She knew it was the wrong prayer, not the one Kate would have wanted. "And take care of her baby."

It felt like throwing diamonds into a river, praying to this God that had never listened to her. "Katie goes to church every Sunday," she reminded Him, just in case.

In the small green hospital room that overlooked the parking lot, Kate lay sleeping. Beside her Mrs. M. sat in a molded plastic chair reading a paperback novel. As always, she moved her lips as she read.

Tully came up beside her, touched her shoulder. "I brought you some coffee." She let her hand rest on Mrs. M.'s shoulder. It had been almost two hours since Kate lost the baby and although Johnny had been called, he was on assignment in Spokane, on the other side of the state.

"I guess it's a blessing it happened early," Tully said.

"Four months isn't early, Tully," Mrs. Mularkey said quietly. "And people who haven't had a miscarriage always say that. It was what Bud said to me. Twice." She looked up. "It never felt like much of a blessing to me. It felt like losing someone I loved. You know about that, don't you?"

"Thanks," she said, squeezing Mrs. Mularkey's shoulder, and then moving closer to the bed. "Now I know what not to say. I just wish I knew what would help."

Kate opened her eyes and saw them.

Mrs. Mularkey stood up, moved next to the bed, standing shoulder to shoulder with Tully.

"Hey," Kate whispered. "How long until Johnny—" At her husband's name, her voice cracked like an egg and she started to shake.

"Did someone say my name?"

Tully spun around.

He stood in the open doorway, carrying a bouquet of flowers that wilted slightly to the left. Everything about him looked disheveled—his unshaven face was a contrasting palette of pale skin and stubbly black beard, his hair was a long, tangled black mess, and his eyes bespoke a bone-deep exhaustion. His Levi's were torn and dirty, his khaki shirt had more wrinkles than an unmade bed. "I hired a private plane. It's going to be a hell of a Visa bill."

He tossed the flowers on a chair and went to his wife. "Hey, baby," he whispered. "I'm sorry it took me so long."

"It was a boy," Katie said, bursting into tears, clinging to him.

Tully heard Johnny start to cry with Kate.

Mrs. Mularkey came up beside her, slipped an arm around her waist.

"He loves her," Tully said slowly. The memory of her night with Johnny had somehow blinded her, trapped her like an insect in the sap of a forgotten time. She'd imagined that Kate was his second choice somehow, his Miss Runner-Up to love.

But this . . . this was no second choice.

Mrs. Mularkey pulled her away from the bed. "Of course he loves her. Come on, let's leave them alone."

They took their coffees and went out into the hallway, where Mr. M. was sitting on an uncomfortable chair. When he looked up, his eyes were bloodshot. "How is she?"

"Johnny's with her now," Mrs. M. said, touching his shoulder.

For the first time in years, Tully felt like an outsider in this family. "I should be with her."

"Don't you worry, Tully," Mrs. M. said, watching her closely. "She'll always need you."

"But things are different now."

"Of course they are. Katie's married. You girls are on separate paths, but you'll always be best friends."

Separate paths.

There it was; the thing she should have seen but somehow hadn't.

They took turns being with Kate during the next few days. On Thursday, it was Tully's time. She called in sick at work and spent the day with Kate. They played cards and watched television and talked. Most of the time, to be honest, Tully just listened. When it was her turn to answer, she tried to say the right thing, but she was pretty sure she failed more often than not. There was a sadness in her friend now, a graying around the edges that was so foreign Tully felt as if she'd stumbled upon some negative version of their friendship. Nothing she said was quite right.

Finally, around eight o'clock, Kate said, "I know you'll think I'm crazy, but I'm going to bed. Johnny will be home in an hour. You can go on home. Go have wild, crazy sex with that new guy, Ted."

"Todd. And I'm not exactly in a make-out mood. Then again . . ." Smiling, she helped Kate up the stairs and got her settled in bed. Then she looked down at her. "You don't know how much I want to say the right thing to make you feel better."

"You do. Thanks." Kate closed her eyes.

Tully stood there a moment longer, feeling uncharacteristically impotent. With a sigh, she went back downstairs and started on the dishes. She was drying the last glass when the door opened quietly, then clicked shut.

Johnny stood there, holding a bouquet of pink roses. With his newly cropped hair and stonewashed jeans and his white Adidas tennis shoes with the tongues hanging out, he looked about twenty years old. In all the years she'd known him, he'd never looked so sad and ruined.

"Hey," he said, putting the flowers on the coffee table.

"You look like you could use a drink."

"How about an IV drip?" He tried to smile. "She asleep?"

"Yeah." Tully grabbed a bottle of scotch from the counter and made him a stiff drink, then she poured herself a glass of wine and went to him.

"Let's sit on the dock," he said, taking the glass from her. "I don't want to wake her up."

Tully got her coat and followed him outside. They sat side by side on the dock, as if they were kids, hanging their legs out over the black waters of Lake Union.

It was still and peaceful out here. A full moon hung in the sky, illuminating the rooflines and reflecting in various windows. The distant hum of cars on the bridge was syncopated by the water slapping against the pilings.

"How are you doing, really?" Tully asked.

"It's Katie I'm worried about."

"I know," she answered, "but I asked about you."

"I've been better." He sipped his drink.

Tully leaned against him. "You're lucky," she said. "She loves you, and when a Mularkey falls in love, it's for life." The minute she said the words, she felt that strange sense of unraveling again. Of loneliness that was somehow just out of view, but moving toward her. For the first time, she wondered what her life could have been like if she'd been like Kate and chosen love. Would she then know how it felt to truly belong somewhere, with someone? She stared out across the water.

"What is it, Tully?"

"I guess I'm jealous of Kate and you."

"You don't want this life."

"What life do I want?"

He put an arm around her. "That's one thing you've always known. You want the networks."

"Does that make me shallow?"

He laughed. "I'm hardly the one to ask. I'll tell you what: I'll start making some calls. Sooner or later we'll find you a network job."

"You'd do that?"

"Of course. But you'll have to be patient. These things take time."

She twisted around and hugged him, whispering, "Thanks, Johnny." He knew her so well. Somehow he'd already known what she'd only just discovered: it was time for her to move on.

As tired as Kate was, she couldn't fall asleep. She lay in bed, staring up at the peaked ceiling, and waited for her husband.

It was in the very core of their relationship, this anxiety of hers. When things went bad, she remembered that she'd been his second choice, and no matter how often she told herself it wasn't true, there was a slim, shadowy version of herself that believed it, worried about it.

It was a destructive neurosis. Like water rising in the Pilchuck River, it eroded everything around it, sent big chunks of earth tumbling away.

Downstairs she heard a sound.

He was home.

"Thank God."

She eased painfully out of bed and went downstairs.

The lights were off. The fire was almost dead; only a faint orange glow remained. At first she thought she'd been wrong, that he wasn't home; then she noticed the shadows on the deck. Two people, sitting side by side, their shoulders touching. Moonlight revealed their shapes, turned them silver against the blackness of the water. She crossed the house quietly, opened the door, and stepped out into the night. A slight breeze ruffled her hair and nightgown.

Tully twisted around, hugged Johnny, whispered something in his ear. His response was muted by the sound of the water slapping the dock. He might have laughed; Kate couldn't be sure.

"You two having a party without me?" She heard the break in her voice and drew in a sharp breath to cover it. In her heart she knew that Johnny hadn't been turning to kiss Tully, but that shadow self of hers wasn't so sure. The ugly, toxic thought was smaller than a drop of blood, yet it poisoned the entire stream.

Johnny was at her side in an instant. He pulled her into his arms and kissed her. When he drew back, she looked around for Tully, but they were alone on the deck.

For the first time in her life, she wished she loved him less. It was dangerous to feel this way; she was like a naked infant exposed to the elements. Fragile and infinitely afraid. He could ruin her someday. Of that she had no doubt.

Tully tried, as the months passed and a new year began, to remain patient and believe in the best, but by the end of May, she'd almost given up hope. Nineteen eighty-eight was not shaping up to be a good year for her. It was early now, on a hot spring day, and she was working hard to enjoy her spot as the replacement anchor. At the end of the broadcast, she headed back to her office.

She was just sitting down at her desk when she heard:

"Line two, Tully."

She picked up the phone, pushed the square white button for line two, which immediately lit up. "Tallulah Hart."

"Hello, Ms. Hart. Dick Emerson here. I'm the VP of programming for NBC in New York. I understand you're looking to move up to the networks."

Tully drew in a sharp breath. "I am."

"We have an opening on the early morning show for a general assignment reporter."

"Really?"

"I'll be seeing nearly fifty candidates next week. The competition will be fierce, Ms. Hart."

"So am I, Mr. Emerson."

"That's the kind of ambition I like to hear." She heard the ruffling of papers on a desk. "I'll have my secretary send you a ticket. She'll call to set you up with a place to stay in the city and the date of your interview. All that work for you?"

"Perfectly. Thank you, sir. You won't be disappointed in me."

"Good. I hate to waste my time." He paused. "And tell Johnny Ryan hi from me."

Tully hung up and dialed Kate and Johnny's number.

Kate answered immediately. "Hello?"

"I'm in love with your husband."

There was a half second's pause. "Oh, really?"

"He got me an interview at NBC."

"Next week, right?"

"You knew?"

Kate laughed. "Of course I knew. He's been working on it for a long time. And yours truly mailed out the tapes."

"With everything that's on your mind, you were still thinking about me?" Tully said, awed.

"You and me against the world, Tully. Some things never change."

"This time I really am going to light the world on fire," she said, laughing. "I finally have a fucking match."

New York City was everything Tully had dreamed it would be. In her first week here, with her new NBC business cards clutched in her hand, she'd walked down these busy streets like Alice in Wonderland, her face perpetually tilted upward. The endless skyscrapers amazed her, as did the restaurants that never closed, the horse-drawn carriages lined up along the park, and the crowds of black-clad people who filled the streets.

She'd spent two weeks exploring the city, choosing a neighborhood, finding an apartment, learning to navigate the subways. It could have been a lonely time—after all, who wanted to see the sights of a magical city like New York alone? But the truth was, she was so excited about her new job that even being solitary didn't bother her. Besides, in the city that never slept, you were never really alone. There were always people in the streets, even in the darkest hours.

And then there was her job. From the moment she first walked into the NBC building as a reporter, she was hooked. She woke every morning at two-thirty so that she could be at the studio by four o'clock. Although she didn't technically need to get there so early, she loved to hang around and help out. She studied Jane Pauley's every movement and mannerism.

Tully had been hired as a general assignment reporter, which meant that she was assigned bits and pieces on other people's stories. At some point, if she was lucky, she'd get to cover a story the big correspondents wouldn't touch with a ten-foot pole—the biggest pumpkin in the state of Indiana or something equally relevant. And she couldn't wait. When she'd paid her dues, she'd get a *real* story to cover, and when she finally got that break, she'd knock it out of the park. Truthfully, when she watched people like Pauley and Bryant Gumbel, she knew how far she had to go. They were gods in her eyes, and she spent every spare minute watching how they did their jobs. At home, she analyzed the broadcasts, recording each one on her videotapes and playing and replaying them.

By the fall of 1989, she'd found her groove and begun to feel less like a cub reporter and more like a young woman poised to make her mark. Last month she'd gotten her first honest-to-God assignment: she'd flown to Arkansas to report on a prize-winning hog. The story never actually made it on air, but she'd done her job and done it well, and she'd learned a lot that trip.

She would have learned more in the studio, she was certain, if the morning show hadn't been in such upheaval. There was a war going on on-set and the whole country knew about it. Last week they'd taken a new publicity photo and Deborah Norville, the host of the early, early show had been on the couch with Jane and Bryant. That one picture sent shockwaves through the network and indeed the country. One article after another appeared; they all claimed that Norville was pushing Pauley out.

Tully kept her head down and stayed away from the gossip. No rumor mill was going to upset her chances for success. Instead, she kept the focus on her job. If she worked harder than anyone else, she might get a replacement shot on the early, early show, *NBC News at Sunrise*. From there, she was sure she'd someday get a crack at the *Today* news nook, and from there, the world would be her oyster.

Eighteen hour workdays didn't leave her much time for a personal life but she still had Katie, even with all the miles between them. They spoke at least twice a week, and every Sunday Tully called Mrs. M. She told them both stories about work pressures and celebrity sightings and life in Manhattan; they responded with details about the new house Kate and Johnny had bought, the trip Mr. and Mrs. M. had planned for the spring, and—best of all—the news that Kate was pregnant again and it was going well.

The days passed like cards falling from a deck, so fast that sometimes they were just a blur of sound and color. But she was on her way. She knew that, and the knowledge kept her going.

Today, an icy cold late December one, just like each of the countless days that had come before it, she spent fourteen hours at the station, then headed tiredly home.

Down on the street, she was captivated by Rockefeller Center at the holidays. Even in the fading gray of an overcast evening, there were people everywhere, shopping, taking pictures of the giant Christmas tree, ice-skating in the seasonal rink.

She was about ready to start walking home when she saw the sign for the Rainbow Room and thought, *What the hell?* She'd been in New York for more than a year now, and although she had made a lot of acquaintances, she hadn't bothered with dating.

Maybe it was the Christmas decorations, or the way her boss had laughed at her when she asked for the holidays off; she wasn't sure. All she knew was that it was Friday night, only a few nights before Christmas, and she didn't feel like going to her quiet apartment. CNN could wait.

The view from the Rainbow Room was everything she'd heard and more. It was as if she were on the bridge of some great mothership from the future, hovering over the multicolored magnificence of Manhattan at night.

It was still early, so there was plenty of seating at the bar and at the tables. She chose a table by the window, sat down, and ordered a margarita.

She was just about to order another one when the bar started filling up. Men and women from Wall Street and Midtown congregated in groups alongside overdressed tourists, commandeering the tables and chairs, lining up three deep at the bar.

"Do you mind if I join you?"

Tully looked up.

A good-looking blond man in an expensive suit smiled down at her. "I'm tired of elbowing my way through the yuppies to get a drink."

An English accent. She was a sucker for that.

"I'd hate to think you were going thirsty." She kicked the chair across from her out just enough for him to sit down.

"Thank God." He flagged down a waiter, ordered a scotch on the rocks for himself and another margarita for her, then collapsed into the chair. "Bloody meat market in here, isn't it? I'm Grant, by the way."

She liked his smile and gave him one of hers. "Tully."

"No last names. Brilliant. That means we don't have to do that whole exchanging of our life stories. We can just have fun."

The waiter delivered the drinks and left them alone again.

"Cheers," he said, tipping his glass against hers. "The view in here is better than I'd been led to believe." He leaned toward her. "You're beautiful, but I expect you know that."

She'd heard those words all her life. Usually they meant nothing to her, bounced off her like raindrops on a metal roof, but for some reason, in this room, with the holidays approaching, the compliment was exactly what she needed to hear. "How long are you in town for?"

"A week or so. I work for Virgin Entertainment."

"Are you making that up?"

"No, really. It's one of Richard Branson's companies. We're scouting U.S. locations for a Virgin Megastore."

"I shudder to think what you sell."

"How naughty of you. It's a music store, for starters anyway."

She sipped her drink, eyeing him over the salted rim, smiling. Kate was always telling her to get out more, to meet people. Just now, it seemed like damned fine advice. "Is your hotel nearby?"

Part Three

THE NINETIES

I'm Every Woman

it's all in me

CHAPTER NINETEEN

Just knock me out. I mean it. If they won't give me drugs, get a base-ball bat and hit me. This breathing is bullsh—aagh!" Kate felt the pain twist through her insides and tear her apart.

Beside her Johnny was saying "Come on . . . ha ha ha . . . you can do it. Breathe ha . . . ha . . . like this. Remember our class? Focus. Visualize. D'you want that statue we—"

She grabbed him by the collar and yanked him close. "So help me God, if you mention breathing again I'm going to take you down. I want drugs—"

And it was back, wrenching, cutting, twisting through her until she cried out. For the first six hours she'd been pretty good. She'd focused and breathed and kissed her husband when he leaned down to her and thanked him when he pressed a cool wet rag to her forehead. In the second six hours she lost her natural sense of optimism. The relentless, gnawing pain was like some horrible creature biting away at her, leaving less and less.

By hour seventeen she was a flat-out, cast-iron bitch. Even the nurse came and went like Speed Racer.

"Come on, baby, breathe. It's too late for drugs. You heard the doctor. It won't be much longer."

She noticed that even as he tried to soothe her, Johnny didn't get too close. He was like some terrorized soldier in a minefield who'd just seen his best friend blown up. He was afraid to move at all.

"Where's Mom?"

"I think she went down to call Tully again."

Kate tried to concentrate on her breathing, but it didn't help. The pain was rising again, cresting. She clung to the bedrails with sweaty hands. "Get . . . me . . . ice . . . chips!" She screamed the last word. It would have been funny, watching Johnny bolt for the door, if she hadn't felt like that girl swimming alone in *Jaws*.

The door to her private room banged open. "I hear someone is being a total bitch-o-rama in here."

Kate tried to smile, but another contraction was starting. "I don't . . . want . . . to . . . do this anymore."

"Changed your mind? Good timing." Tully moved to the side of the bed.

The pain hit again.

"Scream," Tully said, stroking her forehead.

"I'm . . . supposed to . . . breathe through it."

"Fuck that. Scream."

She did scream then, and it felt good. When the pain subsided again, she laughed weakly. "I take it you're against Lamaze."

"I wouldn't call myself a natural childbirth kind of gal." She looked at Kate's swollen belly and pale, sweaty face. "Of course, this is the best birth control commercial I've ever seen. From now on I'm using three condoms every time." Tully smiled, but her eyes were worried. "Are you okay, really? Should I get the doctor?"

Kate shook her head weakly. "Just talk to me. Distract me."

"I met a guy last month."

"What's his name?"

"That would be your first question. Grant. And before you barrel through some idiotic *Cosmo* girl list of how-well-do-you-know-your-man questions, let me say that I don't know squat about him except that he kisses like a god and screws like a devil."

Another contraction hit. Kate arched up and screamed again. As if from a distance she could hear Tully's voice, feel her stroking her forehead, but the pain was so overwhelming she couldn't do anything except gasp. "*Shit*," she said when it was over. "The next time Johnny comes near me I'm going to smack him."

"You were the one who wanted a baby."

"I'm getting a new best friend. I need someone with a shorter memory."

"I have a short memory. Did I tell you I'm seeing someone? He's perfect for me."

"Why?" Kate said, panting.

"He lives in London. We only see each other on the weekends. For totally rocking sex, I might add."

"Is that why you didn't answer when Mom called?"

"We were in the middle of it, but as soon as we finished, I started packing."

"I'm glad to see you have—oh, shit—priorities." Kate was in the middle of another contraction when the door to her room opened again. The nurse was first, followed by her mother and Johnny. Tully stood back, let everyone get in closer. At some point the nurse checked Kate's cervix and called the doctor in. He bustled into the room, smiling as if he'd run into her at the grocery store, and put on some gloves. Then the stirrups came out and it was time.

"Push," the doctor said in an entirely reasonable, pain-free voice that made Kate want to scratch his eyes out.

She screamed and pushed and cried until as quickly as it had begun, the agony was over.

"A perfect little girl," the doctor said. "Dad, do you want to cut the cord?"

Kate tried to lift herself up, but she was too weak. A few moments later, Johnny was beside her, offering her a tiny pink-wrapped bundle. She took her new daughter in her arms and stared down into her heart-shaped face. She had a wild shock of damp black curls and her mother's pale, pale skin, and the most perfect little lips and mouth Kate had ever seen. The love that burst open inside her was too big to describe. "Hey, Marah Rose," she whispered, taking hold of her daughter's grape-sized fist. "Welcome home, baby girl."

When she looked up at Johnny, he was crying. Leaning down, he kissed her with a butterfly softness. "I love you, Katie."

Never in her life had everything been so right in her world, and she knew that, whatever happened, whatever life had in store for her, she would always remember this single, shining moment as her touch of Heaven.

Tully begged for an additional two days off of work so that she could help Kate get settled in at home. When she'd made the call, it had seemed vital, unquestionably the thing to do.

But now, only a few hours after Kate and Marah had been discharged from the hospital, Tully saw the truth. She was about as useful as a dead microphone. Mrs. Mularkey was like a machine. She fed Kate before she even mentioned she was hungry; she changed the baby's handkerchief-sized diapers like a magician; and taught Kate how to breast-feed her daughter. Apparently it was not as instinctual a thing as Tully would have thought.

And what was her contribution? When she was lucky, she made Kate laugh. More often than not, though, her best friend just sighed, looking both remarkably in love with her baby and profoundly worn out. Now Kate lay in bed, holding her baby in her arms. "Isn't she beautiful?"

Tully gazed down at the tiny, pink-swaddled bundle. "She sure is."

Kate stroked her daughter's tiny cheek, smiling down at her. "You should go home, Tully. Really. Come back when I'm up and around."

Tully tried not to let her relief show. "They *do* need me at the studio. Things are probably a real mess without me."

Kate smiled knowingly. "I couldn't have done it without you, you know."

"Really?"

"Really. Now kiss your goddaughter and get back to work."

"I'll be back for her baptism." Tully leaned down and kissed Marah's velvety cheek, and then Kate's forehead. By the time she whispered goodbye and made it to the door, Kate seemed to have forgotten all about her.

Downstairs she found Johnny slumped in a chair by the fireplace. His hair was a shaggy, tangled mess, his shirt was on backward, and his socks didn't match. He was drinking a beer at eleven o'clock in the morning.

"You look like hell," she said, sitting down beside him.

"She woke up every hour last night. I slept better in El Salvador." He took a sip. "But she's beautiful, isn't she?"

"Gorgeous."

"Katie wants to move to the suburbs now. She's just realized this house is surrounded by water, so it's off to some cul-de-sac where they have bake sales and play dates." He made a face. "Can you imagine me in Bellevue or Kirkland with all those yuppies?"

The funny thing was, she could. "What about work?"

"I'm going back to work at KILO. Producing political and international segments."

"That doesn't sound like you."

He seemed surprised by that. When he looked at her, she saw a flash of remembrance; she'd reminded him of their past. "I'm thirty-five years old, Tul. With a wife and daughter. Different things are going to have to make me happy now."

She couldn't help noticing that he'd said *going to.* "But you love gonzo journalism. Battlefields and mortar rounds and people shooting at you. We both know you can't give it up forever."

"You only think you know me, Tully. It isn't like we traded secrets."

She remembered suddenly, sharply, what she was supposed to forget. "You tried."

"I tried," he agreed.

"Katie would want you to be happy. You'd kick ass at CNN."

"In Atlanta?" He laughed. "Someday you'll understand."

"You mean when I'm married, with kids?"

"I mean when you fall in love. It changes you."

"Like it's changed you? Someday I'll have a kid and want to write for the *Queen Anne Bee* again, is that it?"

"You'd have to fall in love first, wouldn't you?" The look Johnny gave her then was so understanding, so knowing, she felt skewered by it. She wasn't the only one who was remembering the past.

She got to her feet. "I gotta get back to Manhattan. You know the news. It never sleeps."

Johnny put down his beer and got to his feet, moving toward her. "You do it for me, Tully. Cover the world."

It sounded sad, the way he said it; she didn't know if what she heard was regret for himself or sadness for her.

She forced herself to smile. "I will."

Two weeks after Tully got home from Seattle, a storm dumped snow on Manhattan, stopping the vibrant city in its tracks. For a few hours, at least. The ever-present traffic vanished almost immediately; pristine white snow blanketed the streets and sidewalks, turned Central Park into a winter wonderland.

Still Tully made it to work at four A.M. In her freezing walk-up apartment, with the radiator rattling and ice collecting on her paper-thin antique windows, she dressed in tights, black velour stirrup pants, snow boots, and two sweaters. Covering it all with a navy-blue wool coat and gray mittens, she braved the elements, angling her body against the wind as she made her way up the street. Snow obscured her vision and stung her cheeks. She didn't care; she loved her job so much she'd do anything to get there early.

Inside the lobby, she stamped the snow off her boots, signed in, and went upstairs. Almost instantly she could tell that much of the staff had called in sick. Only a skeleton crew remained.

At her desk, she immediately went to work on the story she'd been assigned yesterday. She was doing research on the spotted owl controversy in the Northwest. Determined to put a local's "spin" on the story, she was busily reading everything she could find—Senate subcommittee reports, environmental findings, economic statistics on logging, the fecundity of old growth forests.

"You're working hard."

Tully looked up sharply. She'd been so lost in her reading that she hadn't heard anyone approach her desk.

And this wasn't just anyone.

Edna Guber, dressed in her signature black gabardine pantsuit, stood there, one hip pushed slightly out, smoking a cigarette. Sharp gray eyes stared out from beneath an Anna Wintour razor cut of blue-black bangs. Edna was famous in the news business, one of those women who'd clawed her way to the top in a time when others of her sex hadn't been able to come in the front door unless they had secretarial skills. Edna— only the single name was ever used or needed—reportedly had a Rolodex filled with the home numbers of everyone from Fidel Castro to Clint Eastwood. There was no interview she couldn't get and nowhere on earth she wouldn't go to find what she wanted.

"Cat got your tongue?" she said, exhaling smoke.

Tully jumped to her feet. "I'm sorry, Edna. Ms. Guber. Ma'am."

"I hate it when people call me ma'am. It makes me feel old. Do you think I'm old?"

"No, m—"

"Good. How did you get here? The cabs and buses are for shit today."

"I walked."

"Name?"

"Tully Hart. Tallulah."

Edna's gaze narrowed. She looked Tully up and down steadily. "Follow me." She spun on her black boot heel and marched down the hallway, toward the office in the corner of the building.

Holy cow.

Tully's heart was pounding. She'd never been invited into this office, never even met Maury Stein, the big kahuna on the morning show.

The office was huge, with two walls of windows. Falling snow turned everything outside gray and white and eerie. From this vantage point, it felt vaguely like standing inside a snow globe, looking out.

"This one will do," Edna said, cocking her head toward Tully.

Maury looked up from his work. He barely glanced at Tully, then nodded. "Fine."

Edna left the office.

Tully stood there, confused. Then she heard Edna say, "Are you epileptic? Comatose?"

Tully followed her out into the hallway.

"Do you have a pen and paper?"

"Yes."

"I don't need an answer, just do as I ask and do it quickly."

Tully fumbled into her pocket for a pen and found some paper on a nearby desk. "I'm ready."

"First off, I want a detailed report on the upcoming election in Nicaragua. You do know what's going on there?"

"Certainly," she lied.

"I want to know everything about the Sandinistas, Bush's Nicaraguan policy, the blockade, the people who live there. I want to know when Violeta Chamorro lost her virginity. And you've got twelve days to get it done."

"Yes—" She stopped herself from saying ma'am just in time.

Edna came to a stop at Tully's desk. "You've got a passport?"

"Yes. They made me apply for one when they hired me."

"Of course. We'll be leaving on the sixteenth. Before we go—"

"We?"

"Why the hell do you think I'm talking to you? Do you have a problem with this?"

"No. No problem. Thank you. I really—"

"We'll need immunizations; get a doctor here to take care of us and the crew. Then you can start setting up advance interview meetings. Got it?" She looked down at her watch. "It's one o'clock. Brief me on Friday morning at, say, five A.M.?"

"I'll get started right now. And thank you, Edna."

"Don't thank me, Hart. Just do your job—and do it better than anyone else could."

"I'm on it." Tully went to her desk and picked up the phone. Before
she'd even finished punching in the number, Edna was gone.

"Hello?" Kate said groggily.

Tully looked at the clock. It was nine. That meant it was six in Seattle. "Oops. I did it again. Sorry."

"Your goddaughter doesn't sleep. She's a freak of nature. Can I call
you back in a few hours?"

"Actually, I'm calling to talk to Johnny."

"Johnny?" In the silence that preceded the question, Tully heard a
baby start to cry.

"Edna Guber is sending me to Nicaragua. I want to ask him some
background questions."

"Just a second." Kate handed the phone off; there was a sound like
wax paper being balled up and a flurry of whispers, then Johnny came
on the line.

"Hey, Tully, good for you. Edna's a legend."

"This is my big break, Johnny, and I don't want to screw up. I
thought I'd start by picking your brain."

"I haven't slept in a month, so I don't know how much good I'll be,
but I'll do what I can." He paused. "You know it's dangerous down there.
A real powder keg. People are dying."

"You sound worried about me."

"Of course I am. Now, let's start with the relevant history. In 1960
or '61, the Sandinista National Liberation Front, or FSLN, was
founded . . ."

Tully wrote as fast as she could.

For just under two weeks Tully worked her ass off. Eighteen, twenty
hours a day she was reading, writing, making phone calls, setting up meetings. In the few rare hours when she wasn't working or trying to sleep, she
went to the kind of stores she'd never frequented before—camping stores,

military supply outlets, and the like. She bought pocketknives and net-ted safari hats and hiking boots. Everything and anything she could think of. If they were in the jungle and Edna wanted a damn fly swatter, Tully was going to produce it.

By the time they actually left, she was nervous. At the airport, Edna, wearing a pair of razor-pressed linen pants and a white cotton blouse, took one look at Tully's multipocketed khaki jungle attire and burst out laughing.

For the endless hours of their flights, through Dallas and Mexico City and finally onto a small plane in Managua, Edna fired questions at Tully.

The plane landed in what looked to Tully like a backyard. Men—boys, really—in camouflaged clothing stood on the perimeter, holding rifles. Children came out of the jungle to play in the air kicked up by the propellers. The dichotomy of the image was something Tully knew she'd always remember, but from the moment she got out of the plane until she reboarded the flight for home five days later, she had precious little time to think about imagery.

Edna was a mover.

They hiked through guerrilla-infested jungles, listening to the shriek-ing of howler monkeys, swatting mosquitoes, and floating up alligator-lined rivers. Sometimes they were blindfolded, sometimes they could see. Deep in the jungle, while Edna taped her interview with *el jefe*, the general in charge, Tully talked to the troops.

The trip opened her eyes to a world she'd never seen before; more than that, it showed her who she was. The fear, the adrenaline rush, the story; it turned her on like nothing ever had before.

Later, when the story was done and she and Edna were back in their hotel in Mexico City sitting on the balcony outside Edna's room, hav-ing straight shots of tequila, Tully said, "I can't thank you enough, Edna."

Edna took another straight shot and leaned back in her chair. The night was quiet. It was the first time they hadn't heard gunfire in days.

"You did well, kid."

Tully's pride welled to almost painful proportions. "Thank you. I learned more from you in the past few weeks than I learned in four years of college."

"So, maybe you want to go on my next assignment."

"Anywhere, anytime."

"I'm interviewing Nelson Mandela."

"Count me in."

Edna turned to her. The sticky-looking orange glow from the bare outdoor bulb highlighted her wrinkles, caused bags under her eyes. In this light she looked ten years older than usual, and tired; maybe a little drunk. "Have you got a boyfriend?"

"With my work schedule?" Tully laughed and poured herself another shot. "Hardly."

"Yeah," Edna said. "The story of my life."

"Do you regret it?" Tully asked. If they hadn't been drinking she never would have asked such a personal question, but tequila had blurred the lines between them for just this moment in time. Tully could pretend they were colleagues instead of icon/newbie. "Making this your life, I mean?"

"There's a price, that's for sure. For my generation, at least, you couldn't do this job and be married. You could get married—I did; three times—but you couldn't stay married. And forget about kids. When a story broke, I needed to be there, period. It could have been my kid's wedding day and I'd have left. So I've lived by myself." She looked at Tully. "And I've loved it. Every damn second. If I end up dying in a nursing home alone, who gives a shit? I was where I wanted to be every second of my life, and I did something that mattered."

Tully felt as if she were being baptized into the religion she'd always believed in. "Amen to that."

"So, what do you know about South Africa?"

CHAPTER
TWENTY

The first twelve months of motherhood was a riptide of cold dark water that all too often sucked Kate under.

It was embarrassing how ill-equipped she turned out to be for this blessed event that had been her secret girlhood dream. So embarrassing, in fact, that she told no one how overwhelmed she sometimes felt. When asked, she smiled brightly and said motherhood was the best thing that had ever happened to her. It was even true.

Yet sometimes it wasn't.

The truth was that her gorgeous, pale-skinned, dark-haired, brown-eyed daughter was more than a handful. From the moment she came home Marah was sick. Ear infections followed each other like cars on a train; just when one ended, another began. Colic caused her to cry inconsolably for hours at a time. Kate had lost count of the times she'd found herself in the living room in the middle of the night, holding her red-faced, shrieking daughter and quietly crying herself.

Marah would be a year old in three days and she had yet to sleep through the night. Four hours was her record so far. Thus, in the past twelve months, Kate hadn't slept through the night. Johnny always offered to get up. In the beginning he'd even gone so far as to throw back the covers, but Kate had always stopped him. It wasn't that she wanted to play the martyr, although she often felt like one.

Johnny had a job; it was that simple. Kate had given up her career to be a mom. Thus, getting up in the night was her job. At first she'd done it willingly, then at least with a smile. Lately, though, when Marah let out her first wail at eleven o'clock, Kate found herself praying for strength.

There were other problems, too. First off, her looks had gone to hell. She was pretty sure this was yet another ripple in the no-sleep pool. No amount of makeup or moisturizer helped. Her skin, always pale, was J. P. Patches white lately, except for the shadows under her eyes, which were a lovely shade of brown. She'd lost all of her baby weight except for ten pounds, but when you were five-foot-three, ten pounds was two sizes. She hadn't worn anything but sweats in almost a year.

She needed to start on an exercise program. Last week she'd found her old Jane Fonda workout tapes, a leotard, and leg warmers. Now all she had to do was hit play and get going.

"Today's the day," she said aloud as she carried her daughter back to bed and gently tucked her in beneath the expensive pink and white cashmere blanket that had been a gift from Tully. Luxuriously soft, it had become the thing Marah chose to sleep with. No matter what toys or blankets Kate offered, Tully's was the one. "Try to sleep till seven o'clock. Mommy could use it."

Yawning, Kate went back to bed and snuggled up to her husband.

He kissed her lips, lingering as if maybe he wanted to start something, and then he murmured, "You're so beautiful."

She opened her eyes, staring blearily at him. "Okay, who is she? Guilt is the only reason you'd say I was beautiful at this godforsaken hour."

"Are you kidding? With your mood swings lately it's like having three wives. The last thing I want is another woman."

"But sex would be nice."

"Sex would be nice. It's funny you brought that up."

"Funny ha ha, or funny I-can't-remember-the-last-time-we-made-love?"

"Funny that you're getting lucky this weekend."

"Yeah, how's that?"

"I've already talked to your mom. She's taking Marah after the birthday party and you and I are going to have a romantic night in downtown Seattle."

"What if I can't fit into any of my nice clothes?"

"Believe me, I have no problem with nudity. We can order room service instead of going out. Although you're the only one who thinks you haven't lost the weight. Try on something. I think you'll be surprised."

"No wonder I love you so much."

"I'm a god. There's no doubt about it."

She smiled and wrapped her arms around him, kissing him softly.

They had just closed their eyes again when the phone rang. Kate sat up slowly, and looked at the clock: 5:47.

She picked up on the second ring, saying, "Hello, Tully."

"Hey, Katie," Tully said. "How did you know it was me?"

"Lucky guess." Kate rubbed the bridge of her nose, feeling the start of a headache. Beside her, Johnny grumbled something about people who couldn't tell time.

"Today's the day, remember? My report on the reservists Bush called up to active duty. My first honest-to-God important story."

"Oh. Right."

"You don't sound very excited, Katie."

"It's five-thirty in the morning."

"Oh. I thought you'd want to watch the broadcast. Sorry I bothered you. 'Bye."

"Tully, wait—"

It was too late. The dial tone blared at her.

Kate cursed under her breath and hung up the phone. She couldn't seem to do anything right lately. She and Tully had so little in common these days there wasn't much to talk about. Tully didn't want to hear endless "mommy" stories and Kate could only stand so many my-life-and-career-are-great anecdotes. The postcards and calls from distant, exotic places were vaguely irritating.

"She's on *Sunrise* this morning, remember?" Kate said. "She wanted to remind us."

Johnny threw the covers back and turned on the television. They sat up together, listening to Norville's report on the buildup of hostilities in Iraq and the president's response.

Then, suddenly, Tully was on the air. She stood in front of some run-down concrete building, talking to an impossibly fresh-faced kid with a thick red crew cut and freckles. He looked as if he could have been wearing braces and a letterman's jacket ten seconds ago.

But it was Tully who demanded attention. She looked trim and utterly professional and beautiful. She'd tamed her curly auburn hair into a sleek, sophisticated bob and applied just enough makeup to accentuate her eyes.

"Wow," Kate whispered. When had that transformation occurred? She wasn't overblown Tallulah anymore, child of the cocaine-and-glitter eighties. She was reporter Tallulah Hart, as beautiful as Paulina Porizkova, as professional as Diane Sawyer.

"Wow is right," Johnny said. "She looks gorgeous."

They watched the rest of the broadcast. Then he kissed Kate's cheek and headed into the bathroom. Within moments she heard the shower start.

"She looks *gorgeous*," Kate muttered, leaning sideways for the phone.

She punched in Tully's number. The NBC receptionist answered and said she'd need to leave a message.

So Tully was pissed.

"Tell her Katie called to say the story was great."

Tully was probably right there, standing next to the phone, wearing her expensive designer skirt and blouse, digging through her quilted designer handbag, watching the light flash on her phone.

Kate got out of bed and went into the bathroom. There was no point in trying to sleep any more. Marah would waken any minute. In the shower, her husband was singing a very off-key version of an old Rolling Stones' song.

Against her better judgment she looked in the mirror. Steam clouded her reflection but didn't obscure it.

Her hair was straggly and too long. Dark blond roots showed how long it had been since she'd had a foil. She had bags under her eyes the size of open umbrellas and enough cleavage for two women.

No wonder she tried to stay away from reflective surfaces. With a sigh, she reached for the toothpaste and began brushing her teeth. Before she'd finished, she felt Marah wake up.

Turning off the water, she opened the door.

Sure enough, Marah was screaming.

Kate's day had begun.

When the big day arrived, Kate wondered why in the hell she'd planned such a ridiculous birthday party for her daughter. In the morning, after another sleepless night, she got up and began the preparations, putting the finishing touches on the pink Barbie doll cake and wrapping the last few presents. In a moment of obvious madness, she'd invited all the children from Marah's Mommy and Me class, as well as two former sorority sisters who had similarly aged daughters and her parents. Even Johnny had taken the morning off work for the extravaganza. When they all arrived, on time, bearing gifts, Kate immediately got a headache. It didn't help that Marah picked that moment to start screaming, either.

Still, the party went on, with all the women in the living room and the kids on the floor, making more noise than Sherman marching into Atlanta.

"I saw Tully on that really early show the other morning," Mary Kay said. "I was up with Danny."

"I was up, too," Charlotte said, reaching for her coffee. "She looked great, didn't she?"

"That's because she sleeps through the night," Vicki pointed out. "And her clothes don't always have puke on them."

Kate wanted to join in, but she couldn't. Her headache was killing her and she had this nagging sense that something was wrong. It was so acute that when Johnny left the party at just past one, she'd almost pleaded with him to stay.

"You're awfully quiet today," her mother pointed out when the last guest left.

"Marah didn't sleep again last night."

"She never sleeps through the night, and why is that? Because—"

"I know. I know. I need to let her cry." Kate tossed the last of the used paper plates into the trash. "I just can't."

"I let you cry. It took three nights and you never woke up in the wee hours again."

"But I'm a genius. Clearly my daughter is not as bright."

"No, I'm the genius. Clearly *my* daughter is not as bright." Mom looped an arm around Kate's shoulder and led her to the sofa.

Side by side, they sat down. Kate leaned against her mother, who stroked her hair. The gentle, soothing motion transported her back a few decades. "Remember when I wanted to be an astronaut, and you said I was lucky because my generation could have it all? I could have three kids, a husband, and still go to the moon. What a bunch of bullshit that was." She sighed. "It's hard to be a good mother."

"It's hard to be good at anything."

"Amen," Kate said. The truth was that she loved her daughter, ached sometimes with the intensity of that love, but the responsibility was overwhelming, and the pace of life exhausting.

"I know how tired you are. It'll get better. I promise."

No sooner had her mother said the words than her father walked into the room. He'd spent most of the party hiding out in the family room, watching some sports team or another. "We'd best get a move on, Margie. I don't want to get stuck in traffic. Get Marah ready."

Kate felt a flash of panic. Was she ready to be away from her daughter for a night? "I don't know, Mom."

Her mother touched her hand gently. "Your father and I raised two kids, Katie. We can watch our granddaughter for a night. Go out with your husband. Kick up your heels and have some fun. Marah will be safe with us."

Kate knew her mother was right, even knew it was a good thing to do. So why was her stomach clenched?

"You have a lifetime to be afraid," Dad said. "That's what parenting is. Might as well embrace it, kiddo."

Kate tried gamely to smile. "This is it, huh? How you guys felt all the time."

"How we still feel," Dad said. Mom took her by the hand. "Let's go gather Marah's things. Johnny's going to be back in a couple of hours to pick you up."

Kate packed Marah's clothes, making sure she had her pink blanket, her pacifiers, and her beloved Pooh bear. Then she gathered up the formula and bottles and tiny jars of strained fruit and vegetables, and wrote out a feeding and sleeping schedule that would have made an air traffic controller proud.

When she held Marah one last time and kissed her soft cheek, Kate had to hold back tears. It was ridiculous and embarrassing and inevitable, for it didn't matter that motherhood had kicked the hell out of her and ruined her confidence; it had also swamped her so with love that she was only half a person without her daughter.

Kate stood on the porch of her new beachfront Bainbridge Island house, with her hand tented across her eyes until long after the car had disappeared down the driveway.

Then, back inside, she wandered aimlessly for a few moments, not quite certain of how to be alone anymore.

She tried calling Tully again, left another message.

Finally she found herself in her closet, staring at her prepregnancy clothes, trying to figure out what she had that was sexy and grown-up and would fit her. She'd just finished packing when she heard the door downstairs open and close, heard her husband's footsteps on the hardwood floor.

She went down to meet him. "Where are we going, Mr. Ryan?"

"You'll see." He took her hand and got her overnight bag and closed up the house. Out in his car, the radio was on. Loud, like the old days. Bruce Springsteen was singing, *Hey, little girl, is your daddy home . . .*

Kate laughed, feeling young again. They drove down to the ferry terminal and onto the waiting boat. Instead of sitting in their car for the passage, as they usually did, they bundled up in coats and hats and stood on the bow with the tourists. It was five o'clock on this cold January evening, and the sky and Sound were a Monet of lavender and pink. In the distance, Seattle sparkled with a million lights.

"Are you going to tell me where we're going?"

"No, but I'll tell you what we're going to do."

She laughed. "I know what we're going to do."

As the ferry chugged into port, they returned to their car. Once they were off the boat, Johnny maneuvered through the stop-and-go downtown traffic and pulled up in front of the Inn at the Market, where a liveried doorman opened her door and collected her bags.

Johnny came around for her and took her hand. "We're already checked in." To the bellman, he said, "Room 416."

They strolled through the quiet brick courtyard and into the intimate, European-style lobby. On the fourth floor, they went to their room, a corner suite that had a sweeping view of the Sound. Bainbridge Island looked almost purple; the water was steel-blue; the distant mountains were backlit by pink light. On a table by the window a bottle of champagne stood tilted in a silver ice bucket, a plateful of strawberries beside it.

Kate smiled. "I see someone wants to get laid in the worst way."

"What you see is a man who loves his wife." He swept her into his arms and kissed her.

When someone knocked, they broke apart like teenagers, laughing at their own passion.

Kate waited impatiently for the bellman to leave. The second he was gone she began unbuttoning her blouse. "I'm not sure exactly what to wear tonight." When Johnny looked at her—he wasn't smiling now; he looked as hungry as she felt—she unzipped her pants, let them fall to the floor. For the first time in months she didn't worry about her weight gain. Instead she let his gaze be her mirror.

She unhooked her bra, let it dangle from her fingertips and drop to the ground.

"No fair starting without me," he said, wrenching off his shirt, throwing it aside, then unbuttoning his pants.

They fell into bed together and made love as if they hadn't done it in months instead of weeks, with every part of their minds and bodies. Sensation carried Kate away. When he finally entered her with all the pent-up longing of too many passionless nights, she cried out at the joy of it, and everything inside of her, everything she was, melded with this man she loved more than her own life. By the time she came, shuddering hard, holding him against her damp body, she was utterly spent.

He pulled her against him. Naked, panting, they lay entwined, the expensive hotel sheets tangled around their bare legs.

"You know how much I love you, don't you?" he said quietly. They were words he'd said hundreds of times, so often that she knew how they were supposed to sound.

She rolled onto her side, instantly worried. "What is it?"

"What do you mean?" He eased away from her and went to the table, where he poured two glasses of champagne. "Do you want some strawberries?"

"Look at me, John."

Slowly—too slowly—he turned, but he wouldn't meet her gaze.

"You're scaring me."

He went over to the window and stared out. His profile looked sharp suddenly, distant. Damp, tangled hair obscured his cheek. She couldn't tell if he was smiling. "Let's not do this now, Katie. We have all night and all day tomorrow to talk. For now, let's—"

"Tell me."

He put the glass of champagne down on the windowsill and turned to her. Finally, he let his gaze meet hers, and in his blue eyes she saw the kind of sadness that made her breath catch. He went to the bed, knelt beside it so that he was looking up at her. "You know what's going on in the Middle East."

His words were so unexpected that she just stared at him. "What?"

"There's going to be a war, Katie. You know that. The whole world knows it."

War.

The three letters coalesced into something as big and black as a thundercloud. She knew what this was about.

"I have to go." The simple, quiet way he said it was worse than any yell.

"You said you lost your nerve."

"There's the irony; you gave it back to me. I'm tired of feeling like I failed, Katie. I need to prove to myself that I can do it this time."

"And you want my blessing," she said dully.

"I need it."

"You'll go no matter what I say, so why the big act?"

He came up on his knees, took her face in his hands, and held her steady. She tried to pull away, but he wouldn't let her. "They need me. I've got experience."

"I need you. Marah needs you, but that doesn't matter, does it?"

"It matters."

She felt the heat of tears flood her eyes; they blurred her vision.

"If you say no, I won't go."

"Okay, no. You can't go. I won't let you. I love you, Johnny. You could die over there."

He let go of her, sat back on his heels, and stared at her. "Is that your answer?"

The tears fell, streaked down her cheeks. Angrily, she wiped them away. She wanted to say, *Yes. Fuck, yes. That's my answer.*

But how could she deny him this? Not only was it what he wanted, but down even deeper, there was something else, that tattered, ugly remnant of fear that floated to the surface sometimes, reminded her that he'd loved Tully first. It made Kate afraid to deny him anything. She wiped her eyes again. "Promise me you won't die, Johnny."

He climbed into bed and took her in his arms and while she held him as tightly as she could, already it didn't feel safe. It felt as if he were dissolving in her embrace, disappearing bit by bit. "I promise I won't die."

They were empty words, made worse by the fervor with which he spoke.

She couldn't help thinking of this morning, when she'd woken with the feeling that something would go wrong today. "I mean it, Johnny. If you die over there I'll hate you forever. I swear to God I will."

"You know you'll always love me."

The words, and the easy, victorious way he said them made her want to cry all over again. It wasn't until much later, after they'd had a romantic dinner in their room and made love and snuggled into each other's waiting arms, that she thought about what she'd said to him, the terrible, wrenching horror of her threat; the gauntlet she'd thrown down to God.

Tully eased off Grant's naked body and flopped onto the bed, still breathing hard. "Wow," she said, closing her eyes. "That was great."

"Indeed it was."

"I'm so glad you were in town this weekend. This was exactly what I needed."

"You and me both, my love."

She loved listening to his accent, feeling his naked body against hers. This was a moment to hang on to, to cling to, even, because as soon as he left her bed, she knew her unease would come back. She'd been battling it since her call to Kate. Nothing could disrupt her self-confidence or make her feel edgy like being mad at her best friend.

Grant sat up in bed.

She touched his back, thought about asking him to stay the night again, to put off his meeting, but that wasn't the kind of relationship they had. They were friends who met for sex and laughter for a few hours and then went their own ways.

Beside him, the bedside phone rang. He reached for it.

"Don't answer it. I don't want to talk to anyone."

"I gave the office this number." He picked up the phone and answered. "Hello? . . . Grant," he said. "And who are you? Oh, I see." He paused, frowning, then laughed. "I can do that." He held the phone to his naked chest and turned to Tully. "Your best friend forever says—and I quote—that you are to get your lily-white ass out of your bed and come to the damn phone. She says further that if you give her any shit on this of all days that she will beat you until you beg for mercy." He chuckled again. "She sounds serious."

"I'll take the call."

Grant handed her the phone and walked naked toward the bathroom. When he shut the door, Tully brought the phone to her ear and said, "Who is this?"

"Very funny."

"I had a best friend forever once, but she was a real bitch to me, so I figured—"

"Look, Tully, normally I'd grovel for an hour or so and spoon a bunch of humble pie down my throat, but I don't have time for the ritual today. I'm sorry. Your phone call came at a bad time and I was snotty. Okay?"

"What's wrong?"

"It's Johnny. He's going to Baghdad tomorrow."

Tully should have seen this coming. The whole station was buzzing over what was happening in the Middle East. Everyone at the station and around the world was trying to guess when President Bush was going to drop the first bomb. "A lot of journalists are going over there, Katie. He'll be fine."

"I'm scared, Tully. What if—"

"Don't," Tully said sharply. "Don't even think it. I'll follow him from the station. We get most of the news first. I'll watch for you."

"And you'll tell me the truth, no matter what?"

Tully sighed. Their familiar promise didn't sound as airy and hopeful as usual; suddenly it had a dark, ominous edge that she had to force herself to ignore. "No matter what, Katie. But you don't have to worry. This war won't last long. He'll be home before Marah takes her first step."

"I pray you're right."

"I'm always right. You know that."

Tully hung up the phone, listening to the sound of Grant turning on the shower. His humming, which usually made her smile, had no effect. For the first time in a long time she was afraid.

Johnny in Baghdad.

Kate received the first message from Johnny two days after he left. Until then, she'd walked around the house in a daze, never far from the new fax/phone they'd put on the kitchen counter. As she went about the business of her day—changing diapers, reading stories, watching Marah crawl from one potentially dangerous piece of furniture to the next—she thought: *Okay, Johnny: let me know you're alive and well.* He'd told her that phone calls could only be made with dire need (to which she'd argued that her need was dire, and why didn't that count?), but that faxes were not only possible but relatively easy.

And so she'd waited.

When the phone rang at four in the morning, she threw the blanket away and rolled off the sofa, stumbling toward the kitchen, waiting for the message to unfurl.

Before she'd read a word, she started to cry. Just seeing the bold scrawl of his handwriting made missing him almost unbearable.

Dear Katie:

It's crazy here. Flat-out insane. We don't know exactly what's happening—it's a waiting game right now. The journalists are all in the Al-Rashid Hotel in the middle of Baghdad and we've got unprecedented access to both sides. The coverage of this war will change everything. Tomorrow we're leaving the city for the first time. Don't worry, I'll be careful.

Gotta run. Kiss M for me.

Love U

J

After that, the faxes came about once a week. Not nearly often enough.

K—

The bombing started last night. Or should I say this morning? We had a bird's-eye view from the hotel and it was gut-wrenching and horrific and amazing. It was a gorgeous, starry night in Baghdad and the bombs turned this city into hell. An office tower exploded close to the hotel and the heat was like an oven.

Am being careful.

Love U

J

K—

Seventeen hours of bombing and still counting. There will be nothing left when it finally stops. Back to work.

K—

Sorry it's been so long since the last letter. The team is out so much on assignment that I can't get five seconds to myself. But I'm good. Tired. Hell, more than that. Exhausted. The first US female POW was captured last night and I have to say that it hit us all hard. I hope that someday I can tell you how it feels to see all this, but I can't think that way now, not if I want to sleep. Anyway, there's talk that the Iraqis are going to ignite oil wells in Kuwait and we're off to cover it. Kisses to Marah and more to you.

Kate stared down at the last fax she'd received. It was dated February 21, 1991, almost one week ago.

She sat in her living room, watching the war coverage on television. The last six weeks had been the longest, hardest days of her life. She was waiting, always waiting, for a phone call that said he was coming home, for a special report that heralded the end of the war. Now they were saying that the final allied assault should begin any day. A ground assault. That scared her as much as or more than anything else because she knew her Johnny. Somehow, he'd end up on a tank, directing a story that no one else could tell.

The waiting had worn her down to nothing. She'd lost fifteen pounds and hadn't had a good night's sleep since their night at the hotel.

She folded the latest fax in half and placed it on the small pile of others. Every day she told herself she wouldn't unfold them and reread his words; every day she returned to them.

Today she'd begun several chores and left all of them unfinished. Instead, she sat on the couch, watching television. She'd been here for more than two hours.

Marah stood by the coffee table, clutching its wooden edge in her pink, pudgy hands, swaying like a break-dancer and babbling in baby talk. Finally, she plopped down on her diaper-padded butt and immediately began to crawl away from the couch.

"Stay by Mommy," Kate said automatically. On TV, the oil wells were burning; the air above them was a thick cloud of black smoke.

Across the room, Marah found something. Kate could tell by the sudden quiet. She jumped up and went over to the chair by the fireplace.

Johnny's chair.

Don't think about that, she told herself. He'd be back any day to sit there again and read the paper after work.

She bent down and picked up her curious daughter, who looked up at her through huge, bright brown eyes and started to babble. Kate couldn't help smiling at how earnestly Marah was trying to communicate, and as always, her daughter's obvious joy lifted her spirits. "Hey, Munchkin what have you got there?" She carried her back toward the sofa, turning off the TV as she passed it. Enough was enough. She turned on the radio instead. It was tuned to an oldies channel, which always made her shake her head. To her mind the seventies weren't that distant. The Eagles were singing "Desperado."

Kate let the music take her back to an easier time. Holding her daughter close, she danced in the living room, singing along. Marah giggled and bounced in her arms, which made Kate laugh for the first time in days. She kissed her daughter's plump cheek, nuzzled her velvety neck, and tickled her until she screamed happily.

They were having so much fun Kate didn't register instantly that the phone was ringing. When she did hear it, she ran for the radio, turned it down, and answered.

"Mrs. John Ryan?" The connection was scratchy. Clearly long-distance. *Only in dire need.*

She froze, tightened her hold on Marah, who squirmed in her arms. "This is she."

"This is Lenny Golliher. I'm a friend of your husband's. I'm over here in Baghdad with him. I'm sorry to have to tell you this, Mrs. Ryan, there was a bombing yesterday . . ."

The maître d' showed Edna to her regular table, and Tully followed along behind, trying not to gape at all the power brokers and celebrities who were here today for lunch. Clearly 21 was one of the places to be seen in Manhattan. Edna stopped at nearly every table to say hi to someone and she introduced them all to Tully, saying, "Here's a girl you should keep your eye on."

By the time they took their seats, Tully felt as if she were floating. She couldn't wait to call Kate and tell her she'd met John Kennedy, Jr.

She knew the value of what had just happened. Edna had just given her the gift of recognition. "Why me?" she asked when their waiter left.

Edna lit up her cigarette and leaned back. Nodding at someone across the room, she seemed not to have heard the question. Tully was about to ask it again when Edna said quietly, "You remind me of me. That surprises you, I see."

"Flatters me."

"I'm from a little town in Oklahoma. When I got to New York—with a degree in journalism and a job in the secretarial pool—I discovered the ugly truth about this career. Practically everyone is Someone or related to Someone. A nobody has to work damn hard. I don't think I slept more than five hours at a time, had a family holiday, or had sex that meant something for almost a decade."

The waiter brought their food, set it down with an obsequious nod, and disappeared again. Smoking cigarette in hand, Edna began cutting her steak. "When I saw you, I thought, *There's the girl I'll help.* I don't know why except, like I said, you reminded me of me."

"My lucky day."

Edna nodded and went back to her food.

"Ms. Guber?" It was the maître d' again, carrying a phone. "There's an urgent call for you."

She took the phone, said, "Talk." Then she listened for a long time. "What're their names? How? Bomb?" She began taking notes. "Seattle reporter killed, producer wounded."

Tully didn't hear anything after *producer*. Edna's voice turned into white noise. She leaned forward. "Who is it?"

Edna pressed the phone to her chest. "Two guys from the affiliate in Seattle were injured in a bombing. Actually, the reporter was killed. The producer, John Ryan, is in critical condition." She went back to her call. "What was the reporter's name?"

Tully drew in a sharp breath. All she could think was: *Johnny.* She closed her eyes, but it didn't help; in the darkness she collected a dozen painful memories: sitting on the deck of his houseboat, talking about her future . . . dancing at that ridiculous nightclub in the seedy part of downtown all those years ago . . . seeing him look at Marah for the first time, with tears in his eyes. "Oh, my God," she said, getting to her feet. "I have to go."

Edna looked up at her, mouthed, "What is it?"

She could barely form the words; they burned her mouth. "Johnny Ryan is my best friend's husband."

"Really?" Edna looked at her, then said into the phone, "Maury, put Tully on the story. She has an in. I'll call you back," and hung up. "Sit down, Tully."

Numbly, she complied. Her legs had practically given out anyway.

Those memories kept hammering her. "I need to help Katie," she muttered.

"It's a big story, Tully," Edna said.

Tully waved that off impatiently. "I don't care about that. She's my best friend."

"Don't care?" Edna said sharply. "Oh, you care. Everyone wants this assignment, but you have an in. Do you know what that means?"

Tully frowned, trying to switch gears from her worry. It seemed vaguely wrong, to make this about her career. "I don't know."

"Then you're not the woman I thought you were. Why can't you get an exclusive and comfort your friend?"

Tully thought about that. "When you put it that way . . ."

"What other way is there? You can get an interview that no one else will have. A thing like this will put you on the map. Could get you the news nook."

Tully couldn't help but be seduced by that. The news nook was a desk on the morning show's set from which the day's biggest news stories were covered. The recognition factor for anyone assigned there was high. Daily national exposure. Several people had made the jump from news nook to host. "And I can protect Kate from everything while I'm there."

"Exactly." Edna picked up the phone and dialed the number. "Hart can get us an exclusive, Maury. It's as good as done. I'll vouch for her." When she hung up, Edna's look was steely. "Don't let me down."

All the way from the restaurant and back to the office, Tully convinced herself that she'd done the right thing. At her desk, she threw her coat onto the back of her chair and called Kate. The phone rang and rang. Finally the answering machine picked up:

You've reached the Ryan household. Neither Johnny nor Kate can come to the phone right now, but if you'll leave a message we'll get back to you as soon as we can.

At the beep, Tully said, "Hey, Katie, it's me. I just heard—"

Kate picked up the phone and disabled the answering machine. "Hey," she said, sounding completely lost. "You got my message. Sorry about the machine. Those bloodsucking reporters won't leave me alone."

"Katie, how—"

"He's in a hospital in Germany. I'm catching a military flight in two hours. I'll call you when I land."

"Hardly. I'll meet you at the hospital."

"In Germany?"

"Of course. I'm not going to let you go through this alone. Your mom has Marah, right?"

"Right. You mean it, Tully?" Kate's voice lifted on the last question, took on an edge of hope.

"Best friends forever, isn't it?"

"No matter what." On that, Kate's voice broke. "Thanks, Tully."

Tully wanted to say, *That's what friends are for,* but the words stuck in her throat. All she could think of was the exclusive she'd promised Edna.

CHAPTER
TWENTY-ONE

For sixteen hours, Kate rode an emotional pendulum that swung between hope and despair. At first she'd focused on details—calling her parents, packing Marah's things, filling out paperwork. The busy-work had been a lifesaver; without it, there was nothing to do but worry. On the flight, she'd taken sleeping pills for the first time in her life, and though her sleep had been oozy, black, and restless, it was infinitely better than being awake.

Now she was being escorted to the hospital. As she approached the entrance, she saw reporters clotted out front. Someone in the crowd must have recognized her, because they turned in unison, like some suddenly roused beast, and pushed forward.

"Mrs. Ryan, what word do you have on his condition?"

"Is it a head injury?"

"Has he spoken—"

"—or opened his eyes?"

She didn't slow down. If there was one thing a producer's wife knew, it was how to move through the press. They were being as respectful as they knew how to be, given their profession. Although Johnny was one of them and they knew that it could have happened to any of them, a story was a story.

"No comment." She pushed through the crowd and entered the hospital. It was like all such institutions—blank walls, utilitarian flooring, crisply uniformed people bustling down wide corridors.

They'd clearly been alerted to her arrival, because a heavyset woman in a white uniform and starched nurse's cap strode toward her, smiling sympathetically.

"You must be Mrs. Ryan," she said in heavily accented English.

"I am."

"I will take you to your husband's room. The doctor will arrive shortly to speak at you."

Kate nodded.

Thankfully, the woman didn't make small talk as they rode up the elevator. On the third floor, they strode past the nurses' station and turned into his room.

He looked frail and broken, like a child in his parents' bed. She stopped, realizing a second too late that she'd spent too much time imagining a reunion and not enough anticipating this reality. This man bore only the shallowest resemblance to her vibrant, handsome husband.

His head was sheathed in white bandages. The entire left side of his face was swollen and discolored; both his eyes were bandaged. Machines and lines and IVs were clustered around him.

The nurse patted her shoulder and gave her a gentle push toward the bed. "He is alive," she said. "This is what you should see when you look at him."

Kate took the most difficult step of her life. Until that moment, she hadn't even realized that she'd stopped moving. "He's usually so strong."

"He needs you to be strong now."

They were the words Kate needed to hear. She had a job here; the time for feeling too much and falling apart would come later when she was alone. "Thank you," she said to the nurse, and walked toward the bed.

Behind her, the door shut quietly, and she knew they were alone now, she and this man who was and wasn't her Johnny.

"This was not our deal," she said. "I distinctly remember that you promised to be okay. So, I'm going to assume you'll honor that." She wiped her eyes and leaned down to kiss his swollen cheek. "Mom and Dad send their prayers. Marah is with them right now. And Tully is flying over to be with us; you know how pissed she'll be if you don't give her your full attention. You might as well wake up now before she badgers you to death." She tripped over the last word, winced, straightening by sheer dint of will. "I didn't mean that," she whispered, gripping the bedrails tightly. "Can you hear me, John Ryan? Let me know you're in there." She reached down, took his hand in hers. "Squeeze my hand, baby. You can do it." Then: "Say something, damn it. I won't even yell at you for scaring the shit out of me. Not right away, anyway."

"Mrs. Ryan?"

Kate hadn't even heard the door open. When she turned, there was a man standing not more than ten feet away from her.

"I'm Dr. Carl Schmidt. I am in charge of your husband's care."

The polite thing to do would have been to let go, cross the room, and shake Dr. Schmidt's hand, and for all her life Kate had done things correctly, but now she couldn't move, couldn't pretend to be okay. "And?" was all she could say.

"He has suffered a serious head injury, as you no doubt know. He is heavily sedated right now, so we cannot do a comprehensive testing of his brain function. He received excellent medical care in Baghdad. The doctors there removed a section of his skull—"

"They what?"

"Removed a section of his skull to allow the brain to swell. Do not worry. This is most routine in such an injury."

She wanted to say that an appendectomy was routine, but didn't dare. "Why are his eyes bandaged?"

"We don't know yet if—"

The door behind him banged open, cracked against the wall. Tully burst into the room—there was no other word for it—and stopped dead. She was breathing hard and her face was suspiciously bright.

"Sorry it took me so long, Katie. No one would tell me where the hell you were."

"I am sorry," the doctor said. "It is family only in here."

"She is family," Kate said, reaching for Tully's hand. Tully batted away her hand and pulled her into a hug; they cried together, holding on, until finally Kate drew back, wiping her eyes.

The doctor said, "We do not know yet if he will be blind. These are things we will know if he wakes up."

"When he wakes up," Tully said, but her voice was unsteady.

"The next forty-eight hours will tell us much news," the doctor said seamlessly, as if he hadn't been interrupted.

Forty-eight hours. It sounded like a lifetime.

"Keep talking to him," the doctor said. "This couldn't hurt, yes?"

Kate nodded, stepping aside as the doctor moved to the bed and checked Johnny. He made a few notes on the chart and then left.

The minute he was gone, Tully took Kate by the shoulders, gave her a little shake. "We are not going to believe any bad stuff. Herr Doctor doesn't know Johnny Ryan. We do. He promised to come home to you and Marah and he's a man who keeps his promises."

Tully's mere presence buoyed Kate, kept her afloat. The strength that had been so quick to leave her came back. "You'd better listen to her, Johnny. You know what a bitch she can be when she's wrong."

For the next six hours they stayed there, beside his bed. Kate would talk for as long as she could; when she ran out of steam or started to cry, Tully would step in, picking up the conversation.

Somewhere in the middle of the night—Kate had no conception of what time it was—they went down to the empty cafeteria and bought food from vending machines and sat down at a table near the window.

Alone but for the empty tables, they stared at each other.

"What are you going to do about the press?"

Kate looked up. "What do you mean?"

Tully shrugged and sipped her coffee. "You saw the reporters out front. He's a big story, Katie."

"The nurse told me they tried to take pictures of him as he was being wheeled in. One reporter even tried to bribe one of the orderlies on the floor to get a picture of his bandaged face. Cockroaches. No offense."

"None taken. And we're not all that way, Katie."

"He wouldn't want them to know."

"Are you kidding? He's a journalist. He'd certainly advocate giving his colleagues—or at least one colleague—his story."

"You think he wants the world to know that he might be blind or brain-damaged? How could he get work again? No way. This story stays contained until I know how he is."

"They said he might be brain-damaged?"

"They took off a piece of his skull. What do you think?" Kate shuddered. "The world has no business looking under his bandages."

"It's news, Kate," Tully said softly. "If you gave me an exclusive, I could protect you."

"If it weren't for the damn news, he wouldn't be fighting for his life right now."

"I'm not the only one who believes in it."

It was a direct reminder of the thing Johnny and Tully shared, that bond which had always excluded Kate. She wanted to make a smart-ass remark, but she was too tired. She hadn't slept well in weeks and every muscle and sinew in her body ached.

Tully covered Kate's hand with her own. "Let me handle the media for you. Just me. That way you don't even have to think about it."

Kate smiled for the first time in probably twenty-four hours. "What would I do without you, Tully?"

"Are you kidding me? Three days I wait for your call and when you do bother to call, it's to say you need more time?"

Tully leaned closer to the pay phone, trying to squeeze a small bit of privacy out of a very public place. "The family isn't ready to go public yet, Maury. The doctors are respecting their wishes. Surely you can understand that."

"Understand it? Who gives a shit if I understand it? This is world news, Tully, not some damn sorority gossip circle. CNN has reported that he has a head injury—"

"That's officially unconfirmed."

"Damn it, Tully. You're putting me in a hell of a spot. The higher-ups are pissed off. There was talk this morning of pulling you off the story. Dick wants to send—"

"I'll get you something."

"Get me the story today and I'll move you into the news nook next week."

Tully thought for a moment she'd imagined the promise. "You mean it?"

"You have twenty-four hours, Tully. At the end of that time you can be a hero or a zero. It's up to you."

Tully heard him slam the phone down. Through the glass windows of the empty lobby, she could see the reporters clustered along the sidewalk. For three days they'd been waiting for official word on Johnny's condition. In the meantime, they'd reported the known facts—the events that led up to the bombing, the field reports of his injuries, and his backstory in Central America. Additionally, they'd used this to springboard on to other tangentially related general stories, things like the danger to journalists covering wars, the specific challenges of Desert Storm, and the myriad types of injuries that commonly accompany bombings.

She stood there, wondering how in the hell she was going to do this. Everything needed to be done exactly right so that both Maury and Kate got what they wanted. It was up to Tully to make it all happen, and if she did this one thing well, it might change her future. She'd die before she'd let Edna down, and like Edna had said, Tully could do her job and still protect Kate. She'd have to break the story, but how she did it was what mattered.

Carefully. Tactfully. No mention of brain damage or potential blindness. That way everyone got what they wanted.

The news nook.

All her life she'd dreamed of that job, imagined it as the start of everything. She couldn't let go of the opportunity to have it. Surely Kate would understand the importance of that.

Of course.

Smiling, she went in search of her cameraman. They'd start with some establishing shots—background, hospital interior and exterior, that sort of thing. They'd hide the camera as much as they needed to. Fortunately, everyone who mattered knew that Kate had given Tully full access to visit Johnny.

She went to the front door and stepped out into the cold gray afternoon. Her cameraman was standing off to the side, away from the group of reporters. At her signal, he hid his camera under his quilted goose-down coat and headed toward her.

Kate sat in Dr. Schmidt's office, listening. "So the swelling isn't going down," she said, trying not to twist her sweaty hands together. She was so tired, it was a struggle simply to keep her eyes open.

"Not as quickly as we would wish. If soon there is not some improvement I am thinking we will go to surgery again."

She nodded.

"Do not worry yet, Mrs. Ryan. Your husband is very strong. We can see that he is fighting hard."

"How can you tell?"

"Why, because he is still alive. A weaker man would not be here now."

She tried to take strength from that, to truly believe it, but hope was becoming difficult to hold on to. Each passing day had sanded her down, weakened the walls of her denial; in places, fear called itself truth and poked through.

Dr. Schmidt stood. "I must to see a patient now. I will walk with you part of the way back to Mr. Ryan's room."

She nodded and fell into step beside him. For a moment, with him beside her talking in his soft, authoritative voice, she felt a longing for her father.

"Well, this is where I must turn a different way," Dr. Schmidt said, pointing down the hallway toward the radiology department.

Kate nodded. She would have mumbled a simple goodbye, but she didn't trust her voice, and the last thing she wanted to do was to show her weakness.

She stood in the hallway, watching him walk away from her. Near the end of the corridor, he merged into the white-clad sea of bodies and disappeared.

With a sigh, she headed back to Johnny's room. If she was lucky, Tully was there now. Just her friend's presence was a huge help. Honestly, Kate didn't know how she would have made it through the past days without Tully. They'd played cards and told stories and even sang a few old songs together, hoping Johnny would want to wake up to tell them to be quiet. Last night, Tully had found an old episode of *The Partridge Family* broadcast in German. She'd cracked Kate up with her own made-up dialogue that had David Cassidy hot for his TV sister. The nurses had even come in to tell them to be quiet.

Kate turned a corner and saw a tall, long-haired man in a puffy blue coat and ragged jeans standing at the door to Johnny's room. A black video camera rested on his shoulder. He was shooting now; she could tell by the red light on the camera.

She ran down the hall, grabbed the man's puffy coat sleeve, and spun him around. "What in the hell are you doing?" She shoved him so hard he stumbled back, almost fell. It felt good, so good she wished she'd punched him in the face. "Scavenger," she hissed, switching off the camera with one stab of her finger.

That was when she saw Tully. Her best friend stood at the end of Johnny's bed, dressed in a red V-neck sweater and black pants, her hair and makeup camera-ready, holding a microphone.

"Oh, my God," Kate whispered.

"It's not what you think."

"You're not reporting on Johnny's condition?"

"I am, you know I am, but I was going to talk to you about it. Explain everything. I came up to ask you—"

"With a cameraman," Kate said, stepping back.

Tully ran over to her, pleading. "My boss called. They're going to fire me if I don't get this story. I knew you'd understand if I just told you the truth. You know the news and how much this means to me, but I would never do anything to hurt you or Johnny."

"How dare you! You're supposed to be my friend."

"I am your friend." Tully's voice took on an edge of panic. The look in her eyes was so unfamiliar it took Kate a moment to recognize it: fear. "I shouldn't have started filming, I admit it, but I didn't think you'd mind. Johnny sure as hell wouldn't. He's a newsman, like me. Like you used to be. He knows that the story—"

Kate slapped Tully across the face as hard as she could. "He's not your story. He's my husband." On that last word, Kate's voice broke. "Get out. Get away." When Tully didn't move, Kate screamed, "Now. Get the hell out of this room. It's family only."

Beside Johnny's bed, an alarm blared.

White-clad nurses streamed into the room, pushed Kate and Tully aside. They transferred him to a gurney and wheeled him out of the room.

Kate stood there, staring at the empty sheets of his bed.

"Katie—"

"Get out," she said dully.

Tully grabbed her sleeve. "Come on, Katie. We're best friends forever. No matter what. Remember? You need me now."

"You are hardly the kind of friend I need." She wrenched free and ran out of the room.

It wasn't until she was on the second floor, alone in the women's bathroom, staring at the green metal door of the stall, that she cried.

Hours later, Kate sat alone in the family waiting room. At times throughout the day there had been others in here, groups of huddled, glassy-eyed people waiting for news of their loved ones. Now, however, the volunteer at the desk had gone home and the room was empty.

Never before had time crawled so slowly. She had nothing to do, no way to trick her mind into thinking about something else. She tried to flip through the magazines, but none were in English and the pictures didn't hold her attention. Even a phone call home hadn't helped. Without Tully here to buoy her, she felt herself sinking into despair.

"Mrs. Ryan?"

Kate got quickly to her feet. "Hello, Doctor. How did the surgery go?"

"He is most well. There was extensive bleeding in his brain, which we think accounts for the continued swelling. We have now stopped it. Perhaps this will give us reason for new hope, yes? Shall I walk you back to his room?"

It was enough that he was still alive.

"Thank you."

As they passed the nurses' station, he said, "Do you wish me to page your friend, Tallulah? Certainly you don't desire to be alone now."

"I don't want to be alone now, that's true," Kate said. "But Tallulah is no longer welcome here."

"Ah. Well. You must keep believing that he will wake up. I have seen many so-called miracles in my years here. Often, I think faith has its part to play."

"I'm afraid to get my hopes up," she said quietly.

He paused at the closed door of Johnny's room and looked down at her. "I did not say that faith was easy; merely that it was necessary. And you are here, are you not, by his side? This takes its own kind of courage, yes?" He patted her shoulder and left her standing by the door.

She wasn't sure how long she stood there, alone in the stark white hospital; in time, though, she went inside and sat down. In a quiet, halting voice, she closed her eyes and talked to him. About what, she couldn't have said. All she knew was that a voice could offer light in a dark place, and light could lead you out.

The next thing she knew, it was morning. Sunlight glowed through the exterior window, illuminating the beige linoleum floor tiles and gray-white walls.

She unfolded from the chair and stood beside the bed, feeling stiff and sore. "Hey, handsome," she murmured, leaning down to kiss Johnny's cheek. The bandages on his eyes had been removed; she could see now how bruised and swollen his left eye was. "No more bleeding in the brain allowed, okay? When you need attention just try the old-fashioned ways, like getting mad or kissing me."

She kept talking until she ran out of things to say. Finally she turned on the television that hung in the corner. It came on with a thunk and a buzz and showed a grainy black and white picture. "The machine you love so much," she said bitterly, reaching down for his hand. Taking his dry, slack fingers in hers, she held on to him. Leaning down, she kissed his cheek and lingered there. Though he smelled of hospitals and disinfectants and medicines, if she tried hard enough, believed strongly enough, she could smell the familiar essence of him. "The TV is on. You're big news."

No response.

Idly she flipped through the channels, looking for something in English.

Tully's face filled the screen.

She was standing in front of the hospital with her microphone held up to her mouth. Captions along the bottom of the screen translated her words: "For days the world has wondered and worried about John Patrick Ryan, the TV news producer who was seriously injured when a bomb exploded near the Al-Rashid Hotel. Although funeral services were held yesterday for the reporter, Arthur Gulder, who was with him, the Ryan family and the German hospital remained unavailable to journalists. And how can we blame them? This is a time of deep personal tragedy for the Ryan family. John—Johnny to his friends—suffered a serious head trauma in the explosion. A complicated medical procedure was performed on him at an army hospital near Baghdad. Specialists tell me that without this life-saving surgery on site, Mr. Ryan would not have survived."

The picture on screen changed. Now Tully was standing beside Johnny's bed. He lay motionless on the white sheets, his head and eyes bandaged. Though the camera lingered on Johnny for only an instant before returning to Tully's face, the image of him was hard to forget.

"Mr. Ryan's prognosis is uncertain. The specialists with whom I spoke said it is a waiting game to see if the swelling in his brain recedes. If it does, he has an excellent chance of survival. If not . . ." Her voice trailed off as she moved around to the end of the bed. There, she looked directly into the camera. "Everything about this case is uncertain right now, except this: This is a story of heroes, both in the war zone and at home. John Ryan wanted to bring this story to the American people, and I know him well enough to say that he knew the risks he was taking and wouldn't have made another choice. And while he was covering the war, his wife, Kathleen, was at home with their one-year-old daughter, believing that what her husband was doing was important. Like any soldier's wife, it was her sacrifice as much as his that made it possible for John Ryan to do his job." The picture cut back to Tully on the hospital steps. "This is Tallulah Hart, reporting from Germany. And may I say, Bryant, that our prayers are certainly with the Ryan family today."

Kate stared at the television long after the segment had ended. "She made us look like heroes," she said to the empty room. "Even me."

She felt a flutter-soft movement against her palm. It was so gentle that at first she almost didn't notice. Frowning, she glanced down.

Johnny slowly opened his eyes.

"Johnny?" she whispered, half afraid that she was making this up, that the stress had finally cracked her. "Can you see me?"

He squeezed her hand. It was barely a squeeze, really; normally it wouldn't even qualify as a touch, but now it made her laugh and cry at the same time.

"Can you see me?" she asked again, leaning close. "Close your eyes once if you can see me."

Slowly, he closed his eyes.

She kissed his cheek, his forehead, his cracked, dry lips. "Do you know where you are?" she finally asked, pulling back, hitting the nurses' button.

She could see the confusion in his eyes and it scared her. "How about me? Do you know who I am?"

He stared up at her, swallowed hard. Slowly, he opened his mouth and said, "My . . . Katie."

"Yes," she said, bursting into tears. "I'm your Katie."

The next seventy-two hours were a whirlwind of meetings, procedures, tests, and medication adjustments. Kate accompanied Johnny to consultations with ophthalmologists, psychiatrists, physical therapists, speech and occupational therapists, and, of course, Dr. Schmidt. Everyone, it seemed, had to sign off on Johnny's recovery before she could move him to a rehabilitation center near home.

"He is lucky to have you," Dr. Schmidt said at the conclusion of their meeting.

Kate smiled. "I'm lucky to have him."

"Yes. Now I suggest you go to the cafeteria and have some lunch. You have lost too much weight this week."

"Really?"

"Certainly. Now go. I will return your husband to his room when the tests are finished."

Kate rose. "Thank you, Dr. Schmidt. For everything."

He made an it's-nothing gesture with his hand. "This is my job."

Smiling, she headed for the door. She was nearly there when he called her name again. She turned. "Yes?"

"There are not many reporters left, but is it acceptable to report on your husband's condition? We would very much like them to leave."

"I'll think about it."

"Excellent."

Kate left his office and went to the elevator at the end of the hall.

The cafeteria was mostly empty on this late Thursday afternoon. There were a few groups of employees gathered around the rectangular tables and a few families ordering food. It was easy to tell which group was which. The employees were laughing and talking while they ate;

the patients' families were quiet and still, staring down at their food and looking up at the clock every few minutes.

Kate made her way through the tables to the window. Outside, the sky was a dark, steely gray; any moment it would start to rain or snow.

Even with the distortion of the glass, she could see how tired she looked, how spent.

It was odd, but somehow it was harder to be alone with her relief than with her despair. Then, she'd wanted mostly to sit quietly and blank out her mind and try to imagine the best. Now she wanted to laugh with someone, to smile and raise a glass in celebration and say she'd known all along it would end like this.

No. Not someone.

Tully.

For all of Kate's life, Tully had been the first line of celebration, the party just waiting to happen. Her best friend would toast crossing the street safely if that was what Kate wanted.

Turning away from the window, she went over to the table and sat down.

"You look like you could use a drink."

Kate looked up. Tully stood there, dressed in crisp black jeans and a white boat-necked angora sweater. Although her hair and makeup were perfect, she looked tired. And nervous.

"You're still here?"

"You thought I'd leave you?" Tully tried to smile, but it wasn't the real thing. "I brought you a cup of tea."

Kate stared at the Styrofoam cup in Tully's hand. She knew it was her favorite—Earl Grey—doctored with just the right amount of sugar.

It was the only apology Tully knew how to make for what she'd done. If Kate accepted it, she knew that the episode would have to be forgotten—the betrayal and the slap would have to dissolve into nothing so they could step back onto the track that had connected their lives. No regrets, no grudges. They'd be TullyandKate again, or as close to that as grown women could be.

"The story was good," she said evenly.

Tully's eyes pleaded for forgiveness and understanding, but what she said was, "I'm getting the news nook for next week. It's a replacement gig, but it's a start."

Kate thought, *So that's what you sold me out for,* but knew she couldn't say it. Instead, she said, "Congratulations."

Tully held out the cup of tea. "Take it, Katie. Please."

Kate looked at her friend for a long time. She wanted the gift of words—*I'm sorry*—but knew they'd never come. Tully simply wasn't wired that way. Kate had never known exactly how it had happened, Tully's inability to apologize, but she suspected that it had something to do with Cloud. There was some bit of her best friend that had been damaged beyond repair as a child, and this, somehow, was the scar. Finally, she reached for the cup, saying, "Thanks."

Tully grinned and sat down beside her. Before she'd even scooted up to the table, she was talking.

Soon, Tully had Kate laughing. That was the thing about best friends. Like sisters and mothers, they could piss you off and make you cry and break your heart, but in the end, when the chips were down, they were there, making you laugh even in your darkest hours.

CHAPTER
TWENTY-TWO

As bad as that year was, Kate knew every moment that it could have been so much worse. The man she brought home from Germany bore only the merest resemblance to her husband in those first few months. His brain was slow in healing, and sometimes he lost patience with himself when a word outran him or an idea couldn't be latched on to. She spent endless hours with him in rehab, both working with him and his physical therapist and waiting in the lobby with Marah.

From the second they got home, Marah seemed to sense that something was wrong with Daddy, and no amount of cuddling could comfort her. More often than not, she woke screaming in the middle of the night and wouldn't fall silent until Kate brought her into bed with them (a practice which made Mom roll her eyes, light a smoke, and say, "You'll be sorry.")

When the holidays came around, Kate decorated extensively, hoping the sight of their treasured collectibles would somehow knit them all together again and make them the family they'd been before.

During the girlfriend hour, while she sipped her glass of wine and told Aunt Georgia and Mom that she was holding up well, she started to cry.

Mom took her hand. "It's okay, honey. Let it out."

But she was afraid to do that. "I'm fine," she said. "It's been a difficult year, that's all."

The doorbell rang.

Aunt Georgia got up. "That's probably Rick and Kelli."

It was Tully. Standing on the porch, wearing a winter-white three-quarter-length cashmere coat and matching pants, she looked drop-dead gorgeous. There were enough presents in her arms for three families. "Don't tell me you started girlfriend hour without me. If you did, you'll have to start it over."

"You said you had to go to Berlin," Kate said, wishing she'd dressed a little better and put on some makeup.

"And miss Christmas? Hardly." She set the presents down beneath the tree and pulled Kate into a hug.

Kate hadn't realized how much she'd missed her friend until right then.

Tully turned the quiet girlfriend hour into a party. At one o'clock, long after they were supposed to have put the turkey in the oven, Mom and Aunt Georgia and Tully were still dancing to ABBA and Elton John, singing at the top of their lungs.

Kate stood by the tree. The room seemed lit from within suddenly. How was it that Tully could be the life of any party so easily? Maybe it was because she didn't do any of the scut work—no cleaning or cooking or laundry for Tully.

Johnny came up to Kate. She noticed that he was barely limping. "Hey, you," he said.

"Hey."

All around them, people were talking and singing. Aunt Georgia was doing "The Time Warp" with Sean, his girlfriend, and Uncle Ralph. Mom and Dad were talking to Tully, who was swaying to the music with Marah in her arms.

Johnny reached down beneath the tree and found a small box, wrapped in silver and gold paper, with Scotch tape showing along the seams and a red foil bow that was too big. He handed it to her.

"You want me to open it now?"

He nodded.

She peeled back the paper, plucked off the bow, and found a blue velvet box inside. Opening it, she gasped. There lay a fine gold necklace and a diamond-encrusted heart-shaped locket. "Johnny . . ."

"I've done some stupid things in my life, Katie, and for most of them I've paid the price. Lately, you've paid the price, too. I know how hard it's been on you, this past year. And I want you to know this: you are the one thing I've done right in this life." He took the necklace out of the box and put it on her. "I've taken a new job at my old station. You won't have to worry about me anymore. You're my heart, Katie Scarlett, and I'll always be here for you. I love you."

Kate's throat tightened with emotion. "I love you, too."

During college, the cherry trees in the Quad had marked the passing of time. Every season came and went on those spindly gray-brown branches. In the eighties, time had been marked by the streetlamps on the cobblestoned street in front of the Public Market. When the first SEASON'S GREETINGS flag fluttered beneath the lamps, she knew another year had gone by.

In the nineties it was Tully's hair. Every morning, while Kate fed and bathed Marah, she watched the morning show on TV. Like clockwork, Tully's hairdos changed twice a year. First there had been the Jane Pauley extra-short bangs, then the Meg Ryan messy look, then the pixie cut that made her look impossibly young, and most recently, she'd chosen the most talked-about cut in the country—the Rachel.

Every time Kate saw a new hairdo, she winced at how fast time was moving. The years weren't just passing, they were flying by. Already it was the last day of August, 1997. In a little more than a week her baby would be starting second grade.

She hated to admit how much she'd been looking forward to this day.

For the past seven years, she'd been the best mother she knew how to be. She'd diligently recorded every milestone in Marah's baby album and took enough photographs to scientifically document a new life-form. More than that, she enjoyed her daughter so much that she sometimes felt lost in the sea of love that surrounded them. She and Johnny had tried for years to conceive another child, but they had not been so blessed. It had been difficult for Kate to handle; in time, though, she'd accepted her small family and poured herself into making every moment perfect. Finally, she'd found something she was passionate about: motherhood.

But as the months turned into years, she'd begun to feel a tiny itch of dissatisfaction. At first she'd kept it bottled inside of her—after all, what did she have to complain about? She loved her life. She spent what spare hours she did have volunteering in the classroom and at Helper House, the local center that provided assistance to women in need. She even took a few art classes.

It wasn't enough, didn't fill the invisible void, but it made her feel productive and useful. And though the people who loved her—Johnny, Tully, and Mom—repeatedly commented that she seemed to be looking for something more, she ignored them all. It was so much easier to focus on the present, on her daughter. There would be plenty of time later on to search for herself.

Now she stood at the living room window, dressed in her flannel pajamas, staring out at the still-dark backyard. Even in the shadows she could see toys strewn about the deck and yard. Barbies. Beanie Babies. A tricycle lying on its side. A pink plastic Corvette was washing back and forth on the incoming tide.

Shaking her head, she turned away from the view and went to the television, turning it on. As soon as Marah woke up, she was going to make her daughter march outside and pick up the toys. A temper tantrum was sure to follow.

The television came on with a thump. A BREAKING NEWS banner ran beneath Bernard Shaw's grave face. Behind him, a montage of Princess Diana photographs reeled off, one after another. "For those of you just tuning in," Bernard said, "the news from France is that Princess Diana is dead . . ."

Kate stared at the screen, not quite comprehending.

The princess. *Their* princess. Dead?

Beside her, the phone rang. Without looking away from the TV, she answered it. "Hello?"

"You're watching the news?"

"It's true?"

"I'm in London to cover it."

"Oh, my God." Kate stared at the images on the TV—young, shy Diana in her plaid skirt and bomber-type jacket, with her eyes downcast; pregnant Diana, looking hopeful and radiantly happy; elegant Diana, in a gorgeous off-the-shoulder gown, dancing with John Travolta at the White House; laughing Diana, on a ride at Disneyland with her boys; and finally, Diana alone, in a hospital far from home, holding a malnourished black baby.

In those few images were the whole of a woman's life.

"It can be over so fast," Kate said, more to herself than to Tully. She realized a moment too late that Tully had been talking and she'd interrupted her.

"She was just starting to come into her own, too."

Maybe she'd waited too long to try. Kate knew about that, about how frightening it could be to watch your children grow up and your husband go off to work and to wonder what you'd do with the sliver of life that was yours.

Familiar photographs filled the screen: Diana, walking alone at some event, waving to the crowd, then the image changed to the front gates of one of the castles, where flowers were beginning to pile up in remembrance. Life could change so quickly. She'd forgotten that somehow.

"Kate? Are you okay?"

"I think I'll sign up for a writing class at UW," she said slowly. The words felt pulled out of her somehow.

"Really? That's great. You always were a kick-ass writer."

Kate didn't respond. She sank down to the sofa and just stared at the TV, surprised when she began to cry.

Almost immediately, Kate regretted the decision she'd made. Well, that wasn't entirely true. What she actually regretted was that she'd told Tully, who'd told Mom, who'd told Johnny.

"You know, it's a great idea," Johnny said a few nights later as they lay in bed, watching television. "I'll help out with whatever you need me to do."

Kate wanted to give him a laundry list of reasons that it was too burdensome for her schedule. He and Tully made everything sound so easy, as if life were a combo plate you could order and pay for. She knew how wrong they were, how it felt to find that you weren't good enough.

In the end, though, she could lie to herself and make excuses for only so long. When Marah went off to school, waving wildly, Kate was left with the empty hours of her day. Chores and obligations could only fill some of her time.

So, on a hot Indian summer day in mid-September, she dropped Marah off at school, drove onto the midmorning ferry, and merged into the downtown Seattle traffic. At ten-thirty she parked in the visitors' lot at the University of Washington, walked to the Registration Building, and signed up for a single class: Introduction to Fiction Writing.

For the next week, she was a nervous wreck.

"I can't do it," she whined to her husband, feeling sick to her stomach on the day of the first class.

"You can do it. I'll take Marah to school so you won't be stressed about catching the ferry."

"But I am stressed."

He bent down and kissed her, then drew back, smiling. "Get your ass out of bed."

After that, she moved on autopilot—taking a shower, dressing, packing her backpack.

All the way to UW she thought: *What am I doing? I'm thirty-seven years old. I can't go back to college.*

And then she was in the classroom, the only person in the room who was over thirty—including the teacher.

She wasn't sure when she relaxed, but gradually, her stomachache eased. The more the professor talked about writing, about the gift of storytelling, the more Kate felt she belonged here.

From her place at the news desk, Tully finished her on-air banter with the show's cohosts, then turned her attention to the TelePrompTer, reading the news seamlessly. "Chief Tom Koby of the Denver police conceded today that mistakes were made early in the JonBenét Ramsey investigation. Sources close to the case allege that . . ."

When she was done, she gave the camera her trademark smile and turned the show back over to Bryant and Katie. As she was gathering her script and notes, an assistant producer came and whispered in her ear, "Your agent is on the phone, Tully. He says it's urgent."

"Thanks."

She talked to several members of the cast and crew as she made her way out of the studio and up to her office. There, she closed the door and picked up the phone, punching in line one. "This is Tully. Hi, George."

"There's a car waiting for you out front. I'll meet you at the Plaza in fifteen minutes."

"What's going on?"

"Touch up your makeup and move."

She hung up, told everyone who needed to know that she was leaving for a meeting, and left the building.

At the hotel, a liveried bellman appeared instantly to open the car door for her, saying, "Welcome to the Plaza, Ms. Hart."

"Thank you." She handed him a ten-dollar bill and went into the cream and gold marble lobby.

Her agent, George Davison, was waiting for her, looking elegant in a gray Armani suit. "Are you ready to make your dreams come true?"

"You're finally going to do that, huh?"

He led her down the hallway filled with glass cases that held expensive items for sale from the various gift shops and the sparkling jewelry store, and into the airy, high-ceilinged restaurant.

She saw instantly who they were meeting. In a back corner of the room hidden behind the world-class buffet was the president of CBS.

He stood at her arrival. "Hello, Tallulah, thank you for coming."

She missed a step but not her smile. "Hello." She took the seat across from him, watched George sit between them.

"I won't beat around the bush. As you know, *The Today Show* is killing our morning show in the ratings."

"Yes."

"At CBS, we think you're a big part of the show's success. I've particularly noticed your interviewing skills. Amy Fisher and Joey Buttafuoco, the survivors of the Oklahoma City bombing. O.J.'s defense team and Lyle Menendez. You were great."

"Thank you."

"We'd like to offer you the cohost spot on our show, beginning with the first show in '98. Our market research indicates that viewers connect with you. They like and trust you. That's exactly what we need to get our ratings back. What do you say?"

Tully felt as if she might float out of her chair. There was no way to contain her joy or make her smile anything other than huge. "I'm stunned. And honored."

"What's the offer?" George said.

"One million dollars a year for five years."

"Two million a year," George said.

"Done. What do you say, Tully?"

Tully didn't look at her agent. She didn't have to; they'd been dreaming about an offer like this for years. "I say hell, yes. And can I start tomorrow?"

In writing, Kate found her voice again. She woke every morning at six and went into the office she'd set up in the spare bedroom. There, she worked diligently to craft and recraft her sentences, polishing each paragraph until it revealed all that she was trying to say. At some point in this first hour Johnny came in to kiss her goodbye, and then she was alone again until Marah woke and her real-life day began.

She had so much confidence when she was in that pseudo-office of hers, with her fingers on the computer's keyboard. If only she felt so sure of herself now.

She stood in the front of the classroom, with a green blackboard behind her. In the desk/chair sets in front of her, a dozen or so bored-looking kids slumped in their chairs; more than a few appeared to be sleeping. Beside her, the professor—a young guy with long, shaggy hair, wearing Air Jordans and camouflage pants—waited patiently.

Kate took a deep breath and began to read: "The girl in the small room in the ramshackle house was all alone again. Or she thought she was. In this place where the lights didn't work and the windows were covered in black paper and duct tape, it was hard to tell the truth. Should she take a chance and try to escape? That was the question. The last time she'd tried to run, she'd miscalculated and it had cost her. Unconsciously she rubbed the still-tender area along her jaw . . ."

She lost herself in the words she'd written, in the short story that was hers and hers alone. All too quickly it was over, the last sentence read, and she looked up, expecting to see a new respect in the faces that stared up at her.

No such luck.

"Well," the professor said, coming forward. "That was entertaining. It seems we have a budding genre writer in our midst. Who has a comment?"

For the next twenty minutes, they dissected Kate's story, looking for flaws. She listened carefully, refusing to let herself be stung by the criticisms. Who cared that she'd spent almost four weeks on these six pages? What mattered was that she could improve. She could tighten her story and try to master viewpoint and be more careful with her dialogue.

By the end of class, instead of feeling wounded or dejected, she felt empowered, as if a heretofore unseen path had just been revealed. She couldn't wait to get home and try again.

As she packed up her stuff to leave, the professor came over to her, said, "You show real promise, Kate."

"Thank you."

Beaming, she hurried out of the classroom. All the way across campus and through the student parking lot, she imagined new directions for the story, ways to fix it.

So caught up in her imagined world was she that she missed her exit and had to backtrack.

At just past 1:20, she pulled into the parking stall under the cement viaduct and walked across the street to Ivar's Restaurant. Her mother was already seated at a table in the corner. Through the wall of windows, Elliott Bay sparkled in the sunlight. Seagulls wheeled and dropped and dove for french fries thrown by tourists on the pier outside.

"Sorry I'm late," Kate said, sitting down across from her mom, unhooking her fanny pack and letting it rest in her lap. "I hate driving in the city."

"I ordered us both shrimp louies. I know you have to catch the two-ten boat." Mom leaned forward, put her elbows on the table. "Well? Did your professor think your story was better than John Grisham?"

Kate couldn't help laughing at that. "He didn't use those exact words, no. But he did say I had talent."

"Oh." Mom sat back, looking disappointed. "I think your story was brilliant. Even Daddy thought so."

"Dad thinks I'm better than John Grisham, too? And on my very first story. I guess I'm a genius."

"Are you saying our opinion is somewhat inflated?"

"Somewhat. But I love you for it."

"I'm proud of you, Katie," she said softly. "I always wanted to find something like that for me. I guess I made afghans instead."

"You raised two great kids—well, one great one and one pretty good one," Kate teased. "And you stayed married and made everyone happy. You should be proud of that."

"I am, but . . ."

Kate placed her hand on her mother's. They both understood; every at-home mom in the world understood. Ultimately there were prices to be paid for the choices a woman made. "You're my hero, Mom," Kate said simply.

Mom looked at her, tears bright in her eyes. Before she could answer, the waitress returned with their salads and lemonades, put the lunch on the table, and left.

Kate picked up her fork and started eating.

The nausea hit without warning.

"Excuse me," Kate mumbled, dropping her fork and clamping a hand over her mouth as she ran for the restroom. There, in a stiflingly small cubicle, she threw up.

When there was nothing left in her stomach, she went to the sink and washed her hands and face, rinsed out her mouth.

Her whole body felt trembly and weak. Her face in the mirror was bone-pale and drawn. For the first time she noticed the dark shadows under her eyes.

Maybe she was coming down with the stomach flu, she thought. Everyone at playgroup was sick this week.

Still feeling shaky, she returned to the table, under her mother's watchful gaze.

"I'm fine," Kate said, taking her seat. "I took Marah to playgroup this weekend. All the kids were sick." She waited for her mother to respond. When the silence went on and on, Kate finally looked up. "What?"

"Mayonnaise," her mother said. "It made you sick when you were pregnant with Marah, too."

It felt as if the chair beneath Kate just evaporated—poof! disappeared—and she was falling fast. Several annoyances clicked into place and became clues: tender breasts even though she wasn't having her period; trouble sleeping; exhaustion. She closed her eyes and shook her head, sighing. She'd wanted another baby—she and Johnny both did— but it had been so long, they'd given up. And now everything was going so well with the writing. She didn't want to go back to sleepless nights and crying babies and days that left her too tired to answer a question at the dinner table, let alone write a story.

"You'll just take a little longer to get published," her mother said. "You'll be able to do both."

"We wanted another baby," she said, trying to smile. "And I'll still keep writing. You'll see." She almost had herself convinced. "I can do it with two kids."

On Thursday, two days later, she found out she was having twins.

Part Four

THE NEW MILLENNIUM

A Moment Like This

some people wait a lifetime

CHAPTER
TWENTY-THREE

By 2000, Kate rarely paused in the whirlwind chaos of her everyday life to wonder where the years had gone. Contemplation and reflection, like relaxation, were thoughts from another era, ideas from another life. The road not taken, as they used to say. A woman with three children—a ten-year-old girl who was fast approaching puberty and twin boys under two—simply didn't have time to think about herself much, and the number of years that separated her kids' ages created almost two families. She knew now why women had their children closer together. Starting over doubled a mother's exhaustion level.

Her days were consumed by details, and this surprisingly sunny morning in March was no exception. The chores stacked up, one on top of another, until she found herself running from sunrise to well past sunset. The crappy part was that she never seemed to accomplish anything substantial, yet she almost never had an hour to herself. The at-home mother's life: it was a race with no finish line. That was what they talked about in the carpool line as they waited for their kids to leave school. That, and divorce. Every month lately it seemed that one seemingly solid marriage had shown its crumbling clay foundation.

Except today wasn't just another ordinary bead in the strand of her life. Today, Tully was coming to Seattle for a promotional tour. It would be the first time they'd seen each other in months, and Kate couldn't wait. She needed some girlfriend time.

She hurried through her To Do list—dropped Marah off at school, spent too long at Safeway, bought all-new makeup at Rite Aid, made it to the library in time for reading hour, picked up Johnny's dry cleaning, got the boys down for their naps, and cleaned the house.

By two-thirty, as she pulled out of the carpool lane—again—she was exhausted.

"Aunt Tully's coming to spend the night tonight, right, Mommy?" Marah said from the backseat. She looked tiny, wedged in as she was between the boys' dump-truck-sized car seats.

"That's right."

"Are you gonna wear makeup?"

Kate couldn't help smiling at that. She wasn't quite sure how it had happened, but somehow she'd raised a tiny beauty queen. At ten, Marah already had more fashion sense and style sensibility than Kate ever had. She watched in amazement as her tall, slim ten-year-old daughter poured over the teen fashion magazines and memorized designer names. School shopping was a terror. If Marah didn't find exactly what she wanted, she went ballistic. There was rarely any doubt in Kate's mind that her daughter was judging her appearance. More often than not, she knew she was found lacking. "I will definitely wear makeup. I'll even curl my hair, how's that?"

"Can I wear lip gloss? Just this once? All the girls—"

"No. We've had this discussion, Marah. You're too young."

Marah crossed her arms. "I'm not a baby."

"You're not a teenager, either. Believe me, there will be plenty of time for all that." She pulled the car into the garage and parked.

Marah was out of the car and into the house before Kate had time to ask her to help carry stuff in. "Thanks for the help," she muttered, releasing her boys from the car seats. As toddlers, Lucas and William were wild separately; together they were a tornado.

For the next few hours, she did more afternoon chores: in addition to all the regular things, she arranged vases of flowers and placed them throughout the house, positioned and lit scented candles on dressers too high for the boys to reach, and thoroughly cleaned the guest room in case Tully decided she had time to say. Then, with dinner in the oven and the boys trailing along behind her, she went upstairs to get ready. As she passed Marah's room she could hear the patter of feet that meant her daughter was pulling one outfit after another from her closet.

Smiling, Kate went to her own room, parked the boys in the playpen, and, ignoring their screams, took a shower. When she finished drying her hair (trying not to notice how dark her roots were), she opened the bathroom door.

"How you guys doing now?"

Lucas and William sat side by side, their bare pudgy legs splayed out in front of them, babbling to one another in baby talk.

"Good," she said, patting their heads as she passed them.

In her closet, she sighed. Everything she owned was either out of date or too small. She still had some baby weight to lose—the twins had turned her stomach into the Kingdome; that kind of stretching didn't bounce back easily.

Exercising would have helped, and she wished fervently now that she'd fit it into her schedule this winter.

Too late now.

She chose a nice pair of her favorite broken-in Levi's and a pretty black angora sweater that Johnny had given her for Christmas a few years ago, right after he'd taken the job at KLUE. It was one of her only designer garments.

"Come on, boys," she said, scooping them up with practiced ease. Settling one on each hip, she carried them to their bedroom, changed their diapers, and dressed them in the darling sailor boy outfits Tully had sent for their birthday. Then, because it took forever to let them walk down the stairs, she carried them, plopped them on the living room floor with a pile of toys in front of them, and popped in a Winnie-the-Pooh tape. That gave her twenty minutes if she was lucky.

Locking the child gate at the bottom of the stairs, she went into the kitchen and began setting the table. As always, she kept half an eye on the boys while she worked.

"Mom!" Marah shrieked. "They're here!" She thundered down the stairs, jumped over the childproof gate, and ran for the window, pressing her little nose against it.

Kate sidled up to her daughter, pushed the curtains aside. Headlights cut through the darkness. Johnny's car was first; behind it a black limousine crept down the long, treed driveway. The two cars parked in front of the garage.

"Wow," Marah said.

The uniformed driver got out of the limo and came around to the back passenger door, opening it.

Tully emerged slowly, as if she knew she was making an entrance. Dressed in low-rise designer jeans and a crisp white men's-style blouse beneath a navy blazer, she was the very definition of casual chic. Her hair, cut in layers and probably styled by the best hairdresser in Manhattan, was a gorgeous auburn hue that shone in the light from the garage.

"Wow," Marah said again.

Kate tried to suck in her stomach. "I wonder if there's time for liposuction."

Johnny got out of his car and went to Tully. They stood close enough together that their shoulders were touching. Laughing at something the driver said Tully looked up at Johnny, pressing her hand to his chest as she spoke.

They looked perfect together, like models pulled from the pages of a glossy fashion magazine.

"Daddy sure likes Aunt Tully," Marah said.

"He sure does," Kate muttered, but Marah was already gone. Her daughter opened the door and ran to her godmother, who scooped her up and twirled her around.

Tully came into the house like she did everything: in a maelstrom of sound and light. She hugged Kate fiercely, kissed the boys' pudgy

cheeks, handed out more gifts than a Ryan family Christmas, and demanded a drink.

All through dinner, she entertained them, told them stories about
being in Paris for Y2K and the panic that preceded it, about the recent
Oscars ceremony she'd attended and how they'd taped the dress over
her boobs and how the adhesive had failed her at a party when she did
a straight shot.

"Everyone in the room got a shot," she said, laughing, "if you know
what I mean."

Marah hung on Tully's every word. "Was it an Armani?" she asked.

Kate was absolutely dumbfounded to hear Tully say, "Yes, it was,
Marah. I see you know your fashion designers. I'm proud of you."

"I saw pictures in the magazine. They said you were one of the best
dressed."

"You have to work at that," Tully said, beaming. "A whole team of
people work to make me look good."

"Wow," Marah said yet again. "That's so cool."

When Tully had exhausted the celebrity fashion topics, she turned
to world politics. She and Johnny debated the Clinton-Lewinsky scan-
dal and the press coverage of it in fierce detail; Marah jumped in at
every lull with endless questions about teenage celebrities Tully knew
personally and Kate had never heard of. Frankly, the boys were such a
handful it took all of her concentration and effort to keep them quiet.
Kate kept meaning to say something, add a comment or two, but the
boys picked tonight to throw food at each other, and she had to be vigilant to keep them in check.

The dinner seemed to last a nanosecond. When it was over, Marah,
in a pathetically transparent attempt to impress Tully, cleared the table.

"I'll do the dishes," Johnny said. "Why don't you and Tully get some
blankets and sit outside?"

"You're a prince," Tully said. "I'll make a pitcher of margaritas. Katie,
you put Huey and Louie to bed and I'll meet you outside in fifteen
minutes."

Kate nodded and carried the boys upstairs. By the time she was done bathing and dressing and reading to them, it was close to eight o'clock.

Feeling a little weary herself, she went downstairs, where she found Marah curled on Tully's lap.

Johnny met her at the bottom of the stairs. "The margaritas are in the blender. I'll put Marah to bed."

"I love you."

He patted her butt, then turned to his daughter. "I know. Come on, Bunny. Bedtime."

"Aw, Daddy. Do I hafta? I'm telling Aunt Tully about Mrs. Hermann."

"Hop up the stairs and get your pj's on. I'll be up in a minute to read you a story."

Marah hugged Tully tightly, kissed her cheek, and plodded over to where Johnny and Kate stood.

Perfunctorily she kissed Kate goodnight, then went upstairs.

Tully got up and stood by Johnny. "Okay, I've been very patient, which as you know is not my strong suit, but the kids are gone now, so spill the beans."

Kate frowned. "What?"

"You look terrible," Tully said softly. "What's wrong?"

"It's just hormones. Or lack of sleep. The boys exhaust me." She laughed at the ordinary string of excuses. "I'm fine."

"I don't think she knows what's wrong," Johnny said to Tully, as if Kate weren't even here.

"How's the writing going?" Tully asked her.

Kate winced. "Great."

"She isn't writing," Johnny said, and Kate could have coldcocked him for that.

Tully looked disbelieving. "Not at all?"

"Not that I can tell," Johnny said.

"Quit talking about me as if I'm not here," Kate said. "I have a ten-year-old drama queen who plays every sport on the planet, takes dance lessons three times a week, and has a busier social calendar than the *Sex and the City* girls. And don't forget about twin boys who rarely sleep at the same time and break everything they touch. How the hell am I supposed to do all that, make dinner, do the laundry, clean the house, and write a book at the same time?" She looked at them. "I know what you both think. What everyone seems to think. I'm supposed to make time to search for my authentic self. I'm supposed to *need* more than motherhood—and I do, damn it—I just don't know how I'm supposed to do all that and still be in the carpool lane on time."

In the silence that followed her outbreak, a log dropped in the fireplace, made a crackling thump.

Tully looked at Johnny. "You asshole."

"What?" He looked so perplexed, Kate almost laughed.

"She cleans the house and picks up your laundry? Can't you get someone to clean, for God's sake?"

"She never said she needed help."

Kate hadn't realized until that moment how overwhelmed she'd felt. Relief swept through her, loosened the muscles in her back. "I do," she finally admitted to her husband.

Johnny pulled her close and kissed her, whispering, "All you had to do was say something," against her lips. She kissed him back, clung to him.

"Enough making out," Tully said, grabbing her arm. "What we need are margaritas. Johnny, bring them to us on the deck."

Kate let herself be led outside. Once there, she smiled at her friend. "Thanks, Tul. I don't know why I didn't just ask for help."

"Are you kidding? I love bossing Johnny around." She sat down into the nearest Adirondack chair. In front of them, just beyond the ragged yard, lay a silvery ribbon of foamy surf. The quiet, whooshing sound of the water's rise and fall filled the night.

Kate sat in the chair beside her.

Johnny returned, gave them each a drink, and left again.

After a long silence, Tully said, "I say this because I love you, Katie: you don't have to go to every field trip and bake sale. You need to make time for yourself."

"Now tell me something I don't know."

"I read the magazines and watch television. At-home moms are forty percent more likely to—"

"*No*. I mean it. Tell me something I don't know. Something fun."

"Did I tell you about Paris at the turn of the millennium? And I don't mean the fireworks. There was this guy, a Brazilian . . ."

On the first of July 2000, Tully's alarm clock went off, as it did every weekday morning, at three-thirty. With a groan, she smacked the snooze button, wishing just this once she could sleep for ten more minutes, and snuggled back up against Grant. She loved waking up near his arms, although she rarely woke in them. They were each too solitary to meld well, even in sleep. In the years of their on again/off again relationship, they'd been all over the world together, attended dozens of glittering parties and black-tie charity events. The press had dubbed him Tully's "sometime love" and she had always thought it was as apt a nickname as any. Lately, though, she'd been reconsidering.

He wakened slowly, rubbed her arm. "Morning, love," he said in the scratchy, raspy voice that meant he'd smoked cigars last night.

"Am I?" she asked quietly, angling up onto one elbow.

"Are you what?"

He stopped just short of rolling his eyes, but the effect was the same. "That talk again? You're thirty-nine. I know. It doesn't change who we are, Tully. Let's not ruin a good thing, shall we?"

He acted as if she'd asked him to marry her, or knock her up; neither of which was true. She rolled out of bed and walked through her spacious apartment toward the bathroom. There, she turned on the lights.

"Oh, God."

She looked like she'd slept in a Dumpster. Her hair, cut short now and highlighted with blond streaks, stuck out all around her face in a way that only Annette Bening or Sharon Stone could pull off, and the bags under her eyes were carry-on-sized.

No more red-eye flights from the West Coast. She was too damned old to party all weekend in Los Angeles and be at work Monday morning. She hoped no one had snapped a photo of her coming home last night. Ever since John Kennedy, Jr.'s tragic death, the paparazzi had been swarming. Celebrity—and pseudo-celebrity—news was big business.

She took a long, hot shower, washed and dried her hair, and dressed in a pair of designer sweats. By the time she emerged from the steamy room, Grant was waiting for her at the door. In his suit from last night, with his hair messy in a studied way, he looked incredibly handsome.

"Let's play hooky," she said, sliding her arm around his waist.

"Sorry, love. Got a flight to London in a few hours. I'm to see the folks."

She nodded, unsurprised. He always found a reason to leave. Locking her door, they went to the elevator and rode down together. At their separate black town cars, parked one in front of the other on Central Park West, she kissed him goodbye and watched him leave.

She used to love the way he came and went in her life, always arriving unexpectedly and leaving before she could get bored or fall in love. In the past few months, though, she felt as lonely with him as without him.

Her uniformed driver handed her a double-shot latte. "Good morning, Ms. Hart."

She took the coffee gratefully. "Thanks, Hans," she said, getting into the car. Settling back, she tried not to think about Grant or her life. Instead, she stared out the tinted window at the dark streets of Manhattan. This time of day was as close as the city came to sleeping. Only the hardiest of souls were out—garbage collectors, bakers, newspaper deliverymen.

For more years than she wanted to count, she'd lived this routine. Almost from her first day in New York, she'd been waking up at three-thirty A.M. for work. Success had only made long days longer. Since CBS had lured her over, she'd had to include afternoon meetings in addition to her morning broadcasts. Fame and celebrity and money should have allowed her to slow down and enjoy her career, but the opposite had occurred. The more she got, the more she wanted, the more afraid she was of losing it, and the harder she worked. Every job that came her way, she took—narrating a documentary on breast cancer, guest-hosting a super new game show, even being a judge for the Miss Universe contest. And then there were her guest appearances on Leno, Letterman, Rosie, etc. And holiday parades that needed a grand marshal. She made sure no one could forget her.

In her early thirties, it had been easy to keep up the schedule. Back then, she'd been able to work long hours, sleep all afternoon, party all night, and wake up looking and feeling great. But she was approaching forty now, and she was beginning to feel tired, a little old to be running from one job to the next, and in heels, no less. More and more often when she came home from work, she curled up on her sofa and called Kate or Mrs. M. or Edna. Being seen—and photographed—at the It new club or at some red carpet premiere had lost its appeal. Rather, she found herself longing to be with people who really knew her, really cared.

Edna repeatedly told her that this was the deal she'd made; the life she got in exchange for all the success. But what good was success, Tully had asked over drinks last week, if there was no one to share it with you?

Edna had simply shaken her head and said, "That's why they call it sacrifice. You can't have it all."

But what if that was exactly what you wanted: everything?

At the CBS building, she waited for her driver to open her door, then stepped out into the still-black, summer morning. She could already feel heat rising from the street; today would be a scorcher. Somewhere nearby she could hear the thunk-wheeze of a garbage truck loading up.

She hurried to the front door and went inside, nodding to the doorman as she walked to the elevator. Upstairs, at her makeup desk, her savior was already waiting. Dressed in a too-tight red T-shirt that showed off his bulging muscles and form-fitting black leather pants, Tank put one hand on his hip and shook his head. "Someone looks like shit this morning."

"You're being too hard on yourself," Tully said, easing into the chair. She'd hired Tank about five years ago to do her hair and makeup. It was a choice she regretted almost daily.

He pulled the Hermès scarf off her head and removed the dark glasses. "You know I love you, honey, but you gotta quit burning the candle at both ends. And you're getting too thin again."

"Shut up and paint."

As usual, he started on her hair. While he worked, he talked. Sometimes one or the other of them would confide in the other; it was the nature of the business they were in. Time spent together created an intimacy that didn't quite spill over into friendship. A very New York type of relationship. Today, however, Tully kept their conversation light and impersonal. She didn't want to reveal to him that she felt out of sorts. He'd jump on in and tell her how to fix her life.

By five o'clock, she looked ten years younger. "You're a genius," she said, sliding out of the chair.

"If you don't change your ways, missy, you're going to need a surgeon, not a makeup genius."

"Thanks." She flashed him a camera-ready smile and walked away before he could say anything else.

On-set, she stared into the camera and smiled again. Here, in this fake world, she was perfect. She talked easily, laughed at her guests' and co-anchors' jokes, and made everyone who saw her think she could be their friend. She knew that no one in America knew how she really felt right now. No one imagined that Tallulah Hart could possibly want more than she had.

Shopping with the twins and Marah was a headache-inducing event. By the time Kate finished her last stops at Safeway, the library, the drugstore, and the fabric store, she was exhausted, and it wasn't even three o'clock. All the way home the boys cried and Marah sulked. At ten, her daughter had decided that she was too big to sit in the backseat of the car with the babies, and threw a fit now on every excursion. The plan, clearly, was to wear Kate down.

"Stop arguing with me, Marah," she said for at least the dozenth time since they'd left the grocery store.

"I'm not arguing. I'm explaining. Emily gets to sit in the front seat and so does Rachel. You're the only mom who won't—"

Kate pulled into the garage and hit the brakes just hard enough to send the grocery bags flying forward. It was worth it, since it shut Marah up. "Help me carry stuff in."

Marah grabbed a single bag and went inside.

Before Kate could reprimand her, Johnny came into the garage and got a load. Kate and the boys followed him into the house.

As usual, the TV was on, too loud for Kate's taste, and turned to CNN.

"I'll put the boys down for their nap," Johnny said when all the bags were on the counter. "Then I have good news for you."

Kate tossed him a tired smile. "I could use some. Thanks."

Thirty minutes later, he came back downstairs. Kate was at the dining room table, spreading out the fabric for the last few ballet costumes she had to make. Nine down; three to go.

"I'm an idiot," she said, more to herself than to him. "Next time they ask for volunteers, I am *not* going to raise my hand."

He came up behind her, pulled her to her feet, and turned her to face him. "You say that every time."

"Like I said: I'm an idiot. So what's my good news? You're making dinner?"

"Tully called."

"That's my good news? She calls every Saturday."

"She's coming to Marah's recital, and she wants to throw her goddaughter a little surprise party."

She pulled out of his arms.

"You're not smiling," he said, frowning.

Kate was surprised at the flare of anger she felt. "Dance is the only thing Marah and I do together. I was going to have a party for her here."

"Oh."

She could tell her husband wanted to say more, but he was too smart to do it. He knew this wasn't his call.

Finally Kate sighed. She was being selfish and they both knew it. Marah idolized her godmother and would love a surprise party. "What time will she be here?"

CHAPTER
TWENTY-FOUR

On the day of the recital Marah was so nervous and excited she could barely contain her emotions. As usual, the stress of it all turned her into a pint-sized diva given to jumbo-jet-sized tantrums. Now she stood by the dining room table, one hand on her hip, dressed in faded low-rise jeans and a pink top that read Baby One More Time in rhinestones. An inch of skin showed between the bottom of her shirt and the waistband of her jeans. "Where did you put my butterfly barrettes?"

Hunched over the sewing machine, Kate barely glanced up. "They're in your bathroom drawer. Top one. And you're not wearing that top out of the house."

Marah's mouth dropped open. "But it was a birthday present."

"Yeah, well, your Aunt Tully is an idiot."

"Everyone gets to dress like this."

"You're breaking my heart. Really. Now go change. I don't have time to argue with you."

Marah sighed dramatically and stormed back upstairs.

Kate shook her head. It wasn't just the recital. Everything with Marah lately was high drama. Her daughter was either giggling and happy or flat-out pissed. Whenever Mom saw her granddaughter she laughed, lit up a smoke, and said, "Oh, the teen years will be fun. You should start drinking before it's too late."

Kate bent closer to the machine, put her foot on the pedal, and went back to work.

As it turned out, that ended up being the last time she paused for almost two hours. Then, as soon as she'd finished the costumes for the dance recital, she rushed on to her other chores—finding hangers, packing the car, helping the boys brush their teeth, and breaking up fights. Thankfully Johnny took care of dinner and the dishes.

At six o'clock, she herded everyone to the car and helped the boys into their car seats, then took her own seat. "Have I forgotten anything?"

Johnny looked at her. "You have spaghetti sauce on your forehead."

She flipped down the visor and saw herself in the tiny rectangular mirror. Sure enough, she had a streak of red across her brow.

"I didn't take a shower," she said, horrified.

"I wondered about that," Johnny said.

She turned to him. "You *knew?*"

"When I told you it was five o'clock you bit my head off and told me to make dinner."

She groaned. In all the hoopla, she'd forgotten to get herself ready. She was still dressed in her oldest pair of jeans, a baggy UW sweatshirt, and scuffed Adidas. "I look like a bag lady."

"But one who went to college."

Ignoring him, she ran out of the car, hearing Marah shriek behind her, "Wear makeup, Mom!"

Kate dug through her drawers, found a pair of fairly new black stirrup pants and a thigh-length black and white V-neck sweater. Were stirrup pants still in style? She didn't know. Pulling her hair into a ponytail, she anchored it with a white scrunchie, then brushed her teeth and put on mascara and blush.

Outside, a horn honked.

She grabbed a pair of black silk ankle socks and a pair of suede flats and ran back to the car.

"We're going to be late," Marah whined. "Everyone else is probably already there."

"We're fine," Kate said, only slightly out of breath.

They drove through town and parked at the Island Auditorium. Inside, it was pandemonium: twelve girls between the ages of seven and eleven, their harried parents, dozens of rowdy, disinterested siblings, and Miss Parker, their seventy-year-old dance instructor, who demanded strict propriety at all times and somehow managed to corral this wild bunch without ever raising her voice. Kate carried the costumes into the dressing room, where she helped the girls get ready, bobby-pinned and ponytailed and sprayed their hair, and helped them put on a few touches of mascara and lip gloss.

When she was finished, she knelt down in front of her daughter. "You ready?"

"Did you bring the video camera?"

"Of course we did."

Marah grinned at that, showing off her crooked, oversized teeth. "I'm glad you're here, Mommy," she said.

And suddenly it was all worth it: the crazy deadline, the late nights sewing and ironing, the tired, bleeding fingers. She did it all for a split second of togetherness. "Me, too."

Marah hugged her. "I love you, Mommy."

Kate held her tightly, smelling the sweet, powdery scent of her. She thought in that moment how close they were to childhood's end and the start of puberty, and she held on too long. These moments were too rare already.

Marah pulled back, gave her another grin, and ran backstage with her friends. " 'Bye!"

Kate got up slowly and went out to the auditorium, where Johnny sat in the third row, center, with a son on either side of him. She searched the seats around them, looking for Tully. "Is she here yet?"

"No. And she hasn't called, either. Maybe something came up." He grinned. "Like a date with George Clooney."

Smiling, Kate took her seat beside Lucas. All around her, parents and grandparents filed into their seats, bringing out their video cameras as soon as they sat down.

Kate's parents arrived right on time, taking their seats beside her. As always, Mom had the old black Kodak Instamatic dangling from her wrist. "I thought Tully was coming," she said.

"She said she was. I hope nothing happened." Kate held a seat for Tully for as long as she could and then finally let it go.

The lights flickered, and the audience fell silent. Miss Parker, dressed now in pink tights and a knee-length black ballet skirt and black leotard, walked out to center stage. She looked every inch the aging prima ballerina. "Hello, there," she said in her soft, querulous voice. "As you know, I'm—"

The auditorium's back doors banged open. As one, the audience turned.

Tully stood there, looking like she'd just left the Grammys. Her short blond-streaked hair gave her a gamine kind of beauty that made her smile look even bigger. She wore a stunning forest-green silk dress that hung from one shoulder and nipped in at her still-small waist.

Whispers overtook the audience. *Tallulah Hart . . . even prettier in person. . . .* No one was listening to Miss Parker's introduction.

"How does she stay looking so good?" Mom asked, leaning close.

"Plastic surgery and a battalion of makeup artists."

Mom laughed at that and squeezed her hand as if to remind Kate that she was just as pretty.

Waving at the Mularkeys, Tully walked to an empty aisle seat in the front row and sat down.

The house lights dimmed and Maggie Levine, dressed as the blue fairy, danced onstage. Her sister, Cleo, and the rest of the girls followed, pirouetting and prancing in what was supposed to be unison. The little ones watched the more experienced dancers intently, executing every movement a second too late.

The gawkiness only made it more magical. It was all Kate could do not to cry; then Johnny reached over Lucas and held her hand just as

Marah twirled onstage. Halfway through her routine she saw Tully and stopped right in the middle of the stage, waving wildly.

Laughter rippled through the audience when Tully waved back.

When the performance was over, the applause was enthusiastic. The girls took several curtain calls, then giggled and ran for their families.

Marah headed straight for her godmother. She launched herself off the stage and landed in Tully's arms. A crowd formed around them, people wanting autographs and introductions. All the while, Marah beamed with pride.

When the swarm dissipated, Tully headed for the family, hugging them each in turn. She slung an arm around Kate's shoulder and used her other hand to hold on to Marah. "I have a surprise for my god-daughter," she said loudly.

Marah giggled and jumped up and down. "What is it?"

"You'll see," Tully said, winking at Kate. In a pack, the family moved up the aisle and went outside.

There, parked at the curb, was a pink stretch limousine.

Marah screamed.

Kate turned to Tully. "Are you kidding me?"

"Isn't it cool? You wouldn't believe how hard it was to find. Come on, get in, everyone." She opened the door and they all piled into the plush black interior. Tiny red and blue lights illuminated the ceiling.

Marah snuggled close to Tully, held her hand. "This is the best surprise *ever*," she said. "Did you think I was good?"

"You were perfect," Tully said.

They stayed in the car for the entire ferry ride; not once did Marah stop talking to Tully.

On the Seattle side, the car started up again and they were driven around the city as if they were tourists on vacation, then they pulled into a brightly lit porte cochere, where a hotel doorman came out to greet them. He opened the door and bent down. "And which of you lovely ladies is Marah Rose?"

Marah instantly raised her hand, giggling. "I am."

He pulled a single pink rose from behind his back and handed it to her.

Marah looked awestruck. "Wow."

"Say thank you, Marah," Kate said more sharply than she'd intended.

Marah threw her an irritated look. "Thank you."

Tully led them into the hotel. On the top floor, she opened the door to a gigantic suite where all kinds of kid-type play stations had been set up—bouncing rooms and virtual boxing and miniature bumper cars. All the girls from the recital were already there with their families. In the center of the room was a white-draped table. On it was a huge tiered pink cake adorned with tiny frosted ballerinas.

"Aunt Tully," Marah screamed, hugging her. "This is *awesome*. I love you."

"I love you, too, princess. Now go play with your friends."

Everyone stood there for a moment, stunned. Johnny recovered first. Carrying William, he sidled up to Tully. "This is not spoiling her?"

"I wanted to get a pony, but I thought that would be over the top."

Mom laughed. Dad shook his head. "Come on, Margie, Johnny," he finally said. "Let's check out the bar."

When Kate and Tully were alone, Kate said, "You sure know how to make an entrance. Marah will be talking about this for years."

"Too much?" Tully asked.

"Perhaps just a bit."

Tully gave her a bright smile, but it wasn't the real thing. Kate instantly recognized the pretense. "What's wrong?"

Before Tully could answer, Marah came bouncing back, her little face shining with joy. "We all want a picture with you, Aunt Tully."

Kate stood there, watching her daughter practically swoon over her godmother. Although she hated to admit it, she felt a pinch of jealousy. This was supposed to have been their night; hers and Marah's.

Tully sat in the limousine, with Marah's head in her lap, stroking her goddaughter's silky black hair.

Across from them, Kate slept against Johnny, who also had his eyes closed. A small boy lay tucked alongside each of them. They looked like the Hallmark version of family perfection.

The limousine turned onto the beach road.

Tully kissed Marah's soft pink cheek. "We're almost home, princess."

Marah blinked slowly awake. "I love you, Aunt Tully."

Tully's heart closed like a fist around those words, and she felt a swell of almost painful emotion. She used to think that success was like gold, worth sifting through mud for, and that love would always be there, waiting somehow on the riverbanks for her when she was done panning. She couldn't imagine now why she'd thought that, given her background. She ought to have recognized love's scarcity early on. If success were gold, lying in rivers, love was a diamond, buried hundreds of feet beneath the surface of the earth and unrecognizable in its natural form. No wonder it touched her so deeply to hear those words from Marah. They'd been so rare in her life. "I love you, too, Marah Rose."

The limo pulled into the driveway, tires crunching on gravel, and parked. It took forever for the family to get out of the car, walk into the house. They all immediately headed upstairs.

Tully stood in the empty living room, unsure of what to do. The floorboards creaked. She'd tried to merge into the lane of their nighttime routine, but she kept getting in the way, so finally she gave up.

Kate came down the stairs at last, sighing tiredly, holding a pile of afghans in her arms. "Okay, Tully. What's going on?"

"What do you mean?"

Kate grabbed her arm and led her through the toy-strewn house. At the kitchen, Kate paused just long enough to pour two glasses of white wine and then they went outside to the chairs positioned in the grass. The quiet gurgling noise of the waves took Tully back more than twenty years, to those nights they used to sneak out and sit by the river, talking about boys and sharing smokes.

Tully sat down in one of the weathered Adirondack chairs and spread the knitted blanket over her. After all these years and no doubt countless washings, it still smelled of Mrs. M.'s menthol cigarettes and perfume.

Kate drew up her blanketed knees and rested her chin on the bumpy summit, then looked at Tully. "Talk," she said.

"What should we talk about?"

"How long have we been best friends?"

"Since David Cassidy was groovy."

"And you think I can't tell when something's wrong?"

Tully sat back, sipping her wine. The truth was that she wanted to talk about this—it was, after all, part of the reason she'd flown all the way across the country—and yet, now that she was here with her best friend again, she didn't know how to start. Worse than that, she felt like an idiot complaining about what was missing in her life. She had so much.

"I thought you were crazy to give up your career. For four years, every time I called you Marah was screaming in the background. I kept thinking I'd kill myself if that were my life, but you sounded frustrated and pissed off and amazingly happy. I could never quite get it."

"Someday you'll know what it's like."

"No, I won't. I'm almost forty, Kate." She finally looked at Kate. "I guess I was the crazy one, wanting nothing but the career."

"It's a hell of a career."

"Yeah. But sometimes . . . it's not enough. I know that's a greedy thing to say, but I'm tired of working eighteen hours a day and coming home to an empty house."

"You can change your life, you know. But you have to really want to."

"Thank you, Obi-Wan."

Kate stared out at the waves slapping the shore. "In the tabloids last week there was a sixty-year-old woman who gave birth."

Tully laughed. "You are such a bitch."

"I know. Now come on, poor little mega-rich girl, I'll show you to your room."

"I'm going to be sorry I complained, aren't I?"

"Oh, yeah."

They walked through the darkened house. At the guest bedroom door, Kate turned to her. "No more spoiling Marah, okay? She already thinks you hung the moon."

"Come on, Katie. I made more than two million dollars last year, what am I supposed to do with it all?"

"Give it to charity. Just no more pink limos, okay?"

"You are no fun whatsoever, you know that?"

It wasn't until much later, when Tully lay on the bumpy, sagging mattress of the hide-a-bed, staring out the window at the Big Dipper, that she realized she hadn't asked Kate about her own life.

Kate stared at the calendar that hung on the wall by her refrigerator. It seemed impossible to believe that time was passing so quickly, but the proof was right there in front of her. It was November of 2002, and the past fourteen months had changed the world. In September of last year terrorists had flown airplanes into the World Trade Center and the Pentagon, killing thousands. Another plane had been hijacked and ultimately crashed, leaving no survivors. Car and suicide bombers had become part of the nightly news; the search for weapons of mass destruction had begun. Words like *Al-Qaeda* and *Taliban* and *Pakistan* came up in every conversation, were repeated on every broadcast.

Fear changed everyone and everything, and yet, as always, life went on. Hour by hour, day by day, while politicians and military personnel were looking for bombs and terrorists, and while the Justice Department was tearing down Enron's papery walls, families went on with their ordinary lives. Kate continued to run her errands and raise her children and love her husband. If she held on to all of them a little more tightly and kept them closer to home, everyone understood: the world wasn't as safe as it had been before.

Now Thanksgiving was a week away and Christmas lurked just around the corner.

It was the holiday season, the time of year that turned women into card-carrying split personalities. Torn between the joy of the season

and the amount of work that joy required, Kate often had trouble slow-
ing down, remembering to savor the precious moments. There was bak-
ing to do—for the school parties, for the ballet bake sale, for donations
at Helper House—and shopping, of course. As magical as Bainbridge
Island was, when it came time to do serious gift-combing, one was reminded forcibly that this was a body of land surrounded by water.
Thus, malls and department stores were far away. She felt like a moun-
tain climber sometimes, setting out for a vertical ascent without oxygen; the summit was Nordstrom. When you had three kids, it took time
to pick out their presents, and time was in short supply.

Now, as Kate sat in the driver's seat of her car, parked in the first position in the carpool lane, she began her Christmas list. She'd only gotten a few items down when the bell rang and kids poured out of the
middle school.

Marah usually came out of the brick building in a clot of girls. Like
killer whales, preteen girls traveled in pods. But today she was alone,
walking fast, with her head down and her arms crossed tightly.

Kate knew something was wrong. The question was: how bad was
it? Her daughter was twelve years old. That meant hormones were boil-
ing through her body, turning her emotions into a witch's cauldron.
Everything was big drama these days.

"Hey," Kate said tentatively, knowing one wrong word could cause a
fight.

"Hey." Marah climbed into the front passenger seat and reached for
he seatbelt, clicking it into place. "Where are the brats?"

"Evan's birthday party. Daddy's going to pick them up on his way
home."

"Oh."

Kate pulled out of the parking lane and merged into the stop-and-go
traffic on Sportsman's Club Road. All the way home she tried to begin a
conversation, but all her pitches turned out to be strikes. At best Marah
offered a one-word answer, at worst an eye roll or a dramatic sigh. When
they pulled into the garage, Kate gave it one more try. "I'm making cookies for the boys' Thanksgiving party tomorrow. You want to help me?"

Marah finally looked at her. "Those pumpkin-shaped ones with the orange frosting and green sprinkles?"

For a split second her daughter looked like a little girl again, her dark eyes wide with hope, her lips curving into a hesitant smile. Years' worth of parties were between them now, a net of shared memories.

"Of course," Kate said.

"I love those cookies."

Kate had counted on that. "Remember the year Mrs. Norman brought the same kind and you were so mad you made everyone try both just to prove that ours were better?"

Marah finally smiled. "Mr. Robbins got really mad at me. I had to help him clean up after the party."

"Emily stayed to help you."

Marah's smile faded. "Yeah."

"So, you want to help me?"

"Sure."

Kate took care not to react too sharply to that. Although she wanted to grin and say how happy she was, she simply nodded and followed her daughter into the house and then into the kitchen. She'd learned a few things in the last turbulent year about dealing with preteen girls. While they were virtual roller coasters of emotion, you needed to be calm, always.

For the next three hours they worked side by side in the big country-style kitchen. Kate reminded her daughter how to sift ingredients together and showed her how to grease a cookie sheet the old-fashioned way. They talked about little things, this and that; nothing important. Kate was gauging the scene like a hunter. Instinctively, she knew when the time was right. They'd just frosted the last of the cookies and were stacking the dirty dishes by the sink when Kate said, "You want to make another batch? We could take them over to Ashley's house."

Marah went very still. "No," she said in a voice almost too quiet to be heard.

"But Ash loves them. Remember when—"

"She hates me," Marah said, and just like that the floodgates opened. Tears gathered in her eyes.

"Did you two have a fight?"

"I don't know."

"How can you not know?"

"I just don't, okay?" Marah burst into tears and turned away.

Kate lunged for her daughter, grabbed her sleeve, and pulled her into a fierce hug. "I'm right here, Marah," she whispered.

Marah hugged her tightly. "I don't know what I did wrong," she wailed, sobbing.

"Sshh," Kate murmured, stroking her daughter's hair as if she were still little. When Marah's crying finally subsided, Kate drew back just enough to look down at her. "Sometimes life is—"

Behind them the door banged open. The twins burst into the house, yelling at each other, making their toy dinosaurs fight. Johnny came in after them, chasing them down. William bumped into an end table, upsetting a glass of water that shouldn't have been left there. The sound of shattering glass rang through the room.

"Uh-oh," William said, looking up at Kate.

Lucas laughed. "Wil-lie's in tro-uble," he chanted.

Marah wrenched free, and ran upstairs, slamming the door shut behind her.

"Lucas," Johnny said. "Stop teasing your brother. And stay back from the glass on the floor."

Kate sighed and reached for a towel.

The next day, Kate pulled into the school drive-through lane just three minutes before the lunch bell rang. Parking illegally, she hurried into the office, signed Marah out for the day, and then walked down to her classroom. Last night, after the moment of conversation and connection between them, Marah had shut Kate out again. No amount of prompting could restart the engine, and so Kate had had to formulate plan B. A surprise attack.

Peering through the rectangular glass window, she knocked once, saw the teacher wave at her, and went inside.

Most of the kids smiled at her and said hello. That was one of the benefits of constant volunteering: everyone knew you. All the kids looked happy to see her—or at least happy for this disruption in class.

All the kids except one.

Marah's face wore the what-are-you-doing-at-school-embarrassing-me grimace. Kate was more than familiar with it. She knew the middle school rules: parents should be invisible.

The bell rang and the kids ran from the room, talking loudly.

When they were alone, Kate went to Marah.

"What are you doing here?"

"You'll see. Get your things. We're leaving."

Marah stared up at her, obviously assessing the situation from every possible social angle. "Okay. I'll meet you at the car, okay?"

Ordinarily Kate would make a comment about that and force Marah to walk out with her, but her daughter was emotionally fragile right now. That was why Kate was here. "Okay."

The easy victory surprised Marah. Kate smiled at her, touched her shoulder. "See you in a minute."

Actually, it took a bit longer than that, but not much. In no time, Marah was in the passenger seat, buckling up. "Where are we going?"

"Well, first we're going out to lunch."

"You got me out of school to have lunch?"

"And something else. A surprise." Kate drove to the diner-style restaurant that was next door to the brand-new multiplex theater on the island.

"I'm going to have a cheeseburger, fries, and a strawberry milkshake," Kate said when they were seated.

"Me, too."

After the waitress took their orders and left, Kate looked at her daughter. Slouched down in the blue vinyl seat, she looked thin and angular, a girl bursting into adolescence. Her black hair, messy and unkempt now, would someday be a crowning glory, and her brown eyes revealed every nuance of emotion she felt. Now she looked bereft.

The waitress delivered their shakes. Kate took a sip. It was probably her first ice-cream product since the twins' birth and it tasted like Heaven. "Ashley still being mean to you?" she finally said.

"She hates me. I don't even know what I did to her."

Kate had been thinking a lot about what to say, how to handle this first heartbreak. Like all mothers, she would do anything in the world to keep her daughter safe and whole, but some dangers couldn't be fully protected against, they could only be experienced and then understood. That was one of the many lessons this country had learned this year, and even though some things had changed for them all, some things had stayed the same.

"In fifth grade, I had two very best friends. For years, we did everything together—showed our horses at the fair, had slumber parties, hung out at the lake in the summer. Grandma called us the three horseketeers. And then one summer, when I was almost fourteen, they stopped liking me. I still don't know why. They started hanging around with boys and went to parties and they never called me again. Every day I went to school and sat on the bus by myself and ate lunch by myself, and every night I cried before I went to sleep."

"Really?"

Kate nodded. "I can still remember how much it hurt my feelings."

"What happened?"

"Well, when I was at my very most miserable—and I mean miserable, you should have seen me with my braces and dork-o-rama glasses—"

Marah giggled.

"I got up and went to school."

"And?"

"And Aunt Tully was waiting at the bus stop. She was the coolest-looking girl I'd ever seen. I figured she'd never want to be friends with me. But you know what I found out?"

"What?"

"Inside, where it counts, she was as scared and lonely as I was. We became best friends that year. Real friends. The kind that don't purposely hurt your feelings or stop liking you for no reason."

"How do you make friends like that?"

"That's the hard part, Marah. To make real friends you have to put yourself out there. Sometimes people will let you down—girls can be really mean to each other—but you can't let that stop you. If you get hurt, you just pick yourself up, dust off your feelings, and try again. Somewhere in your class is the girl who will be friends with you all through high school. I promise. You just have to find her."

Marah frowned at that, thinking.

The waitress delivered their meals, left the bill, and walked away.

Before she took a bite of her cheeseburger, Marah said, "Emily's nice."

Kate had hoped Marah would remember that. She and Emily had been inseparable in grade school but had drifted apart in recent years. "Yes, she is."

Kate saw her daughter finally smile, and it lit Kate up inside, that tiny change. They talked about little things through lunch, mostly fashions, about which Marah already obsessed and Kate knew next to nothing. When she'd paid the bill and they were ready to leave, Kate said, "There's one more thing." She reached into her handbag and pulled out a small wrapped package. "This is for you."

Marah tore off the shimmery paper, revealing the paperback book that had been beneath it.

"*The Hobbit*," Marah said, looking up.

"In that year when I had no friends, I wasn't completely alone. I had books to keep me company, and that is the start of one of my favorite stories of all time. I must have read *The Lord of the Rings* ten times in my life. I don't think you're quite ready for *The Hobbit* yet, but someday soon, maybe in a few years, something will happen to hurt your feelings again. Maybe you'll feel alone with your sadness, not ready to share it with me or Daddy, and if that happens, you'll remember this book on your nightstand. You can read it then, let it take you away. It sounds silly, but it really helped me when I was thirteen."

Marah looked slightly confused by the receipt of a gift she was too young to enjoy, but she said, "Thank you," anyway.

Kate stared at her daughter for just a moment longer, feeling a pinch in her chest. It was going by so fast, these baby/little girl years were almost gone.

"I love you, Mommy," Marah said.

To the world at large, perhaps this was an ordinary moment in an ordinary day, but to Kate it was extraordinary. This was the reason she'd chosen to stay home instead of work. She judged the meaning of her life in nanoseconds, perhaps, but she wouldn't trade this instant for anything. "I love you, too. That's why we're playing hooky for the rest of the day. We're going to go to a matinee of *Harry Potter and the Chamber of Secrets.*"

Marah slid out of the booth, grinning. "You're the best mommy ever."

Kate laughed. "I just hope you remember that when you're a teenager."

CHAPTER
TWENTY-FIVE

Tully remembered the years by the stories she covered. In 2002, she vacationed in Europe, St. Barts, and Thailand. She went to the Oscars, won an Emmy, graced the cover of *People* magazine, and redecorated her apartment, but none of that stayed with her. What she remembered were the stories. She'd covered the launch of Operation Anaconda against the Taliban, the escalating violence in the region, the trial of Milosevic for crimes against humanity, and the start of the war against Iraq.

By the spring of 2003, she was exhausted, worn down by the violence. When she finally returned home, it wasn't much better. Everywhere she went she was in a crowd, and nowhere did she feel more isolated than in a group of people who fawned over her, and sucked up to her, but didn't really know her.

Although no one who watched her on television would notice it, she was quietly coming undone. Grant hadn't called her in almost four months, and the last time they'd spoken before that it hadn't gone well.

I just don't want what you want, love, he'd said, not even bothering to look sad when he said it.

And what is that? she'd snapped back, surprised to feel tears sting her eyes.

What you always want: more.

It shouldn't have surprised her. God knew she'd heard the same thing often enough in her life. She could even admit the truth of it. She did want more lately. She wanted a real life, not this perfect, glittery cotton candy one she'd created for herself.

But she had no real idea how to go about starting over at her age. She loved her job too much to give it up; besides, she'd been famous and rich for so long that she couldn't imagine being ordinary again.

Now, beneath a surprisingly warm sun, she walked down the busy streets of Manhattan, watching the fast-moving locals dodging between brightly dressed tourists. Today was the first sunny day after a long snowy winter, and nothing changed the mood of New York like the sun. People poured out of their boxy apartments, put on their walking shoes, and went outside. To her right, Central Park was a green oasis. For a moment, when she looked at it, she saw her own past: the Quad at UW; kids running around, throwing Frisbees, playing hacky sack. It had been twenty years since she'd left the campus for the last time. So much life had happened in those years, but right now it all felt as close as her own shadow.

Smiling, she shook her head to clear it. She'd have to call Katie tonight and tell her about this senior moment.

She was just about to start walking again when she saw him.

Down a low green hillside, standing on the paved path, watching two teenage girls roller-skate around him.

"Chad."

It was the first time she'd said his name aloud in years and it tasted as sweet as almond liquor. Just the sight of him peeled back the carapace of years and made her feel young again.

She walked down to the start of the path and turned toward him. A huge tree spread out above her like an umbrella, blocking out the sunlight, making her instantly cold.

What would she say to him after all these years? What would he say to her? The last time they'd been together he'd asked her to marry him; they'd never seen each other again. He'd known her so well then, enough that he hadn't stuck around to be told no. But they'd loved each other. With the wisdom of time and the passing of years, she knew that. She knew, too, that love didn't evaporate. It faded, perhaps, lost its weight like bones left out in the sun, but it didn't go away.

It occurred to her suddenly, sharply, that she wanted to be in love. Like Johnny and Kate. She wanted not to feel so damned alone in the world.

She faltered only once as she walked toward him. Out of the shadows and into the sunlight.

And there he was, standing in front of her, the man she'd never quite been able to evict from her dreams. She said his name aloud, too quietly for him to hear.

He looked up and saw her, his smile fading slowly. "Tully?"

She saw his mouth move and felt him say her name, but just then a dog barked and a pair of skateboarders rumbled past her.

And then he was moving toward her. It was like every movie she'd ever seen, every dream she'd ever had. He pulled her into his arms and held her.

Too soon, though, he let go of her and stepped back. "I knew I'd see you again."

"You always had more faith than I did."

"Almost everyone does," he said, smiling. "So how are you?"

"I'm on CBS. I do—"

"Believe me," he said gently, "I know. I'm proud of you, Tully. I always knew you'd get to the top." He studied her for a long time, then said, "How's Katie?"

"She married Johnny. I hardly see them lately."

"Ah," he said, nodding as if a question had been answered.

She felt exposed by his glance. "Ah, what?"

"You're lonely. The world isn't enough after all."

She frowned up at him. They were standing so close that the merest move would be a kiss, but she couldn't imagine crossing that small distance. He looked younger than she remembered, more handsome. "How do you do that?" she whispered.

"Do what?"

"Dad, watch this!"

As if from far away, Tully heard the girl's voice. She turned slowly around, saw two young women roller-skating toward them. She'd been wrong before; they were older than teenagers. One was the spitting image of Chad—sharp features, black hair, eyes that crinkled when she smiled.

But it was the other woman who held her attention. Maybe thirty, thirty-five, with a bright smile and a ready laugh. She wore the colors of a tourist: brand-new jeans, thick pink cable-knit sweater, aqua-blue hat and gloves.

"My daughter. She's in grad school at NYU," Chad said. "And Clarissa. The woman I live with."

"You still live in Nashville?" It was like rolling a log uphill, pushing those words out. The last thing she wanted was to make ordinary conversation with him. "Still teaching bright-eyed believers about the news?"

He took her by the shoulders, turned her to face him. "You didn't want me, Tully," he said, and this time she heard the gruffness of deep emotion in his voice. "I was ready to love you forever, but—"

"Don't. Please."

He touched her cheek in a fleeting, almost desperate caress.

"I should have come to Tennessee with you," she said.

He shook his head. "You have big dreams. That was one of the things I loved most about you."

"Loved," she said, knowing it was foolish to be hurt.

"Some things just don't happen."

She nodded. "Especially when you're too afraid to let them."

He took her in his arms again and held her with more passion in that instant than Grant had tendered in years. She waited for a kiss that never came. Instead, he let her go, then took her arm and walked her back up to the road.

In the sudden coldness of shade, she shivered and leaned against him. "Give me some advice, Wiley. I seem to have screwed up my life."

Out on the sunny sidewalk, he faced her again. "You're successful beyond your wildest dreams and it still isn't enough."

She winced at the look in his eyes. "I guess I should have stopped to smell a few of those flowers. Hell, I didn't even see them."

"You're not alone, Tully. Everyone has people in their life. A family."

"I guess you've forgotten Cloud."

"Or maybe you have."

"What do you mean?"

He glanced down to the park, where his daughter was holding hands with his girlfriend; one was teaching the other to skate backward. "I lost a lot of years with my daughter. One day I just decided it had been too long and I went to find her."

"You always were an optimist."

"That's the funny thing. So were you." He leaned down, kissed her on the cheek, and drew back. "Keep lighting the world on fire, Tully," he said, and then walked away.

They were almost the exact same words he'd written to her all those years ago. She hadn't recognized the sad desperation in them when they were letters on a piece of paper. Now she saw the truth: they were both an encouragement and an indictment. What good did it do to light the world on fire if she had to watch the glow alone?

If there was one thing Tully had always done well, it was to ignore unpleasantness. For most of her life she'd been able to box up bad memories or disappointments and store them deep in the back of her mind, in a place so dark they couldn't be seen. Sure, she dreamed about the bad times, and woke occasionally in a cold sweat with memories on the oily surface of consciousness, but when daylight came, she pushed those thoughts back into their hiding place and found it easy to forget.

But now, for the first time, she'd found something she could neither file away in the darkness nor forget.

Chad. Seeing him like that, standing there in her adopted city, had shaken her to the core. She couldn't seem to dislodge the memory. There was so much she hadn't said to him, hadn't asked.

In the three months since they'd run into each other, she found herself remembering every detail, going over the seconds like a forensic scientist, looking for clues to the meaning of it all. He became a kind of marker for everything she'd given up for this life of hers. The road she hadn't taken.

And even worse than all of that was the memory of what he'd said about Cloud. _You're not alone, Tully. Everyone has a family_. Those weren't precisely the words, but they were close enough. The gist of it.

Like a cancerous cell, the idea replicated in her mind and grew. She found herself thinking of Cloud, really thinking. She focused on the times her mother came back for her instead of the times she left. It was dangerous, Tully knew, to hang on to the positive when so much negative existed, and yet, she wondered suddenly if that had been her mistake. Had she been so intent on hating her mother, on shelving and forgetting the disappointments, that she'd missed the meaning of Cloud's many returns?

The thought of that, the hope of it, wouldn't fit in her box, wouldn't remain in the dark.

Finally, she quit running from the idea and sat down and studied it. That had led her to this strange and frightening journey. She had taken two weeks off of work, called it a vacation, packed a suitcase, and boarded a plane heading west.

A little less than eight hours after she left Manhattan, she was on Bainbridge Island, pulling up to the Ryan house in a sleek black limousine.

Now Tully stood in the driveway, listening to the car drive away, tires crunching on gravel. From beyond the house, in the backyard, she could hear waves washing onto the pea-gravel beach. That meant the tide was coming in. On this beautiful sunny early summer afternoon, the old-fashioned farmhouse looked like something out of a photo album of the Good Life. A fresh coat of stain made the shingles look like caramel and the white, glossy trim caught the sunlight and kept it.

Flowers ran riot through the yard, creating bursts of color everywhere she looked. Toys and bikes lay scattered about, reminding her sharply of the old days, back when they'd been the Firefly Lane girls. Their bikes had been magic carpets to another world.

Come on, Katie. Let go.

Tully smiled. She hadn't thought about that summer in years. 1974. The beginning of it all. Meeting Kate had changed her life, and all because they'd dared to reach out for each other, dared to say, *I want to be your friend*.

She walked up the weed-veined concrete path to the front door. Even before she got to the stoop, she could hear the noise coming from within. It didn't surprise her. According to Kate, the first half of 2003 had been wild and crazy. Marah hadn't eased into the teen years; she'd lurched. And the boys had gone from loud, into-everything toddlers to louder, even more destructive five-year-olds. Every time Tully called, it seemed, Kate was driving someone somewhere.

Tully rang the doorbell. Normally, of course, she'd just walk in, but normally, she'd be expected. This trip had been so spur-of-the-moment that she hadn't called ahead. To be honest, she hadn't really expected to make it. She'd thought she'd chicken out along the way. But here she was.

The sound of footsteps shook the old house. Then the door opened and Marah stood there. "Aunt Tully!" she shrieked, launching herself forward.

Tully caught her goddaughter and held her tightly. When they drew apart, she stared at the girl in front of her, a little nonplussed. It had been only seven or eight months since she'd seen Marah—a blip of time—and yet the girl in front of her was a stranger. A near-woman, Marah was taller than Tully, with milky pale skin, penetrating brown eyes, lush black hair that fell in a waterfall down her back, and cheekbones to die for. "Marah Rose," she said. "You're all grown up. And you're *gorgeous*. Have you tried modeling?"

Marah's smile made her even more breathtakingly beautiful. "Really? My mom thinks I'm a baby."

Tully laughed. "You, my dear, are no baby." Before she could say more, Johnny came down the stairs, holding a squirming boy in each arm. Halfway down, he saw her and stopped. Then he smiled. "You shouldn't have let her in, Marah. She's got a suitcase."

Tully laughed and closed the door behind her.

"Katie," Johnny yelled up the stairs. "You better come down here. You won't believe who has come to visit." He put the boys down on the floor at the base of the steps and went to Tully, drawing her into his arms. She couldn't help thinking how good it felt simply to be held. It had been a long time.

"Tully!" Kate's voice rose above the other sounds in the room as she hurried down the stairs and pulled Tully into a hug. When Kate drew back, she was smiling.

"Now, what in the hell are you doing here? Don't you know I need *notice* for one of your trips? Now you'll give me crap about the haircut I need and the foil I missed."

"Don't forget the makeup you don't have on. But I could give you a makeover. I'm good at that. It's a gift."

The past enveloped them, made them laugh.

Kate linked arms with Tully and led her to the sofa. There, with her suitcase positioned at the door like a bodyguard, they spent at least an hour catching up on each others' lives. At around three o'clock they moved their little party to the backyard, where the boys and Marah competed with Kate for Tully's attention. When darkness began to fall, Johnny fired up the barbeque, and on a picnic table in the grass, beneath a dome of stars and beside the placid Sound, Tully had her first home-cooked meal in months. Afterward, they played a rousing game of Candy Land with the boys. While Kate and Johnny were upstairs putting the twins to bed, Tully sat out in the backyard with Marah, each wrapped against the night's chill in yet another of Mrs. Mularkey's famous afghans.

"What's it like to be famous?"

Tully hadn't really thought about that in years; she'd simply taken it for granted. "It's pretty great, actually. You always get the best tables, get into all the best places; people give you free stuff all the time. Everyone waits for you. And since I'm a journalist instead of a movie star, the paparazzi leave me alone for the most part."

"Parties?"

Tully smiled. "It's been a while since I cared about parties, but yeah, I get invited to a lot of them. And don't forget the clothes. Designers send me dresses all the time. All I have to do is wear them."

"Wow," Marah said. "That is so totally cool."

Behind them, a screen door screeched open and banged closed. There was the sound of something—a table, maybe—being dragged across the deck. Then the music started. Jimmy Buffet, "Margaritaville."

"You know what that means," Kate said, appearing beside them with two margaritas.

Marah immediately whined, "I'm old enough to stay up. Besides, there's no school tomorrow. It's a teacher contract day."

"Bedtime, little one," Kate said, bending down to offer Tully a drink.

Marah looked at Tully as if to say, *See? I told you she thinks I'm a baby.* Tully couldn't help laughing. "Your mom and I were once in a hurry to grow up, too. We used to sneak out of the house and steal my mother's—"

"Tully," Kate said sharply. "The old stories won't interest her."

"My mom sneaked out of the house? What did Grandma do?"

"She put her on restriction for life. And made her wear clothes from the sale rack at Fred Meyer," Tully answered.

Marah shuddered at the thought.

"Polyester," Kate added. "For an entire summer I was afraid to be near open flames."

"You two are lying to me," Marah said, crossing her arms.

"Us? Lie? Never," Tully said, taking a sip of her drink.

Marah got out of her chair, gave them a long-suffering sigh, and headed back into the house. As soon as the door banged shut, Tully and Kate laughed.

"Tell me we weren't like that," Tully said.

"My mom swears I was. You were little Miss Perfect around her. Until you got us arrested, that is."

"The first chink in the armor."

Laughing, Kate sat down in the Adirondack chair beside her, wrapping herself in one of her mom's afghans.

Tully hadn't realized how tense she'd been, how tight her neck and shoulders had become, until that moment, when she began to relax. As always, Kate was her safety net, her security blanket. With her best friend beside her, she could finally trust herself. She leaned back in her chair and stared up at the night sky. She'd never been one of those people who felt insignificant beneath the heavens, but suddenly she understood why some people did; it was a matter of perspective. She'd spent so much of her life in a rush for the finish line that she'd been left out of breath. If she'd paid a little more attention to the scenery and a little less to the goal line, she might not be here now, a forty-two-year-old single woman searching for the tattered remnant of a family.

"So, are you going to make me ask?" Kate finally said.

There was no point in hiding the truth, although she had an almost instinctive need to do just that. The music changed to ABBA, "Knowing Me, Knowing You." "I saw Chad," she said quietly.

"A few months ago, right? In Central Park?"

"Yeah."

"And seeing him then made you jump on a plane and fly out to see me now. I completely understand."

Before Tully could answer, the door opened behind them again and Johnny walked out, holding a beer. Dragging another chair over to where they were, he sat down. The three of them formed a ragged semicircle in the grassy yard and faced the dark Sound. Moonlight illuminated the waves that lapped against the sand. "Has she told you yet?"

"What are you two, telepaths?" Tully said. "I was just getting started."

"Actually," Kate said, "she reminded me that she saw Chad a couple of months ago."

"Ah," Johnny said, nodding as if that explained Tully's unexpected cross-country trip.

"What does that mean, *ah?*" she asked, irritated suddenly. It was exactly what Chad had done.

"He's your Moby-Dick," Johnny answered.

Tully gave him a look. "I never said a thing about his dick."

"Come on, Tully," Kate said, putting her hand on her husband's arm. "What's the matter?"

She looked at both of them, sitting so close together, a wife and husband who still laughed together and touched each other after so many years of marriage, and her chest felt tight with longing. "I'm tired of being alone," she finally said. She'd held the words back so long that when they finally came out they sounded worn, as polished as beach stones.

"What about Grant?" Johnny asked.

"I thought you said Chad lived with a woman," Kate said, leaning forward.

"This isn't really about Chad. I mean, it is, but not in the way you think. He pointed out that I have a family," Tully said.

Kate drew back. "You mean Cloud?"

"She's my mother."

"Biologically speaking. A reptile is a better parent, and they bury their eggs and leave."

"I know you're only trying to protect me, Kate, but it's easy for you to discount her. You *have* a family."

"She hurts you every time you see her."

"But she kept coming back. Maybe that meant something."

"She kept leaving, too," Kate said gently. "And each time it broke your heart."

"I'm stronger now."

"What are you two actually *saying*? It's like you're speaking in code," Johnny said.

"I want to go find her. I've got her last known address—I send money every month. I thought maybe if I could get her into a treatment program we'd have a chance."

"She's been in treatment a lot," Kate pointed out.

"I know, but never with support. Maybe that's all she needed."

"I'm hearing a lot of maybes," Kate said.

Tully looked from Kate to Johnny and finally back to Kate. "I know it's crazy and it probably won't work and no doubt I'll end up sobbing or drinking or both, but I'm tired of being so damned alone and I don't have a lover or kids to count on. What I do have is a mother, as flawed as she is. And Katie, I want you to come help me find her. It shouldn't take more than a few days."

Kate looked completely taken aback by that. "What?"

"I want to find her. I can't do it alone."

"But . . . I can't just leave for a few days. The elementary school carnival is tomorrow. I'm the games chairman. I have to be there to run the games and distribute the prizes."

Tully's breath came out in a rush of disappointment. "Oh. Well. What about this weekend?"

"I'm sorry, Tul. Really. Mom and I are running the church food drive on Saturday and Sunday. If I didn't show up it would be a real mess. On Monday and Tuesday I'm volunteering at the Parks and Rec Department, but maybe I could go with you for a few days at the end of next week."

"If I wait I won't go," Tully said, trying to gather the courage to do it alone. "I guess I can go by myself. I was just worried—"

"You should go with a crew," Johnny said.

Tully looked at him. "What do you mean?"

"You know, film it. You're a big star with a poor-little-rich-girl story. I don't mean to sound insensitive, but your viewers would love to go on this journey with you. My boss would skip on tacks to air it."

Tully turned the unexpected idea around in her head. It was dangerous for her, certainly; she could be humiliated by her mother. Then again, she could be triumphant, too. A mother-daughter reunion would be TV gold. It surprised her, frankly, that she hadn't thought of it herself. An intimate portrait like this could make her Q rating—her recognition factor—skyrocket. Was it worth the risk?

What she needed was a producer who cared about her.

She looked at Johnny. "Come with me," she said, angling toward him. "Be my producer."

Kate sat up straighter. "What?"

"Please, Johnny," Tully pleaded. "I need *you* if this is going to happen. I wouldn't trust anyone else. It'll give you national exposure. I'll call your boss. Fred and I are friends from way back. And like you said, he'd kill for an exclusive on it."

Johnny looked at his wife. "Katie?"

Tully held her breath, waiting for her friend's answer.

"It's up to you, Johnny," Kate said at last, though she didn't look happy about it.

Johnny sat back. "I'll talk to Fred. Assuming he's on board, we'll get started tomorrow. I'll call Bob Davies to run the camera." He grinned. "It'll be nice to get out of the station for a few days, anyway."

Tully laughed. "That's *great*."

The screen door banged open; Marah rushed out into the yard. "Can I go with you, Daddy? There's no school tomorrow, and you said you wanted me to see you work sometime."

Tully took Marah's hand, pulled her goddaughter down into her lap. "That's a fantastic idea. That way you'll get to see what a great producer your dad is and your mom won't have to worry about you while she's volunteering at school."

Beside her, Kate groaned.

She turned to her best friend. "It's okay, isn't it, Katie? It's just a few days. And besides, it will show Marah how lucky she is to have you for a mom. I'll have her back in time for school on Monday. I promise."

Johnny stood up and flipped his cell phone open. Punching in numbers, he walked into the house. His voice started strong and trailed away as he went inside. "Fred? Johnny here. Sorry to bother you, but . . ."

"Kate?" Tully said, leaning close. "Tell me it's okay."

Her best friend's smile was slow in coming. "Sure, Tully. Take my whole family if you want."

CHAPTER
TWENTY-SIX

Y ou always get hurt by her," Kate said, hours later, when the lights of Seattle, shimmering between the black Sound and the starless sky, had begun to darken.

Tully sighed, staring at the foamy rope of water breaking along the shore. It was barely visible. Finishing her third margarita, she put the empty glass on the grass beside her. "I know."

Tully fell silent. In truth, her head was spinning and she was beginning to worry about this idea of hers.

"Why Johnny?" Kate finally asked. She sounded hesitant, as if perhaps she hadn't meant to say it out loud.

"He'll protect me. If I say cut, he'll cut. If I say throw it in the trash, he will."

"I don't think so."

"He will. For me. And d'you know why?"

"Why?"

"You." She lurched awkwardly to her feet, unwilling to analyze this decision anymore.

Kate was beside her in an instant, steadying her.

"What would I do without you, Katie?" Tully said, leaning against her best friend.

"We'll never have to find out. Come on, now, I'll help you to your room. You need some sleep."

Kate maneuvered her into the house and down the hall to the guest bedroom.

There, Tully fell into bed, staring blearily up at her best friend. Now, with the room tumbling around her, she realized how stupid an idea this documentary was, how firmly she'd planted herself in harm's way. She could be hurt . . . again. If only she had Kate's life; then Tully wouldn't have to take this risk.

"You're so lucky," she murmured, starting to fall asleep. "Johnny . . ." She meant to continue *and the kids love you*, but the words got tangled up in her head and before she could finish she was crying, and then she was asleep.

The next morning she woke with a blinding headache. It took her longer than usual to do her hair and makeup—and Johnny yelling at her to hurry didn't help—but finally she was ready to go.

Johnny pulled Kate into a hug and kissed her. "It shouldn't take more than two days," he said in a voice so quiet Tully knew she wasn't supposed to be able to hear. "We'll be back before you can miss us."

"It'll feel like longer," Kate said. "I already miss you."

"Come on, Mommy," Marah said sharply. "We need to go. Right, Aunt Tully?"

"Give your mom a kiss goodbye," Johnny said.

Marah dutifully went to Kate and kissed her. Kate held her daughter until she started to squirm, then let her go.

Tully felt a clutch of jealousy at their intimacy; they were such a beautiful family.

Johnny led Marah out to the car and began loading their suitcases into the back.

Tully looked at Kate. "You'll be here, right? In case I need to call?"

"I'm always here, Tully. That's why they call it being an at-home mom."

"Very funny." Tully glanced down at her stuff. On top was a pile of notes she'd taken in the most recent phone conversation with her lawyer. It was a list of the last addresses they had for Cloud. "Okay, then. I'm out of here." She grabbed her bag and went out to the car.

When they reached the end of the driveway, she twisted around in her seat.

There was Kate, still standing at the front door, with two little boys hanging on to her, waving goodbye.

Their first stop, only two hours later, was at a mobile home park in Fall City. Cloud's last known address. But her mother had apparently moved out a week ago and no one yet had a forwarding address. The man they spoke to thought Cloud had moved to a campground in Issaquah.

For the next six hours they drove from place to place, following leads—Tully, Johnny, Marah, and a cameraman who called himself Fat Bob for good reason. At every stop, they filmed a segment of Tully talking to people at the various campgrounds and communes. Several people knew who Cloud was, but no one seemed to know where to find her. They went from Issaquah to Cle Elem to Ellensburg. Marah hung on Tully's every word.

They were finishing a late night dinner in North Bend when Fred called with a report that Cloud's last monthly check had been cashed at a bank on Vashon Island.

"We could have been there in an hour," Johnny muttered.

"You think we'll find her?" Tully asked, pouring sugar into her coffee. It was the first time they'd been alone all day. Fat Bob was in the van and Marah had just gone to the restroom.

Johnny looked at her. "I think we can't make people love us."

"Including our parents?"

"Especially our parents."

She felt a hint of their old connection again. They'd had that in common, she recalled. Lonely childhoods. "What's it like, Johnny, being loved?"

"That's not the question you want to ask. You want to know what it's like to love someone." He gave her a grin that made him look like a kid again. "Besides yourself, I mean."

She leaned back. "I need new friends."

"I won't pull back, you know. You better be okay with that. You've got me on this story now. The camera will be there, seeing all of it. If you want to back out, this is the time."

"You can protect me."

"That's what I'm telling you, Tully. I won't. I'll follow the story. Like you did in Germany."

She understood what he was saying. Friendship ended when the story rolled; it was an axiom of journalism. "Just try to shoot me from the left. It's my good side."

Johnny smiled and paid the bill. "Go get Marah. If we hurry, we might be able to catch the last ferry."

In fact, they missed the last ferry and ended up sleeping in three rooms in a run-down hotel near the dock.

The next morning Tully woke with a pounding headache that no amount of aspirin could tame. Still, she got dressed and put on her makeup and ate breakfast at some greasy spoon diner that Fat Bob recommended. By nine in the morning they were on the ferry, headed to a berry-growing commune on Vashon Island.

Every step of the way, every mile driven, the camera was on Tully. As she interviewed the tellers at the bank where the last check was cashed and showed the old and creased picture of her mother—the only photo she had of her—she maintained her smile.

It wasn't until almost ten o'clock when they pulled up to the SUNSHINE FARMS sign that she began to lose her grip.

The commune was like others she'd seen: long, rolling acres covered in crops, shaggy-looking people dressed in the modern-day equivalent of sackcloth and ashes, rows of Sani-Cans. The main difference was the housing. Here, people lived in domed tents called yurts. There were at least thirty of them lining the river.

Johnny pulled into a parking stall and got out of the van. Fat Bob followed suit, sliding the van door open and then slamming it shut.

Marah said worriedly, "Are you okay, Aunt Tully?"

"Be quiet, Marah," Johnny said. "Move over here by Daddy."

Tully knew they were waiting for her; still she sat there. People waited for her all the time; it was one of the perks of celebrity.

"You can do this," she said to the scared-looking woman in the rearview mirror. She'd spent a lifetime shellacking her heart, creating this hard casing around it, and now she was purposely peeling it away, exposing her vulnerability. But what choice did she have? If she and her mother were ever going to have a chance, someone had to make the first move.

Cautiously, she opened the door and stepped out.

Fat Bob and his camera were right there.

Tully took a deep breath and smiled. "We're at the Sunshine Farms commune. We've been told that my mother has lived here for almost a week, although she hasn't yet sent this address to my attorney, so we don't know if she's planning to stay."

She walked up to the long row of tables, covered by cedar lean-tos, where tired-looking women sold their wares. Berries, jams, syrups, berry butters, and Holly Hobbie–type handicrafts.

No one seemed to care that a camera was coming their way. Or a celebrity.

"I'm Tallulah Hart, and I'm looking for this woman." She held out the picture.

Fat Bob moved to her left, stayed close. People had no idea how close cameras sometimes needed to be to capture nuances of emotion.

"Cloud," the woman said without smiling.

Tully's heart skipped a beat. "Yes."

"She's not at Sunshine anymore. Too much work for her. Last I heard she was out at the old Mulberry place. What has she done?"

"Nothing. She's my mother."

"She said she didn't have any kids."

Tully knew the camera caught her reaction to that, her flinch of pain. "That's hardly surprising. How do we get to the Mulberry place?"

As the woman gave directions, Tully felt a wave of anxiety. She walked away, went over by a fence to be alone. Johnny came up beside her, leaning close.

"Are you okay?" he asked softly enough that the camera couldn't pick up the question.

"I'm scared," she whispered, looking up at him.

"You'll be fine. She can't hurt you anymore. You're Tallulah Hart, remember?"

That was what she needed. Smiling, feeling stronger, she pulled back and broke free, looking at the camera. She didn't bother to wipe the tears from her eyes. "I guess I still want her to love me," she revealed quietly. "Let's go."

They climbed back into the van and drove out to the highway. On Mill Road they turned left and drove down a bumpy, rutted gravel road until an old beige mobile home came into view. It sat on blocks in a grassy field, surrounded by rusted, broken-down cars. A refrigerator lay on its side in the front yard; a threadbare, broken recliner beside it. Three ragged-looking pit bulls were chained to the fence. They went crazy when the van pulled into the yard, barking and snarling and jumping forward.

"It's *Deliverance*," Tully said, giving a weak smile as she reached for the door handle.

They all got out at once, moving forward in formation: Tully in the lead, advancing with false confidence; Fat Bob beside or in front of her, capturing every instant on tape; and Johnny behind them, holding Marah's hand, reminding her to keep quiet.

Tully went up to the front door and knocked.

No one answered.

She tried to listen for footsteps, but the barking dogs made that impossible.

She knocked again, and was just about to give in to relief and say, *No luck!* when the door swung open to reveal a huge, straggly-haired man in boxer shorts. A tattoo of a woman in a hula skirt covered the left half of his swollen, hairy belly.

"Yeah?" he said, scratching his underarm.

"I'm here to see Cloud."

He cocked his head to the right and stepped out of the trailer, moving past her, going toward his dogs.

Tully's eyes watered at the smell that came from the mobile home. She wanted to turn to the camera and say something witty, but she couldn't even swallow, she was so nervous. Inside, she found piles of junk and old food containers. There were flies everywhere and pizza boxes full of leftover crusts. But mostly what she saw were empty booze bottles and a bong. A huge pile of pot lay on the kitchen table.

Tully didn't point it out or make a comment.

Fat Bob mirrored every step, filmed her journey through this mobile home hell.

She went to the closed door behind the kitchen, knocked, and opened it, revealing the grossest bathroom of all time. She slammed the door shut and went to the next door. There, she knocked twice and then turned the knob. The bedroom was small, made smaller by the piles of clothes everywhere. Three empty half-gallon Monarch Gin bottles lined the bedside table.

Her mother lay curled in the fetal position on the unmade bed, with a ragged blue blanket wrapped around her body.

Tully bent close, noticing now how grayed and wrinkled her mother's skin had become. "Cloud?" She said the name three or four times, and got no response at all. Finally she reached out, touched her mother's shoulder, gently at first and then not so gently. "Cloud?"

Fat Bob got into position, pointed the camera at the woman in bed.

Slowly, her mother opened her eyes. It took her a long time to focus; she had a vague, vacant look. "Tallulah?"

"Hey, Cloud."

"Tully," she said as if just remembering the nickname her daughter preferred. "What are you doing here? And who the hell is that guy with the camera?"

"I'm here looking for you."

Cloud sat up slowly, reaching into her dirty pocket for a cigarette. When she lit up, Tully noticed how palsied her mother's hand was. It took three tries to touch the tip to the flame. "I thought you were in New York, getting rich and famous." She glanced nervously at the camera.

"I'm both," Tully said, unable to squelch the pride in her voice. She hated it that still, after all the disappointments, she craved this woman's admiration. "How long have you been living here?"

"What do you care? You live in some fancy place while I'm rotting away."

Tully looked at her mother, noticing the wild, unkempt hair now threaded with gray; the baggy, stained cargo pants with the ragged, torn hem; the worn flannel shirt that was buttoned wrong. And her face. Lined, dirty, and grayed from cigarettes and alcohol and a life poorly lived. Cloud was barely sixty and she looked fifteen years older. The fragile beauty of her youth was gone now, scrubbed away by harsh excess. "You can't want this, Cloud. Even you . . ."

"Even me, huh? Why did you come looking for me, Tully?"

"You're my mother."

"We both know better than that," Cloud cleared her throat and looked away. "I need to get away from here. Maybe I could stay with you for a few days. Take a bath. Eat something."

Tully hated the tiny lurch of emotion that followed those words. She had waited a lifetime for her mother to want to come home with her, but she knew how dangerous a moment like this could be. "Okay."

"Really?" The disbelief on Cloud's face revealed how little faith they had in each other.

"Really." And for an instant, Tully forgot the camera was even there. She dared to imagine the impossible: that they could become mother and daughter instead of strangers. "Come on, Cloud. Let me help you to the car."

Tully knew she shouldn't believe in the possibility of forging a connection with her mother, but the idea created a dizzying cocktail of hope that, once drunk, made her light-headed. Maybe she could finally have a family of her own.

The camera caught it all: Tully's hope and fear and need. On the long drive home, while Cloud slept slumped in the corner, Tully spilled

her heart to the lens. She answered Johnny's questions with an unprecedented honesty, revealing at last how wounded she'd been by her distant mother.

Now, though, Tully added a new word.

Addicted.

For as long as she'd known her mother, Cloud had been hooked on
drugs or booze or both.

The more Tully thought about that, the more it seemed like the
cause of their problems.

If she could get her mom into rehab and help her through the program, maybe they could make a new start. So sure of this was she that
she called her boss at CBS and asked for more time off so that she could
be a good daughter and help her broken mother heal.

"Are you sure that's a good idea?" Johnny asked when she got off the
phone.

They were in the sitting room of the luxurious Cascade Suite at the
Fairmont Olympic Hotel in Seattle. By the window, Fat Bob sat in an
overstuffed chair, capturing this whole conversation on tape. Cameras
and equipment covered most of the floor; huge lights created a staging
area along the couch. Marah lay curled catlike in an overstuffed chair,
reading a book.

"She needs me," Tully said simply.

Johnny shrugged and said nothing more, just looked at her.

"Well." She stood up, stretching. "I think I'll hit the sack." To Fat Bob,
she said, "That's it for the night. Go get a good night's sleep. We'll start
again at eight."

Fat Bob nodded, packed up his gear, and headed to his room down
the hall.

"Can I sleep with Aunt Tully?" Marah said, letting her book fall to
the floor.

"It's okay with me," Johnny said, "if Tully doesn't mind."

"Are you kidding? A slumber party with my favorite goddaughter is a
perfect end to the day."

After Johnny went to his own room, Tully played mommy to

Marah—telling her to brush her teeth and wash her face and get into her jammies.

"I'm too old for jammies," Marah informed her smartly, but when she climbed into bed, she snuggled up to Tully like the little girl she'd been only a few short years ago.

"This was so awesome, Aunt Tully," she said sleepily. "I'm going to be a TV star, too, when I grow up."

"I don't doubt it."

"If my mom lets me, which she probably won't."

"What do you mean?"

"My mom won't let me do anything."

"You do know that your mom is my best friend, right?"

"Yeah," she answered grudgingly.

"Why do you think that is?"

Marah twisted around and looked at her. "Why?"

"Because your mom rocks."

Marah made a face. "My mom? She never does anything cool."

Tully shook her head. "Marah, your mother loves you no matter what and she's proud of you. Believe me, princess, that's the coolest thing in the world."

The next morning Tully got up early and went to the bedroom door across the hall. There, she paused, gathering her nerve, and knocked. When no one answered, she quietly opened it.

Her mother was still asleep.

Smiling, she left the suite and closed the door quietly behind her. At Johnny's door, she paused and knocked.

He answered quickly, dressed in one of the hotel's robes, his hair dripping wet. "I thought we were starting at eight."

"We are. I'm just going to get Cloud some clothes to take to rehab and some breakfast for all of us. Marah's still asleep."

Johnny frowned. "You're moving awfully fast, Tully. The stores aren't open yet."

"I've always been fast. You know that, Johnny. And everything is open for Tallulah Hart. It's one of the perks of my life. You have a key to my room?"

"Yeah. I'll go over there now. You be careful."

Ignoring his concern, she went to the Public Market and stocked up on croissants, beignets, and cinnamon rolls. Cloud needed to pack on a few pounds. Then she went to La Dolce, where she bought her mother jeans, tops, shoes, underwear and bras, as well as the thickest jacket she could find. She was back at the hotel by nine.

"I'm home," she called out, kicking the door shut behind her. "And wait till you see what I've got." She draped the garment bags over the sofa and set the bags on the floor.

At the small table in the sitting room, she began setting out the rolls and beignets.

Fat Bob was in the corner, shooting her entrance.

She gave him her best smile. "My mother needs to put on a few pounds. This should do it. I got practically every coffee Starbucks sells. I don't know what she likes."

Johnny sat on the sofa, looking tired.

"It's like a morgue in here." Tully went to her mother's door and knocked. "Cloud?"

There was no answer.

She knocked again. "Cloud? Are you in the shower? I'm coming in." She opened the door.

The first thing she noticed was the smell of cigarettes and the open window. The bed was empty.

"Cloud?" She went to the bathroom, which was still damp and cloudy with steam. Thick Egyptian cotton towels lay in a heap on the floor. The washrag and hand towel were stained with dirt and lying in the sink.

Tully backed slowly out of the steamy bathroom and faced Johnny and the camera. "She left?"

"A half an hour ago," he said. "I tried to stop her."

Tully was stunned by how betrayed she felt, like that ten-year-old girl again, abandoned on the Seattle street. Worthless and unwanted.

Johnny came over to her, took her in his arms, and held her. She wanted to ask him *why*, ask what was wrong with her that no one ever stayed, but the question caught in her throat. She clung to him for too long, taking the comfort he offered. He stroked her head, whispered, *Shhh*, in her ear as if she were a child.

In time, though, she remembered where she was and pulled back, forcing a smile for the camera. "Well, there it is. The end of the documentary. I'm done, Bob." Sidestepping Johnny, she went back into her room, where she heard Marah singing in the shower. Tears stung her eyes, but she refused to let them fall. Her mother wouldn't break her again. She'd been a fool to even think there could be a different ending than this one.

Then she noticed the empty nightstand beside her. "The bitch stole my jewelry."

She closed her eyes and sat on the end of the bed. Pulling a cell phone out of her pocket, she hit Kate's number and listened to the ringing. When her friend answered, Tully didn't even bother with hello. "There's something wrong with me, Katie," she said quietly, her voice trembling.

"She ditched you?"

"Like a thief in the night."

"Tallulah Rose Hart, you listen to me right now. You are going to hang up the phone and get down to the ferry right now. I'll take care of you. Got it? And bring my family with you."

"You don't have to yell. I'm coming. We all are. But you better have alcohol ready for me when I get there. And I'm not mixing it with that gross juice your kids drink."

Kate laughed. "It's the morning, Tully. I'll make you breakfast."

"Thanks, Kate," Tully said quietly. "I owe you one."

When she looked up she saw Fat Bob. He was filming all of this from the doorway, with Johnny standing beside him.

But it wasn't the red light on the camera or the knowledge of her public humiliation or the all-seeing lens that broke her.

It was Johnny and the sad, knowing way he looked at her that finally made her cry.

CHAPTER
TWENTY-SEVEN

The documentary aired two weeks later, and even Kate, who was used to Tully's amazing successes, was caught off guard by the public's reaction. It caused a media frenzy. For years Tully had been seen on camera as the cool, witty professional, following stories and reporting on them with her journalist's detachment.

Now the public learned how she'd been disappointed and abandoned. They saw beyond the journalist to the woman within, and they couldn't stop talking about her. The phrase heard most often was, *just like me*.

Before the documentary, the public respected Tully Hart. Afterward, they adored her. She graced the cover of *People* and *Us* in the same week. The documentary—and segments from it—were played and replayed on entertainment news shows. America, it seemed, couldn't get enough of Tully Hart.

But while everyone was watching Tully and the sad encounter with her estranged mother, Kate saw something else entirely on that tape, and she watched it just as obsessively.

She couldn't help noticing the way Johnny looked at Tully at the end, when Cloud's disappearance was revealed, the way he'd gone to her and taken her in his arms.

And then there was the quiet talk Tully and Johnny had had out at Sunshine Farms. They'd edited out whatever words had been exchanged and gone to an establishing shot of the commune, but Kate couldn't help wondering what they'd said to each other.

She studied their body language like a primatologist, but in the end she had only what she'd had in the beginning: two old friends working together on an emotional documentary and a wife who'd worried for a long time about them.

That should have been the end of it. If nothing else had happened, Kate would have boxed up her old jealousies and put them away again, just as she'd done dozens of times over the years.

But something *had* happened.

Syndiworld, the second largest syndication company in the world, had seen the documentary and offered Tully her own one-hour show, of which she would be a majority interest owner.

The idea had rocked Tully's world, offered her a way to be herself on camera, to show the world who she really was and how she really felt. No more three A.M. start times, either. The minute she heard the idea, she said it was exactly what she needed, but even so, she'd put down two conditions: first, they had to shoot in Seattle; second, John Ryan had to be her producer. Neither of these had she bothered to clear with her friends.

Kate and Johnny had been on the back porch, talking over drinks after a long day, when the first phone call had come in.

Johnny had laughed at Tully's offer, told her to find a producer who specialized in prima donnas.

Then Tully mentioned a salary in the millions.

Now, two days later, Kate sure as hell wasn't laughing. She and Johnny were in the living room, trying to keep their voices down because the kids were in bed. Tully was back in New York, no doubt sitting by the phone, waiting to see if once again she'd get her way.

"I don't know why you're fighting me on this, Katie," Johnny said, pacing in front of the window. "It will change our lives."

"What's wrong with our life now?"

"Do you understand how much money they're offering us? We could pay off this house and send the kids to Harvard for medical degrees. And I could do a few shows that *mattered*. Tully said I could spotlight places in the world that are in trouble. Do you know what that would mean to me?"

"Is that how you want your career to be from now on—starting everything with, *Tully said*?"

"Are you asking if I can work for her? The answer is hell, yes. I've worked for a lot worse people than Tully Hart."

"Maybe I'm asking if you should be working for her," Kate said softly.

He stopped in his tracks and turned to look at her. "You've got to be kidding me. Is that what this is about? One night a million years ago?"

"She's an incredibly beautiful woman. I just think . . ." She couldn't finish, couldn't put her old fears and insecurities into words.

The look he gave her was so hot she felt herself melting, disappearing. "I don't deserve that."

She watched him storm up the stairs, heard the bedroom door slam shut.

She sat there a long time, staring down at her wedding ring. Why was it that some memories could never be erased? Slowly, she turned off all the lights, locked all the doors, and went upstairs.

At their closed door she paused, taking a deep breath. She knew what she had to do now, what she had to say. She'd hurt his feelings and insulted him. They both knew this was the opportunity of a lifetime. Her insecurities and jealousy couldn't stand in the way of that.

She had to go to him, say she was sorry, and tell him she was foolish to be afraid, that she believed in his love like she believed in sunshine and rain. It was true, too. She did.

Because of all that, she should be proud of Johnny and happy for this chance and what it meant to him. That was what marriage was, a team sport, and this was her time to be cheerleader. But even knowing all that, she couldn't quite be happy.

Instead, she was afraid.

Yes, they'd be rich. Maybe even powerful.

But at what cost?

Tully finished off her contract, had an emotional, celebrity-studded last broadcast, and said goodbye to New York. She found a new penthouse in the Emerald City and spent the next month in closed-door meetings, coming up with the plans for her new show, which she was calling *The Girlfriend Hour with Tully Hart* in honor of the Mularkeys' holiday tradition. She and Johnny had spent long hours working together like the old days, hiring staff and designing the set and devising show concepts.

By August of 2003, much of the advance work was done and she realized that yet again she'd been so busy with work that she'd forgotten to have a life. Even with Kate just across the bay, Tully had hardly seen her. So she picked up the phone and invited her best friend and god-daughter to spend the day with her.

"Sorry," Kate said. "I can't come into the city."

"Come on," Tully pleaded. "I know I haven't called enough this summer, but Johnny and I have been working twelve-hour days."

"Tell me something I don't know. You see him more than we do."

"I've missed you."

There was a pause, then: "I've missed you, too, but today is no good for me. The boys have some friends coming over."

"How about if I take Marah off your hands? Yeah," Tully said, warming to the idea. "I could take her to Gene Juarez for a manicure and a makeup lesson. Maybe a facial. It'd be great. A girl's day out."

"She is too young for a spa, Tully." Kate laughed, but it sounded a little strained. "And you can forget the makeover. She is not allowed to wear makeup until ninth grade."

"No one is too young for a spa, Kate, and you're crazy to forbid makeup. Remember when your mom tried that? We just put it on at the bus stop. Don't you want her to learn the right way to apply it?"

"Not yet."

"Come on," Tully cajoled. "Put her on the eleven-fifteen boat. I'll meet her at McDonald's. You said you two are always fighting anyway."

"Well . . . I guess that would be okay. But no R-rated movies, no matter how much she begs."

"Okay."

"Maybe that'll put her in a good mood. Tomorrow we're going school shopping, which is only slightly less painful than a root canal without anesthesia."

"Maybe I'll take her to Nordstrom, get her something special."

"Forty dollars."

"What?"

"That's how much you can spend. Not one dollar more, and Tully, if you buy her anything that shows off her belly—"

"I know. I know. Britney Spears is the Antichrist. Got it."

"Good. I'll go tell Marah."

Exactly one hour and twelve minutes later, Tully directed her driver to pull up beside the McDonald's on Alaskan Way. She could tell by the honking that it was an illegal place to park, but what did she care?

She rolled down the window and saw Marah running toward her. "Over here," she called, getting out of the car.

Marah hugged her tightly. "Thank you so much for getting me out of the house. Mom's been ragging on me all day. What are we going to do?"

"How about makeovers at Gene Juarez?"

"Awesome."

"And after that, we can do whatever you want."

"You're so totally awesome," Marah said, gazing at Tully with the purest expression of adoration she'd ever seen.

Tully laughed. "We both are. That's why we're a perfect team."

CHAPTER
TWENTY-EIGHT

The *Girlfriend Hour* was a runaway success from the first day it aired. Suddenly Tully was more than a journalist or a morning news anchor; she was a bona fide star. Everything about the show had been designed to play to her strengths and highlight her talent.

What she did well—what she'd always done well—was talk to people.

And she connected, not only with the camera, but with her guests, her audience, and her viewers. In the first two weeks of the show, she became a sensation. Her picture graced the covers of *People, Entertainment Weekly, Good Housekeeping,* and *In Style.* Syndiworld had trouble keeping up with demand; that was how fast her show was growing into new markets.

Best of all was: she owned it. Sure, she shared ownership with Syndiworld and the Ryans had a small piece, but she was the powerhouse. As anyone knew, half as successful as *Oprah* was damned successful.

Now she sat in her office, going over the notes for the taping that would start in—she looked up at the clock—twenty-five minutes.

This was one of her celebrity shows. A smiling, don't-we-just-love-each-other interview. To be honest, there was still enough of the journalist left in Tully to bristle at these segments, but the businesswoman overruled her. The public simply couldn't get close enough to their stars these days. Johnny put up with these segments in exchange for his change-the-world bits.

There was a knock on the door, then a respectful, "Ms. Hart?"

She spun around in her chair. "Yes?"

"Your goddaughter is here. For the take-your-daughter-to-work segment?"

"Great!" Tully shot to her feet. "Let her in."

The door opened farther, revealing Johnny, who stood there dressed in faded jeans and a navy blue cashmere sweater. "Hey," he said.

"Hey."

Beside him, Marah couldn't keep still, she was so excited. "Hi, Aunt Tully. Daddy said I could be with you all day."

Tully walked over to them. "I couldn't ask for a better daughter. You ready to see what it's like to make a show work?"

"I can hardly wait."

Tully turned to Johnny, realizing a second too late that she was too close. She could see a tiny place by his ear where he'd missed shaving.

"I'll be in my office if you need me. Don't buy her a car or a horse while she's here."

"How about something small?"

"Normally I'd say fine, but with you small could be a diamond."

"I was thinking of a *Girlfriend Hour* tote bag."

"Perfect."

Tully smiled up at him. "You're my producer. You have to say I'm perfect."

He stared down at her. "The whole world thinks you're perfect."

A lot of years were suddenly between them, conversations and moments and opportunities she'd walked away from. At least that was what she was thinking about; she no longer knew him well enough to read his expressions. Even though they worked together every day, they were always surrounded by people and focused on work. On the weekends, when she went to his house, he was Katie's husband, and Tully kept her distance.

He didn't move, didn't smile.

Tully smiled and backed away, hoping her smile looked real. "Come on, Marah, let's go play mother/daughter. I have Lindsay Lohan in the green room. You can ask her how she got started."

On a bright Wednesday in the first full week of September, Kate stood on the sidewalk outside of Ordway Elementary School. The parking lot, which only moments before had been clogged with buses pulling up to the curb and cars—mostly SUVs and minivans—inching through the carpool lane, was now empty and quiet. The bell had rung and fallen silent; the principal had gone back inside the squat, low-roofed brick building to start his day. Directly overhead, two flags flapped in the early autumn breeze.

"Are you still crying?" Tully tried to sound reassuring, but her voice was too honest for that. There was the merest hint of laughter behind the words.

"Bite me, and I mean that in the nicest possible way."

"Come on, I'm taking you home."

"But . . ." Kate glanced at the window at the far end of the school. "One of them might need me."

"They're going into kindergarten, not open-heart surgery, and you've got things to do."

Kate sighed, wiping her eyes. "I know it's stupid."

Tully squeezed her hand. "It's not stupid. I remember my first day of school. I was so jealous of the kids who had moms that cried."

"I really appreciate you being here for me today. I know how hard it is for you to leave the studio."

"My producer gave me the day off," she said with a smile. "I think he has the hots for my best friend."

Together, they walked down the tree-lined sidewalk to their parking spot. Kate climbed into the driver's seat of her new blue SUV and started up the engine.

Tully immediately leaned forward in her own seat and popped a CD into the stereo. Rick Springfield's voice blared through the speakers, singing "Jessie's Girl."

Kate laughed. By the time they'd driven out of the school lot, stopped at the coffee stand drive-through for their lattes, and arrived back home, she definitely felt better.

In her messy, toy-strewn living room, she collapsed into Johnny's favorite overstuffed chair and put her feet up on the ottoman. "What now, fearless leader? Are we going shopping?"

"In the ridiculous three hours we have, not likely. You should have put them in the all-day program."

Kate had heard it before. "I'm well aware of your opinion on that. I happen to like my kids around me."

"Actually, I have a better plan, anyway." Tully flopped down on the sofa. "We're going to talk about your writing."

Kate almost dropped her latte. "M-my writing?"

"You always said you were going to start writing again when the boys were in school."

"Give me some time, will you? They just started. Let's talk about the show instead. Johnny tells me that—"

"I can see through your feeble tactics. You think I'll forget everything else if you talk about me."

"It's usually true."

"Touché. So, what will you write about?"

Kate felt exposed suddenly. "It's an old dream, Tully."

"Well, you're getting old, so it's perfect."

"Has anyone ever told you that you're a coldhearted bitch?"

"Only the men who date me. Come on, Katie. Talk to me. I see how tired you are all the time. I know you need something more in your life."

This was the last thing that Kate would have expected; that Tully, as on top of the world as she was, would notice her depression. At the realization, the fight went out of her. In truth, she was exhausted lately by the pretense, anyway. "It's more than just that. I feel . . . lost. What I have should be enough, but somehow it isn't. And Marah is wearing me down. Everything I do is wrong. I love her so much and she treats me like last year's shoes."

"It's the age."

"That excuse is wearing a little thin. Maybe I should let her take the modeling class she's so jazzed about. I just hate to think of her in a world like that."

"P.S.: We're talking about you, here," Tully said. "Look, Katie, I don't know what you're going through, but I know about wanting more. Sometimes you have to fight for the thing that will complete you."

"Says the woman who has to borrow my family when she needs one."

Tully smiled. "We're quite a pair, aren't we?"

For the first time in what felt like forever, Kate laughed. "We always have been. I'll tell you what: I'll think about writing if you think about falling in love."

Tully looked at her. "Maybe it would be easier to think about spending the day on the beach." She paused. "I haven't heard from Grant since I moved out here."

"I know," Kate said. "I'm sorry. But I don't think he was the one for you. If you two had been right for each other you'd have fallen in love."

"That's what people like you think," Tully said quietly, and then brightened. "Come on, let's make margaritas."

"Now you're talking. I'll get drunk on the first day of kindergarten, and in the morning, no less. Perfect."

The Ordway Halloween Carnival was only seven days away and Kate had foolishly volunteered to design and make the photograph staging area. Between shopping for supplies, painting the backdrops, and building the faux haunted house set, she was overwhelmed with work. Add to that driving responsibilities that came with getting Marah to her modeling class, and she was emotionally close to the edge most of the time.

But she was supposed to be writing her book. Johnny and Tully and Mom expected it of her. She expected it of herself. She'd been certain that once the boys started school she'd find the time.

Unfortunately, she'd forgotten the kindergarten timetable. Frankly, she'd barely dropped the boys off before it was time to pick them up, and Johnny, who'd always been so much help, now spent more waking hours at the studio than he did at home.

So Kate did what she'd always done: she kept moving, hoping no one would notice that she didn't smile as easily as she used to, or sleep as well.

This morning at six o'clock, she kissed Johnny awake, then went down the hall to waken Marah. From that moment on, she was caught in the whirlpool of other people's needs. She drove carpool and went shopping and met the decorating committee for an hour of hammer-and-nails-type work.

She got so caught up in the work she almost missed picking up the boys. Late, she ran for her SUV and sped across the island, pulling into the pickup lane as most of the cars were leaving. She honked at the boys and waved them over.

Her phone rang. "Hello?" she answered, reaching behind her to unlock the back door.

"Mom?" Marah said.

"What's wrong?"

Marah laughed, but it was definitely contrived. "Nothing. I don't want you to spaz out, but I'm scheduling a family meeting for seven o'clock tonight."

"A *what?*"

"A family meeting. Well, sort of. I don't want Lucas or William there."

"Let me get this straight: you want to have a meeting with your dad and me at seven."

"And Tully."

"What trouble are you in?"

"Way to believe the worst in me. I just want to talk."

A thirteen-year-old girl wanting to talk to her parents? Specifically, Marah wanting to talk to Kate? That was like a snowfall in July. "Okay," Kate said slowly. "You sure you're not in trouble?"

"I'm sure. See you. 'Bye."

Kate stared at the phone in her hand. "What's going on?" she wondered aloud, but before an answer floated to the surface, the car door behind her opened, the boys climbed into the backseat, and Kate was tossed onto the surf of her everyday life.

There was shopping to do, and cooking, and at three she was back in the carpool lane, picking up Marah.

"You sure you don't want to talk about something now?" she asked.

Marah sat slouched against the window in the passenger seat, with her long black hair covering most of her downcast face. As usual, she wore low-rise jeans, flip-flops (even though it was raining), a skimpy pink T-shirt, and a surly expression. The expression was the one accessory she never left home without.

"If I wanted to talk now I wouldn't have scheduled a meeting. Sheesh. Get a clue, Mom."

Kate knew she shouldn't let her daughter talk to her like that, and usually she didn't, but today she didn't feel like fighting, so she let it go.

At home, Kate went straight up to her bathroom, took two aspirin, and changed into her sweats. Ignoring her headache, she got the boys settled at the kitchen table with their sticker books and started dinner.

Before she knew it, it was six o'clock and Johnny opened the door. "Hey," he said, ushering Tully into the house. "Look who came home with me for the big meeting."

Kate looked up from the tacos she was making. "Hey, you two." She covered the saucepan and turned the stove's heat down to low, then went out to meet them. "You don't know what's going on, do you?"

"Me? I hardly know anything," Tully said.

After that, the evening seemed alternately to drag and to fly. Kate watched her daughter all through dinner, trying to glean a hint about what was to come, but by the end of the meal she was no closer to an answer than she'd been this afternoon.

"Okay," Marah finally said at almost exactly seven o'clock when the dishes were done and the boys were upstairs watching a movie. She stood by the fireplace, looking both nervous and young. "Aunt Tully thought I should be—"

"Tully knows what this is about?" Kate asked.

"Uh. No," Marah said quickly. "Just in general, she thinks I shouldn't throw stuff at you. I should be respectful and let you know how much something matters to me."

Kate glanced at Johnny, who rolled his eyes in response.

"So, here it is," Marah said, wringing her hands together. "There's a conference in New York in November that I just have to go to. It's where a bunch of agents and photographers come looking for models. Tully thinks Eileen Ford could definitely pick me. And my modeling class teacher invited me personally."

Kate sat there, too stunned to speak right away. *New York. Tully thinks . . . Invited me personally.* Which arrow should she pull out first?

"I assume this costs money," Johnny said.

"Oh. Right." Marah nodded. "Three thousand dollars, but it's a bargain at that price. Everyone who is anyone will be there."

"And the dates?"

"November fourteenth through the twenty-first."

"During school?" Kate said sharply.

"It's just a week—" Marah began, but Kate cut her off.

"Just a week? Are you kidding?"

Marah glanced nervously at Tully. "I can take my homework and do it at night and on the plane, but if I get discovered, I wouldn't need to finish high school anyway. I'd have tutors."

"How many of the kids in your modeling class were invited to attend?" Johnny asked, sounding calm and reasonable.

"Everyone," Marah answered.

"Everyone?" Kate got to her feet. "Everyone? That's not anything special, then, it's some racket to wring money out of us. You actually think—"

"Kate," Johnny said, giving her The Look.

She yanked hard on her temper, took a deep breath. "I didn't mean that, Marah. I just . . . you can't miss a week of school, and three thousand dollars is a lot of money."

"I'll pay it," Tully said.

Kate had never wanted to hit her best friend more. "She can't miss school."

"I could—"

Kate held up a hand for silence. "Don't say more," she said to Tully.

Marah burst into tears. "See?" she yelled at Tully. "She thinks I'm a baby and she won't let me do anything."

Johnny got to his feet. "Marah, come on, you're thirteen years old."

"Brooke Shields and Kate Moss were millionaires by fourteen because their mothers *loved* them, right, Tully?" She wiped her eyes and looked at Johnny. "Please, Daddy?"

He shook his head. "I'm sorry, honey."

Marah spun on her heel and ran upstairs; all the way up, until she slammed her bedroom door, they could hear her crying.

"I'll go talk to her," Johnny said, sighing as he headed for the stairs.

Kate turned to her best friend. "Are you *insane?*"

"It's a modeling school, not a crack house."

"Damn it, Tully, she doesn't need to be in that screwed-up world. I've told you that before. It's dangerous."

"I'll help her through it. I'll go with her."

Kate was so mad she could hardly breathe. Once again Tully had made Kate look bad in front of Marah, and frankly, she didn't need any help screwing up her relationship with her daughter. "You're not her mother. I am. You can whoop it up with her and have a blast and live like the world is your Never-Never Land. It's my job to keep her safe."

"Safe isn't everything," Tully said. "Sometimes you have to take a risk. Nothing ventured, nothing gained."

"Tully, you don't know what in the hell you're talking about. My thirteen-year-old daughter is not going to New York City on some scam of a modeling trip, and you are certainly not going to chaperone her. The subject is closed."

"Fine," Tully said. "I was just trying to help."

Kate heard the hurt in her friend's voice, but she was too tired, and this was too important, to let herself yield. "Fine. And next time my daughter comes to you with a plan that includes skipping a week of school or modeling in a faraway place, I would appreciate it if you'd let me discuss it with her."

"But you don't. You two just scream at each other. Even Johnny says—"

"You've talked to Johnny about this?"

"He's worried about you and Marah. He says it's like World War II around here some nights."

That was about the third sucker punch tonight, and it hurt so much she said, "You better leave, Tully. This is a family matter."

"But . . . I thought I was family."

"Goodnight," Kate said quietly, then walked out of the room.

CHAPTER
TWENTY-NINE

Tully should have gone straight home and tried to forget the whole thing, but by the time the ferry pulled back into downtown Seattle, she was a wreck. Instead of turning left on Alaskan Way, she turned right and hit the gas.

In record time she was in Snohomish, driving past the altered landmarks of her youth. The town was a tourist stop now, full of trendy cafés and upscale antique shops.

None of it mattered much to her; what changed, what stayed the same . . . she didn't care. Even under the best of circumstances, she was only barely connected to the yesterdays of her life, and tonight was far from the best of circumstances. Still, when she turned onto Firefly Lane, it was like rocketing into the past.

She turned onto the paved driveway and drove up to the small white farmhouse with the glossy black trim. Over the years Mrs. Mularkey had turned the ragged yard into an English-style garden full of flowers. In this late autumn, the whole garden seemed to glow golden. The yard and hanging baskets were a riot of red geraniums, visible in the orangey porch light.

Tully parked the car and went to the front door, ringing the bell.

Mr. M. answered, and for a second there, standing on the porch, looking up at him, Tully felt her whole life flash before her eyes. He looked older, of course, with a vanishing hairline and an expanding waistline, but dressed as he was in a white T-shirt and worn jeans, he looked so much like he used to that she felt young again, too. "Hey, Mr. M."

"You're here late. Everything okay?"

"I just needed to talk to Mrs. M. I won't stay long."

"You know you're welcome to stay as long as you want." He stepped back to let her in, then went to the base of the stairs and yelled up, "Margie, come on down. Trouble's here." He flashed Tully a smile that coaxed out one of her own.

In no time, Mrs. M. came down the stairs, zipping up the red velour robe she'd worn for as long as Tully had known her. No matter how many expensive robe-and-nightgown sets Tully sent Mrs. M. over the years, this old red one remained her favorite. "Tully," she said, pulling off her big beige-rimmed bifocals. "Is everything okay?"

There was no point in lying. "Not really."

Mrs. M. went straight to the wet bar in the living room—an addition in the late eighties—and poured two glasses of wine. Handing one to Tully, she led the way into the living room and sat down on the new leopard-print sofa. Behind their heads the wall was full of family photos now. Jesus and Elvis still held center stage, but around them were dozens of school photos of Marah and the twins; Johnny and Kate's wedding pictures; Sean's graduate school graduation photos; and a few here and there of Tully. "Okay, what's the problem?"

Tully sat down in the newest edition of Mr. Mularkey's favorite recliner. "Kate is mad at me."

"Why?"

"Marah called me last week and wanted to talk to me about a modeling thing in New York—"

"Oh, boy."

"I offered to help her talk to her folks about it, but the second Kate heard about it, she went wacko. She refused to even listen to Marah."

"Marah is thirteen years old."

"That's old enough to—"

"No," Mrs. M. said crisply, then she smiled gently. "I know you're just trying to help, Tully, but Kate's right to try to protect Marah."

"Marah hates her."

"That's how it seems with thirteen-year-old girls and their mothers. You don't know, maybe, because Cloud was so different, but girls and their mothers often go through a rough patch. You don't make it better by giving the kids everything they want."

"I'm not suggesting they should give her everything, but she has real talent. I think she could be a supermodel."

"And if she were, what would happen?"

"She'd be rich and famous. She could be a millionaire by seventeen."

Mrs. M. leaned forward. "You're mega-rich, right?"

"Right."

"Does that make you whole? Is success worth what Marah would give up for it—her childhood, her innocence, her family? I have watched some of those made-for-TV movies about young models. There's all kinds of drugs and sex and such around them."

"I'd watch out for her. What matters is that she has found something she loves. That should be nurtured, not ignored. And I'm afraid Marah and Kate won't find their way back. You should hear how Marah talks about her."

"You're worried about Marah," Mrs. M. said, eyeing Tully over the rim of her glass. "I think you're looking at the wrong player. Kate is the one who needs you now."

"Kate?"

"The problems with Marah are eating her up alive. Those two have to figure out how to talk to each other without screaming or crying." She looked at Tully. "And you need to be Katie's friend first."

"Are you saying it's my fault?"

"Of course not. I'm saying that Katie needs her best friend beside her. You two have always been each other's armor and sword. I know how much Marah idolizes you—and how much you like to be idolized." She smiled knowingly. "But you can't take sides in this unless it's Katie's."

"I just wanted to—"

"She's not your daughter."

And there it was. Tully hadn't realized until just now, this second, what had driven her to get so involved. She loved Marah, sure, but there was more to it than that, wasn't there? And Mrs. M. had seen it. Marah was the perfect child for Tully—gorgeous, ambitious, a little selfish. Best of all, she thought Tully was flawless. "So, what do I say to Marah?"

"That she has her whole life in front of her. If she's as good and talented as you believe, she'll make it when she's old enough to handle it."

Tully sat back in the recliner, sighing. "How long do you think Kate will stay mad at me?"

Mrs. M. laughed. "You two have more ups and downs than an Internet stock. Everything will be fine. Just quit trying to be Marah's best friend and be there for Katie."

Kate never tired of the view from her own back porch. Tonight, on this crisp late October evening, the sky above Seattle was an endless, star-filled black. In the glorious moonlight, every skyscraper looked sharp and distinct, so much so it was easy to imagine you could actually see the individual squares of glass and granite and steel.

Sounds were clearer here by the water as well. Maple leaves turned color and fell from the nearby trees, landing like quickened footsteps on the marshy ground; squirrels scurried from branch to branch, no doubt gathering their food for a cold they sensed was drawing near, and as always there was the tide, moving forward and back against the shore with a rhythm connected to the faraway moon. Here, on her back porch, only the seasons changed, and each gave the landscape an amazing new look.

Only a few feet behind her, through an antique wooden door, the changes came fast enough to leave you breathless. Her teenage daughter was sprouting like a tree, blooming every day into another variation of who she would someday become. Moods twisted her up and left her looking sometimes like a girl who'd just washed up onshore, unable to quite remember who she was and who she wanted to be.

Kate's baby boys were growing up, too. Kindergartners now, they were beginning to make their own friends and choose their own clothes and selectively answer her questions. In the blink of an eye, they, too, would be approaching adolescence, pinning magazine pictures to their bedroom walls and demanding privacy.

So fast . . .

She stood on the porch a few minutes longer, until the sky was charcoal-gray and the stars appeared above the distant city, then she went back inside, locking the door behind her.

The house was quiet, empty downstairs. As she made her way through the living room, she picked up several toy dinosaurs that lay scattered in front of the TV.

Upstairs, she turned the doorknob quietly, opening the door to the boys' room, expecting to see them sleeping. What she saw was a tent of sheets on William's bed, and the telltale light from a flashlight glowing through the red and blue Star Wars images.

"I know two little boys who are supposed to be asleep."

Giggles erupted from the makeshift tent.

Lucas was the first to emerge. With his spiky black hair and gap-toothed grin, he looked like Peter Pan being caught by Wendy. "Hi, Mommy."

"Lucas," William hissed from inside, "pretend you're sleeping."

Kate went to the bed and gently pulled the sheets back.

William stared up at her, flashlight in one hand, gray plastic *T. rex* in the other. "Oops," he said, then laughed.

Kate opened her arms. "Give Mommy a hug."

They launched themselves at her, enthusiastic as always. She held them tightly, smelling the sweet, familiar baby shampoo scent of their hair. "Do you guys need another bedtime story?"

"Read us about Max, Mommy," Lucas said.

Kate reached for the book and settled in her usual position—seated against the headboard, legs stretched out, with a boy tucked on either side of her. Then she opened *Where the Wild Things Are* and began to read. Max was halfway through his adventure when they fell asleep.

She tucked William in, kissed his cheek, and carried Lucas to his bed. "'Night, Mommy," he murmured as she put him down.

"'Night." She turned off the flashlight and left the room, closing the door behind her.

Across the hall, Marah's door was shut; a slice of light ran beneath it.

She paused, wanting to go in, but it would just start another fight. Nothing Kate said or did was right anymore, and in the weeks since the modeling fiasco, it had grown even more tense. Instead, she knocked on the door, said, "Lights out, Marah," and waited for her daughter to comply.

Then she walked down the hall and went into her own room.

Johnny was already in bed, reading. At her entrance, he glanced up. "You look exhausted."

"Marah," was all she said. All she had to say.

"I think it's more than that."

"What do you mean?"

Taking off his glasses, he set them on the nightstand and began gathering up the papers spread out around him. Without looking up, he said, "Tully tells me you're still mad at her."

Kate could tell by his voice and the studious way he avoided looking at her that he'd wanted to mention this for a while. *Men,* she thought. You had to be an anthropologist, studying clues to know what they were thinking. "She's the one who hasn't called."

"But you're the one who is mad."

Kate couldn't deny that. "Not crazy-mad or pissed off, just irritated. That crap she pulled with Marah's modeling . . . she could at least have admitted she was wrong."

"Tully, apologize?"

Kate couldn't help smiling. "I know. I know. But how come I always have to be the one to let things go? How come I always have to make the first call?"

"You just do."

It was true; always had been. Friendships were like marriages in that way. Routines and patterns were poured early and hardened like cement.

Kate went into the bathroom, brushed her teeth, and climbed into bed with him.

He turned off the bedside lamp and rolled over to face her. Moonlight shone through the window and illuminated his profile. He held his arm out, waiting for her to snuggle up to him. She felt a surge of love for him that was surprisingly sharp, given their years together. He knew her so well, and there was a cashmere comfort in that; it wrapped around and warmed her.

No wonder Tully had so many sharp angles and harsh edges; she'd never let herself be softened by love, wrapped up in it. Without kids or a husband or a mother's love, she'd grown selfish. And so, yet again, Kate would let go of her anger without an apology. She shouldn't have let it simmer so long anyway. It was remarkable how quickly time passed. Sometimes it felt as if they'd just had the blowup. What mattered now was not the words, spoken or withheld, but rather the years of friendship.

"Thanks," she whispered. Tomorrow she'd call Tully and invite her over to dinner. Like always, that would put an end to their fight. They'd move effortlessly back onto the road of their friendship.

"For what?"

She kissed him gently, touched his cheek. Of all the views she loved, this man's face was her favorite. "Everything."

On a gray, drizzly morning in mid-November, Kate turned her car into the middle school parking lot and joined the snakelike line of SUVs and minivans. In the stop-and-go traffic, she glanced to her right.

Marah sat slouched in the passenger seat, looking surly. Her expression and her mood had been dark ever since the blowup over the modeling class in New York.

Before, Kate now saw, there had been bricks between her and her daughter. Lately there was a wall.

Usually it fell to Kate to smooth over any of the rough patches in the road their family traveled. She was the peacemaker, the referee, and the mediator, but nothing she said had worked. Marah had stayed angry for weeks now and it was taking a toll on Kate. She wasn't sleeping well. It pissed her off, too, these silent treatments, because she knew Marah was manipulating her, trying to break Kate down.

"Are you excited about the banquet?" she forced herself to ask. At least it was something to say. The whole eighth grade was excited about the winter banquet, as they should be. The parents—including Kate—had expended a huge amount of effort to create a magical night for the kids.

"Whatever," Marah said, looking out the window, obviously searching for friends in the crowd of kids outside the school. "You're not going to chaperone, are you?"

Kate refused to be wounded by the remark. She told herself it was normal; she'd been telling herself that a lot lately. "I'm the decorations chairman. You know that. I'm hardly going to work on this event for two months and then not see our work."

"So you'll be there," Marah said dully.

"Dad and I both will. But you'll still have fun."

"Whatever."

Kate came to the drop-off lane and stopped. "The Mularkey family school bus is here," she said. Behind her, the boys giggled at the familiar joke.

"That is so totally lame," Marah said, rolling her eyes.

Kate turned to her daughter. "'Bye, honey. Have a nice day. Good luck on your social studies test."

"'Bye," Marah said, slamming the door.

Kate sighed and glanced in the rearview mirror. The twins were playing together in the backseat, making their plastic dinosaurs fight. "Girls," she whispered under her breath, wondering why it was that adolescent girls simply had to be mean to their mothers. Clearly it was normal behavior; she'd spent enough time with her friends and peers to know that. So normal it was probably part of evolution. Maybe the species needed girls who thought they were grown up at thirteen for some bizarre, hidden reason.

A few minutes later she dropped the boys off at school (kissed them both goodbye—in public) and began her own day. First off was a stop at Bainbridge Bakers, where she got a latte, then she dropped off some books at the library and headed down to Safeway. By ten-thirty, she was home again, standing in her kitchen, putting the groceries away.

Just as she was closing the fridge door, she heard the familiar *Girlfriend Hour* theme music coming from the TV in the living room, and she followed it. She rarely watched the show all the way through—how could she, with her busy schedule?—but she always turned it on so she knew what the episodes were about. Both Johnny and Tully sometimes quizzed her.

Kate hitched her leg over the end of the sofa and sat down.

On-screen, the theme music died down and Tully walked onto the cozy, we're-just-a-couple-of-girls-hanging-out-in-your-family-room set. As usual, she looked beautiful. Last year she'd decided to let her hair grow out into a sleek shoulder-length bob, and she'd returned to her natural reddish-brown color. The sophisticated girl-next-door cut and color only emphasized her high cheekbones and chocolaty eyes. A few well-placed shots of collagen had given her perfect lips, which she coated in just a hint of gloss but almost no color.

"Welcome back to *The Girlfriend Hour*," she was saying now, trying to be heard over the din of applause. Kate knew that people sometimes stood in line for six hours to be in the studio audience, and why not? *The Hour*, as it was called by fans and media alike now, was fun and breezy and occasionally even inspiring. No one ever quite knew what Tully would say or do next. It was part of what kept people tuning in, and Johnny made sure that everything ran like a well-oiled machine. True to her word, Tully had made them all rich, and Johnny, in turn, always made Tully look good.

Tully sat onstage, in the cream-colored chair that was hers. The pale color made her look more vibrant, larger than life. She leaned forward to talk intimately with both the audience and the camera.

Kate was instantly hooked. While she watched Tully reveal her makeup and hair secrets to the rest of America, Kate paid bills and dusted the Levolor blinds and folded laundry. After the show, she clicked off the television and sat down again to work on her Christmas list. She was so engrossed in this project, it took her a moment to realize her phone was ringing. She glanced around, saw the cordless phone on the floor under a pile of Legos, and answered it. "Hello?"

"Kate, is this you?"

"Yes."

"Thank goodness. It's Ellen, from Woodward. I'm calling because Marah isn't in her fourth-period class. If you forgot to sign her out, that's—"

"I didn't forget," Kate said, realizing how sharp she sounded. "Sorry, Ellen. Marah is supposed to be in class. Let me guess: Emily Allen and Sharyl Burton are absent, too."

"Oh, boy," Ellen said. "Do you know where they are?"

"I have a pretty good idea. When I find them I'll call you. Thanks, Ellen."

"Sorry, Kate."

She hung up the phone and glanced at the clock: 12:42.

It didn't take an advanced degree to figure out where the girls were. Today was Thursday, the day the new movies opened at the Pavillion. Coincidentally, that new teen queen—Kate couldn't remember her name—had a new movie out.

Kate grabbed her purse and headed out, pulling into the Pavillion lot at just before one. Trying not to be royally pissed took some real effort, and by the time she'd spoken to the manager, walked through the darkened theaters, found the girls, and herded them back into the lobby, she was losing the battle.

But her anger was nothing compared to her daughter's.

"I can't *believe* you did that," Marah said when they reached the parking lot.

Kate ignored the tone and said tightly, "I told you you could see the Saturday matinee with your friends."

"If my room was clean."

Kate didn't bother to answer. "Come on, girls. Out to the car. They're waiting for you at school."

The girls climbed quietly into the backseat, murmuring how sorry they were.

"I'm not sorry," Marah said, slamming her door and yanking her seat belt into place. "We only missed dumb old algebra."

Starting the car, Kate drove out of the parking lot and onto the main road. "You are supposed to be in school. Period."

"Oh. Like *you'd* never take me out of class to see a movie," Marah said. "I must have dreamed I saw Harry Potter on a school day."

"In the no-good-deed-goes-unpunished category," Kate said, trying not to raise her voice.

Marah crossed her arms. "Tully would understand."

Kate pulled into the circular drive in front of the middle school and parked. "Okay, girls, they're waiting for you at the office."

Emily groaned. "My mom's gonna flip out."

When they were alone in the car, Kate turned to her daughter.

"Dad would understand," Marah said. "*He* knows how much movies and modeling mean to me."

"You think so?" Kate pulled out her cell phone and hit the speed-dial list, then handed it to Marah. "Tell him."

"Y-you tell him."

"I didn't skip school and go to the movies." She held the phone out.

Marah took it, put it to her ear. "Daddy?" Marah's voice instantly softened and tears filled her eyes.

Kate felt a clutch of jealousy. How was it that Johnny had maintained such a lovely relationship with their daughter when it was Kate who was practically the kid's indentured servant?

"Guess what, Daddy? Remember that movie I told you about, the one where the girl finds out that her aunt is really her mom? I went to see it today and it was totally . . . What? Oh." Her voice fell to a near-whisper. "During fourth period, but . . . I know." She listened for a few moments and then sighed. "Okay. 'Bye, Dad." Marah hung up the phone and handed it back to Kate. For a split second, she was a little girl again. "I can't go see the movie this weekend."

Kate wanted nothing more than to seize the instant's possibility and pull Marah into her arms for a hug, to hang on to her little girl for just a moment and say, *I love you*, but she didn't dare. Motherhood at times like this—most times—was about the steel in your spine, not the bend. "Maybe next time you'll think about the consequences of an action."

"Someday I'll be a famous actress and I'll tell the TV that you were totally no help at all. None. I'll give all the credit to Aunt Tully, who believes in me." She got out of the car and started walking.

Kate followed, fell into step beside her. "I believe in you."

Marah snorted. "Ha. You never let me do anything, but as soon as I can I'm moving in with Tully."

"When hell freezes over," she muttered under her breath. Thankfully, she and her daughter had no more opportunity to speak. When they stepped into the school, the principal was waiting for them.

The summer before Marah started high school was hands down the worst summer of Kate's life. A thirteen-year-old daughter in middle school had been bad; in retrospect, though, it looked a hell of a lot better from a distance. A fourteen-year-old girl getting ready for high school was worse.

It didn't help that for the last year Johnny had been working sixty hours a week, either.

"You are not going to wear jeans that show the crack of your butt to school," Kate said, striving to keep her voice even. In her busy end-of-the-summer schedule, she'd budgeted four hours to buy Marah's school clothes. They'd been in the mall two hours already and the only thing in their arms was hostility.

"Everyone is wearing these jeans at the high school."

"Everyone except you, then." Kate pressed a pair of fingertips to her throbbing temples. She was vaguely aware of the boys running through the store like banshees, but she let that go for now. If she was lucky, maybe security would come and lock her up for failing to control her children. Right now a little solitary confinement sounded heavenly.

Marah threw the jeans on a rounder and stomped off.

"Do you even know how to walk away anymore?" Kate muttered, following her daughter.

By the time they were finished, Kate felt like Russell Crowe in *Gladiator*: beaten, bloodied, but alive. No one was happy. The boys were whining over the *Lord of the Rings* action figures she'd denied them, Marah was fuming over the jeans she hadn't gotten and the practically see-through blouse that had also gotten away, and Kate was angry that school shopping could so drain her energy. The only good news was that she'd drawn her line in the sand and defended it. Kate hadn't completely won the day, but neither had Marah.

On the drive home from Silverdale, the car was divided into two discernible halves: the backseat was noisy, boisterous, and full of fighting; the front seat was frigid and silent. Kate kept trying to make conversation with her daughter, but every sentence was an unreturned volley; by the time they'd turned down the gravel driveway and parked in the garage, she felt utterly defeated. That vague triumph over holding the line, being a mother and not a friend, had lost its luster.

Behind her, the boys unhooked their seat belts and climbed over each other in their haste to get out. Kate knew that whoever got to the living room first controlled the remote.

"Take it easy," she said, glancing at them in the rearview mirror.

They were tangled together like lion cubs trying to crawl out of a hole.

She turned to Marah. "You got some lovely things today."

Marah shrugged. "Yeah."

"You know, Marah, life is full of—" Kate stopped herself midsentence and almost laughed. She'd been about to offer one of her mother's life-is speeches.

"What?"

"Compromises. You can go around seeing what you did get, or you can focus on what you didn't. The choice you make will ultimately determine what kind of woman you become."

"I just want to fit in," Marah said in a voice that was unexpectedly small. It reminded Kate how young her daughter really was, and how frightening it was to start high school.

Kate reached out, gently tucked some hair behind Marah's ear. "Believe me, I remember the feeling. I had to wear cheap, secondhand clothes to school when I was your age. The kids used to make fun of me."

"So you know what I mean."

"I know what you mean, but you can't get everything you want. It's that simple."

"It's a pair of jeans, Mom. Not world peace."

Kate looked at her daughter. For once, she wasn't scowling or turning away. "I'm sorry we fight so much."

"Yeah."

"Maybe we could sign you up for that new modeling class, after all. The one in Seattle."

Marah jumped on that scrap like a hungry dog. "You'll *finally* let me go off-island? The next session starts Tuesday. I checked. Tully said she'd pick me up from the ferry." Marah smiled sheepishly. "We've been talking about it."

"Oh, you have, have you?"

"Daddy said it would be okay if I kept my grades up."

"He knows, too? And no one talks to me? Who am I, Hannibal Lecter?"

"You get mad pretty easily these days."

"And whose fault is that?"

"Can I go?"

Kate had no choice, really. "Okay. But if your grades—"

Marah launched herself out of her seat and into Kate's arms. She held her daughter tightly, reveling in the moment. She couldn't remember the last time Marah had initiated a hug.

Long after Marah had run into the house, Kate was still sitting in the car, staring after her daughter, wondering if the modeling class was a good idea. That was the sly, ruinous thing about motherhood, the thing that twisted your insides with guilt and made you change your mind and lower your standards: giving in was so damned easy.

It wasn't that she didn't want Marah to take the classes, precisely. It was that she didn't want Marah on that difficult road so young. Rejections, corruption, beauty that went no deeper than the skin, drugs, and anorexia. All that lay beneath the surface of the modeling world. Self-esteem and body image were too fragile in the teen years. God knew a girl could fall off the track even without the burden of constant beauty-based rejection.

In short, Kate wasn't afraid her gorgeous daughter wouldn't make it in the world of runways and taped-on clothing. Rather, she was afraid she would, and then her childhood would be lost.

Finally, she left the car and went inside, muttering, "I should have held firm."

The mother's lament. She was trying to figure out how to backtrack (impossible now) when the phone rang. Kate didn't even bother answering. In these last few weeks of summer, she'd learned one true thing: teenage girls lived on the phone.

"Mom! It's Grandma for you," Marah screamed down the stairs. "But don't take too long. Gabe is gonna call me."

She picked up the phone and heard the exhalation of smoke on the other end. Smiling, she ignored the groceries and plopped onto the couch, curling up under an afghan that still smelled like her mother. "Hey, Mom."

"You sound terrible."

"You can tell that from my breathing?"

"You have a teenage daughter, don't you?"

"Believe me, I was never this bad."

Mom laughed; it was a horsey, hacking sound. "I guess you don't remember all the times you told me to butt out of your life and then slammed the door in my face."

The memory was vague but not impossible to recall. "I'm sorry, Mom."

There was a pause. Then Mom said, "Thirty years."

"Thirty years what?"

"That's how long before you'll get an apology, too, but you know what's great?"

Kate groaned. "That I might not live that long?"

"That you'll know she's sorry long before she does." Mom laughed. "And when she needs you to babysit, she'll *really* love you."

Kate knocked on Marah's door, heard a muffled, "Come in."

She went inside. Trying to ignore the clothes and books and junk scattered everywhere, she picked her way to the white four-poster bed, where Marah sat, knees drawn up, talking on the phone. "Could I talk to you for a minute?"

Marah rolled her eyes. "I gotta go, Gabe. My mom wants to talk to me. Later." To Kate, she said, "What?"

Kate sat on the edge of the bed, remembering suddenly all the times this very scene had played out in her own teenage years. Her mother had started every reconciliation with a life-is speech.

She smiled at the memory.

"What?"

"I know we've been fighting a lot lately, and I'm sorry about that. Most of the time it's because I love you and I want the best for you."

"And the rest of the time, what's it about then?"

"Because you've really pissed me off."

Marah smiled at that, just a little, and sidled left to make room for Katie, just as Kate had once done for her own mother.

She moved more fully onto the bed and cautiously reached down to hold her daughter's hand. There were lots of things she could say right now, conversations she could try to knit out, but instead she just sat there, holding her daughter's hand. It was the first quiet, connected moment they'd spent together in years and it filled her with hope. "I love you, Marah," she said finally. "It was you, more than anyone else, who showed me what love could be. When they put you in my arms for the first time . . ." She paused, feeling her throat tighten. Her love for this child was so enormous, so overwhelming. Sometimes in the day-to-day war zone of adolescence, she almost forgot that. She smiled. "Anyway, I was thinking we should do something special together."

"Like what?"

"Like the anniversary party for Dad's show."

"You mean it?" Marah had been begging for this opportunity for weeks. Kate had repeatedly said she was too young.

"We could go shopping together, get our hair done, get beautiful dresses—"

"I love you," Marah said, hugging her.

She held on to her daughter, reveling in the moment.

"Can I tell Emily?"

Before Kate had even said, "Sure," Marah was reaching for the phone, punching in numbers. As she headed for the door and closed it behind her, she heard Marah said, "Em, you won't believe this. Guess where I'm going on Saturday—"

Kate closed the door and went to her own room, thinking about how quickly things changed with kids. One minute you were an old Eskimo woman, floating away from everyone, forgotten; the next you were climbing Mount Rainier, stabbing your flag in the snow. The changes could leave you dizzy sometimes, and the only way to survive was to enjoy the good moments and not dwell too much on the bad.

"You're smiling," Johnny said when she entered the room. He was sitting up in bed, wearing the drugstore reading glasses he'd grudgingly purchased.

"Is that so remarkable?"

"Frankly, yes."

She laughed. "I guess it is. Marah and I had a bad week. She got invited to an overnight party with boys—I still can't believe it—and I told her she couldn't go."

"So why the smile?"

"I invited her to the anniversary party. We'll make a girl's day out of it. Shopping, manicures, haircuts, the works. We'll need to get a suite at the hotel, or get a rollaway."

"I'll be the luckiest guy in the room," he said.

Kate smiled at him, feeling hopeful for the first time in longer than she could remember. She and Marah would have a perfect mother-daughter evening. Maybe it would finally tear down that wall between them.

Tully should have been on top of the world. Tonight was the anniversary party for her show. Dozens of people had been working for months to make it the event of the year in Seattle. Not only were the locals expected to attend, but the RSVPs indicated a celebrity-studded night. In short, everyone who was anyone would be here, and they were coming to honor her, to applaud her phenomenal success.

She glanced around the glittery, traditional ballroom of the Olympic Hotel. Actually, she thought it was called something else these days—chains kept acquiring and selling the property—but to Seattleites, it was and would always be the Olympic.

The room was full of her peers, her colleagues, her partners, many of her A-list celebrity guests, and a few of her key employees. Everyone she saw raised a glass in celebration. They all loved her.

And not one of them really knew her.

There it was. Edna had been unable to come, and Grant hadn't even returned her phone call. The latest tabloid she'd read claimed he was marrying some starlet, and although the news shouldn't bother Tully, it did. It made her feel old and lonely, especially tonight. How was it that she'd reached this age alone? Without a special person with whom she could share her life?

A waiter passed by her and she tapped his shoulder, snagging a second glass of champagne from his tray. "Thanks," she said, flashing the Tallulah Hart smile, looking around the ballroom for the Ryans. They still weren't here. She was drifting in a sea of acquaintances.

She downed the champagne and went in search of another drink.

―――――

The day of beauty with her daughter was everything Kate had hoped it would be. For the first time in ages, they didn't fight. Marah even listened to Kate's opinions on things. After they'd chosen their gowns—a one-shouldered black silk gown for Kate and a beautiful pink chiffon strapless one for Marah—they checked into the Gene Juarez day spa, where they got manicures and pedicures, haircuts, and their makeup done.

Now they were in Marah's bedroom in the suite at the Olympic. Crowded into the bathroom, they stood side by side, studying themselves in the mirror.

Kate knew she'd never forget the sight of them so close together: the tall, gangly daughter with the exquisite face, smiling so broadly her eyes tilted up, with her skinny arm around Kate's bare shoulder.

"We totally rock," Marah said.

Kate smiled. "Totally."

Marah kissed her cheek impulsively, said, "Thanks, Mom," and grabbed her beaded evening bag from the bed on her way to the door. "Here I come, Daddy," she said, opening it, stepping into the sitting room.

"Marah," she heard him say, whistling. "You're gorgeous."

Kate followed her daughter into the room. She knew she wasn't as shapely as she'd once been, or quite as pretty, but in this dress, with Johnny's diamond-heart necklace at her throat, she felt beautiful, and when she saw the way her husband smiled, she felt sexy, too.

"Wow," he said, coming toward her. Leaning close, he kissed her. "You look hot, Mrs. Ryan."

"You, too, Mr. Ryan."

Laughing, the three of them left the room and went down to the ballroom, where hundreds of people were already celebrating.

"Look, Mom," Marah whispered, sidling close. "It's Brad and Jennifer. And there's Christina. Wow. I can't wait to call Emily."

Johnny took Kate's hand and led her through the crowd to the bar, where he got two drinks and a Coke for Marah.

Then they eased back and stood there, sipping their drinks and surveying the crowd.

Even in a room like this, Tully stood out in a flowing silk gown the color of Burmese emeralds. She sailed toward them, waving, her gown rippling behind her. "You guys look *fabulous*," she gushed, laughing.

Kate couldn't help noticing that Tully appeared a little unsteady on her feet already. "Are you okay?"

"Couldn't be better. Johnny, we need to say a few things onstage after dinner. Then we'll go to the dance floor to get the ball rolling?"

"Don't you have a date?" Johnny asked.

Tully's smile faltered. "Marah can be my date for the evening. You don't mind if I borrow her, do you, Katie?"

"Well—"

"Why should she care?" Marah said, gazing at Tully in adoration. "She sees me every day."

Tully leaned close to Marah. "Ashton is here. Do you want to meet him?"

Marah practically swooned. "Are you kidding?"

Kate watched them walk away, hand in hand, heads cocked together like a pair of cheerleaders talking about the captain of the football team.

After that, the night lost some of its luster for Kate. Sipping her champagne, she followed her husband around the room, smiling when she was supposed to, laughing when it seemed appropriate, saying, "I'm an at-home mom," when asked, and watching how those few words—a sentence that made her so proud—could kill a conversation.

All the while, she watched Tully pretend that Marah was her daughter, introducing her to one celebrity after another, letting her have sips of her champagne.

When it was finally time for dinner, Kate took her place at the head table, with Johnny on one side of her and the president of Syndiworld on the other. Tully held court all through the meal. There was no other way to describe it. She was lively, animated, funny; every person seated around her—especially Marah—seemed awestruck.

Kate tried not to let any of it get to her. A few times she even tried to get her daughter's attention, but it was impossible to compete with Tully.

Finally, she couldn't stand it anymore. She made an excuse to Johnny and headed for the bathroom. In line, every woman there seemed to be talking about Tully, remarking on how gorgeous she looked.

"And did you see the girl she's with—"

"I think it's her daughter."

"No wonder they look so close."

"I wish my daughter treated me like that."

"So do I," Kate murmured too quietly to be heard. She stared at herself in the mirror, seeing a woman who'd done her best to look beautiful for her husband and daughter, only to fade into the wallpaper beside her best friend. She knew it was ridiculous to feel so hurt and excluded. It wasn't her night, after all. Still . . . she'd had such high hopes.

That was her mistake.

She'd pinned her happiness to a teenage girl's chest. *Idiot.* The realization made her almost smile. She certainly knew better than that. Feeling better, more in control of her silly emotions, she headed back to the party.

CHAPTER THIRTY

Tully shouldn't have drunk so much. She stood on the stage, holding Johnny's hand to keep herself steady. "Thank you all," she said, flashing her smile to the crowd. *"The Girlfriend Hour* is so successful because of you." She lifted a glass to everyone, and they answered with applause. It occurred to her in a burst that her sentence hadn't been quite right, had maybe made no sense, but since she couldn't remember what she'd said, it was hard to tell.

She turned to Johnny, put her arm around him. "It's our turn to dance."

The band started up; they were playing a slow song. Tully took his hand and led him out to the dance floor. She was still laughing when she recognized the song: "Crazy for You."

Touch me once and you'll know it's true.

It was the song he and Kate had first danced to at their wedding.

Tully tilted her head and looked up at him; suddenly she was remembering what she shouldn't remember: the last time she'd danced in his arms. The song had been "Didn't We Almost Have it All?" and when the dance was over, he'd kissed her. If she'd chosen differently back then, reached for love instead of fame, maybe he would have loved her, given her Marah and a home.

In the pale golden light from the old-fashioned chandelier, he looked as handsome as she'd ever seen him. He had the kind of dark Irish looks that only improved with age. Somehow the way he looked at her, so seriously, reminded her of the old days, when he'd been just a little broken by life, and she'd made him laugh for that one romantic night.

"You always were a good dancer," she said, and as she said it, she felt a little flare of caution go up. She was drunk; she needed to draw away, but it felt so good to be in a man's arms, and it wasn't like anything would happen.

He twirled her easily around and pulled her close again.

The crowd clapped in approval.

"I shouldn't have had so much champagne. I can't follow your lead."

"Following has never been your strong suit."

And with those few words, she remembered all of it again, the details. Memories came crashing through the walls she'd built to contain them. She stopped and looked up at him. "What happened to us?"

"Was there ever an 'us,' Tully, really?" he asked quietly. The way he said it, so easily, so quickly, made her wonder if he'd been wanting to ask the question for years. She couldn't tell if his smile was rueful or indulgent; all she knew was that they were no longer dancing, but he hadn't let her go.

"I wouldn't let there be."

"Kate thinks I never got over you."

Tully knew that, had always known it. Without ever actually talking about their shared past with Johnny, she and Kate had tucked it away in the name of friendship. There in the dark was where it should remain, but as always with Tully, booze and loneliness weakened her, and so, despite her best intentions, she found herself asking, "Did you?"

By the time Kate returned to the party, the band had begun to play.

"Crazy for You."

The song always made her smile. At the entrance to the ballroom, she paused, looking around. The dinner tables were emptying out. Lines were forming again at the bar. She saw Marah in the corner, talking to a remarkably skinny girl in a dress that was smaller than a handkerchief.

"Perfect."

Tamping down a flare of irritation, she kept moving. That was when she caught a flash of emerald-green silk and the world seemed to drop away from her.

Tully was on the dance floor, hanging all over Johnny. He held her with an easy familiarity, as if they'd spent a lifetime together. Although they should have been dancing, they were just standing there, a still pair amid the colorful swirl of the other dancers. Tully was looking up at him as if she'd just asked him to take her to bed.

Kate couldn't draw a breath. For a terrible moment, she thought she might be sick.

You were always his second choice.

She knew that; making peace with it over the years was not the same as changing it.

The song ended and Johnny stepped back from Tully. Turning, he saw Kate. Through the jeweled array of gowns, their gazes met. There, in front of anyone who might be watching, she started to cry. Embarrassed, she walked out of the ballroom.

Okay, she ran.

Downstairs, at the elevators, she pushed the button impatiently. "Come on . . . come on . . ." She didn't want anyone to see her crying.

The bell rang and the door opened. She stepped inside, backing up against the wall, and crossed her arms. It took long seconds of impatient waiting to realize she'd forgotten to press a button.

The doors were about to close when a hand pushed through.

"Go away," she said to her husband.

"We were dancing."

"Ha!" Kate pressed the button for their floor, then wiped her eyes.

He stepped inside. "You're being ridiculous."

The elevator whisked them to their floor; doors opened. She walked away from him. "Fuck you," she yelled behind her, finding her key and opening her door. She went into the room, slammed the door shut behind her.

Then she waited.

And waited.

Maybe he went to Tully—

No.

She didn't really believe that. Her husband might carry a torch for Tully, but he was an honorable man, and Tully was her best friend.

That was what she'd somehow forgotten in her jealous snit.

She opened the door, saw him sitting in the hallway, one leg stretched out, his bow tie hanging slack around his throat. "You're still here."

"You have our key. I hope you're going to apologize."

She went to him, knelt beside him. "I'm sorry."

"I can't believe you'd think—"

"I don't."

She took his hand and pulled him to his feet. "Dance with me," she said, hating the tiny emphasis she put on *me*.

"There's no music."

She put her arms around his neck and started to sway her hips, slowly moving closer toward him until his back was to the wall and she was pressing against him.

She unzipped her dress, let it fall to the floor.

Johnny glanced down the hallway. "Katie!" He opened her purse, got the key, and opened the door. They hurried into their room and fell onto the sofa, kissing with a passion that felt both familiar and new.

"I love you," he said, moving his hand down toward her panties. "Try not to forget it, okay?"

She was too breathless to answer, so she nodded and unzipped his pants, shoving the fabric aside. She vowed to herself that she wouldn't let her insecurities run rampant again, wouldn't forget his love.

Two weeks later, Tully stood at the window of her enormous office, staring out. She'd known for ages that something was missing in her life. She'd hoped that moving back to Seattle and starting her own show would somehow fill that empty place inside of her, but she hadn't been so lucky. Now she was simply more famous, endlessly wealthy, and still vaguely dissatisfied.

As always when she was unhappy, she turned to her career for the fix. It had taken her a while to come up with the answer, a course of action that would challenge and fulfill her, but in the end, she'd figured it out.

"You're insane," Johnny said, pacing in front of the window that looked out over Elliott Bay. "Format is king in television. You know that. Our ratings are second only to *Oprah*, and last year you were nominated for an Emmy. Companies can't line up fast enough to provide giveaways and promos to our audience. These are indicators of success."

"I know," she said, distracted for a moment by her own reflection. In the window glass, she looked thin and worn out. "But I'm not a rule-follower, you know that. I need to shake things up a bit. Mix it around. A live show would do that."

"Why do you need to do this? What more do you want?"

That was the $64,000 question. Why was it that she never had enough? And how could she possibly make Johnny, of all people, understand?

Kate would understand, even if she disagreed, but her best friend was too busy lately to talk much. Maybe that was part of what was wrong. She felt . . . disconnected from Kate. Their lives were on such different paths these days. They'd hardly spoken since the anniversary party. "You're going to have to trust me on this, Johnny."

"It could turn all *Jerry Springer* in an instant, and our credibility would be shot to hell." He moved in toward her, frowning slightly. "Talk to me, Tul."

"You couldn't understand," she said, giving him the only truth she knew.

"Try me."

"I need to make a mark."

"Twenty million viewers watch you every day; what's that, nothing?"

"You have Katie and the kids."

She saw when understanding dawned. He gave her the poor-Tully look; no matter how far she ran or high she climbed, that look seemed somehow to follow her. "Oh."

"I need to try this, Johnny. Will you help me?"

"When have I ever let you down?"

"Only when you married my best friend."

He laughed and headed for the door. "One try, Tully. Then we assess. Fair enough?"

"Fair enough."

The deal stayed with her in the weeks that followed. She put her nose to the grindstone and worked like a maniac, giving up her ever-meager pretense of a social life.

Now, finally, the moment of truth had arrived, and she was worried. What if Johnny was right and her brilliant idea degenerated into melodrama?

There was a knock at her office door.

"Come in," she said.

Her assistant, Helen, a recent graduate of Stanford, poked her head in. "Dr. Tillman is here. He's in the green room. I put the McAdams family in the employee lunchroom and Christy is in Ted's office."

"Thanks, Helen," she said distractedly as the door closed.

She'd almost forgotten how this felt, the scary/exhilarating feeling that you might fail. The past years had given her such insulation. Now it was as if she were new again, starting out, trying something only she believed in.

She checked herself in the mirror one last time, pulled the white makeup protector away from her collar, and headed for the studio. On-stage she found Johnny doing about ten things at once, barking out orders.

"You ready?" he asked.

"Honestly? I don't know."

He walked over, talking into his headpiece as he neared. Pulling the mic away from his mouth, he said quietly to her alone, "You'll be great, you know. I trust you."

"Thanks. I needed to hear that."

"Just be yourself. Everyone loves you."

At his signal, the audience began streaming into the studio. Tully ducked backstage and waited for her cue. When the red lights lit up, she walked onstage.

As always, she stood there a moment, smiling, letting the strangers' applause wash through her, fill her to overflowing.

"Today we have a very special show for you. My guest, Dr. Wesley Tillman, is a noted psychiatrist who specializes in addiction recovery and family counseling . . ."

Behind her, a huge screen played a film clip of an overweight man with thinning hair. He was trying not to cry, and losing the battle. "My wife is a good woman, Tallulah. We've been married for twenty years and we have two beautiful children. The problem is . . ." He paused, wiping his eyes. "Booze. It used to be just cocktail hour with friends, but lately . . ."

The clip showed the disintegration of a family in sound and images.

When it ended, Tully turned back to the audience. She could see how moved they were by the piece. Several women already looked close to tears. "Mr. McAdams is like too many of us, living lives of quiet desperation because of a loved one's addiction. He swears that he's tried everything to convince his wife to go into treatment and quit drinking. Today, with Dr. Tillman's help, we're going to try something radical. Mrs. McAdams is backstage, alone, right now. She believes she's won a trip to the Bahamas and is here to collect it. In fact, though, her family—with Dr. Tillman's professional help—is going to confront her about her alcoholism. Our hope is that we can force her to see the truth and seek treatment."

There was a moment of silence in the audience.

Tully held her breath. *Go along with me.*

Then applause.

It was all Tully could do not to laugh. She glanced over at Johnny, who was standing in the shadows by Camera 1, giving her a boyish grin and a thumbs-up.

This would help her, fill her up. She would genuinely help this family and America would love her for it.

She stepped back to introduce her guests and from that moment on, the show moved forward like a runaway train. Everyone in the room climbed aboard and loved the ride; they clapped, they moaned, they cheered, they cried. Like an expert ringmaster, Tully controlled it all. She was in the zone; no doubt about it. This was as good as she'd ever been on TV.

Winter came all at once that November, settling over the island in a gray and rainy pall. Naked trees shivered in the cold, clung to their blackened, dying leaves as if to let go would mean defeat. Fog rose from the Sound, morning after morning, obscuring the view and changing ordinary noises into muffled, faraway echoes. Ferries honked as they came in and out of port, the sound a mournful dirge in the haze.

It should have provided the perfect setting in which to write a gothic thriller. At least that was what Kate told herself when she began, secretly, to write again.

Unfortunately, it wasn't as easy as she remembered.

She reread what she'd just written, then sighed and hit the delete key, watching the letters blink out of existence one by one until she was left once more with a blank blue screen. She tried to come up with a better way to say it, but only more clichés came to her. The tiny white cursor mocked her, waited.

Finally, she pushed away from her desk and stood up. She was too tired to imagine worlds and people and dramatic events right now. It was time to make dinner anyway.

Lately it seemed that she was always exhausted, and yet, when she went to bed she rarely slept well.

She flicked off the light in Johnny's office, closed up her laptop, and went downstairs.

Johnny looked up from *The New York Times*. "eBay suck you in again?"

She laughed. "Of course. Were the boys good?"

He leaned forward, tousled their hair. "As long as I sing along with *poor unfortunate souls*, they're happy as clams."

She couldn't help smiling at that. *Little Mermaid* was this week's favorite movie. That meant they watched it every day if they could.

The front door banged open and Marah was home, looking excited. "You'll never guess what happened to me today."

Johnny put down his paper. "What?"

"Christopher, Jenny, Josh, and I are going to the Tacoma Dome to see Nine Inch Nails. Can you believe it? Josh asked *me*."

Kate took a deep breath. She'd learned to react slowly with Marah.

"A concert, huh?" Johnny said. "Who are these kids? How old are they?"

"Josh and Chris are juniors. And don't worry, we'll wear our seat belts."

"When is the concert?" he asked.

"Tuesday."

"On a school night? You think you're going on a date, with a junior, to a concert, on a school night." Kate looked at Johnny. "That's wrong on so many levels."

"When does it start?" Johnny asked.

"Nine. We should be home by two o'clock."

Kate couldn't help herself: she laughed. She had no idea how her husband could stay so reasonable. "*Should* be home by two o'clock? You must be joking, Marah. You're fourteen years old."

"Jenny's fourteen and she gets to go. Daddy?" Marah turned to Johnny. "You have to let me go."

"You're too young," he said. "Sorry."

"I'm not too young. Everyone gets to do stuff like this except me."

Kate's heart went out to Marah. She remembered being in a hurry to grow up, how sharp that need could be in a girl. "I know you think we're too strict, Marah, but sometimes life—"

"Oh, please. Not another lame life-is speech." With a snort, she ran upstairs and slammed her bedroom door shut.

Kate felt a wave of exhaustion so profound she almost sat down. Instead, she looked at her husband. "I'm so glad I came downstairs."

Johnny smiled. It came easily, too. How was it that he could do the same battles with Marah that Kate did, but manage to come out unscathed? And loved? "Your timing with her is always impeccable." He stood up, kissed her. "I love you," he said simply.

She knew it was meant to be a Band-Aid, those words, and she appreciated it.

"I'll go make dinner and then try talking to her. Give her some time to cool down."

He sat back down, returned to his paper. "Call Jenny's mom and tell her she's an idiot."

"I'll leave that to you." She went into the kitchen and started dinner. For almost an hour, she lost herself in slicing vegetables for stir-fry, and making Marah's favorite teriyaki marinade. At six o'clock, she tossed the salad, put the biscuits in the oven, and set the table. Usually that was Marah's job, setting the table, but there was no point in asking for help tonight.

"Okay," she said, coming back into the living room, where Johnny was sprawled on the floor with his boys, building something out of Legos. "I'm going in."

Johnny looked up. "The Kevlar vest is in the coat closet."

In the comforting wake of his laughter, Kate went upstairs. At the closed door to her daughter's room, which sported a yellow KEEP OUT sign, she paused, steeling herself, then knocked.

There was no answer.

"Marah?" she said after a moment. "I know you're upset, but we need to talk about this."

She waited, knocked again, and opened the door.

In the jumble of clothes and books and movies, it took Kate a moment to process what she was seeing.

An empty room.

With an open window.

Just to be sure, she checked everywhere—in the closet, under the bed, behind the chair. She checked the bathroom, too, and the boys' room and even her own. By the time she'd searched the entire upstairs, her heart was pounding so fast she felt light-headed. At the top of the stairs, she held onto the banister for support. "She's gone," she said, hearing the crack in her voice.

Johnny looked up. "Huh?"

"She's gone. I think she climbed out her window and went down the trellis."

He was on his feet in a second. "Son of a bitch."

He ran outside. Kate followed.

They stood beneath her bedroom window, seeing where her weight had broken the white wooden trellis and ripped through the ivy. "Son of a bitch," Johnny said again. "We need to start calling everyone she knows."

Even on a cold night like this, Tully loved being on the deck of her condo. It was a big, stone-tiled space that had been designed to replicate an Italian villa's terrace. Big, leafy trees grew from terra-cotta planters, their branches strung with tiny white lights.

She went to the railing and stared out. From here, she could hear the bump and grind of the city far below and smell the salty air of the Sound. In the distance, beyond the expanse of gray water, she could see the forested outline of Bainbridge Island.

What were the Ryans doing tonight? she wondered. Were they gathered around that big old-fashioned trestle table of theirs, playing board games? Or maybe Marah and Kate were curled up on the couch together, talking about boys. Or maybe she and Johnny had stolen a moment together to kiss—

The phone rang in her apartment. It was just as well. Thinking about Kate's family only made Tully feel more lonely.

She went through the open pocket doors and closed them behind her, then answered the phone. "Hello?"

"Tully?" It was Johnny. His voice was tight, unfamiliar.

She was immediately worried. "What is it?"

"Marah ran away. We don't know when exactly, probably about an hour and fifteen minutes ago. Have you heard from her?"

"No. I haven't. Why did she run away?" Before Johnny could answer, Tully's doorman buzzed her. "Just a second, Johnny. Hold on." She ran to the intercom, pressed it. "What is it, Edmond?"

"There's a Marah Ryan here to see you."

"Send her up." Tully released the button. "She's here, Johnny."

"Thank God," he said. "She's there, honey. She's fine. We'll be right over, Tully. Don't let her leave."

"Don't worry." Tully hung up the phone and went to the door. As the penthouse unit, hers was the only door on this side of the building, so she opened it and stood there, trying to look surprised when Marah stepped out of the elevator.

"Hey, Aunt Tully, I'm sorry to come here so late."

"This isn't late. Come on in." She stood back, let Marah enter the condo first. As always, she was struck by her goddaughter's remarkable beauty. Like most girls her age, she was too thin, a jangle of points and hollows, but none of that mattered. She was the kind of girl who'd be called coltish until she was thirty; that was when she'd settle into her body like royalty.

Tully went to her. "What happened?"

Marah flopped onto the couch and sighed dramatically. "I got invited to a concert."

Tully sat beside her. "Uh-huh."

"At the Tacoma Dome."

"Uh-huh."

"On a school night." Marah gave her a sideways glance. "The boy who asked me is a junior."

"That's, what, sixteen, seventeen?"

"Seventeen."

Tully nodded. "I went to see Wings in the Kingdome when I was about your age. What's the trauma?"

"My parents think I'm too young."

"They said no?"

"How lame is that? Everyone gets to do stuff like this except me. My mom won't even let me drive with boys who have their license. She still picks me up from school every day."

"Well, sixteen-year-old boys are notoriously bad drivers, and sometimes it's not . . . safe to be alone with them." She thought about that night in the woods, all those years ago. "Your mom is just protecting you."

"But we'll be in a group."

"A group. That's different. Nothing can happen as long as you all stay together."

"I know. I think she's worried about their driving."

"Oh. Well, I could take you guys in a limo."

"You'd do that?"

"Sure. Solves all the problems. Chaperone. Driver. We'll have a blast. I'll make sure no one gets hurt."

Marah sighed. "It won't work."

"Why not?"

"Because my mom is a bitch and I hate her."

That caught Tully off guard, shocked her so much that she couldn't think of what to say. "Marah—"

"I mean it. She treats me as if I'm a child. She doesn't respect my privacy. She tries to pick my friends and tell me what I can do. No makeup, no thongs, no belly ring, no staying out after eleven, no tattoos. I can't wait to get away from her. Believe me, once I graduate, it's sayonara, Mom. I'm going straight to Hollywood to be a star like you."

That last bit flattered Tully so much she almost forgot what had preceded it. She had to force herself back on track. "You're not being fair to your mom. Girls your age are more vulnerable than you think. A long time ago, when I was your age and thought I was invincible, I—"

"You'd let me go to the concert if you were my mom."

"Yes, but—"

"I wish you were my mom."

Tully was surprised by how deeply she felt those words. They found a soft spot inside her. "You two will get past this, Marah. You'll see."

"No, we won't."

For the next hour Tully tried to crack through Marah's anger, but it was a durable shell, impossible to breach. She was stunned by how easily Marah claimed to hate Katie, afraid that these two would never repair their damaged relationship. If there was one thing Tully knew, it was how ruined you could be without a mother's love.

Finally, the intercom buzzed and Edmond's voice came through: "The Ryans, Ms. Hart."

"They know I'm here?" Marah said, popping to her feet.

"It couldn't have been hard to figure out," Tully said, going to the intercom. "Let them up, Edmond. Thanks."

"They're going to kill me," Marah said, pacing, wringing her hands, and all at once she was a child again, gangly and tall and gorgeous, but still a child, scared that she was going to be in trouble.

Johnny was the first to walk through the open door. "Damn it, Marah," he said, "you scared the hell out of us. We didn't know if you'd been kidnapped or run away—" He broke his sentence off, as if he were afraid to say more.

Kate came up behind him.

Tully was stunned at the sight of her friend. She looked tired and sick and smaller somehow, as if she'd just taken a beating.

"Katie?" Tully said, worried.

"Thanks, Tully," she answered, giving her a wan smile.

"Aunt Tully said she'd take us to the concert in her limo," Marah said. "And chaperone us."

"Your aunt is a moron," Johnny snapped. "Her wacko mother dropped her on her head. Now get your stuff. We're going home."

"But—"

"No buts, Marah," Kate said. "Get your things."

Marah put on a real show—sighing, stomping, uttering, whining. Then she gave Tully a fierce hug, whispered, "Thanks for trying," and left the condo with Johnny.

Tully waited for Kate to say something.

"Don't promise her things without asking us, okay?" was all Kate said; her voice was a monotone, not even angry. "It just makes it harder." She turned to leave.

"Katie, wait—"

"Not tonight, Tul. I'm exhausted."

CHAPTER
THIRTY-ONE

Tully was worried about Kate and Marah. For most of the past week, she'd tried to figure out how to fix things between them, but nothing had come to her. Now she was at her desk, looking over her script notes for today.

Her phone rang. It was her assistant. "Tully. The McAdamses are here. From the rehab show."

"Send them in."

The couple that walked through her door on that icy November morning bore only the most surface resemblance to the people who'd been on her first live show. Mr. McAdams had lost at least twenty pounds and no longer walked hunched over, with his head pulled down into his shoulders. Mrs. McAdams had cut her hair, put on makeup, and was smiling. "Wow," Tully said, "you two look great. Please, sit down."

Mr. McAdams held his wife's hand. Together they sat down on the expensive black leather sofa that faced the windows. "We're sorry to bother you. We know how busy you are."

"I'm never too busy for friends," Tully said, giving them her PR smile. Hitching one leg over the end of her desk, she looked down at them.

"We just wanted to say thank you," Mrs. McAdams said. "I don't know if you know anyone with a drug or alcohol problem . . ."

Tully's smile faded. "I do, actually."

"We can be mean and selfish and angry and resistant. I wanted to change. Lord knows, I wanted to quit every day, but I didn't. Until you put the spotlight on me and I actually saw my life."

"You can't imagine how you've helped us," Mr. McAdams said. "We just wanted to say thank you."

Tully was so moved by their words it took her a moment to respond. "That's what I wanted to do with the live show: change someone's life. It means a lot to me that it worked."

Her phone rang.

"Excuse me." She answered it. "What is it?"

"John is on line one, Tully."

"Thanks. Put him through." When he came on the line, she said, "Too lazy to walk fifty feet to my office? You must be getting old, Johnny."

"I need to talk to you, and not over the phone. Can I buy you a beer?"

"Where and when?"

"Virginia Inn?"

She laughed. "God, I haven't been there in years."

"Liar. Come to my office at three-thirty."

She hung up the phone and turned her attention back to the McAdamses, who were standing now.

"Well," Mr. McAdams said, "we've said what we came to. I hope you can help other folks like you've done for us."

She went to them, shook their hands. "Thank you. If you don't mind, can I schedule a follow-up show for next year? To show America your progress."

"Sure."

She walked them to the door, said goodbye, and went back to her desk. For the next few hours, while she made notes for tomorrow's show, she found herself smiling.

She'd done some good with her show. She'd changed the McAdamses' lives.

At three-thirty, she closed up the folder, grabbed her coat, and went to Johnny's office. Together, talking about ideas for the upcoming shows, they walked up the block toward the Public Market and turned into the dank, smoky bar on the corner.

He led her to the back wall, took a seat at one of the small wooden tables by the window. Before she even sat down, he flagged down a waitress, ordered a Corona for himself and a dirty martini for her. She waited until the drinks were delivered before she said, "Okay, what's wrong?"

"Have you talked to Kate lately?"

"No. I think she's pissed at me over the concert. Or maybe it's still the modeling thing. Why?"

He ran a hand through his unruly hair. "I can't believe I'm going to say this about my own daughter, but Marah's being a first-rate bitch. Slamming doors, yelling at her brothers, ignoring her curfew, refusing to do her chores. She and Kate battle all day, every day. It's wearing Kate out. She's lost weight. Isn't sleeping."

"Have you thought about boarding school?"

"Kate would never go." He smiled tiredly at his own joke. "Honest to God, Tully. I'm worried about her. Will you talk to her?"

"Of course, but it sounds like she needs more than a friendly talk. Should she see someone?"

"Like a shrink? I don't know."

"Depression is common in at-home moms. Remember that show we did on it?"

"That's what worries me. I need you to find out if it's something I should worry about or not. You know her so well."

Tully reached for her drink. "You can count on me."

He smiled, but it looked tired. "I know that."

On Saturday, Tully called Johnny first thing in the morning. "I've got it," she said when he answered.

"What are you going to do?"

"Take her to the Salish Lodge. Get her relaxed and massaged. That sort of thing. And we'll talk."

"She'll tell you she's busy and blow you off."

"Then I'll kidnap her."

"You think you can make it work?"

"Have you ever seen me fail?"

"Okay. I'll pack a bag and leave it by the door, then I'll take the kids out so she'll have no excuses." He paused. "Thanks, Tully. She's lucky to have a friend like you."

Tully ended that call and immediately made another one, and then another.

By nine A.M., she had everything set up. Packing quickly, she threw what she needed in her car and drove to a store on Capitol Hill for a few supplies, then continued to the ferry. The wait on shore and then the crossing seemed to take forever, but eventually she drove into Kate's driveway.

The front yard had a wild, untended look about it, as if long ago a young mother had spent her spring months outside, planting bulbs and perennials, with her babies in blankets on the grass around her, and over the years, as those kids had grown up and chosen their own summer pursuits, the time for gardening had been lost. All those plants still thrived in the short, hot blast of a Northwest summer, though, returning year after year as reminders of an earlier time, growing up and out and into one another, just like the family that lived in the house. Now, in the midst of a cold, gray November's day, every plant looked leggy and brown. Leaves lay strewn everywhere, multicolored splashes hung on dying roses.

Tully parked her Mercedes in front of the garage and got out. As she picked her way through the bikes and skateboards and action figures strewn across the gravel path, she couldn't help admiring how homey this place was, even at this time of year. The shingled house, built in the twenties for a wealthy lumber baron's weekends, wore a new, crisp coat of caramel-hued stain; bright glossy white trim outlined the mullioned windows, beneath which were flower boxes filled with the last blooming geraniums of the season.

On the front porch, she squeezed past a freestanding clown/punching bag and knocked on the door.

Kate answered, wearing a pair of worn black leggings and an oversized T-shirt. With her blond hair badly in need of both a cut and a color, she looked ragged. Worn out. "Oh," she said, tucking the hair behind her right ear. "What a nice surprise."

"I'm going to ask you once, nicely, to come with me."

"What do you mean, come with you? I'm right in the middle of something. The boys' Little League team is having a quilting fundraiser. As soon as I finish—"

Tully pulled a bright yellow squirt gun out of her pocket and pointed it at Kate. "Don't make me shoot you."

"You're going to shoot me?"

"I am."

"Look, I know how much you love drama, but I don't have time for it today. I've got to quilt about fifty bits of fabric before—"

Tully pulled the trigger. A stream of cold water snaked through the air and hit Kate full in the chest. Moisture seeped through her cotton T-shirt, leaving a stain.

"What the—"

"This is a kidnapping. Don't make me aim for your face, although you appear to need a shower, frankly."

"Are you *trying* to piss me off?"

She handed Kate a black blindfold. "I had to go into that creepy sex toys store on Capitol Hill for that, so I hope you appreciate it."

Kate looked utterly confused, as if she didn't quite know if she should laugh or be pissed. "I can't just leave. Johnny and the kids will be back in an hour, and I need to—"

"No, they won't." Tully looked past her, into the cluttered living room. "There's your suitcase."

Kate spun around. "How—"

"Johnny packed it this morning. He's my accomplice. Or my alibi, if you give me trouble. Now get your suitcase."

"You expect me to go somewhere with only the things my husband thinks I need? I'll open that suitcase and find sexy lingerie, a tooth-brush, and clothes I outgrew two years ago."

Tully shook the blindfold. "Put it on or I'm going to shoot you again." She started to squeeze the trigger.

Finally Kate threw up her hands. "Fine. You win." She put on the blindfold, saying, "You know, of course, that intelligent criminals blind-fold their victims *before* the crime. I think it has something to do with thwarting identification."

Tully bit back a smile and went into the living room, where she grabbed the suitcase and then gently guided Kate to the car.

"It's not every kidnap victim that gets to ride in a Mercedes."

Tully popped a CD into the stereo. Within minutes they were rock-eting across the Agate Pass Bridge, and winding their way through the reservation land, where the local tribes' boarded-up fireworks stands lined the highway.

"Where are we going?" Kate asked.

"That's my business, not yours." Tully turned up the volume on Madonna singing "Papa Don't Preach." In no time at all they were singing along. They knew the words to one song after another, and every song took them back in time to when they were young. Madonna. Chicago. The Boss. The Eagles. Prince. Queen. "Bohemian Rhapsody" was their particular favorite sing-along. They tossed their heads in time with the music in a perfect imitation of Garth and Wayne.

It was just past two o'clock when Tully pulled into the driveway of their destination. "We're here. The doorman is looking at you funny so you might want to remove the blindfold."

Kate whipped it off just as the doorman welcomed her to the Salish Lodge and opened her door. As if from everywhere at once, they could hear the distant roaring of Snoqualmie Falls, but from here they couldn't actually see it. The ground vibrated with the force of the falling water. The air was heavy and moist.

Tully led the way to the front desk, checked in, and followed the bellman to their room, which was a corner suite with two bedrooms, a

fireplace in the sitting room, and view of the rushing, whitecapped Snoqualmie River as it moved toward the falls.

The bellman gave her their spa schedule; she gave him a healthy tip,
and then she and Kate were alone.

"First things first," Tully said. She'd been on television long enough
to know when a script was needed. She'd devised a format and schedule
for the entire duration of their stay. She opened her suitcase, pulled out
two limes, a shaker of salt, and the most ridiculously overpriced tequila
she'd ever seen. "Straight shots."

"You are insane," Kate said. "I haven't had a straight shot since—"

"Don't make me shoot you. I'm running out of water."

Kate laughed. "Okay. Pour up, bartender."

"One more," Tully said right away.

Kate shrugged and drank up.

"Okay. Bathing suits. Put yours on. There's a robe in your bedroom."

As usual, Kate did as she was told.

"Where are we going?" she asked as they walked down the glossy
slate floor of the lodge's main floor.

"You'll see."

They came to the spa and followed the signs to the hot tub.

In a back corner, they came to a beautiful steaming pool surrounded
by Northwest and Asian styled accents. The air smelled of lavender and
roses. Lush green plants in ceramic and bronze pots made it almost feel
as if you were outdoors.

They climbed down into the hot, bubbling water.

Kate immediately sighed and leaned back. "This is Heaven."

Tully stared at her best friend, seeing now, amid the softening curtain of steam, how tired she looked. "You look terrible," she said gently.

Kate opened her eyes slowly. Tully could see anger flash across her
face, but as quickly as it flared, it died. "It's Marah. Sometimes when she
looks at me, I actually see hate in her eyes. I can't tell you how much
that hurts."

"She'll grow out of it."

"That's what everyone says, but I don't believe it. If there was just some way I could force her to talk to me, and to listen. We tried counseling, but she refused to participate."

"You can't make a kid open up. Only peer pressure can get them to do anything, right?"

"Oh, they'll open up. You just can't believe anything they say. According to Marah, I'm the only mother in the world who's so grossly overprotective."

Tully saw the deep unhappiness in her friend's eyes and although she tried to believe it was just ordinary motherhood stress, suddenly she was afraid. No wonder Johnny was so worried. Last year Tully had interviewed a young mother who was overwhelmed and depressed. A few months after the interview the woman had swallowed a bottle of pills. The very thought of that terrified her. She *had* to find a way to help Kate. "Maybe you should see someone."

"You mean a shrink?"

Tully nodded.

"I don't need to talk about my problems. I need to be more organized, that's all."

"Organization is hardly your problem. You don't have to go on every field trip or make costumes for every kid's play or cookies for every bake sale. And they can ride the damn bus to school."

"You sound like Johnny. I suppose now you're going to tell me that everything would be better if I did all this and wrote a book, too. Well, I tried. I've been trying." Kate's voice broke. Tears welled in her eyes. "Where's the tequila?"

"Excellent idea. We haven't been totally toasted in years."

"Like, fer sure." Kate laughed.

"We have massages in thirty minutes, though, so we'll have to wait a while."

"Massages." Kate looked at her. "Thanks, Tully. I needed this."

It wasn't enough by a long shot. Tully could see that now. Katie needed real help, not a few shots of tequila and a mud wrap, and she needed her best friend to find the answer. "If you could change one thing in your life, what would it be?"

"Marah," she said softly. "I'd get her to talk to me again."

Like magic, Tully knew what to do. "Why don't you come on my show? You and Marah. We'll do a mother-daughter segment. Live would be best so she knows there's no editing. She'll see how much you love her and how lucky she is."

Hope took ten years off Kate's face. "You think it would work?"

"You know how badly Marah wants to be on TV. She'd never let herself look bad in front of the camera. She'd have to listen to you then."

That tired desperation finally left Kate's eyes. In its stead was a bright anticipation. "What would I do without you, Tully?"

Tully's smile felt too big for her face. She could help her friend through all this, maybe even save her life. Just like they promised all those years ago. "We'll never have to find out."

"Will your makeup people hide my wrinkles?"

Tully laughed. "Believe me, when they get done, you'll look younger than Marah."

"Perfect."

Kate returned from the spa with a new attitude. The moment she walked into the house, Marah started in on her, complaining about some event she couldn't attend because of her curfew, but for once the words were arrows that found no target and clattered uselessly to the ground. *Soon*, Kate thought, smiling to herself, *soon we'll find a way back to each other*.

She put her clothes away, took a nice long bath, then gathered her boys into her arms for a story. They were just falling asleep when Johnny poked his head in.

"Shh," she said, closing the book. Kissing each little forehead, she tucked the boys into bed, then went to her husband.

"Did you guys have a good time?" Johnny said, pulling her into his arms.

"Great. Tully has a plan—"

Downstairs, the doorbell rang. Marah's voice followed: "I'll get it!"

Johnny and Kate frowned at each other. "It's Sunday night," Kate said. "She's not allowed to have kids over on a school night."

But when they got downstairs, they saw Mom and Dad in the living room, carrying suitcases.

"Mom?" Kate said. "What's going on?"

"Tully sent us over to watch the kids for a week. The car outside is going to take you two to the airport. Tully said to pack bathing suits and sunscreen. That's all you get to know."

"I can't leave work," Johnny said. "We've got Senator McCain on."

"Tully's your boss, isn't she?" Dad said. "I guess if she says you're taking a vacation, you're taking a vacation."

Kate and Johnny looked at each other. They'd never taken a vacation away from the kids.

"It might be nice," he said, smiling.

For the next hour, they ran through the house, packing, making lists, gathering telephone numbers. Then they kissed the kids—even Marah—thanked Mom and Dad, and went out to the waiting limousine.

"She doesn't do anything halfway," Johnny said, sliding into the plush, dark interior.

Kate snuggled beside him. "I feel more relaxed already and we're still in our driveway."

The car engine started, purred.

"Do you know where we're going?" Johnny asked the driver.

"The tickets are in the pocket across from you, sir."

Johnny reached for the envelope, opened it. "Kauai," he said.

It was where they'd gone on their honeymoon. Kate closed her eyes, picturing the swaying palm trees and pinkish sand of Anini Beach.

"No fair going to sleep," Johnny said.

"I'm not sleeping." She twisted around, draped herself across his lap. "Thanks for helping Tully to kidnap me."

"I've been worried about you."

"I've been worried about me, too. But I feel better now."

"How much better?"

She glanced at the open window that separated them from the driver. "Close the window and I'll show you."

"Are we talking sex?"

"We're talking sex," she said, unbuttoning his shirt. "But if you'd hit the damn button, we'd be doing more than talking."

He smiled slowly. "Oh, I'll hit it."

CHAPTER
THIRTY-TWO

K ate and Johnny returned home, rested and refreshed, on the night before the big broadcast. The next morning, Kate woke up at five o'clock to go to the bathroom and found it impossible to go back to sleep.

The house was quiet and dark. She didn't bother turning on lights as she went from room to room, picking up toys and putting them away. She still couldn't quite believe today was going to happen. She'd waited so long, and prayed so hard, for a change in her relationship with Marah that she'd almost given up hope. Tully, and this program, had given it back to her. Even Johnny seemed optimistic. He'd done as Tully asked—or demanded, actually—and relinquished control over the segment. For this one broadcast, he was going to be simply an audience member, a father supporting his family.

In the bathroom, after she'd taken a shower and gotten dressed, Kate stared at herself in the mirror, trying not to notice the lines that had begun to collect in the corners of her eyes as she practiced what she would say. "That's right, Tully. I've given up my career to be an at-home mom. Frankly, I think it would have been easier to work."

The audience would laugh at that.

"I still want to be a writer someday, but it's so hard to balance work and motherhood. And Marah needs me more now than she did as a toddler. Everyone talks about the terrible twos, but in my house, it's the terrible teens. I miss the days when I could put her in a playpen and know that she was safe."

A murmur of agreement would certainly follow that remark.

She went downstairs, made breakfast for everyone, and set it out on the table. The boys were down the stairs in record time, clambering over each other in their quest for the perfect chair.

When Marah came downstairs, clearly excited for the taping, Kate couldn't contain her excitement.

This was going to work. She knew it.

"Stop grinning, Mom. You're creeping me out," Marah said, pouring milk into her oatmeal bowl and carrying it to the table.

"Leave your mom alone," Johnny said, walking past her. He paused behind Kate, squeezed her shoulders, and kissed the back of her neck. "You look gorgeous."

She turned and put her arms around him, gazing into his eyes. "I'm glad you're going to be my husband today and not her producer. I need you in the audience."

"Don't thank me. Tully pushed me completely on the outside. No one on-set is allowed to tell me anything or show me a script. Tully wants me to be surprised."

From that moment on, the day flew forward like the *Millennium Falcon* in hyperspace. It wasn't until they were on the ferry, crossing the bay, that she started to get nervous.

The audience would laugh at her, say she should have done more with her life, been more.

She'd look fat.

She was so caught up in her negative fantasies that when they parked she couldn't get out of the car. "I'm scared," she said to Johnny.

Marah rolled her eyes and walked away.

Johnny took her arm, unhooked her seat belt, and eased her out of the car.

"You'll be great," he said, leading her into the elevator. In the studio, there were people everywhere, running to and fro, yelling at one another. Johnny leaned close. "It's just like your old days in news, remember?"

"Kate!"

She heard her name ring through the busy hallway and looked up. Tully, looking thin and gorgeous, was coming at her with open arms.

Tully pulled her into a fierce embrace, and Kate finally felt herself relaxing. This wasn't just a TV show; it was Tully's show. Her best friend would make sure Kate did well.

"I'm a little nervous," Kate confided.

"A little?" Marah said. "She's been acting like Rain Man."

Tully laughed at that and looped her arm through Kate's. "There's nothing to worry about. You're going to be great. Everyone is excited to have you and Marah on the show." She led them to the makeup room and left them there.

"This is exciting," Kate said, sitting in front of the giant mirror. The makeup artist—a woman named Dora—immediately went to work on Kate's face.

Marah sat in the chair beside her. Another makeup artist went to work on her.

Kate stared into the mirror. In no time, a stranger emerged beside her: the woman Marah would someday become. In her daughter's made-up face, she saw the future, recognized a truth that had until now been hidden from her beneath the pretty gauze of childhood. Soon Marah would be dating, and then driving, and then going off to college.

"I love you, Munchkin," she said, purposely using the nickname that had gone out of fashion with Winnie-the-Pooh lunch boxes and Tickle Me Elmo. "Remember when we used to dance to those old Linda Ronstadt songs?"

Marah looked at her. For a second—just that—they were Mommy and Munchkin again, and though it didn't last, couldn't last in the hurricane of the teen years, it filled Kate with hope that after today they'd come together again, be as inseparable as they'd once been.

Marah looked poised to say something, then she smiled instead. "I remember."

Kate wanted to hug her daughter, but that would never have the desired effect. Physical contact, she had learned, was the surest way to put distance between them.

"Kathleen and Marah Ryan?"

She twisted around in her chair, saw a young, pretty woman with a clipboard standing behind her. "We're ready for you."

Kate reached out for Marah, who was excited enough to take her hand. They followed the woman up to the greenroom, where they were put to wait.

"There's water in that fridge, and feel free to eat anything in that basket," the woman said. Then she handed Kate a lapel microphone and the corresponding pack that attached to her waistband. "Tallulah said you'd know how to work this?"

"It's been a while, but I think I can still manage. I'll show Marah. Thanks."

"Great. I'll come and get you when it's time. As you know, we're live today, but don't let that worry you. Just be yourself."

And then she was gone.

This was really happening. It meant so much to her, this chance to reconnect with her daughter.

An instant later there was a knock on the door.

"We're ready for you, Kathleen," the woman said. "Marah, stay here. We'll come for you in a minute."

Kate headed for the door.

"Mom!" Marah said sharply, as if she'd just remembered something important. "I need to tell you something."

Kate looked back, smiling. "Don't worry, honey. We'll be great." Then she followed the woman down the busy corridor. Through the walls she could hear applause, even a smattering of laughter.

At the edge of the stage, the woman paused. "When you hear your name, you'll walk out."

Breathe.

Suck in your stomach. Stand up straight.

She heard Tully say, "And now I'd like you all to meet my good friend Kathleen Ryan . . ."

Kate stumbled around the corner and found herself standing beneath the bright glare of the stage lights. It was so disorienting that it took her a second to process her surroundings.

There was Tully, standing center stage, smiling at her.

Behind her was Dr. Tillman, the psychiatrist who specialized in family counseling.

Tully swept over to her side, took her arm. Beneath the swell of applause, she said, "We're live, Katie, so just roll with it."

Kate glanced over at the screen behind them. There was a huge image of two women shouting at each other. Then she looked at the audience.

Johnny and her parents were in the front row.

Tully faced them. "Today we're talking about overprotective mothers and the teenage daughters who hate them. Our goal is to get a dialogue going, to break up the logjam of communication that comes with adolescence and get these two talking again."

Kate actually felt the blood drain from her face. "What?"

Behind her, Dr. Tillman moved from his place in the shadows to a chair onstage. "Some mothers, especially the controlling, domineering type, actually damage their children's fragile psyches without ever really seeing what they're doing. Children can be like flowers, trying to blossom in too small a space. They need to break out, make their own mistakes. We don't help them by wrapping them in rules and rigid expectations and pretending that we can keep them safe."

The full impact of what was happening hit Kate.

They were calling her a bad mother, on national television, with her family right here.

She wrenched her arm away from Tully. "What are you doing?"

"You need help," Tully said, sounding reasonable and just a little sad. "You and Marah both do. I'm scared for you. So is your husband. He begged me to help. Marah wants to confront you about it, but she's afraid."

Marah walked onstage, smiling brightly at the audience.

Kate felt the start of tears, and the vulnerability fueled her anger. "I can't believe you'd do this to me."

Dr. Tillman came forward. "Come on, Kathleen, Tully is being your friend here. You're crushing your daughter's tender spirit. Tully just wants you to address your parenting style—"

"She's going to help me be a better mother?" She turned to Tully. "You?" Then she looked at the audience. "You're taking advice from a woman who doesn't know the first thing about love or family or the hard choices women have to make. The only person Tully Hart ever loved is herself."

"Katie," Tully said in a low, warning voice. "We're live."

"That's all you care about, isn't it? Your ratings. Well, I hope they keep you warm when you're old, because you won't have anything or anyone else. What the hell do you know about motherhood or love?" Kate stared at her, feeling sick enough that she thought she might throw up. "Your own mother didn't love you. And you'd sell your soul for fame. Hell, you just did." She turned back to the audience. "There's your icon, folks. A woman so fucking warm and *caring* that she's probably never told a single human being she loved them."

Kate wrenched off her microphone and power pack and threw them on the floor. As she stormed offstage, she snagged Marah's arm and pulled her along.

Backstage, Johnny rushed at her, took her in his arms, and held her tightly, but even his body heat couldn't reach her. Her parents and the boys ran up behind him, creating a circle around Kate and her daughter. "I'm sorry, honey," he said. "I didn't know . . ."

"I can't believe Tully would do that," Mom said. "She must have thought—"

"Don't," Kate said sharply, wiping her eyes. "I don't care what she thought or wanted or believed. Not anymore."

Tully ran out into the hallway, but Kate was gone.

She stood there too long, then turned and went back onstage, where she stared at a sea of unfamiliar faces. She tried to smile, she really did, but for once her cast-iron will failed her. She heard the quiet murmuring of the crowd; it was the sound of sympathy. Behind her, Dr. Tillman was talking, filling the void with words she could neither follow nor understand. She realized that he was keeping the show going since they were live.

"I just wanted to help her," she said to the audience, interrupting him. She sat down on the edge of the stage. "Did I do something wrong?"

Their applause was loud and went on and on, their approval as unconditional as their presence. It should have filled up the empty places in her, that had always been their role, but now the applause didn't help.

Somehow she made it through the rest of the broadcast.

Finally, though, she was as alone onstage as she felt. The audience had filed out and her employees had all left. None had had the courage to even speak to her on the way out. She knew they were angry at her for ambushing Johnny, too.

As if from a great distance, she heard footsteps. Someone was coming toward her.

Dully, she looked up.

Johnny stood there. "How could you do that to her? She trusted you. *We* trusted you."

"I was just trying to help her. You told me she was falling apart. Dr. Tillman told me that drastic situations call for drastic measures. He said suicide was—"

"I quit," he said.

"But . . . tell her to call me. I'll explain."

"I wouldn't count on hearing from her."

"What do you mean? We've been friends for thirty years."

Johnny gave her a look so cold she began to shake. "I think that ended today."

Pale morning light came through the windows, brightening the white-painted sills. Outside, seagulls cawed and dove through the air; the sound, combined with the waves slapping against the shore, meant that the ferry was chugging past their house.

Ordinarily, Kate loved these morning noises. Even though she'd lived on this beach for years now, she still loved to watch the ferries pass by, especially at night when they were lit like floating jewel boxes.

Today, though, she didn't even smile. She sat in bed, with a book open in her lap so that her husband would leave her alone. As she stared at the pages, the type blurred and danced like black dots on the creamy paper. Yesterday's fiasco kept playing in her mind, over and over. She saw it from a dozen angles. The title: Overprotective mothers and the teenage daughters who hate them.

Hate them.

Crushing your daughter's tender spirit . . .

And Dr. Tillman, coming toward her, saying she was a terrible parent; her mother in the front row, starting to cry; Johnny jumping from his seat, shouting something to a cameraman that Kate couldn't hear.

She still felt shell-shocked by all of it, numb. Beneath the numbness, though, was a raw and terrible anger that was unlike anything she'd felt before. She had so little experience with genuine anger that it scared her. She actually worried that if she started screaming, she'd never stop. So she kept the lid on her emotions and sat quietly.

She kept glancing at the phone, expecting Tully to call.

"I'll hang up," she said. And she would. She was actually looking forward to it. For all the years of the friendship, Tully had pulled shit like this (well, nothing really like this), and it had fallen to Kate to apologize, whether it was her fault or not. Tully never said she was sorry; she just waited for Kate to smooth things over.

Not this time.

This time Kate was so hurt and angry, she didn't care if they stayed friends or not. If they were to get back together, Tully was going to have to work for it.

I'll hang up a lot of times.

She sighed, wishing the thought made her feel better, but it didn't. She felt . . . broken by yesterday.

There was a knock at her door. It could be any member of her family. Last night they'd circled the wagons around her, treating her like a breakable princess, protecting her. Mom and Dad had spent the night; Kate thought her mom was on suicide watch, that was how overbearing she was. Dad kept patting her shoulder and saying how pretty she was, and the boys, who didn't know exactly what was wrong but sensed that it was big, hung on her constantly. Only Marah stood back from the drama, watching it all from a distance.

"Come in," Kate said, sitting up taller, trying to look more durable than she felt.

Marah walked into the room. Dressed for school in low-rise jeans, pink UGG boots, and a gray hoodie sweatshirt, she tried to smile, but it was a failure. "Grandma said I had to talk to you."

Kate was relieved beyond measure simply by her daughter's presence. She moved to the middle of her bed and patted the empty place beside her.

Marah sat opposite her instead, leaning back against the silk-upholstered footboard, with her legs drawn up. Ragged holes in her favorite jeans showed the knobby curl of her knees.

Kate couldn't help longing for the time when she could have scooped her daughter into her arms and held her. She needed that now. "You knew about the show, didn't you?"

"Tully and I talked about it. She said it would help us."

"And?"

Marah shrugged. "I just wanted to go to the concert."

The concert. It hurt Kate deeply, that simple, selfish answer. She'd forgotten about the concert and Marah's running away. The trip to Kauai had cleared her mind of all of that.

No doubt as Tully had intended. It had also gotten Johnny out of the way so he couldn't stop the plan.

"Say something," Marah said.

But Kate didn't quite know what to say, how to handle this. She wanted Marah to understand how selfish she'd been and how deeply that selfishness had hurt Kate, but she didn't want to load guilt on her. The weight of this debacle fell on Tully. "Did it occur to you when you and Tully were hatching this plan that I might be hurt and embarrassed by it?"

"Did you think that I'd be hurt or embarrassed by not getting to go to the concert? Or rockin' midnight bowling? Or to—"

Kate held up a hand. "So it's still about you," she said tiredly. "If this is all you have to say, you can leave. I don't have the strength to fight with you now. You were selfish and you hurt my feelings, and if you can't see that and take responsibility for it, I feel sorry for you. Get out. Go."

"Whatever." Marah got off the bed, but she moved slowly. At the door, she paused and turned around. "When Tully comes over—"

"Tully won't be coming over."

"What do you mean?"

"Your idol owes me an apology. That's not something she's good at. I'd say it's something else you two have in common."

For the first time, Marah looked scared. And it was at the prospect of losing Tully.

"You better think about how you're treating me, Marah." Kate's voice broke on that; she struggled to sound in control. "I love you more than the world and you're hurting me on purpose."

"It's not my fault."

Kate sighed. "How could it be, Marah? Nothing ever is."

It was exactly the wrong thing to say. Kate knew it the second she said it, but she couldn't take it back.

Marah yanked open the door and slammed it shut behind her.

Quiet came instantly. Somewhere outside a rooster crowed and a pair of dogs barked at each other. She heard people walking around downstairs. The floorboards of this old house creaked with the movement.

Kate looked at the phone, waiting for it to ring.

———

"I think it was Mother Teresa who said that loneliness is the worst kind of poverty," Tully said, sipping her dirty martini.

The man to whom she spoke looked startled for a moment, as if he were driving on some dark, empty stretch of road and a deer had suddenly bounded into his path. Then he laughed, and there was so much in the sound, a shared camaraderie, a hint of superiority, an undercurrent of privilege. No doubt he'd learned to laugh like that in the hallowed halls of Harvard or Stanford. "What do people like us know about poverty or loneliness? There must be one hundred people here, at your birthday party, and God knows the champagne and caviar didn't come cheap."

Tully stood there, trying—and failing—to remember his name. He was her guest; she ought to know who in the hell he was.

And why had she made such a ridiculously transparent remark to a stranger?

Disgusted with herself, she finished the martini—her second—and walked over to the makeshift bar that had been set up in the corner of her penthouse. Behind the tuxedoed bartender, the glittering starburst of the Seattle skyline was a magical combination of bright lights and black sky.

She waited impatiently for her third martini, making small talk with the bartender. The minute the drink was ready, she set a course for the terrace, sailing past the table overflowing with foil- and ribbon-wrapped gifts. She knew without opening a single package the kind of gifts she'd received: champagne glasses from Waterford or Baccarat; silver bracelets and frames from Tiffany; Montblanc pens; perhaps a cashmere throw or a pair of blown-glass candlesticks. The kind of expensive presents that strangers and co-workers gave each other when they'd reached a certain economic status.

There wouldn't be anything personal in any of those beautifully wrapped packages.

She took another sip of her martini and went out onto the deck. From the railing, she saw the barest outline of Bainbridge Island. Moonlight painted the forested hills silver. She wanted to look away but couldn't. It had been three weeks since the broadcast. Twenty-one days. Her heart still felt cracked beyond repair. The things Kate had said to her kept running on an endless loop through her mind. And when she managed to forget, she saw them in print, in *People* magazine or on the Internet. *Her own mother didn't even love her . . . there's your icon: a woman so warm and caring, she's probably never said I love you to another human being . . .*

How could Kate have said that? And then not called to apologize . . . or to say hello . . . or even to wish her a happy birthday?

She finished the drink and set the empty glass on the table beside her, still staring out across the black expanse of water. Behind her, she heard the phone ring. She knew it! She ran back into the condo, pushed through the people crowded in her living room, and went into her bedroom, slamming the door shut behind her.

"Hello," she said, a little out of breath.

"Hey, Tully, happy birthday."

"Hey, Mrs. M. I knew you'd call. I could come down and see you and Mr. M. right now. We could—"

"You have to make things right with Katie."

She sat down on the end of her bed. "I was only trying to help."

"But you didn't help. Surely you see that?"

"Did you hear the things she said to me on TV? I was trying to *help* her and she told all of America . . ." She couldn't even say it. That was how much it still hurt. "She owes me an apology."

There was a long pause on the other end, then a tired sigh. "Oh, Tully."

She heard the disappointment in Mrs. M.'s voice, and she felt like a kid again in the police station. No words came to her, for once.

"I love you like a daughter," Mrs. M. finally said. "You know that, but . . ."

Like a daughter. There was a whole sea in that single word, an ocean of distance.

"You have to see how you hurt her."

"What about how she hurt me?"

"What your mother did to you is a crime, Tully." Mrs. M. made a sad sound, then said, "Bud is calling me. I better go. I'm sorry for the way things are, but I need to go now."

Tully didn't even say goodbye. She just quietly hung up the phone. The truth she'd been trying to outrun landed on her chest, so heavy she could hardly breathe.

Everyone she loved was a member of Kate's family, not her own, and when the chips were down, they took sides.

And where was she left, then?

As the old song said, alone again. Naturally.

She got up slowly, and returned to her party, surprised that she'd been so blind. If there was one central lesson of her life, it was this: people leave. Parents. Lovers.

Friends.

In the room full of acquaintances and colleagues, she smiled brightly, made small talk, and went straight to the bar.

It wasn't so hard to act normal, to pretend she was happy. It was what she'd done for so much of her life. Acted.

Only with Katie had she ever really been herself.

By the following autumn, Kate had stopped waiting for Tully to call. In the long months of their estrangement, she'd settled—albeit uncomfortably—into a rarefied and contained world, a kind of snow globe of her own creation. At first, of course, she'd cried about their lost friendship, ached for what had been, but in time, she accepted that there would be no apology from Tully, that if one were to be offered it would have to—as always—come from her.

The story of their lives.

Kate's ego, usually such a fluid and convenient thing, became solid on this point. For once, she would not yield.

And so the time passed, and the curved glass walls of the snow globe hardened. Less and less often she thought of Tully, and when she did, she learned to stop crying about it and go on.

But it exhausted her, drained her. As the weather had begun to turn cold again, it took all her effort to get up in the morning and take a shower. By November, washing her hair had been such a daunting prospect that she'd avoided it altogether. Cooking dinner and doing the dishes sapped so much energy that halfway through she had to sit down.

That all would have been okay, and by that she meant acceptable levels of depression, if only it had ended there. Last week, unfortunately, she'd been too tired to brush her teeth in the morning, and she'd driven the kids to school in her pajamas.

"I don't know why that's such a big deal," she'd said to her husband that night when he asked her about it. He'd taken a job at his old station, and the lessened responsibilities gave him too much time to notice Kate's flaws. "It's just a slip in personal hygiene. It's not like I went postal."

"You're depressed," he'd said, pulling her against him on the sofa. "And frankly, Kate, you don't look good."

That had hurt, although, to be honest, not as much as it should have. "So make me an appointment with a plastic surgeon. I hardly need a physical exam. I see my doctors regularly. You know that."

"Better safe than sorry," was his answer, and so now, here she was on the ferry, going in to the city. The truth was—although she wouldn't have admitted it to her husband—she was glad to be going in. She was tired of being depressed, tired of feeling worn out. Maybe a prescription of some kind would help; a pill to forget a thirty-year friendship that had ended badly.

When the ferry docked, she drove off the bumpy ramp and merged into the early morning traffic. It was a gray dismal day that matched her mood. She drove through downtown and negotiated the hill up to the hospital, where she found a parking spot in the garage, then walked across the street and into the lobby. After a quick check-in, she headed for the elevator.

Forty minutes later, after she'd read every article in the newest edition of *Parents* magazine, she was led back to an examination room, where a nurse took all the usual stats and information.

When she was left alone again, Kate picked up the new *People* and flipped it open.

There was a picture of Tully, mugging for the camera, tilting up an empty champagne glass. She looked gorgeous in a black Chanel dress and glittery, beaded shrug. Below the photograph, it read: *Tallulah Hart at a gala charity event at the Chateau Marmont, with her date, media tycoon Thomas Morgan.*

The door opened. Dr. Marcia Silver stepped into the room. "Hey, there, Kate. It's good to see you again." Sitting down on her wheeled stool, she glided forward, reading Kate's chart. "So, is there anything you want to tell me?"

"My husband thinks I'm depressed."

"Are you?"

Kate shrugged. "A little blue maybe."

Marcia made a note in the chart. "It's been almost exactly twelve months since your last appointment. Way to go."

"You know us Catholic girls. Rule-followers."

Marcia smiled and closed the chart, reaching for her gloves. "Okay, Kate, we'll start with the pap smear. Slide on down to the end here . . ."

For the next few minutes Kate gave herself over to the little indignities that came with female health care: the speculum, the probing, the sampling. All the while she and Dr. Silver made stilted, impersonal conversation. They talked about the weather, the latest show at the 5th Avenue Theater, and the approaching holidays.

It wasn't until nearly thirty minutes later, when the exam had moved to her breasts, that Marcia actually stopped making chitchat. "How long have you had this discoloration on your breast?"

Kate glanced down at the quarter-sized red patch beneath her right nipple. The skin was slightly puckered like an orange peel. "Nine months or so. Maybe a year, come to think of it. It started as a bug bite. My family doctor thought it was an infection and put me on antibiotics. It went away for a while and then came back. Sometimes it feels hot— that's how I know it's an infection."

Marcia stared down at Kate's breast, frowning. Kate added: "I had my mammogram on time. Everything was clean."

"I see that." Marcia went to the wall phone, punched in a number, and said, "I want to get Kate in for a breast ultrasound. Now. Tell them to fit her in. Thanks." She hung up and turned around.

Kate sat up. "You're scaring me, Marcia."

"I hope it's nothing, Kate, but I want to be sure, okay?"

"But what—"

"Let's talk when we know what's going on. Janis will take you down to radiology. Okay? Is your husband here?"

"Should he be?"

"No. I'm sure it's fine. Oh, here's Janis."

Kate's mind was a whirl. Before she knew it, she was dressed again and being shepherded up three floors and down the hall. There, after an interminable wait, she endured another breast exam, more clucking and frowning, and an ultrasound.

"I always do my self-exams," she said. "I haven't felt a lump."

Above her, as she lay in the dark room, the nurse and radiologist exchanged a look.

"What?" Kate said, hearing fear in her voice now.

When the ultrasound was over, she was again shuffled out of the exam room and deposited back in the waiting room. Like all the other women in the small room, she read magazines, trying to concentrate on random sentences and Bundt cake recipes; anything except the results of the ultrasound.

It'll be fine, she told herself whenever the worry crept through. *Nothing to worry about.* Cancer wasn't something that crept up on you; certainly not breast cancer. There were warning signs and she watched for them religiously. It had already struck her family once with Aunt Georgia, so they were vigilant. One by one, the other women left; still Kate waited.

Finally, a plump, doe-eyed nurse came for her. "Kathleen Ryan?"

She stood up. "Yes?"

"I'm going to take you across the hall. Dr. Krantz is waiting to do a biopsy on you."

"Biopsy?"

"Just to be sure. Come on."

Kate couldn't seem to move; she could barely nod. Clutching her purse, she stumbled along behind the nurse. "My last mammogram was clear, you know. I do regular self-exams, too."

She wished suddenly that Johnny were here, holding her hand, telling her everything was going to be fine.

Or Tully.

She took a deep breath and tried to control her fear. Once, several years ago, she'd had a bad pap smear and needed a biopsy. It had ruined a weekend, waiting for results, but in the end she'd been fine. Remembering that, clinging to it like a life ring in cold, turbulent water, she followed the silent nurse to the office down the hall. The sign by the door read: THE GOODNO FOUNDATION CANCER CARE CENTER.

CHAPTER
THIRTY-THREE

Tully was awakened by the phone ringing. She came awake hard, looked around. It was 2:01 in the morning. She reached over and answered. "Hello?"

"Is this Tallulah Hart?"

She rubbed her eyes. "Yes. Who is this?"

"My name is Lori Witherspoon. I'm a nurse at Harborview Hospital. We have your mother here. Dorothy Hart."

"What happened?"

"We're not sure. It looks like a drug overdose, but she was pretty badly beaten up, too. The police are waiting to question her."

"Did she ask for me?"

"She's unconscious. We found your name and number in her things."

"I'll be right there."

Tully got dressed in record time and was on the road by 2:20. She pulled into the parking lot at the hospital and went to the desk.

"Hello. I'm here to see my mother, Cl—uh, Dorothy Hart."

"Sixth floor, Ms. Hart. Go to the nurses' desk."

"Thanks." Tully went upstairs and was directed to her mother's room by a tiny woman in a pale orange nurse's uniform.

Inside the shadowy room there were two beds. The one nearest the door was empty.

She shut the door behind her, surprised to find that she was frightened. For the whole of her life, she'd been wounded by her mother. She'd loved her as a child, inexplicably; hated her as a teenager; and ignored her as a woman. Cloud had broken her heart more times than she could count, and let her down on every possible occasion, and yet, even after all of that, Tully couldn't help feeling something for her.

Cloud was asleep. Bruises covered her face, blackened one eye; her lip was split open and seeped blood. Short gray hair, apparently cut with a dull knife, was matted to her head.

She didn't look anything like herself; rather, she looked like a frail old woman who'd been beaten by more than someone's fists—by life itself.

"Hey, Cloud," Tully said, surprised to find that her throat was tight. She gently stroked her mother's temple, the only place on her face that wasn't bloodied or bruised. As she felt the velvety soft skin, she realized that the last time she'd touched her mother had been in 1970, when they'd held hands on that crowded Seattle street.

She wished she knew what to say to this woman, with whom she had a history but no present. So she just talked. She told her about the show and her life and how successful she'd become. When that started to sound hollow and desperate, she talked about Kate and their fight and how it had left her feeling so alone. As the words formed themselves and spilled out, Tully heard the truth in them. Losing the Ryans and Mularkeys had left her devastatingly alone. Cloud was all she had left. How pathetic was that?

"We're all alone in this world, haven't you figured that out by now?"

Tully hadn't noticed her mother wake up, and yet she was conscious now, and looking at Tully through tired eyes. "Hey," she said, smiling, wiping her eyes. "What happened to you?"

"I got beat up."

"I wasn't asking what put you in the hospital. I was asking what happened to you."

Cloud flinched and turned away. "Oh. That. I guess your precious grandmother never told you, huh?" She sighed. "It doesn't matter now."

Tully drew in a sharp breath. This was the most meaningful conversation they'd ever had; she felt poised on the edge of some essential discovery that had eluded her for all her years. "I think it does."

"Go away, Tully." Cloud turned her face into the pillow.

"Not until you tell me why." Her voice trembled on that question; of course it did. "Why didn't you ever love me?"

"Forget about me."

"Honestly, I wish I could. But you're my mother."

Cloud turned back and stared at her, and for a moment, no longer than it took to blink, Tully saw sadness in her mother's eyes. "You break my heart," she said quietly.

"You break mine, too."

Cloud smiled for a second. "I wish . . ."

"What?"

"I could be what you need, but I can't. You need to let me go."

"I don't know how to do that. After everything, you're still my mother."

"I was never your mother. We both know that."

"I'll always keep coming back," Tully said, realizing just then that it was true. They might be damaged, she and her mother, but they were connected, too, in a strange and profound way. This dance of theirs, as painful as it had always been, wasn't quite over. "Someday you'll be ready for me."

"How do you keep hold of a dream like that?"

"With both hands." She would have added, *no matter what,* but the promise reminded her of Kate and hurt too much to utter aloud.

Her mother sighed and closed her eyes. "Go away."

Tully stood there a long time, her hands curled around the metal bed rails. She knew her mother was pretending sleep; she also knew when it became real. When intermittent snores filled the silence, she went to the small closet in the room, found a folded-up blanket, and grabbed it. That was when she noticed the small pile of clothes folded neatly in the corner on the closet's bottom self. Beside it was a brown paper grocery bag, rolled closed at the top.

She covered her mother with the blanket, tucked it up beneath her chin, and returned to the closet.

She wasn't sure why she went through her mother's things, what she was looking for. At first, it was the stuff she'd expected: dirty, worn clothes, shoes with holes along the soles, a makeshift toiletry set in a plastic baggie, cigarettes and a lighter.

Then she saw it, coiled neatly at the bottom of the sack—a frayed piece of string, knotted into a circle, with two pieces of dried macaroni and a single blue bead strung on it.

The necklace Tully had made in her Bible study class and given to her mother on that day, so many years ago, when they'd left Gran's house in the VW bus. Her mother had kept it, all this time.

Tully didn't touch it. She was afraid somehow that she'd find it existed only in her mind. She turned to her mother, went to the bed. "You kept it," she said, feeling something brand-new open up inside her. A kind of hope—not the spit-shined little-girl variety, but something tarnished and worn; more reflective of who they were and where they'd been. Still, it was there, under all the rust and discoloration: hope. "You know how to hold on to a dream, too, don't you, Cloud?"

She sat down on the molded plastic chair by the bed. Now she had a genuine question for her mother, and she intended to get an answer.

Sometime around four o'clock, she slumped in her chair and fell asleep.

The trilling of her cell phone wakened her. She unfolded slowly, painfully, rubbing the crick in her neck. It took her a moment to realize where she was.

The hospital.

Harborview.

She stood up. Her mother's bed was empty. She wrenched open the closet doors.

Empty. The bag was crumpled into a ball and left behind.

"Shit."

Her cell phone rang again. She glanced at the incoming number. "Hey, Edna," she said, sinking back into the chair.

"You sound awful."

"Bad night." She wished she'd touched the necklace now; already it was taking on the blurry edges of a dream. "What time is it?"

"Six, your time. Are you sitting down?"

"Coincidentally, I am."

"Do you still take off part of November and all of December?"

"So that my crew can enjoy the holidays with their families?" she said bitterly. "I do."

"I know you're usually busy with that friend of yours—"

"Not this year."

"Good. Then maybe you'd like to come to the Antarctic with me. I'm doing a documentary on global warming. I think it's an important story, Tully. Someone of your stature would get it watched."

The offer was a Godsend. A moment before she'd been wanting to get away from her own life. You couldn't get much farther than Antarctica. "How long will we be gone?"

"Six weeks; seven at the most. You could fly back and forth, but it's a hell of a trip."

"Sounds perfect. I need to get away. How soon can we leave?"

Naked, Kate stood in front of the mirror in her bathroom, studying her body. All her life she'd been engaged in a guerrilla-type war with her reflection. Her thighs had always been too fleshy, no matter how much weight she lost, and her tummy pooched out after three kids. She did sit-ups at the gym, but still her middle sagged. She'd stopped wearing sleeveless shirts about three years ago—arm jiggle. And her breasts . . . Since the boys' births, she'd started wearing heavier-molded, less sexy bras, that was for sure, and she tightened the straps to pull her boobs into place.

Now, though, when she looked at herself, she saw how little all of that mattered, what a waste of time it had been.

She stepped closer, practicing the words she'd chosen, rehearsing. If ever there was a moment in her life that required strength, this was it.

She reached for the pile of clothes on the counter and began dressing. She'd chosen a pretty pink cashmere V-neck sweater—a Christmas present from the kids last year—and a worn, soft-as-lambskin pair of Levi's. Then she brushed her hair, pulled it away from her face and made a ponytail. She even put on some makeup. It was important that she look healthy for what was to come. When there was nothing else she could do, she left the bathroom and went into her bedroom.

Johnny, who'd been seated on the end of the bed, stood quickly and turned to her. She could see how hard he was trying to be strong. Already his eyes were bright.

It should have made her cry, too, that shiny evidence of his love and fear, but somehow it made her stronger. "I have cancer," she said.

He already knew it, of course. The past few days, spent waiting for the test results, had been agonizing. Last night they'd finally gotten the doctor's call. They'd held hands while she gave them the information, assuring each other before she spoke that it would be fine. But it hadn't been fine; not even close to fine.

I'm sorry, Kate . . . stage four . . . inflammatory breast cancer . . . aggressive . . . already spread . . .

At first Kate had been furious—she'd always done everything right, looked for lumps, gotten her mammograms—and then the fear set in.

Johnny took it even harder than she did, and she saw quickly that she needed to be strong for him. Last night, they'd lain awake all night, holding each other, crying, praying, promising each other they'd get through it. Now, though, she wondered how they'd do it.

She went to him. He curled his arms around her and held her as tightly as he could, and still it wasn't close enough.

"I have to tell them."

"We have to." He stepped back slightly, loosened his hold just enough to look down at her. "Nothing will change. Remember that."

"Are you kidding? They're going to take away my breasts." Her voice caught on that; fear was a crack in the road that tripped her up. "Then they'll poison and burn me. And all that is supposed to be the good news."

He stared down at her, and the love in his eyes was the most beautiful, heart-wrenching thing she'd ever seen. "Between us, nothing will change. It doesn't matter how you look or feel or act. I'll love you forever, just like I do now."

The emotions she'd worked so hard to submerge floated up again, threatened to consume her. "Let's go," she said quietly. "While I've still got the nerve."

Hand in hand, they walked out of their bedroom and went downstairs, where the kids were supposed to be waiting for them.

The living room was empty.

Kate could hear the television in the family room. It blared out the *bleep-thump* of video games. She let go of her husband and went to the corner, by the hall. "Boys, come on out here."

"Aw, Mom," Lucas whined, "we're watching a movie."

She wanted to say, *Keep on watching, forget it,* so badly it actually hurt to say, "Come on, please. Now."

Behind her, she heard her husband go into the kitchen and pick up the phone.

"Downstairs, Marah. Right now. No, I don't care who you're talking to."

Click.

Kate heard him hang up. Instead of going to him, she went to the couch and sat down, perching stiffly on the cushion's edge. She wished suddenly that she'd put on a heavier sweater; she was freezing.

The boys rushed into the room together, fighting with plastic swords, laughing.

"Take that, Captain Hook," Lucas said.

"I'm Peter Pan," William complained, pretending to stab his brother. "En garde!"

At seven, they were just beginning to change. The little-boy freckles were fading; baby teeth were falling out. Every time she looked at them lately, some baby trait had been lost.

Three years from now they'd be almost unrecognizable.

The thought scared her so much that she clutched the sofa's arm and closed her eyes. What if she weren't here to see them grow up? What if—

No bad thoughts.

It had become her mantra in the past four days. Johnny came up beside her, sat down close, and took her hand in his.

"I can't believe you picked up the phone," Marah said, coming down the stairs. "That is so totally an invasion of my privacy. And it was Brian."

Kate counted silently to ten, calmed herself enough to breathe, and opened her eyes.

Her children were in front of her, standing there, looking either bored (the boys) or irritated (Marah).

She swallowed hard. She could do this.

"Are you gonna say something?" Marah demanded. "Because if you're just gonna stare at us, I'm going back upstairs."

Johnny started to come out of his seat. "Damn it, Marah."

Kate put a hand on his thigh to stop him. "Sit down, Marah," she said, surprised to hear how ordinary she sounded. "You, too, boys."

The boys plopped onto the carpet like marionettes whose strings had been cut, landing in side-by-side heaps.

"I'll stand," Marah said, flinging her hip out and crossing her arms. She gave Kate the old you're-not-the-boss-of-me glare, and Kate couldn't help feeling a pinch of nostalgia.

"You remember when I went into the city on Friday?" Kate began, feeling the acceleration of her heartbeat and the slight breathlessness that accompanied it. "Well, I had a doctor's appointment."

Lucas whispered something to William, who grinned and punched his brother.

Marah looked longingly up the stairs.

Kate squeezed her husband's hand. "Anyway, there's nothing for you to worry about, but I'm . . . sick."

All three of them looked at her.

"Don't worry. They're going to operate on me and then give me a bunch of medicine and I'll be fine. I might be tired for a few weeks, but that should be about it."

"You promise you'll be okay?" Lucas said, his gaze steady and earnest and only a little afraid.

Kate wanted to say, *Certainly of course,* but such a promise would be remembered.

William rolled his eyes and elbowed his brother. "She just said she'd be fine. Will we get out of school to go to the hospital?"

"Yes," Kate said, actually finding a smile.

Lucas rushed forward to hug her first. "I love you, Mommy," he whispered. She held on to him so long he had to wrench free. The same thing happened with William. Then, as one, they turned and went to the stairs.

"Aren't you going to finish your movie?" Kate asked.

"Naw," Lucas said. "We're going upstairs."

Kate glanced worriedly at her husband, who was already rising. "How about a game of basketball, boys?"

They jumped on the idea and all went outside.

Finally, Kate looked at Marah.

"It's cancer, isn't it?" her daughter asked after a long silence.

"Yes."

"Ms. Murphy had cancer last year and she's fine. And Aunt Georgia, too."

"Exactly."

Marah's mouth trembled. For all her height and pseudo-sophistication and makeup, she looked suddenly like a little girl again asking Kate to leave the night-light on. Wringing her hands together, she moved toward the sofa. "You'll be fine, right?"

Stage four. Already spread. Caught it late. She put a lid on those thoughts. They could do her no good. Now was a time for optimism.

"Right. The doctors say I'm young and healthy, so I should be fine."

Marah lay down on the couch, snuggled close, and put her head in Kate's lap. "I'll take care of you, Mommy."

Kate closed her eyes and stroked her daughter's hair. It seemed like only yesterday she'd been able to hold her in her arms and rock her to sleep, only yesterday that Marah had curled into her lap and cried for their lost goldfish.

Please God, she prayed, *let me get old enough that someday we're friends . . .*

She swallowed hard. "I know you will, honey."

The Firefly Lane girls . . .

In Kate's dream, it is 1974, and she is a teenager again, riding her bike at midnight with her best friend beside her in a darkness so complete it is like being invisible. She remembers the place in vivid detail: a meandering ribbon of asphalt bordered on either side by deep gullies of murky water and hillsides of shaggy grass. Before they met, that road seemed to go nowhere at all; it was just a country lane named after an insect no one had ever seen in this rugged blue and green corner of the world. Then they saw it through each other's eyes . . .

Let go, Katie. God hates a coward.

She woke with a start, feeling tears on her cheeks. She lay there in her bed, wide awake now, listening to a winter storm rage outside. In the last week she'd lost the ability to distance herself from her memories. Too often lately she returned to Firefly Lane in her dreams, and no wonder.

Best friends forever.

That was the promise they'd made all those years ago, and they'd believed it would last, believed that someday they'd be old women together, sitting in their rocking chairs on a creaking deck, talking about the times of their lives, and laughing.

Now she knew better, of course. For more than a year she'd been telling herself that it was okay, that she could go on without her best friend. Sometimes she even believed it.

Then she'd hear the music. Their music. Yesterday, while she'd been shopping, a bad Muzak version of "You've Got a Friend" had made her cry, right there next to the radishes.

She eased the covers back and got out of bed, careful not to waken the man sleeping beside her. For a moment she stood there, staring down at him in the shadowy darkness. Even in sleep, he wore a troubled expression.

She took the phone off its hook and left the bedroom, then walked down the quiet hallway to the deck. There, she stared out at the storm and gathered her courage. As she punched in the familiar numbers, she wondered what she would say after all these silent months, how she would start. *I've had a bad week . . . my life is falling apart . . .* or simply: *I need you.*

Across the black and turbulent Sound, the phone rang.

And rang.

When the answering machine clicked on, she tried to marshal her need into something as small and ordinary as words. "Hey, Tul. It's me, Kate. I can't believe you haven't called to apologize to me—"

Thunder echoed across the sky; lightning flashed in staccato bursts. She heard a click. "Tully? Are you listening to this? Tully?"

There was no answer.

Kate sighed and went on. "I need you, Tully. Call me on my cell."

Suddenly the power went out, taking the phone connection with it. A busy signal bleated in her ear.

Kate tried not to take it as a sign. Instead, she went back inside and lit a candle in the living room. Then, on this day of her surgery, she did one special thing for each member of her family, a little reminder that she was here. For William she found the DVD of *Monsters, Inc.* that he'd misplaced. For Lucas she put together a sack full of his favorite snacks for the waiting room. She charged Marah's cell phone and put it by her bed, knowing how adrift her daughter would feel today if she couldn't call her friends. Finally, she found every set of keys in the house, tagged them, and set them on the counter for Johnny. He lost them almost daily.

When she couldn't think of anything else to do for her family, she went to the window and watched the storm die. Slowly, the dewy world lightened. Charcoal clouds turned to a gorgeous pearlized pink. Seattle looked shiny and new, huddled as it was beneath the rising sun.

A few hours later, her family began to gather around her. The whole time they were together, having breakfast and packing their things into the car, she found herself glancing at the phone, expecting it to ring.

Six weeks later, when they'd taken both her breasts and poured poison into her blood and irradiated her flesh until it looked raw and burned, she was still waiting for Tully to call.

On January second, Tully came home to a cold, empty apartment.

"Story of my life," she said bitterly, tipping the doorman, who carried her bulky designer suitcases into the bedroom.

When he left, she stood there, uncertain of what to do. It was nine o'clock on a Monday night, and most people were home with their families. Tomorrow, she'd go back to work and be able to lose herself in the daily routine of the empire she'd created. In no time at all she'd let go of the images that haunted her during the holidays, had even followed her to the ends of the earth last month. Literally. She'd spent Thanksgiving, Christmas, and New Year's in the frozen south, huddled around their heat source, singing songs and drinking wine. To the naked eye, and the ever-present camera, it had looked like a good time.

But too often when she'd crawled into her down sleeping bag, wearing her hat and mittens, and tried to sleep, she heard the old songs banging around in her head, making her cry. More than once she'd wakened with ice on her cheeks.

She tossed her purse on the sofa and glanced at the clock, noticing that the red numbers were flashing 5:55. The power must have gone out while she was gone.

She poured herself a glass of wine, got out a piece of paper and a pen, then sat down at her desk. The numbers on the answering machine were flashing, too.

"Great." Now she'd have no idea who had tried to call her after the outage. She hit the replay button and began the slow, arduous task of going through her messages. Halfway through, she made a note to speak to her assistant about voice mail.

She was barely paying attention when Kate's voice roused her.

"Hey, Tul. It's me. Kate."

Tully sat up sharply and hit the rewind button.

"Hey, Tul. It's me. Kate. I can't believe you haven't called to apologize to me."

A loud Click. Then: "Tully? Are you listening to this? Tully?" and then another click followed by a loud busy signal. Kate had hung up.

That was all there was. It was over. There were no more messages on the machine.

Tully felt a disappointment so sharp it actually made her flinch. She played and replayed the message until all she could hear was the accusation in Kate's voice.

That wasn't the Kate she remembered, the girl who'd promised all those years ago to be friends forever. That girl would never have called to taunt Tully like this, to berate her and then hang up.

I can't believe you haven't called to apologize to me.

Tully stood up, trying to distance herself from this voice that had invaded her home, tricked her into hoping. She hit the erase all button and backed away.

"I can't believe you haven't called *me*," she said to her empty apartment, trying not to notice how thick her voice sounded.

She went to her purse and burrowed through the mess inside for her cell phone. Finding it, she scrolled through her huge contact list for a name she'd added only a few months ago, and hit send.

When Thomas answered, she tried to sound flirty and light, but it was hard to pretend; a weight seemed to be sitting on her chest, making it hard to breathe. "Hey, Tom I just got back from the icy beyond. What are you doing tonight? Nothing? That's great. How about getting together?"

It was pathetic how desperate she suddenly felt. But she couldn't be alone tonight, couldn't even sleep in her own apartment.

"I'll meet you at Kells. Say, nine-thirty?"

Before he even said, "It's a date," she was on her way.

CHAPTER
THIRTY-FOUR

Two thousand six saw *The Girlfriend Hour* rise even higher in the ratings. Week after week, month after month, Tully created magic with her selection of guests and her rapport with the audience. She had definitely reached the top of her game and seized control of the board. No longer did she let herself think about what she didn't have in her life. Just as she'd done at six and ten and fourteen, she boxed all that negative stuff up and put it in the shadow box.

She went on. It was what she'd always done in her life when disappointment set in. She tucked her chin, squared her shoulders, and set a new goal for herself. This year, she was starting a magazine. Next year it would be a retreat for women. After that, who knew?

Now she sat in her newly decorated office in a corner of the building that didn't face Bainbridge Island, talking to her secretary on the phone. "Are you kidding me? He's canceling the show, forty minutes before we're scheduled to start taping? I have a studio full of people waiting to see him." She slammed the phone back onto the hook, then hit the intercom. "Get Ted in here."

A few minutes later, there was a knock at the door and her producer walked into her office. His cheeks were pink from exertion and he was breathing hard. "You wanted to see me?"

"Jack just canceled."

"Now?" Ted glanced at his watch. "Son of a bitch. I hope you told him the next time he has a movie out he can pitch it on the radio."

Tully flipped open her calendar. "It's June first, right? Call Nordstrom and the Gene Juarez Spa. We'll do mothers' makeovers for summer. Give away a bunch of clothes and stuff. It'll suck, but it's better than nothing."

From the moment Ted left her office, the whole team was in high gear. People were tracking down new guests, calling the various spa and department store contacts, and keeping the studio audience entertained. The adrenaline was so high that everyone, including Tully, worked at supersonic speed, and the taping of the new segment began only one hour late. Judging by the audience's applause, it was a rousing success.

After the show, as always, Tully stayed around and talked with her fans. She posed for photographs and signed autographs and listened to one story after another about how she'd changed someone's life. It was her favorite hour of any day.

She had just returned to her office when her intercom buzzed. "Tallulah? There's a Kate Ryan on line one."

Tully's heart missed a beat; the hope she felt pissed her off. She stood at the corner of her huge desk and pushed the intercom button. "Ask her what she wants."

A moment later, her secretary was back on the line. "Ms. Ryan says you need to pick up the phone and find out for yourself."

"Tell her to go fuck herself." Tully wished she could take the words back as soon as she'd said them, but she didn't know how to bend now. During their long estrangement, she'd had to stay angry just to get by. Otherwise the loneliness would have been unbearable.

"Ms. Ryan says, and I quote: 'Tell that bitch to get her designer-clad ass out of her ridiculously expensive leather chair and come to the phone.' She also says that if you ignore her on this of all days she's selling those pictures of you with a bad perm to the tabloids."

Tully almost smiled. How could two sentences peel back so many years and blast through the sediment of so many bad choices?

She picked up the phone. "You're the bitch, and I'm pissed at you."

"Of course you are, you narcissist, and I'm not apologizing, but that doesn't matter anymore."

"It matters. You should have called long before—"

"I'm in the hospital, Tully. Sacred Heart. Fourth floor," Kate said. Then she hung up.

"Hurry up," Tully said to her driver for at least the fifth time in as many blocks.

When the car pulled up in front of the hospital, she got out and ran for the glass doors, pausing for a moment while the sensors engaged. The second she stepped inside, people swarmed around her. Usually she factored what she called fan maintenance into her schedule—thirty minutes at every location to meet and greet—but now she didn't have time. She pushed through the crowd and went to the front desk. "I'm here to see Kathleen Ryan."

The receptionist stared up at her in awe. "You're Tallulah Hart."

"Yes, I am. Kathleen Ryan's room, please."

The receptionist nodded. "Oh. Right." She glanced at her computer screen, entered a few keys, and said, "Four-ten East."

"Thanks." Tully headed for the elevators, but noticed that she was being followed. Her fans would nonchalantly enter the elevator with her. The brave ones would initiate conversation between floors. The weirdos might follow her out.

She took the stairs instead, thankful by the third flight that she attended daily aerobics classes and worked with a personal trainer. Still, she was out of breath when she reached the fourth floor.

Just down the hall, she found a small waiting area. The television was turned on to her show—a rerun from two years ago.

She knew the moment she stepped into the small room that it was Bad, this thing with Kate.

Johnny sat there, in an ugly blue love seat, with Lucas curled up beside him. With one son's head in his lap, Johnny was reading to the other.

Marah was in a chair beside William, with her eyes closed, listening to an iPod through tiny headphones. She moved to the beat of music only she could hear. The boys were so big; it was a painful reminder of how long Tully had been apart from them.

Beside Marah, Mrs. Mularkey sat, staring intently at her knitting. Sean was beside his mother, talking on his cell phone. Georgia and Ralph were watching TV in the corner.

By the looks of it, they'd been here a long time.

It took a huge act of will to step forward. "Hey, Johnny."

At the sound of her voice, they all looked up, but no one said anything and suddenly Tully remembered the last time they'd all been together.

"Kate called me," she explained.

Johnny eased out from under his sleeping son and stood up. There was only a beat of awkwardness, a clumsy pause, before he took her in his arms. She could tell by the ferocity of his embrace that it was more to comfort himself than her. She clung to him, trying not to be afraid. "Tell me," she said, more harshly than she intended, when he let go of her and stepped back.

He sighed and nodded. "We'll go into the family room."

Mrs. M. stood up slowly.

Tully was struck by how much Mrs. M. had aged. The woman looked frail and a little hunched. She'd stopped dyeing her hair and it was snow-white. "Katie called you?" Mrs. M. said.

"I came right away," she said, as if speed mattered now, after all this time.

Then Mrs. M. did the most amazing thing: she hugged Tully, enveloped her once again in an embrace that smelled of Jean Naté perfume and menthol cigarettes, with just a hint of hairspray to give it spice.

"Come on," Johnny said, breaking up the hug, and leading the way to another room. Inside there was a smallish fake wood conference table and eight molded plastic chairs.

Johnny and Mrs. M. sat down.

Tully remained standing. No one spoke for a moment and every passing second was a turn of the screw. "Tell me."

"Kate has cancer," Johnny said. "It's called inflammatory breast cancer."

Tully had to concentrate on each breath to remain upright. "She'll have a mastectomy and get radiation and chemotherapy, right? I have several friends who have fought—"

"She's already had all of that," he said gently.

"What? When?"

"She called you several months ago," he said, and this time his voice had an edge she'd never heard before. "She wanted to have you at the hospital with her. You didn't return her call."

Tully remembered the message, word for word. *I can't believe you haven't called to apologize to me. Tully? Are you listening to this? Tully?* And the click. Had something happened to the rest of the message? Had the power gone out or the tape hit its end?

"She didn't say anything about being sick," Tully said.

"She *called*," Mrs. M. said.

Tully felt tackled by guilt, overcome. She should have sensed something was wrong. Why hadn't she just picked up the phone? Now all that time had been lost. "Oh, my God. I should have—"

"None of that matters now," Mrs. M. said.

Johnny nodded and went on. "The cancer has metastasized. Last night she had a minor stroke. They got her into the OR as quickly as possible, but once they were inside, they saw there was nothing they could do." His voice broke.

Mrs. M. laid her hand on his. "The cancer is in her brain now."

Tully thought she had known fear before—like on that Seattle street when she was ten years old, or when Katie had had her miscarriage, or when Johnny had been hurt in Iraq—but nothing had felt like this. "Are you saying . . ."

"She's dying," Mrs. M. said quietly.

Tully shook her head, unable to think of what to say. "W-where is she?" The question came out sounding choppy and broken. "I need to see her."

A look passed between Johnny and Mrs. M.

"What?" Tully said.

"They're only allowing one person in at a time," Mrs. M. said. "Bud is in there now. I'll go get him."

As soon as Mrs. M. left, Johnny moved even closer, said, "She's frag- ile right now, Tul. Her faculties have been impacted by the cancer in her brain. She has good moments . . . and not-so-good moments."

"What are you saying?" Tully asked.

"She might not know who you are."

The walk to Kate's room was the longest journey of Tully's life. She felt people all around her, talking quietly among themselves, but never had she felt more alone. Johnny led her to a doorway and stopped there.

Tully nodded, trying to gather strength as she walked into the room.

Closing the door behind her, she reached for a smile, found one that was the best she could do under the circumstances, and went toward the bed, where her friend lay sleeping.

Angled up to a near-sit, Kate looked like a broken doll against the stark white sheets and piled pillows. She had no hair or eyebrows left, and her bald head was a pale oval that nearly disappeared against the pillowcase.

"Kate?" Tully said quietly, moving forward. The moment she heard her voice she winced. It sounded too loud in this room, too alive some- how.

Kate opened her eyes, and there was the woman Tully knew, the girl she'd sworn to be best friends with forever.

Put your arms out, Katie. It's like flying.

How had it happened, after all their decades together, that they were estranged now? "I'm sorry, Katie," she whispered, hearing how small the words were; all her life she'd hoarded those few and simple words, kept them tucked inside her heart as if to let them out would harm her. Why, of all the lessons she should have learned from her mother, had she held on to this most hurtful one? And why hadn't she called when she'd heard Kate's voice on the answering machine?

"I'm so sorry," she said again, feeling the burn of tears.

Kate didn't smile or give any indication of welcome or surprise. Even the apology—as little and late as it was—seemed to have no effect. "Please say you remember me."

Kate just stared up at her.

Tully reached down, let her knuckles graze Kate's warm cheek. "It's Tully, the bitch who used to be your best friend. I'm so sorry for what I did to you, Katie. I should have told you that a long time ago." She made a tiny, desperate sound. If Kate didn't remember her, remember them, she didn't think she could bear it. "I remember when I first met you, Katie Mularkey Ryan. You were the first person who ever really wanted to know me. Naturally I treated you like shit at first, but when I got raped you were there for me." The memories overtook her. She wiped her eyes. "You're thinking I'm only talking about me, right? Typical, you say. But I remember you, too, Katie; every second. Like when you read *Love Story* and couldn't figure out what *sonovabitch* meant because it wasn't in the dictionary . . . or when you swore you'd never French-kiss because it was gross-o-rama." Tully shook her head, fighting to keep it together. Her whole life was in the room with them now. "We were so damned young, Katie. But we're not young anymore. You remember that first time I left Snohomish, and we wrote about a million letters? We signed them *Forever friends* . . . or *Best friends forever*. Which was it . . ."

Tully spun out the story of their years; sometimes she even laughed, like when she told about riding their bikes down Summer Hill or running from the cops on the night they got busted. "Oh, here's one you'll know. Remember when we went to *Pete's Dragon* because we thought it was an action movie, only it was a cartoon? We were the oldest kids in the theater, and we came out singing 'You and Me Against the World,' and we said it would always be that way—"

"Stop."

Tully drew in a sharp breath.

There were tears in her friend's eyes, and more streaking down her temples. They'd formed a small gray patch of wetness on the pillow behind her head. "Tully," Kate said in a soft, swollen voice, "did you really think I could forget you?"

Tully's relief was so huge she felt weak in the knees. "Hey," she said. "You didn't have to go so far to get my attention, you know." She touched her friend's bald head, let her fingers linger on the baby-soft skin. "You could have just called."

"I did call."

Tully flinched. "I'm so sorry, Katie. I—"

"You're a bitch," Kate said, smiling tiredly. "I've always known that. And I could have called back, too. I guess no one stays friends for more than thirty years without a few broken hearts along the way."

"I am a bitch," Tully said miserably, her eyes welling up. "I should have called. It was just . . ." She didn't even know what to say, how to explain this dark rip that had always been inside of her.

"No looking back, okay?"

"That only leaves ahead," Tully said, and the words were like bits of broken metal, sharp and cold.

"No," Kate said. "It leaves now."

"I did a show on breast cancer a few months ago. There's a doctor in Ontario doing amazing things with some new drug. I'll call him."

"I'm done with treatments. I've had them all and none has worked. Just . . . be with me."

Tully took a step back. "I'm here to watch you die. Is that what you're telling me? Because I say no fucking way to that. I won't do it."

Kate looked up at her, smiling just a little. "That's all there is, Tully."

"But—"

"Do you really think Johnny just gave up on me? You know my husband. He's just like you and we're almost as rich. For six months I saw every specialist on the planet. I did conventional and unconventional and naturopathic remedies. I even went to that faith healer in the rain forest. I have kids; I did everything I could to stay healthy for them. None of it worked."

"So what do I do?"

Kate's smile was almost like the old days. "That's my Tul. I'm dying of cancer and you ask about you." She laughed.

"That's not funny."

"I don't know how to do this."

Tully wiped her eyes. The truth of what they were really talking about pressed in on her. "We'll do it like we've done everything else, Kate. Side by side."

Tully came out of Kate's room shaken. She made a small sound, a kind of gasp, and covered her mouth with her hand.

"You can't hold it in," Mrs. M. said, coming up to her.

"I can't let it out."

"I know." Mrs. M's voice cracked, stumbled. "Just love her. Be there for her. That's all there is. Believe me, I've cried and argued and bargained with God, I've begged the doctors for hope. All that's past now. She's most worried about the kids. Marah especially. They've had such a rough go of it—well, you know about that—and Marah seems to have shut down for all of this. No tears, no drama. All she does is listen to music."

They walked back out to the waiting room, only to find everyone gone.

Mrs. M. looked at her watch. "They're in the cafeteria. You want to join us?"

"No, thanks. I think I need some fresh air."

Mrs. M. nodded. "It's good to have you back, Tully. I missed you."

"I should have taken your advice and called her."

"You're here now. That's what matters." She patted Tully's arm and walked away.

Tully went outside, surprised to find that it was light out here, warm and sunny. It seemed vaguely wrong that the sun was still shining while Kate lay up in that narrow bed, dying. She walked down the street, her watery eyes hidden behind huge, dark sunglasses so that no one would recognize her. The last thing she wanted now was to be stopped.

She passed a coffee shop, heard a bit of music waft through the door as someone came out. *Bye, bye, Miss American Pie.*

Her legs gave out on her, and she went down, hard, scraping her knees on the concrete sidewalk, but she didn't notice, hardly cared, she was crying so hard. She'd never felt so swollen with emotion; it was as if she couldn't handle it all. Fear. Sorrow. Guilt. Regret.

"Why didn't I call her?" she whispered. "I'm so sorry, Katie," she said, hearing the hollow desperation in her voice, feeling sick that now the words came so easily, when it was too late to matter.

She didn't know how long she knelt there, her head bowed, sobbing, thinking of all their times together. It was a bad part of Capitol Hill, full of homeless people, so no one stopped to help her. Finally, feeling spent and shaky, she climbed back to a standing position and stood there, feeling as if she'd been beaten up. The music took her back in time, reminded her of so many shared moments. *Swear we'll always be best friends.*

"Oh, Katie . . ."

And she was crying again. Quieter this time.

She walked dully up one street and down another until something in one of the display windows caught her eye.

There, in a store on the corner, she found what she hadn't even realized she'd been looking for. She had the gift wrapped and ran all the way back to Kate's room.

She was out of breath when she opened the door and went inside.

Kate smiled tiredly. "Let me guess: you've got a film crew with you."

"Very funny." She eased around the curtain and stood by the bed. "Your mom tells me you're still having trouble with Marah."

"It's not your fault. She's scared of all this and she doesn't know how easy it is to say you're sorry."

"I didn't."

"You always were her role model." Kate closed her eyes. "I'm tired, Tully . . ."

"I have a present for you."

Kate opened her eyes. "What I need can't be bought."

Tully tried not to react to that. Instead, she handed Kate the beautifully wrapped gift and helped her open it.

Inside was a hand-tooled, leather-bound journal. On the first page, Tully had written: *Katie's story*.

Kate stared down at the blank page for a long time, saying nothing.

"Katie?"

"I was never really a writer," she finally said. "You and Johnny and Mom all wanted it for me, but I never did it. Too late now."

Tully touched her friend's wrist, feeling how fragile and thin it was; the tiniest pressure could leave a bruise. "For Marah," she said quietly. "And the boys. Someday they'll be old enough to read it. They'll want to know who you were."

"How do I know what to write?"

Tully had no real answer for that. "Just write what you remember."

Kate closed her eyes, as if the thought alone were too much to bear. "Thanks, Tully."

"I won't leave you again, Katie."

Kate didn't open her eyes, but she smiled just a little. "I know."

Kate didn't remember falling asleep. One minute she was talking to Tully, and the next—she was waking up in a dark room that smelled of fresh flowers and disinfectant.

She'd been in this room for so long it almost felt like home, and sometimes, when her family's hope was more than she could bear, this small beige room comforted her with its silence. Within these blank walls, when no one else was around, she didn't have to pretend to be strong.

But right now she didn't want to be here. She wanted to be at home, in her own bed, in her husband's arms rather than watching him sleep in the hospital bed on the other side of the room.

Or with Tully, sitting on the muddy banks of the Pilchuck River, talking about David Cassidy's newest album and sharing a bag of Pop Rocks.

The memory made her smile, and with it came a lessening of the fear that had wakened her.

She knew she wouldn't fall back asleep without medication and she didn't want to wake the night nurse. Besides, she had little enough life left to her; what was the point in sleeping?

It had only been in the last few weeks that such morbid thoughts had come to her. Before that, in the months since her diagnosis—what she thought of as D-Day—she did everything she was supposed to do, and she did it with a smile for everyone in the room.

Surgery—*Sure, cut me open and take my breasts.*

Radiation—*Absolutely. Burn me up.*

Chemotherapy—*Another dose of poison, please.*

Tofu and miso soup—*Yum. May I have some more?*

Crystals. Meditation. Visualization. Chinese herbs.

She'd done it all, and done it with vigor. Even more important, she'd believed in all of it, believed she'd be cured.

The effort had winded her; the belief had broken her.

She sighed and rubbed her eyes. Leaning sideways, she turned on the bedside lamp. Johnny, who'd grown used to her weird waking/sleeping schedule, rolled onto his side and murmured, "You okay, baby?"

"I'm fine. Keep sleeping."

Mumbling something, he rolled back over. In no time, she heard his quiet snore.

Kate reached over for the journal Tully had bought her. Holding it, she traced the leather etchings and the gold-edged sheets of paper.

It would hurt to do this; of that she had no doubt. To pick up a pen and write down her life, she'd have to remember it all, who she was, who she'd wanted to be. Those memories would be painful, both the good and the bad would wound her.

But her children would see through the illness to *her,* the woman they would always remember, but never truly have time to know. Tully was right. The only gift Kate could give them now was the truth of who she was.

She flipped the journal open. Because she had no clear idea of where to start, she simply began to write.

Panic always comes to me in the same way. First, I get a knot in the pit of my stomach that turns to nausea, then a fluttery breathlessness that no amount of deep breathing can cure. But what causes my fear is different every day; I never know what will set me off. It could be a kiss from my husband, or the lingering look of sadness in his eyes when he draws back. Sometimes I know he's already grieving for me, missing me even while I'm still here. Worse yet is Marah's quiet acceptance of everything I say. I would give anything for another of our old knock-down drag-out fights. That's one of the first things I'd say to you now, Marah: Those fights were real life. You were struggling to break free of being my daughter but unsure of how to be yourself, while I was afraid to let you go. It's the circle of love. I only wish I'd recognized it then. Your grandmother told me I'd know you were sorry for those years before you did, and she was right. I know you regret some of the things you said to me, as I regret my own words. None of that matters, though. I want you to know that. I love you and I know you love me.

But these are just more words, aren't they? I want to go deeper than that. So, if you'll bear with me (I haven't really written anything in years), I have a story to tell you. It's my story, and yours, too. It starts in 1960 in a small farming town up north, in a clapboard house on a hill above a horse pasture. When it gets good, though, is 1974, when the coolest girl in the world moved into the house across the street . . .

CHAPTER
THIRTY-FIVE

From her place in the makeup chair, Tully stared at herself. It was the first time, in all her years spent in seats like this, that she'd really noticed how huge the mirrors were. No wonder it was so easy for a celebrity to get lost in her own reflection.

She said, "I don't need makeup, Charles," and got out of the chair.

He stared at her, gape-mouthed, his own seriously overstyled hair falling across his face. "You're kidding me, right? You're on in fifteen."

"Let them see me as I am."

She walked around the studio, her fiefdom, watching her employees scurry around, running to and fro to make sure everything went off without a hitch, and that was no mean feat, given that she'd called everyone at three yesterday to change the theme of today's live show. She knew that several of her producers and bookers had worked late into the night to put it together. She herself had been up until almost two in the morning, doing research. She'd faxed and e-mailed dozens of the best oncologists in the world. She'd spent hours on the phone, relaying every bit of information on Kate's case that she'd been able to glean. Every specialist said the same thing.

There was nothing Tully could do. No amount of fame or success or money would help her now. For the first time in years, she felt ordinary. Small.

But, for once, she had something important to say.

The theme music started, and she walked onto her stage.

"Welcome to *The Girlfriend Hour*," she said as she always did, but then something went wrong, just stopped. She looked at her audience and saw strangers. It was an odd and disconcerting moment. For most of her life, she'd sought approval from crowds like this, and their unconditional support had buoyed her.

They noticed something was wrong and fell silent.

She sat down on the edge of the stage. "You're all thinking I'm skinnier in person and older. And that I'm not as pretty as you'd thought."

The audience laughed nervously.

"I'm not wearing makeup."

They burst into applause.

"I'm not fishing for compliments. I'm just . . . tired." She glanced around. "You have been my friends for a long time. You write to me, e-mail me, come to my events when I'm in your city, and I've always appreciated it. In return, I've given you my honest self or as close as I can without some kind of medication. Do you remember a show from a few years ago, when my best friend, Kate Ryan, was ambushed on this very stage? By me?"

There was a nervous rumbling, a shaking and nodding of heads.

"Well, Kate has breast cancer."

A murmur of sympathy.

"It's an extremely rare kind of cancer that starts not with a lump, but with a rash or a discoloration. Kate's family physician diagnosed it as a bug bite and prescribed antibiotics. Unfortunately, this happens to too many women, especially younger women. It's called inflammatory breast cancer and it can be aggressive and all too deadly. By the time Kate was diagnosed, it was already too late."

There wasn't a sound from the audience.

Tully looked up through a blur of tears. "Dr. Hilary Carleton is here to talk about inflammatory breast cancer, and to educate you about the symptoms: the rashes, the localized heat, the discolorations, the puckered skin, and the inverted nipples, to name a few. She'll remind us all that we need to look for more than just lumps. The doctor has brought a woman with her—Merrilee Comber from Des Moines, Iowa—who first noticed a small scaly patch near her left nipple . . ."

The show rolled forward as they all did, on the wheels of Tully's personality. She interviewed guests and showed pictures and reminded her audience of millions not only to get yearly mammograms but to watch for any changes in their breasts. At the end of her broadcast, instead of her usual *We'll talk tomorrow* tagline, she looked into the camera and said, "Katie, you're the best friend I have and the best mother I know. Except for Mrs. M., who is good, too." Then she smiled at her audience and said simply: "This will be my last show for a long while. I'm taking time off to be with Katie. As all of you would."

She heard a gasp following her announcement; this time the sound came from backstage.

"This show is, after all, just that: a show. Real life is with friends and family, and as an old friend pointed out to me a while ago: I do have a family. And she needs me now." She unclipped her microphone, dropped it to the floor, and left the stage.

On Kate's last night in the hospital, Tully convinced Johnny to take the kids home, and she took his place in the room's other bed. She pushed the bed across the linoleum floor until it practically butted up to Katie's. "I brought you a tape of my last show."

"You *would* think that's what a dying woman wanted to watch."

"Ha ha." Tully put the tape in the machine and hit play, then crawled into her bed. Like a pair of eighth-grade girls at a slumber party, they watched the taped broadcast.

When it was over, Kate turned to her. "I'm glad to see you'll still use me to bump up your ratings."

"I'll have you know that was poignant and powerful. And important."

"You think that's true of everything you do."

"Do not."

"Good comeback."

"You wouldn't know good TV if it bit you in the ass."

Kate smiled, but it was as washed out as her complexion. With her bald head and sunken eyes, she looked impossibly young and fragile.

"Are you getting tired?" Tully said, sitting up. "Maybe we should go to sleep."

"I noticed that you apologized to me on air. In your own way." Her smile expanded. "I mean, without admitting you were a bitch or actually saying the words. You meant that you were sorry."

"Yeah, well, you're on morphine. You probably saw me fly, too."

Kate laughed, but it soon dissolved into coughing.

Tully sat up quickly. "Are you okay?"

"Hardly." She reached for the plastic glass on the table by her bed. Tully leaned over and guided the straw to her mouth. "I started the journal."

"That's great."

"I'll need you to help me remember," she said, putting the glass back. "So much of my life happened with you."

"Seems like our whole lives. God, Katie, we were such babies when we met."

"We're still kids," Katie said softly.

Tully heard the sadness in her friend's voice; it matched her own. The last thing she wanted to think about right now was how young they were. For years they'd teased each other about getting old. "How much have you written?"

"About ten pages." When Tully fell silent, Kate frowned. "You aren't going to demand to read it?"

"I don't want to intrude."

"Don't do that, Tully," Kate said.

"Do what?"

"Treat me as if I'm dying. I need you to be . . . you. It's the only way I remember who I am. Deal?"

"Okay," she said quietly, promising the only thing she had to give: herself. "It's a deal." She had to force a smile and both of them knew it. Some lies, it was obvious, would be unavoidable in the days ahead. "You'll need my input, of course. I was a witness to every important moment of your life. And I have a photographic memory. It's a gift. Like my ability to apply makeup and highlight hair."

Kate laughed. "There's my Tully."

Even with self-regulated pain meds, Kate found leaving the hospital a difficult endeavor. First of all, there was the crowd: her parents, her kids and husband, her aunt and uncle, her brother, and Tully. Second, there was just so much movement—out of bed, into the wheelchair, out of the wheelchair, into the car, out of the car, into Johnny's arms.

He carried her through the comfortable, pretty island house that smelled of scented candles and last night's dinner, just as it always had. He'd made spaghetti last night; she could tell. That meant tomorrow night it would be tacos. His two recipes. She rested her cheek against the soft wool of his sweater.

What will he cook for them when I'm gone?

The question made her draw in a sharp breath, which she forced herself to release slowly. Being home would hurt like this sometimes; so would being with her family. In a strange way, it would have been easier to spend her final days at the hospital, without all these reminders around her.

But easier wasn't the point anymore. Time with her family was what mattered.

Now they were all in the house, scattering like soldiers to their different tasks. Marah had herded the boys into their room to watch television. Mom was busy making casseroles; Dad was probably mowing the lawn. That left Johnny, Tully, and Kate, making their way down the hallway toward the guest room, which had been redecorated for her homecoming.

"The docs wanted you in a hospital bed," Johnny said. "I've got one, too, see? We'll be like Ricky and Lucy in our twin beds."

"Of course." She'd meant to sound matter-of-fact, to simply acknowledge what they both knew: soon she would have trouble sitting up and the bed would help, but her voice betrayed her. "Y-you painted," she said to her husband. The last time she'd seen this room it had been barn-red with white trim and red and blue furniture—a casual, beachy look with lots of painted antique pieces and shells in glass bowls. Now it was pale green, almost celery-colored, with rose accents. Family photos were everywhere, in white porcelain frames.

Tully stepped forward. "Actually, I did it."

"Something to do with shysters," Johnny said.

"Chakras," Tully corrected him. "It's stupid, I'm sure, but . . ." She shrugged. "I did a show on it once. Couldn't hurt."

Johnny carried Kate to her bed and tucked her in. "The bathroom down here is all set up for you. Everything has been installed—railings and a shower seat and all the stuff they recommended. A hospice nurse will be coming by . . ."

She wasn't sure when she closed her eyes. All she knew was that she was sleeping. Somewhere a radio was playing "Sweet Dreams (Are Made of This)" and she could hear people talking in the distance. Then Johnny was kissing her and telling her she was beautiful and talking about the vacations they would someday take.

She awoke with a start. The room around her was dark now; she'd slept through the remaining daylight hours, obviously. Beside her, a eucalyptus-scented candle burned. The darkness lulled her for a moment, made her think she was alone.

Across the room, a shadow moved. Someone breathed.

Kate hit the button on her bed and moved to a sit. "Hey," she said.

"Hey, Mom."

She grew accustomed to the darkness and saw her daughter, sitting in a chair in the corner. Although Marah looked tired, she was so beautiful that Kate felt a cinching in her chest. Being home again made her see everything and everyone with perfect clarity, even in this gray darkness. When she looked at her teenage daughter, with her long black hair kept out of her eyes with little girl barrettes, she glimpsed the whole arc of life—the child she'd been, the girl she was, the woman she'd become.

"Hey, baby girl." She smiled and leaned sideways to turn on the bed-side lamp. "But you aren't my baby anymore, are you?"

Marah stood up and moved forward, twisting her hands together. For all of her grown-up beauty, the fear in her eyes made her look ten years old again.

Kate tried to figure out what she should say. She knew how much Marah wanted everything to be normal, but it simply wasn't. From now on the words they said to each other would be weighted, remembered. That was a simple fact of life. Or of death.

"I've been mean to you," Marah said.

Kate had waited years for this moment, actually dreamed of it in the days when she and Marah had been at war; now she saw it from a distance and knew that those battles were just ordinary life—a girl trying to grow up and a mother trying to hang on. She'd give anything for another fight, actually; it would mean they had time.

"I was a bitch to grandma, too. That's what teen girls do: rag on their mothers. And your Aunt Tully was a bitch to everyone."

Marah made a sound that was half snort, half laughter, and pure relief. "I won't tell her you said that."

"Believe me, honey, it will come as no surprise to her. And I want you to know something: I'm proud of your big personality and spirit. It will take you far in this life." On those last words, she saw her daughter's eyes fill with tears. Kate opened her arms and Marah leaned down to her, pulling her into a fierce embrace.

Kate could have held on forever, that was how good it felt. For years, Marah's hugs had been perfunctory at best, or a reward for getting her way. This was the real thing. When Marah drew back she was crying. "Remember when you used to dance with me?"

"When you were really little, I'd hold on and twirl you around until you giggled. Once I did it so long you threw up all over me."

"We shouldn't have stopped," Marah said. "I shouldn't have, I mean."

"None of that," Kate said. "Put down the bed rail and sit by me."

Marah struggled with the rail, but finally got it down. She climbed into the bed and pulled her knees up.

"How's James?" Kate asked.

"I'm into Tyler now."

"And is he a nice boy?"

Marah laughed at that. "He's totally hot, if that's what you mean. He asked me to the junior prom. Can I go?"

"Of course you can. But you'll have a curfew."

Marah sighed. Some habits were in the teen DNA; the disappointed sigh, it seemed, simply couldn't be overcome, not even by cancer. "Okay."

Kate stroked her daughter's hair, knowing she should say something profound here, something that would be remembered, but nothing extraordinary came to her. "Did you apply for a summer job at the theater?"

"I'm not gonna work this summer. I'll be home."

"You can't put your life on hold, honey," Kate said quietly. "That's not how this is going to work. You said a summer job would help you get into USC anyway."

Marah shrugged, looked away. "I decided to go to UW, like you and Aunt Tully."

Kate worked to keep her voice level, to imply that this was simply an ordinary teen/parent talk and not a glimpse of the rocky future. "The USC drama school is the best around."

"You don't want me that far away."

That was true. Kate had gone out of her way to tell her defiant daughter that California was too far away and that drama was not a smart major.

"I don't want to talk about college," Marah said, and Kate let it go for now.

Their conversation drifted into other ports. For the next hour, they just talked. Not about It, the big thing on the horizon and how it would change them all. Instead they talked about boys and writing and the movies that were out.

"I got the lead in the summer play," Marah said after a while. "I wasn't going to try out because you were sick, but Daddy said I should."

"I'm glad you did. I know you'll be amazing."

Marah launched into a long monologue about the play, the costumes, and her part. "I can't wait for you to see it." Her eyes widened in realization of what she'd said, the subject she'd unintentionally broached. She slid off the bed, looking desperate to change the subject. "I'm sorry."

Kate reached up and touched her cheek. "It's okay. I'll be there."

Marah stared down at her. They both knew it could end up being a broken promise. "Remember when I was in middle school and Ashley stopped being my friend and I didn't know why?"

"Of course."

"You took me out to lunch and it was like we were friends."

Kate swallowed hard, tasting the bitterness of tears in the back of her throat. "We've always been friends, Marah. Even when we didn't know it."

"I love you, Mom."

"I love you, too."

Marah wiped her eyes and bolted out of the room, closing the door quietly behind her.

It opened a moment later, so fast Kate barely had time to wipe her eyes before she heard Tully say, "I've got a plan."

Kate laughed, grateful to be reminded that life could still be funny and surprising, even now. "You always do."

"Will you trust me?"

"To my everlasting ruination, yes."

Tully helped maneuver Kate into the wheelchair and wrapped her in blankets.

"Are we going to the North Pole?"

"We're going outside," Tully answered, opening the French doors that led out to the deck. "Are you warm enough?"

"I'm sweating. Grab that pouch off the nightstand, will you?"

Tully grabbed the pouch, dropped it in Kate's lap, and then took control of the wheelchair.

The yard on this cool June night was stunningly, unexpectedly beautiful. Stars blanketed the sky and cast pinpricks of light onto the jet-black

Sound. A full moon hung poised above the glittering distant city lights. The grassy lawn rolled down toward the water. Blue moonlight illuminated a trail of toys and bikes left on the side of the wide hard-packed dirt path that led to the beach.

Tully maneuvered her off the deck, down a wide wooden ramp that was a very new addition; then she paused. "Close your eyes."

"It's dark out, Tully. I hardly need—"

"I can't wait forever."

Kate laughed. "Fine. I'm doing it so you don't throw one of your tantrums."

"I do not throw tantrums. Now close your eyes and put your arms out from your sides, like an airplane's wings."

Kate closed her eyes and extended her arms.

Tully pushed the wheelchair over the bumpy bit of grass. There, at the lip of the slow hill that rolled down to the beach, she paused. "We're kids again," she whispered into Kate's ear. "It's the seventies and we've just sneaked out of your house and gotten our bikes." She began to push the chair forward; it went slowly, bumping over the uneven grass, dipping in potholes, and still Tully talked. "We're on Summer Hill, riding without our hands, laughing like crazy people, thinking we're invincible."

Kate felt the breeze along her bare head, tugging at her ears, making her eyes water. She could smell the evergreen trees and rich, black earth. She put her head back and laughed. For a moment, just a heartbeat really, she was a kid again, on Firefly Lane with her best friend beside her, believing she could fly.

When the ride was over and they were on the beach, she opened her eyes and looked up at Tully. In that moment, that one poignant smile, she remembered everything about them. The starlight looked like fireflies, falling down around them.

Tully helped her into one of the beach chairs, and then sat down beside her.

They sat side by side, as they'd done so often in the past, talking about nothing that mattered, this and that.

Kate glanced back at the house, saw that no one was on the deck, and leaned toward Tully, whispering, "Do you really want to feel like a kid again?"

"No, thanks. I wouldn't change places with Marah for the world. All that angst and drama."

"Yeah, you're a real drama-free zone." Grinning at her own wit, Kate dug into the purple pouch on her lap and pulled out a fat white doobie. At Tully's awestruck expression, Kate laughed and lit up. "I have a prescription."

The sweet, strangely old-fashioned scent of marijuana mingled with the tangy sea air. A cloud of smoke darted between them and disappeared.

"You are totally bogarting the joint," Tully said, and they both laughed again. Just that word—*bogart*—sent them spiraling back to the seventies.

They passed it back and forth and kept talking, giggling. They were so caught up in *then* that neither of them heard footsteps coming up behind them.

"I turn my back on you girls for ten minutes and you're smoking pot." Mrs. Mularkey stood there, dressed in faded jeans and a sweatshirt from the nineties—maybe even the eighties—her snow-white hair in a lopsided, scrunchied ponytail. "You know that leads to worse things, don't you? Like the crack or LSD."

Tully tried not to laugh; she really did. "Just say no to crack."

"That's a lesson I tried to teach Marah in choosing her pants," Kate said, giggling.

Mrs. M. pulled up another Adirondack chair and positioned it beside Kate. Then she sat down and angled toward her.

For a moment they all sat there, staring at one another while smoke drifted into the air.

"Well?" Mrs. M. finally said. "I taught you to share, didn't I?"

"Mom!"

Mrs. M. waved her hand. "You girls from the seventies think you're so cool. Let me tell you, I was around for the sixties, and you've got nothing on me." She took the joint and put it in her mouth, taking a long, deep drag, holding it, and blowing it out. "Hell, Katie, how do you think I got through the teen years when my two girls were sneaking out of the house at night and riding their bikes in the dark?"

"You knew about that?" Tully said.

Kate laughed. "You said it was booze that got you through."

"Oh," Mrs. M. said. "That, too."

At one o'clock in the morning they were in the kitchen raiding the refrigerator when Johnny walked in and noticed the pile of junk food on the counter. "Someone has been smoking pot."

"Don't tell my mom," Kate said.

At that, her mom and Tully burst out laughing.

Kate leaned back in her wheelchair, grinning loopily up at her husband. Cast in the pale and distant light from the hallway, wearing his drugstore bifocals and an old Rolling Stones T-shirt, he looked like a hip professor. "I hope you've come to join the party."

He moved toward her, bent down, and whispered, "How about a private party?"

She put her arms around his neck. "You read my mind."

He scooped her into his arms, said goodnight to everyone, and carried her to their new room. She hung on tightly, her face buried in the crook of his neck, and smelled the last hint of aftershave he'd put on this morning. It was the cheap stuff the kids gave him every Christmas.

In the bathroom, he helped her to the toilet and let himself be her crutch as she brushed her teeth and washed her face. By the time she was dressed for bed, she was exhausted. She hobbled slowly across the room, clutching Johnny's arm. Halfway there, he swept her up again and carried her to bed, tucking her in. "I don't know how I can sleep without you in bed with me," she said.

"I'm right there. Ten feet away. If you need me in the night, just yell."

She touched his face. "I always need you. You know that."

His face crumpled at that; she saw the toll her cancer had taken on him. He looked old. "And I need you." He leaned down and kissed her forehead.

That scared her more than it should have; the forehead kiss was for old people and strangers. She grabbed his hand, said desperately, "I won't break."

Slowly, still looking at her, he kissed her lips, and for a glorious moment, time and tomorrow fell away. It was just them; when he drew back, she felt colder.

If only there was something they could say; words that would ease them over this bumpy road.

"Goodnight, Katie," he said at last, and turned away from her.

"'Night," she whispered back, watching him go to his own bed.

CHAPTER
THIRTY-SIX

For the next week Kate soaked in the early summer sun; her days were spent huddled under her treasured afghans in a chair by the beach, writing furiously in her journal, or talking with her kids or her husband or Tully. Evenings were taken up by conversation; Lucas and William told the longest, most run-on stories in the world. By the end of them, everyone was laughing. Afterward, the adults sat around the fire. More and more often they talked about the old days, back when they'd been too young to know that they were young, when the whole world had seemed open to them and dreams were as easy to pick as daisies. The funniest part of all was watching Tully try to take over the household duties. She burned dinners, bitched about an island world where no one delivered food to your home, ruined laundry, and repeatedly received instructions about how to operate the vacuum. Kate especially loved it when she heard her friend mutter, "This at-home shit is *hard*. Why didn't you ever tell me? No wonder you looked tired for fifteen years."

In any other circumstances it would have been the time of Kate's life. For once she was the center of attention.

But no matter how hard they all tried to be normal, their life was a dirty window that couldn't be wiped clean. Everything, every moment, was coated by illness. As always, it fell to Kate to lead the way, to be the smiling, optimistic one. They were all okay as long as she remained strong and resilient. Then they could talk and laugh and carry on the pretense of ordinary life.

It was exhausting, all this propping up of their feelings, but what choice did she have? Sometimes when the burden was too great she upped her pain meds and curled up with Johnny on the couch and simply fell asleep. When she woke up, invariably she was ready to smile again.

Sunday mornings were especially overwhelming. Today, everyone was here—Mom, Dad, Sean and his girlfriend, Tully, Johnny, Marah and the twins. They took turns telling stories so that there was rarely a lull in the conversation.

Kate listened and nodded and smiled and pretended to eat, even though she was nauseous and in pain.

It was Tully who noticed. In the process of passing the quiche Mom had made, she looked up at Kate, said, "You look like shit."

They all agreed.

Kate tried to make a joke, but her mouth was too dry to form words.

Johnny swept her out of her chair and carried her to her room.

When she was back in bed, medicated again, she stared up at her husband.

"How is she?" Tully said, coming into the room, standing beside Johnny.

Kate saw them there, together, shoulder to shoulder, and loved them so much it hurt. As always there was a pinch of jealousy, too, but that was as familiar to her as the beat of her heart.

"I was hoping to feel good enough to go shopping with you," Kate said. "I wanted to help Marah pick out her prom dress. You'll have to do it, Tully." She tried to smile. "Nothing too revealing, okay? And watch out for the shoes. Marah thinks she can wear high heels, but I worry . . ." Kate frowned. "Are you two listening to me?"

Johnny smiled at Tully. "Did you say something?"

Tully put a hand to her chest in a Scarlett O'Hara protestation of innocence. "Me? You know how rarely I talk. People often say I'm too quiet."

Kate maneuvered her bed up to a sit. "What's with the comedy act? I'm trying to tell you something important."

The doorbell rang. "Who could that be?" Tully said. "I'll go check."

Marah poked her head in the room. "They're here. Is she ready?"

"Who is here? Am I ready for what?" No sooner had the words left Kate's mouth than the parade into her room began. First came a man in coveralls, pushing a rolling rack full of floor-length gowns. Next, Marah and Tully and Mom crowded into the small space.

"Okay, Dad," Marah said. "No boys allowed."

Johnny kissed Kate's cheek and left the room.

"The only good thing about being rich and famous," Tully said, "well, there are *lots* of good things about it, but one of the best is that if you call Nordstrom's and say please send me every prom dress you have in sizes four through six, they do it."

Marah came to the side of the bed. "I couldn't pick out my first prom dress without you, Mom."

Kate didn't know if she wanted to laugh or cry, so she did both.

"Don't worry," Tully said. "I explicitly told the saleswoman to leave the skanky dresses in the store."

At that, they all laughed.

As the weeks passed, Kate felt herself weakening. Despite her best efforts and her purposely optimistic attitude, her body began to fail in a dozen little ways. A word she couldn't find, a sentence she couldn't finish, a trembling weakness in her fingers that wouldn't still, a nausea that all too often became unbearable, and the cold. She was always chilled to the bone.

And then there was the pain. By late July, when the nights began to grow longer and had the sweet sultry taste of a ripe peach, she had nearly doubled her morphine dosage and no one cared. As her doctor said, "Addiction isn't your problem now."

She was a good enough actress that no one seemed to notice how weak she was becoming. Oh, they knew she had to use the wheelchair to get to the beach, and that she often fell asleep well before the nightly movie started, but in these days of summer, the household was in a constant state of flux. Tully had taken over Kate's daytime routine as best she could, which left Kate time to work on her journal. Sometimes, lately, she worried that she wouldn't have time to finish it, and the thought scared her.

The funny thing was that dying didn't. Not so much anymore. Oh, she still had panic attacks when she thought about The End, but even those were becoming less frequent. More and more often, she just thought: *Let me rest.*

She couldn't say that, though. Even to Tully, who'd listen to her for hours and hours. Whenever Kate brought up the future, Tully flinched and made a smart-ass comment.

Dying was a lonely business.

"Mom?" Marah said quietly, pushing the door open.

Kate forced herself to smile. "Hi, honey. I thought you were going over to Lytle Beach today with the gang."

"I was going to."

"What changed your mind?"

Marah stepped forward. For a moment, Kate was disoriented by the sight of her own daughter; she'd had a growth spurt again. At almost six feet, she was filling out, too, becoming a woman before Kate's eyes. "I need to do something."

"Okay. What is it?"

Marah turned around, looked down the hall, then back to Kate. "Could you come into the living room?"

Kate's desire to say no swelled, almost overtook her, but she said "Of course," and put on her robe, mittens, and knitted cap. Fighting nausea and exhaustion, she got slowly out of bed.

Marah took her by the arm and steadied her, becoming for a moment the mother; she led her into the living room, where, despite the heat of the day, a fire burned in the fireplace. Lucas and William, still in their jammies, sat together on the couch.

"Hi, Mommy," they said at once, flashing their gap-toothed grins.

Marah positioned Kate next to the boys, tucked her robe around her legs, and then sat down on the other side of her.

Kate smiled. "This is like those plays you used to stage when you were little."

Marah nodded and snuggled in close to her. When she looked at Kate, though, she wasn't smiling. "A long time ago," she said in an unsteady voice, "you gave me a special book."

"I gave you lots of books."

"You told me that someday I'd be sad and confused and I'd need it."

Kate wanted to pull away suddenly, distance herself, but she was held in place by her children. "Yes," was all she could say.

"For the last few weeks, I've tried to read it a bunch of times and I couldn't."

"It's okay—"

"And I figured out why. We all need it." She reached over to the end table and picked up the paperback copy of *The Hobbit* Kate had given her. It felt like a lifetime ago now, the day she'd given this favorite novel to her daughter, passed it on. A lifetime ago, and an instant.

"Yippee!" William said. "Marah's gonna read to us."

Lucas elbowed his brother. "Shut up."

Kate put an arm around her boys and stared at her daughter's earnest, beautiful face. "Okay."

Marah leaned back, settled in close to Kate, and opened the book. Her voice was only a little wobbly at the start, but as the story took hold, she found her strength again. "In a hole in the ground, there lived a hobbit . . ."

August ended too quickly and melted into a lazy September. Kate tried to experience every moment of every day, but even with a positive outlook, there was no way to avoid the ugly truth: she was fading.

She clung to Johnny's arm and concentrated on her walking. One slippered foot in front of the other; keep breathing. She was so tired of being wheeled around in her chair, or carried like a child, but walking was more and more difficult. She had headaches, too; blistering ones that sometimes left her winded and unable to remember the people and things around her.

"Do you need your oxygen?" Johnny asked, bending close to her ear so the kids wouldn't hear.

"I sound like Lance Armstrong during the Tour de France." She tried to smile. "No, thanks."

He got her settled on the deck in her favorite chair and tucked the wool blanket around her. "Are you sure you'll be okay while we're gone?"

"Of course. Marah needs to get to rehearsal and the boys would hate to miss Little League. And Tully will be home any minute."

Johnny laughed. "I don't know. I can produce an entire documentary in the time it takes her to grocery-shop for one meal."

Kate smiled, too. "She is learning a lot of new skills."

After he left, the house behind her settled into an unfamiliar silence. She stared out at the glittering blue Sound and the tiara of a city on the opposite shore, remembering suddenly when she'd lived over there, near the Public Market; a young career girl with shoulder pads and cinch belts and slouch boots. That was when she first saw Johnny and tumbled into love. She still remembered so many of their moments—when he'd first kissed her and called her Katie and said he didn't want to hurt her.

Reaching into the bag at her side, she pulled out her journal and stared down at it, tracing the leather pattern on the cover. It was almost finished now. She'd written it all down, or as much as she could remember, and it had helped her as much as she'd hoped it would someday help her kids.

She opened to the page where she'd left off and began to write.

That's the funny thing about writing your life story. You start out trying to remember dates and times and names. You think it's about facts, your life; that what you'll look back on and remember are the successes and failures, the time line of your youth and middle age, but that isn't it at all.

Love. Family. Laughter. That's what I remember when it's all said and done. For so much of my life I thought I didn't do enough or want enough. I guess I can be forgiven my stupidity. I was young. I want my children to know how proud I am of them, and how proud I am of me. We were everything we needed—you and Daddy and I. I had everything I ever wanted.

Love.

That's what we remember.

She closed the journal. There was nothing more to say.

Tully came home from the grocery store feeling triumphant. She put the bags on the counter, emptied them one by one, then opened a can of beer and went outside.

"That grocery store is a jungle, Kate. I guess I went down the up lane, or in the out lane, I don't know. You'd have thought I was Public Enemy Number One. I never heard so much honking."

"We at-home moms don't have long to shop."

"I don't know how you did it all. I'm exhausted by ten o'clock every morning."

Kate laughed. "Sit."

"If I roll over and play dead do I get a biscuit?"

Kate handed her her journal. "You get this. First."

Tully drew in a sharp breath. For all of the summer, she'd seen Kate writing on these pages, at first quickly and easily, and gradually more slowly. In the last few weeks, everything had been slow going for her.

She sat down slowly—slumped, actually—unable to say anything past the lump in her throat. She knew it would make her cry, but it would make her soar, too. Reaching out, she held Kate's hand and then opened the journal to the first page.

A sentence jumped out at her.

The first time I saw Tully Hart, I thought: Wow! Look at those boobs.

Tully laughed and kept reading. Page after page.

We're sneaking out?

Of course. Get your bike. And: I'll just shave your eyebrows to give them shape . . . oops . . . that's not good . . .

Your hair is coming out . . . maybe I should read the directions again . . .

Laughing, Tully turned to her. These words, these memories had, for a glorious moment, made everything normal. "How could you be friends with me?"

Kate smiled back. "How could I not?"

Tully felt like an imposter as she slipped into Kate and Johnny's bed. She knew it made sense, her being in this room, but on this night it felt more wrong than usual. Reading the journal had reminded Tully of everything she had with Kate; everything they were losing.

Finally, sometime after three, she fell into a fitful sleep. She dreamed of Firefly Lane, of two girls riding their bikes down Summer Hill at night. The wind smelled of freshly cut hay and the stars were bright.

Look, Katie, no hands.

But Kate wasn't there. Her empty bike clattered down the road, the white plastic streamers fluttering from the ends of the molded plastic grips.

Tully sat up, breathing hard.

Shaking, she got out of bed and put her robe on. Out in the hallway she passed dozens of mementos, photos of this life they'd shared for decades, and two closed bedroom doors. Behind them, the kids were asleep, probably suffering through similar dreams.

Downstairs, she made a cup of tea and went to the deck, where the cool dark air allowed her to breathe again.

"Bad dreams?"

Johnny's voice startled her. He was in one of the Adirondack chairs, looking up at her. In his eyes she saw the same sadness that filled every pore of her skin and cell of her body.

"Hey," she said, sitting in the chair beside his.

A cool breeze came off the Sound, whistling eerily above the familiar whooshing of the waves.

"I don't know how to do this," he said quietly.

"That's the same thing Katie said to me," she said, and just like that, the realization of how similar they were made Tully ache all over again. "It's quite a love story you two have."

He turned to her, and in the pale moonlight she saw the tense line of his jaw, the tightening around his eyes. He was holding it all in, trying so hard to be strong for all of them.

"You don't have to do it with me, you know," she said quietly.

"Do what?"

"Be strong."

The words seemed to release something in him. Tears shone in his eyes; he crumpled forward, saying nothing; silently his shoulders shook.

She reached out and took his hand, held it tightly while he cried.

"For twenty years, every time I turn around, you two are together."

Tully and Johnny both turned.

Kate stood in the open doorway behind them, bundled up in a huge terrycloth robe. Bald and impossibly thin, she looked like a child playing dress-up in her mother's clothes. She'd said things like this to both of them before; they all knew it, but this time she was smiling. She looked somehow both sad and peaceful.

"Katie," Johnny said, his voice raw, his eyes shining. "Don't . . ."

"I love you both," she said, not moving toward them. "You'll comfort each other . . . take care of each other and the kids . . . after I'm gone—"

"Don't," Tully said, starting to cry.

Johnny was on his feet. He gently picked his wife up and kissed her for a long, long time.

"Take her up to your bed, Johnny," Tully said, trying to smile now. "I'll sleep in the guest room."

Johnny carried her upstairs with so much care she couldn't help thinking that she was sick. He put her on her side of the bed. "Turn on the fire."

"Are you cold?"

To the bone. She nodded and tried gingerly to sit up as he crossed the room and flicked the switch for the gas fireplace. With a whoosh, blue and orange flames shot up from the fake log, tinting the dark room with a soft golden light.

When he came back and settled in beside her, she reached up slowly, traced the outline of his lips with the tip of her finger. "You first ravished me on the floor in front of a fire, remember?"

He smiled; like a blind woman, she felt his lips curve with the sensitive pad of her finger. "If I remember correctly, you were doing the ravishing."

"And what if I wanted to ravish you now?"

He looked so scared that she wanted to laugh, but it wasn't funny. "Can we?"

He took her in his arms. She knew they were both thinking that she'd lost so much weight there was almost nothing left of her.

Nothing left of her.

She closed her eyes and tightened her hold around his neck.

The bed seemed so big suddenly, like a sea of soft white cotton compared to the bed downstairs that had become hers.

Slowly, Kate took off her robe and peeled out of her nightgown, trying not to notice how white and sticklike her legs were. Even worse was the battlefield that had been her breasts. She looked ruined, like a little boy, only there were the scars.

Johnny stripped out of his clothes, kicked them aside, and climbed back into bed beside her, drawing the covers up to their hips.

Her heart was thumping hard as she looked at him.

"You're so beautiful," he said, and leaned forward to kiss her scars.

Relief and love cracked her open inside. She kissed him, her breath coming hard and ragged already. In their twenty years of marriage they'd made love thousands of times, and it was always great, but this was different; they had to be so gentle. She knew he was terrified of breaking her bones. She hardly remembered later how it had all happened, how she'd come to be on top of him; all she knew was that she needed every part of him, and everything that she was, that she'd ever been, was irrevocably tied up with this man. When he finally entered her, slow and easy, filling her, she came down to meet him, and in that glorious second, she was whole again. She bent down and kissed him, tasting his tears.

He cried out her name so loudly she silenced him with her palm; if she'd had any breath left she would have laughed at his outburst and whispered, *The kids!*

But her own orgasm, seconds later, made her forget everything except the pleasure of this sensation.

Finally, smiling, feeling young again, she snuggled up against him. He put an arm around her and pulled her close. They lay there a long time, half sitting against the mound of pillows, watching the firelight, saying nothing.

Then, quietly, Kate said what had been on her mind for a long time. "I can't stand to think of you alone."

"I won't ever be alone. We've got three kids."

"You know what I mean. I'd understand if you and Tully—"

"Don't." He looked at her finally, and in the eyes she knew as well as her own she saw a pain so deep she wanted to weep.

"It was always you. Just you, Katie. Tully was a one-night stand, a long time ago. I didn't love her then and I never have. Not for a second. You're my heart and soul. My world. How can you not know that?"

She saw the truth in his face, heard it in the tremble in his voice, and she was ashamed of herself. She should have known this all along. "I do know that. I'm just so worried about you and the kids. I hate to think . . ."

This conversation was like swimming through acid; it burned through flesh and bone. "I know, baby," he said finally. "I know."

CHAPTER THIRTY-SEVEN

The day of the summer play dawned crisp and clear. A beautiful Northwest autumn afternoon. Kate wanted to help Marah prepare for the big event, but she was too weak to do much. Smiling took effort. The pain behind her eyes was constant now, like the bleating beat of an alarm clock that couldn't be turned off.

And so Kate handed over her duties to Tully, who performed them like a champ.

Kate slept through most of it. By the time night had fallen, she was as rested as she could be and ready to face the challenge of what lay ahead.

"Are you sure you're up to this?" Tully asked at six forty-five.

"I'm ready. Maybe you should put some makeup on me so I don't scare little kids."

"I thought you'd never ask. And I brought you a wig to wear—if you want it."

"I'd love it. I would have thought of it myself if I had any brain cells left." She reached for her oxygen mask and took a few hits.

Tully left the room and returned with her makeup kit.

Kate angled her bed up and closed her eyes. "This feels like the old days."

Tully talked as she worked her magic, penciling on eyebrows, gluing on lashes. Kate let herself be carried away on the tide of her friend's voice. "I have a gift, you know. Do you have a razor?"

Kate meant to laugh. Maybe she even did.

"Okay," Tully finally said. "Time to try on the wig."

Kate blinked, realizing she'd fallen asleep, and grinned. "Sorry about that."

"Don't worry about me. I love it when people fall asleep while I'm talking."

Kate pulled the stocking cap off her head and the mittens off her hands. She was always freezing cold.

Tully put the wig on, positioned it, then helped Kate dress in a black wool dress with tights and boots. In the wheelchair, they wrapped her in blankets, then Tully wheeled her over to the mirror. "Well?"

She stared at her reflection—pale, thin face with eyes that looked huge beneath the drawn-on eyebrows, brightly blond shoulder-length hair, perfectly red lips. "Great," she said, hoping she sounded honest.

"Good," Tully said. "Let's round the troops up and go."

A half an hour later, they pulled up to the auditorium. They were so early that no other cars were yet in the parking lot.

Perfect.

Johnny put Kate in the wheelchair, covered her in blankets, and led the way to the front doors.

Inside, they took up most of the first row, saving places for the rest of the family; Kate's wheelchair was positioned on the end of the aisle.

"I'll be back in thirty minutes with your folks and the boys," Johnny said to Kate. "Do you need anything else?"

"No."

When he was gone, she and Tully sat in the shadows of the empty auditorium. Kate shivered and tightened the blankets around her. Her head was pounding and she felt sick to her stomach. "Talk to me, Tully. About anything."

Tully didn't miss a beat. She started talking about yesterday's rehearsal, then went on to her troubles with the carpool protocol.

Kate closed her eyes, and suddenly they were kids again, sitting by the Pilchuck River, wondering how their lives would unfold.

We'll be TV journalists. Someday I'll tell Mike Wallace that I couldn't have done it without you.

Dreams. They'd had so many of them, and a surprising number had come true. The funny thing was that she hadn't valued them all highly enough when she'd had the chance.

Leaning back in her seat, she said quietly, "Do you still know the guy who runs the drama program at USC?"

"I do." Tully looked at her. "Why?"

Kate felt Tully's scrutiny on her profile. Without making eye contact, she straightened her wig. "Maybe you could call him. Marah would love to go there." With the words came the thought: *I won't be there for her.* For any of it. Marah would go off to college without her . . .

"I thought you didn't want her to be in the arts."

"It scares the hell out of me to think of my baby in Hollywood. But you're a TV star. Her dad's a news producer. The poor kid is surrounded by dreamers. What chance did she ever have?" She reached over, squeezed Tully's hand. More than anything, she wanted to look at Tully, but she couldn't do it, didn't dare. "You'll watch out for her and the boys, right?"

"Always."

Kate felt the start of a smile; that one word released a little of her sadness. One thing about Tully: she kept her word. "And maybe you'll look up Cloud again."

"It's funny you'd mention that. I was planning on it. Someday."

"Good," Kate said softly but firmly. "Chad was right, and I was wrong about that. When you get . . . to the end, you see that love and family are all there is. Nothing else matters."

"You're my family, Katie."

"I know. You'll need more after—"

"Please don't say it."

Kate looked at her friend. Bold, brassy, larger-than-life Tully, who'd barreled through the years like a lion in a jungle, always the king. Now she was quiet, afraid. The very idea of Kate's death had unraveled her, made her smaller. "I'm going to die, Tully. Not saying it won't change it."

"I know."

"Here's what I want you to know: I loved my life. For so long I was waiting for it to start, waiting for *more*. It seemed like all I did was drive and shop and wait. But you know what? I didn't miss a thing with my family. Not a moment. I was there for all of it. That's what I'll remember, and they'll have each other."

"Yes."

"I'm worried about you, though," Kate said.

"You would be."

"You're afraid of love, but you've got so much of it to give."

"I know I've spent a lot of years whining about being alone, and I've had a history of hooking up with inappropriate or unavailable men, but the truth is my career has been my love, and mostly it's been enough. I've been happy. It's important to me that you know that."

Kate gave her a tired smile. "I'm proud of you, you know. Have I told you that often enough?"

"And I'm proud of you." Tully looked at her best friend, and in that one look, thirty plus years crowded in between them, reminded them both of the girls they'd been and the dreams they'd shared, and of the women they'd become. "We've done all right, haven't we?"

Before Kate could answer, the auditorium doors banged open and people streamed in.

Johnny, Mom, Dad, and the boys took their seats just as the house lights flickered.

Then the stage lights came on, the heavy red velvet curtains parted slowly, dragging across the wooden stage at their hem, and revealing the poorly painted set of a small town.

Marah walked onstage, dressed in a high school drama version of a nineteenth century gown.

When Marah began to speak, it was magic.

There was no other word for it.

Kate felt Tully's hand close over hers, squeeze gently. When Marah walked offstage, to a standing ovation, Kate's heart swelled with pride. She leaned against Tully and whispered, "Now I know why I gave her your middle name."

Tully turned to her. "Why?"

Kate tried to smile, but couldn't. It took almost a full minute before she could find enough voice to say, "Because she's the best of both of us."

The end came on a bleak and rainy October night. With everyone she loved standing around her bed, she said goodbye to them one by one, whispering one last special thing to each of them. Then, as rain hit the window and darkness fell, she closed her eyes for the last time.

Kate's last To Do list concerned her funeral and Tully followed it to the letter. The Catholic church on the island was filled with photographs and flowers and friends. Not surprisingly, Kate had chosen Tully's favorite flowers rather than her own.

For days Tully focused on nothing else. She handled the details and took care of everything while the Ryans and the Mularkeys sat together on the beach, holding hands and occasionally remembering to talk.

Tully prepared herself for the day, as well, reminding herself that she was a professional; she could smile her way through anything.

But when the time came, and they actually pulled up in front of the church, she panicked. "I can't do this," she said.

Johnny reached for her hand. She waited for comforting words, but he had none.

While they sat there in silence, with the kids in the backseat, all of them staring at the church, the Mularkeys pulled up beside them and parked.

It was time. Like a flock of black crows, they came together, hoping for strength in numbers. Holding hands, they walked past the throng of mourners and up the massive stone church steps and into the church.

"We're in the left front row," Mrs. M. said, sidling close.

Tully looked down at Marah, who was crying quietly, and the sight broke her.

She wanted to comfort her goddaughter, tell her it would be okay, but they both knew better than that. "She loved you so much," she said, getting a strange and sudden glimpse of their future then. They'd be friends someday, she and Marah. In time, Tully would give her the journal and they'd share the stories of who her mother had been, and those stories would bind them together and bring Kate back for a few precious moments.

"Come on," Johnny said.

Tully couldn't move. "You guys go up. I'm just going to stand here for a minute."

"Are you sure?"

"I'm sure."

Johnny squeezed her shoulder and then ushered the boys and Marah forward. Mr. and Mrs. M., Sean, Georgia, and the rest of the family followed; they all ducked into the front row and sat down.

Up front an organ began to play a slow, plodding version of "You and Me Against the World."

Tully didn't want to be here for this. She didn't want to listen to pathetic music that was designed to make you cry, or listen to the priest tell stories about the woman he'd known, who was only a shadow of the woman Tully knew. Most of all, she didn't want to see the montage of pictures of Kate's life splashed on a giant screen above her coffin.

Before she could even think about it, she turned and walked out.

Sweet, fresh air filled her lungs. She gulped it greedily, trying to calm down. Behind her, through the door, she heard the music change to "One Sweet Day."

She closed her eyes, leaning back against the door.

"Ms. Hart?"

Startled, she opened her eyes and saw the funeral director standing on the bottom step. She'd met him once before, when she'd brought clothes for the burial and pictures for the montage. "Yes."

"Mrs. Ryan asked me to give you this." He held out a big black box.

"I don't understand."

"She entrusted me with this box and asked me to give it to you on the day of her funeral. She said you'd be standing out front when it started."

Tully smiled at that, even though it hurt like hell. Of course Kate would know. "Thanks."

She took the box and walked down the steps and across the parking lot. Across the street, she sat down on an iron park bench.

There, she took a deep breath and opened the box. On top lay a letter. Kate's bold, left-slanted handwriting was unmistakable.

Dear Tully—

I know you won't be able to stand my fucking funeral. You're not the star. I hope you at least had the photos of me airbrushed. There are so many things I should say to you, but in our lifetime we've said them all.

Take care of Johnny and the kids for me, okay? Teach the boys how to be gentlemen and Marah how to be strong. When they're ready, give them my journal and tell them about me when they ask. The truth, too. I want them to know it all.

It's going to be hard on you, now. That's one of the things I regret the most. So, here's what I have to say in my beyond-the-grave letter (very dramatic, don't you think?):

I know you'll be thinking that I left you, but it's not true. All you have to do is remember Firefly Lane, and you'll find me.

There will always be a TullyandKate.

It was signed:

BFF ♥
Kate

She pressed the letter to her chest.

Then she looked down in the box again. There were three things left.

A Virginia Slims cigarette with a yellow sticky note on it that read, *Smoke me*.

An autographed picture of David Cassidy that said, *Kiss me*, and an iPod with headphones that said, *Play me and dance*.

Tully laughed through her tears and lit up the cigarette, taking a drag and coughing on the exhale. The smell of smoke immediately made her think of their nights on the banks of the Pilchuck River, lying against fallen logs, staring up at the Milky Way.

She closed her eyes, put her head back, and tilted her face to the cool autumn sun. A breeze touched her face and tangled in her hair, and with it, she thought: *Katie*.

Suddenly she felt her friend beside her, above her, all around her, inside her. She heard Kate in the whispering of the wind overhead and the skudding of the golden leaves across the pavement.

She opened her eyes, gasping at the certainty that she wasn't alone.

"Hey, Katie," she whispered, then put on the headphones and hit play.

"Dancing Queen" blared out at her, sweeping her back in time.

Young and sweet, only seventeen.

She stood up, unsure of whether she was laughing or crying. All she really knew was that she wasn't alone, that Kate wasn't gone. They'd had more than three decades of good times and bad times and everything in between, and nothing could take that away. They had the music and the memories, and in those, they would always, always be together.

Best friends forever.

There, standing in the middle of the street, all by herself, she started to dance.

Dear Reader,

In the two decades of my writing career, I have never before been tempted to add any kind of postscript or letter to a novel, and truthfully, I tried to avoid it here. As you can plainly see, that plan failed miserably. The problem, it seems, is the book you've just read.

As you may or may not be able to tell, the writing of Firefly Lane was a very personal journey for me. I grew up in the late seventies in western Washington, a place and time that felt oh-so-dangerous and turbulent back then and now seems sweetly innocent in comparison to today's world. I went to the University of Washington and joined a sorority. All of the music mentioned throughout the story reminds me of those long-gone days. Goodbye Yellow Brick Road was the first album I bought with my own money.

And I lost my mother to breast cancer. Like so many women, I have spent a lifetime being on the lookout for danger signs. I do my self-exams and have my yearly mammograms; I do everything I'm supposed to do.

That's why inflammatory breast cancer, or IBC, is so frightening. It presents in sly and unexpected ways. Often family physicians overlook or misdiagnose the symptoms, and as we all know, when it comes to cancer, timing is everything. So I want to urge women to add the IBC warning signs to their list of symptoms to look for, and I'd add that if something feels wrong, don't be afraid to ask questions or get second opinions. We women know our bodies; we know when something doesn't feel or look right. We need to embrace our knowledge of ourselves and not take no for an answer.

I know it can be scary and difficult, but fear is no excuse to turn away. If you find yourself hesitating, or giving in to your fear, look to a friend for help and support. That's the best thing about being a woman—we're always there for each other. As Tully and Kate would say: no matter what.

Thank you for reading.

Kristin

FIREFLY LANE

by Kristin Hannah

About the Author

- In Her Own Words

Behind the Novel

- A Trip Down "Memory Lane"
- Kate and Tully's Letters
- Kristin Hannah and Her Readers
- And more!

Keep on Reading

- Recommended Reading
- Reading Group Questions

For more reading group suggestions
visit www.readinggroupgold.com

ST. MARTIN'S GRIFFIN

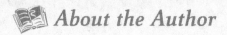

In Her Own Words

I was born in Southern California and grew up at the beach, making sand castles and playing in the surf. But my parents were adventurers, and when I was about eight years old, they decided to follow the call of the wild, and thus began the journey to the blue and green majesty of the Pacific Northwest. We headed up the Coast Highway in a VW bus, with my brother and sister and I singing songs and arguing in the back seat—pretty much like all family vacations everywhere, I think. Even as a young girl, I remember being amazed by the towering trees and the blue, blue sky.

I definitely grew up as a Northwest girl. Like Kate and Tully, I went to the University of Washington and studied communications. Afterward, I went on to law school.

It was then, while studying law, that my life was turned on its head. My mother was diagnosed with breast cancer. On one of my daily visits to her hospital bedside, she said the words that would change my life: "I know you think you love the law, but really you're going to be a writer."

A writer??? I was at the tail end of seven years of college, poised to be a lawyer, and now my mom was telling me that writing was in my future? I didn't understand and certainly didn't believe, but because she did—and because it was a dark time and I was too young and there were questions I didn't want to face—we began working on a novel together. I still remember that as one of the best times of my life, and even of our relationship. I never got around to writing the book (I mean, I was going to be a lawyer, thank you very much), I had the bar exam to

> *"I think the dream of writing was as much my mom's own as it was her gift to me."*

study for. After my mom passed away, I boxed all the research material up and stored it in my closet.

Fate, apparently, considered me a slow learner, because a few years later, when I was married and pregnant with my son, I discovered that pregnancy was not going to be easy for me. At about fourteen weeks, I was put on bedrest by the doctor. Now, I'm not great at math, but let me tell you, that's a long time to lie down.

In no time, I'd read every book in the house and started asking my husband for cereal boxes to read; in short, I was a goner. That's when my darling husband reminded me of the book I'd started with my mom.

And there was everything I needed, right there in my closet. A last great gift from my mother. I pulled out the boxes of research material, dusted them off, and began writing. By the time my son was born, I'd finished a first draft and found an obsession.

All these years later, as I approach the age my mother was when she was diagnosed, I see the magic of it all. I know why she saw the writer's temperament in me, and why she knew me so well. I hope someday to give my son just one piece of advice that good (and to say it only once).

I think the dream of writing was as much my mom's own as it was her gift to me. In a lot of ways I feel I'm writing for both of us. And of all my novels, *Firefly Lane* is the one she would have loved the most.

It is absolutely the most personal of my novels, and as I'm sure is obvious to anyone who has read it, my mother's spirit was always by my side as I was writing. It is not often that I write a novel that has a message above and beyond the story itself. Generally, I strive to entertain my readers; hopefully to make them laugh a little and perhaps cry a little. With *Firefly Lane*, I had a deeper mission as well. I became aware that too many women of my generation didn't know about inflammatory breast cancer and how deadly it can be. I felt I was in a unique position to get the dialogue started, and I've been told by countless readers that this book made them aware of the danger. I've gotten many letters from women who have been helped by simply being made aware of IBC. Many of you have been prompted to get a checkup. When it comes to cancer, knowledge and early detection can save your life, and we all can make a difference. So thanks so much to all of you who have embraced this novel and passed it along to your best friend or your mother or your daughter. You're helping me get the message out there.

"It is, at its heart, a profoundly personal novel."

A Trip Down "Memory Lane"

Dear Readers,

I mentioned previously in this material that Firefly Lane
*would have been my mother's favorite novel of mine, and
here's why. This book, more than any other I've written,
hits close to home for me. It is, at its heart, a profoundly
personal novel. There are so many correlations to my own
life. First and foremost—the clothes. Yes, I remember
wearing them all—elephant-leg bell bottoms, tie-dyed
T-shirts, Earth shoes, shoulder pads, stirrup pants, leg
warmers, and last but not least—polyester. And how
about those hairstyles? Each one named after and
forever immortalized by the celebrity who made it
famous. These were the pictures we brought into our
small-town beauty salons and tried religiously to follow: the Marcia Brady center-part, long and straight;
the Farrah Fawcett; the Dorothy Hamill (this was for
my senior picture, in which I was in soft focus and
staring down at a rose); the horrifying asymmetrical
(am I the only one who remembers this???); the Linda
Evans; and last but by no means least, the Rachel.*

*Since I went to the University of Washington, I remem-
ber a lot of locations used in the book. Anyone interested
in a* Firefly Lane *memory lane tour should try: The Last
Exit coffee house (is it even still there?), Kells pub in
Pioneer Square, which is still a great time, Starbucks in
the Public Market, a ferry ride from Seattle to Bainbridge
Island, Goldie's tavern in the U District, Greek row at
the University of Washington (I'm sure you can still find
a ton of parties happening there on Saturday nights), and
the view of Seattle at night from Rockaway Beach.*

*As a little treat, I've also included some extra pages—
extra material, I guess you'd say—from* Firefly Lane.
They are some of the letters Kate and Tully wrote back

and forth to each other during their high school years in the seventies. This is just a sampling; there are more on KristinHannah.com, as well as my playlist for the novel. And please, once you check out the Web site, stick around and join me on the blog. I love hearing from readers.

Kristin Hannah

Kate and Tully's Letters

Dear Kate,

Your last letter cracked me up. I would have called, but I'm in lockdown again. Got caught smoking a doobie in the girl's bathroom. (Don't tell your mom—I know you won't.) This isn't like that time in the tenth grade. This time I wasn't even doing it. I was just there. That's the thing about Catholic girls' schools—they always expect the worst. When I got home my grandma was PISSED. Anyway, I'm on double restriction which means I can't even use the phone. It is totally bogus but there's nothing I can do. So, write lots and give me all the news that's fit to print. It'll be good practice for our future careers in TV news.

Friends 4 ever

Tully

p.s. Do you think I should go with Talullah for my professional name or make up something intelligent sounding?

Dear Tully,

At least you're doing stuff. Snohomish is the boringest place on Earth. NOTHING ever changes here. That's

*why everyone still talks about you. My curfew is ten
o'clock, even in the summer. I can't even stay up late
enough to watch the Bicentennial celebration. How
grody is that? I keep telling my mom she's making me
miss history but she just laughs. Man, next year is
going to blow chips. I wish you were here. I can't wait
'til we get our dorm room together. It'll rock. We'll
party hardy every night.*

*Mom's calling me down for dinner. Tuna Helper.
Again. I'd rather eat my own shoe.*

Best Friends 4 ever

Kate

*p.s. Do you think I really have a future career in TV
news???*

Dear Kate—

*Last night I snuck out of the house and met up with
some SENIOR boys from O'Dea. We saw Wings at the
Kingdome. It was the coolest night ever. I wish you'd
been there. I know Paul McCartney is old, but he's
still a stone cold fox. And Ted Frumm asked me out
while they played "Band on the Run." He's the captain of the football team. What should I do???*

Will write back soon, good buddy. 10-4.

Friends 4 ever,

Tully

*p.s. Of course you have a future in news. We're a team,
aren't we? And you're lucky your mom watches out for
you. Boys can be real jerks. The Bicentennial shit was
pretty lame anyway.*

Want to read more letters?
Visit www.KristinHannah.com.

Kristin Hannah and Her Readers

I have been lucky enough to be able to talk with dozens of book groups around the country, and I can honestly say that I learn something every time I do it. Here are some of the questions that come up often.

Q: What influenced you to want to write a novel about female friendship?

A: The truth is that I'd been longing to read a big, complex, emotional book about friendship for years. I wanted the story of my generation, as seen through the eyes of two women who had managed to stay friends for most of their lives. I kept waiting and waiting for someone else to write it, and I guess I finally got tired of waiting. I figured if I wanted to read it, I'd better write it.

As I've gotten older, I've really begun to see how profoundly important we women are to each other. As I said in the book, men and careers and even children can come and go in our lives, but our friendships are forever. That may sound a little flip, and it is, but there's a real thread of truth in it. Especially when I was maneuvering through the battlefield that comes when you're parenting a teenager...I really needed my friends to keep me laughing. And I wanted to write a kind of valentine to those friends.

Q: Why did you choose Seattle as the setting for *Firefly Lane*?

A: I chose Seattle because it's such a deep part of who I am. I've lived here for most of my life, and I've seen my little corner of the world change and grow. We've gone from a sleepy little REI-clad town to a glittering, dot com urban sprawl. So many of the places from my youth are gone now, and I wanted to remember the physical reminders of those bygone days. One of the best parts of writing this book was

"There's nothing like motherhood to make us reassess how we were as daughters."

remembering what Seattle used to be like. And while Kate and Tully are definitely Northwest girls, I hear from readers all across the country who relate to them. In the end, I really believe that we're all living versions of the same life.

Q: In a way, *Firefly Lane* is as much about mothers and daughters as it is about best friends. How did you use the differing female relationships to further the story?

A: Honestly, I believe that the mother-daughter relationship is magical, complex, transformative, potentially dangerous, and deeply powerful. We all are touched by this relationship and more than that, I believe we're formed by it. There's nothing like motherhood to make us reassess how we were as daughters. Obviously, that's a big part of *Firefly Lane*. Much of how Kate and Tully interact, indeed who they are at their deepest levels, is colored by the differences in how their mothers raised them.

One of my favorite parts of the novel is the circle of Kate's relationship with her mom. First we see her as an angry teenager, slamming the door in her mother's face...and then we see her as a mother, standing on the other side of that door. There's a real symmetry in that, a real reflection of how our lives unfold. I have often wished in the past few years that my mom were here to help me as I raised my own teenage son. As a girl, I thought I knew it all. Now I know I don't know much. And somewhere, my mom is laughing.

Q: A big component of *Firefly Lane* is the dichotomy of choices women face today. How do you balance the competing demands of motherhood and work?

A: I was very lucky to have landed in this career.

Kristin Hannah and Her Readers

What I love most about it is the opportunity it has afforded me to be both a stay-at-home mom and a working mom. For all the formative years in my son's life, I was able to be there for him—every class party and field trip and sporting event. I was always able to put down my writing and put my son first. Until, of course, he realized how embarrassing I was and begged me to stop putting him first. A moment I well remember coming to with my own mom.

There was a price to be paid for all that flexibility, of course. I couldn't write as fast as a lot of other writers, I couldn't travel to promote the books, and I had to miss a lot of social moments with friends, but in the end, I wouldn't have changed a thing. I was lucky to be able to drop him off at school and then come home and do work that fulfilled me. I feel extremely blessed. What I took away from having a foot in both camps, so to speak, is the knowledge that we women tend to feel that whatever we're doing, it's not quite enough. When I was at school, I sometimes worried that I should have been writing, and when I was writing, I often thought I wasn't "present" enough for my family. It's all a trade-off, I guess. That's one of my major themes in *Firefly Lane*—that we need to accept that we are good enough, that all we can do is our best. The whole supermom/super woman thing is an idea that needs to be retired. We're just women, and while we are super, we don't have super powers.

Q: Are you Kate or Tully?

A: While I would love to say that there's a little bit of Tully in me, I'm definitely more like Kate. I identified with her from the very beginning. Like me, she was a small-town girl who had to get up in the predawn hours to go feed her horses, who read *The Lord of the Rings* during every family camping trip,

"I was lucky to . . . do work that fulfilled me."

and who felt lost amid the masses at the sprawling University of Washington. All of that was me, to a great extent; thus, the problem in this book was for me to distance myself from Kate, to see her with some perspective.

Tully was much more problematic to write. I had a really difficult time understanding her. It took me a long time to get a handle on the way abandonment had shaped her. The truth is that I fell in love with Tully. I loved her ambition, her heart, her oversized desires and impossible dreams; I also felt sorry for her. She was so broken by her mother that for all of her grandiose ideas, she could never truly love herself, and therefore, she couldn't love or be loved by anyone else. Except Kate, who saw through all the drama and defenses and loved Tully anyway. And isn't that what a lasting friendship is about?

Q: Can you tell us a little bit about your next book?

A: My next novel, *True Colors* (turn to page 501 for an exclusive sneak peek!), is a complex, poignant portrait of a family in crisis. It's about sisters, betrayal, vengeance, sibling rivalry, honor, honesty, and ultimately what it means to be a family. Raised on a small horse farm in the Pacific Northwest, the Grey sisters have always been close. There's Winona, who has struggled with her weight for years, and yearns for her father's approval; and Vivi Ann, the beautiful, bright-eyed romantic for whom everything comes easily, her father's love most of all; and Aurora, the level-headed middle sister who sees everything too clearly. For years, the sisters have banded together against the cold, distant father who demands everything and gives nothing in return, but when impetuous Vivi Ann follows her heart, events are set in motion that will shake their family to its very foundation. Lies will be told,

Keep on Reading

hearts will be broken, and a man's life will hang in the balance.

I have to say I really adore the characters in this book. It's a big, dramatic story that's part family drama, part legal thriller, part love story, and altogether compelling.
I don't think you'll be able to put it down once you pick it up. Enjoy!

And one last note:

I have to admit that I came late to the whole Internet party. I was dragged kicking and screaming into the new millennium. With great reluctance (and more than a bit of whining), I updated my Web site and set about the task of blogging.

Who would have thought I'd enjoy it??? You could have knocked me over with a feather.

Another opportunity that has arisen out of the Web site has been the ability to "talk" to book groups (via speakerphone) during their meetings. It has been an absolute blast. I have met great women from all over the country—many of whom remember dancing to ABBA and dreaming about David Cassidy and drinking Boone's Farm. We talk about all kinds of things— writing, reading, the books themselves, and what it's like to be writer. So if you belong to a book group and you've chosen *Firefly Lane*, please jump on board the Web site and tell me you'd like to set up a book club phone chat with me. I can't promise to fulfill all the requests, but I will certainly do my best.

Thanks!

"I have met great women from all over the country."

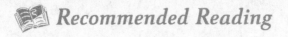

This is the fun part—getting to recommend books and tell you why I think you should be reading them. The only problem, of course, is that there are so many wonderful books out there and we all have only so much time. Still...here goes:

To Kill a Mockingbird by Harper Lee. Okay, okay, I know it's a no-brainer. But I honestly believe this is one of the best novels ever written. I love the prose, the characters, and the message. On top of all that, it's a story you can't put down.

The Prince of Tides by Pat Conroy. What can I say about this one that hasn't been said? Conroy is truly one of our greatest American writers. I love the lyricism of his voice and the poetry of his thoughts.

The Shadow of the Wind by Carlos Ruiz Zafón. Love, love, love this story. Gorgeous imagery, beautiful language, compelling characterizations, and a story that hooked me from page one. You can't do better than that.

It, The Stand, and *The Shining* by Stephen King. I'm a real fan of King's. I could have listed several more titles, but I figure that anyone who hasn't read him can start with these three and be hooked for good. The man just rocks the written word.

As I Lay Dying by William Faulkner. This is my favorite Faulkner novel, and that's really saying something. I love the way the beautiful language contrasts with the dark, gritty reality of the story. Also loved *The Sound and the Fury*, btw...

Turtle Moon by Alice Hoffman. This book just really resonated with me. Also, it was my first Alice Hoffman book. Her voice is absolutely beautiful and unlike anyone else's.

Middlemarch by George Eliot. I just read this recently—somehow I missed it in college, and although it took a while to get into it, once this story hooked me, it hooked me big time. Like Tolstoy's *Anna Karenina*, this novel is a substantial investment of time, but well worth the effort.

Harry Potter and the Deathly Hallows by J. K. Rowling. Obviously, when I chose this book, I mean the whole of the series. I loved every segment of Harry's journey, but the final novel knocked my socks off. As a reader, I was captivated and saddened and elated; as a writer, I was awed and humbled. I can't recommend these books highly enough.

The Lord of the Rings by J. R. R. Tolkien. The novel of my youth, period. You'll see it play a part in *Firefly Lane*, particularly because of its impact on me.

One Hundred Years of Solitude by Gabriel García Márquez. This is simply a beautiful, mesmerizing, original novel—and there's nothing simple about any of that.

The Witching Hour and *Interview with the Vampire* by Anne Rice. Fabulously conceived, beautifully written, and ultimately compelling, these are my favorite two Rice books.

Romeo and Juliet by William Shakespeare. No list of must-reads is complete without the ultimate wordsmith. This is my favorite.

 *Reading Group Questions*

 Reading Group Gold

1. One of the first things Tully says to Kate is a lie. Indeed, Tully is quick to lie throughout her life. Do you think this trait is her way of hiding the shames in her past or is it a willful reinterpretation of self? Do these lies and manipulations, big and small, help her ultimately to be more honest about who she is or do they undermine her ability to face her own shortcomings?

2. From her earliest memory, Tully feels abandoned by her mother and father. How does this sense of being unwanted influence her life? How does her troubled relationship with her mother lead to the decisions she makes in her life? Do children have an obligation of some kind to forgive their parents, even in the face of repeated disappointment? How much do you think childhood heartaches make us who we are?

3. The Kate-Johnny-Tully triangle is one of the central threads of the novel. How does Johnny really feel about Tully? How does Tully feel about him?

4. Kate believes she is Johnny's second choice for love. How does Johnny contribute to her insecurities? How does Tully? How much of a relationship is set in the beginning and how are changes made as we grow?

5. When Chad leaves Tully, she rationalizes away her broken heart by saying, "if he really loved me, he would wait for me." What does this reveal about Tully's perception of romantic love? How do these perceptions set the stage for the rest of her life? Do you believe that Tully will ever fall in love?

Keep on Reading

6. Near the end of the novel, when their friendship is on the rocks, both women feel wronged. Certainly Kate has ample reason to feel betrayed, but what about Tully's similar belief? Do you understand why Tully was upset, too? Do you believe that a friend should always reach out, even when great pain has been caused? Or do you believe that true friends would never hurt each other?

7. Kate is continually striving to live up to the "supermom" ideal, and continually feels that she has failed in this attempt. Do you think she has succeeded or failed? Discuss the idealized vision society has set up for both working moms and at-home moms. Who do you think has the harder road, and how can women best balance the various responsibilities of their lives? Kate often felt that society discounted her choice to be a stay-at-home mom, and that even her family wanted her to somehow "do more" or "be more." Do you think she was right or wrong to feel this way?

8. At which moment in the novel did you first notice a hint of tension between Tully and Kate? Who do you feel was to blame for this turning point?

9. Music plays an important role in this novel. What musical memories do you have of your teen years, your twenties, and today? Do you feel, as we get older, that music plays less of a role in our lives? Why do you feel that music so profoundly impacts us when we're "coming of age"?

10. What do you feel Kate was most jealous about with regards to Tully? And what was Tully the most envious of in Kate's life? Jealousy is often wanting what we cannot have. Do you feel that these characters truly could not have the things they wanted? If not, why not?

11. Under what circumstances do you feel a betrayal is unforgivable? Do you feel that any of these characters crossed that line?

12. What role do you see Tully playing in Mara's life, after the pages of the novel are closed? Johnny's life?

13. In the end, Kate comes full circle in her life and accepts the choices she has made, and in fact, discovers that she would do it all over again. She is fully at peace with who she is for perhaps the first time. How is this acceptance a gift to her children, her husband, and her best friend? And where do you think Tully ends up in terms of her own self worth? How will Kate's illness change her life?

DON'T MISS...

#1 *New York Times* Bestselling Author of *The Nightingale*

KRISTIN HANNAH

A NOVEL

THE FOUR WINDS

CHAPTER ONE

The next morning, Elsa woke late. She pushed the hair from her face. Fine strands were stuck to her cheek; she'd cried in her sleep.

Good. Better to cry at night when no one could see. She didn't want to reveal her weakness to this new family.

She went to the washstand and splashed lukewarm water on her face, then she brushed her teeth and combed her hair.

Last night, as she'd unpacked, she'd realized how wrong her clothes were for farm life. She was a town girl; what did she know about life on the land? All she'd brought were crepe dresses and silk stockings and heels. Church clothes.

She slipped into her plainest day dress, a charcoal-gray with pearl buttons and lace at the collar, then pulled up her stockings and stepped into the black heels she'd worn yesterday.

The house smelled of bacon and coffee. Her stomach grumbled, reminding her she hadn't eaten since yesterday's lunch.

The kitchen—a bright yellow wallpapered room with gingham curtains and white linoleum flooring—was empty. Dishes drying on the counter attested to the fact that Elsa had slept through breakfast. What time did these people waken? It was only nine.

Elsa stepped out onto the porch and saw the Martinelli farm in full sunlight. Hundreds of acres of harvested wheat fanned out in all directions, a sea of rough burnished gold, with the homestead part taking up a few acres in the middle of it all.

A driveway cut through the fields, a brown ribbon of dirt bordered by cottonwoods and fencing. The farm itself consisted of the house, a big wooden barn, a horse corral, a cow paddock, a hog pen, a chicken coop, and a windmill. Behind the house were an orchard, a small vineyard, and a fenced vegetable garden. Mrs. Martinelli was in the garden, bent over.

Elsa stepped down into the yard.

Mr. Martinelli came out of the barn and approached her. "Good morning," he said. "Walk with me."

He led her along the edge of the wheat field; the shorn crop struck her as broken, somehow, devastated. Much like herself. A gentle breeze rustled what remained, made a shushing sound.

"You are a town girl," Mr. Martinelli said in a thick Italian accent.

"Not anymore, I guess."

"This is a good answer." He bent down, scooped up a handful of dirt. "My land tells its story if you listen. The story of our family. We plant, we tend, we harvest. I make wine from grapes that I brought here from Sicily, and the wine I make reminds me of my father. It binds us, one to another, as it has for generations. Now it will bind you to us."

"I've never tended to anything."

He looked at her. "Do you want to change that?"

Elsa saw compassion in his dark eyes, as if he knew how afraid she'd been in her life, but she had to be imagining it. All he knew about her was that she was here now and she'd brought his son down with her.

"Beginnings are only that, Elsa. When Rosalba and I came here from Sicily, we had seventeen dollars and a dream. That was our beginning. But it wasn't what gave us this good life. We have this land because we worked for it, because no matter how hard life was, we stayed here. This land provided for us. It will provide for you, too, if you let it."

Elsa had never thought of land that way, as something that anchored a person, gave one a life. The idea of it, of staying here and finding a good life and a place to belong, seduced her as nothing else ever had.

She would do her best to become a Martinelli through and through, so she could join their story, perhaps even take it as her own and pass it on to the child she carried. She would do anything, become anyone, to ensure that this family loved the baby unconditionally as one of their own. "I want that, Mr. Martinelli," she said at last. "I want to belong here."

He smiled. "I saw that in you, Elsa."

Elsa started to thank him, but was interrupted by Mrs. Martinelli, who called out to her husband as she walked toward them carrying a basket full of ripe tomatoes and greenery. "Elsa," she said, coming to a stop. "How nice to see you up."

"I . . . overslept."

Mrs. Martinelli nodded. "Follow me."

In the kitchen, Mrs. Martinelli took the vegetables from her basket and laid them on the table, plump red tomatoes, yellow onions, green herbs, clumps of garlic. Elsa had never seen so much garlic at one time.

"What can you cook?" she asked Elsa, tying an apron on.

"C-coffee."

Mrs. Martinelli stopped. "You can't cook? At your age?"

"I'm sorry, Mrs. Martinelli. No, but—"

"Can you clean?"

"Well . . . I'm sure I can learn to."

Mrs. Martinelli crossed her arms. "What can you do?"

"Sew. Embroider. Darn. Read."

"A lady. *Madonna mia.*" She looked around the spotless kitchen. "Fine. Then I will teach you to cook. We will start with arancini. And call me Rose."

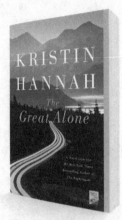
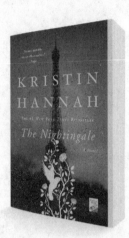